# Bad Girls
# Finish First

Also by Shelia Dansby Harvey

*Illegal Affairs*

# Bad Girls
# Finish First

## SHELIA DANSBY HARVEY

KENSINGTON PUBLISHING CORP.
http://www.kensingtonbooks.com

DAFINA BOOKS are published by

Kensington Publishing Corp.
850 Third Avenue
New York, NY 10022

All Kensington titles, imprints and distributed lines are available at special quantity discounts for bulk purchases for sales promotion, premiums, fund-raising, educational or institutional use.

Special book excerpts or customized printings can also be created to fit specific needs. For details, write or phone the office of the Kensington Special Sales Manager: Kensington Publishing Corp., 850 Third Avenue, New York, NY 10022. Attn. Special Sales Department. Phone: 1-800-221-2647.

Dafina Books and the Dafina logo Reg. U.S. Pat. & TM Off.

ISBN 0-7582-0823-5

First Kensington Trade Paperback Printing: April 2006
10  9  8  7  6  5  4  3  2  1

Printed in the United States of America

# Bad Girls
# Finish First

# 1

Reverend David Capps stood at the curb of the airport passenger arrival section watching for his ride. Mid-January snow flurries whipped at the tail of his leather trench coat. All the other passengers stood inside the airport, but David, his six-foot-four frame unbowed by the Austin wind, was invigorated by the cold. David spotted a Mercedes S500 coming his way and began waving. The driver rolled up and popped the trunk so that David could store his overnight bag.

When David got in, Senator Michael Joseph asked, "Why were you waving so hard, man? There's no way I could miss you—big black man dressed all in black." He eyed David from head to toe. "With those sunglasses on, I might have mistaken you for a baller, but overlook you? Couldn't happen."

"It's good to see you too, Michael," David said. He sat back and made a show of adjusting his Armani sunglasses. "And in case you haven't noticed, it may be snowing, but the sun is out." He turned to Michael. "You're looking good for an old man."

That was an understatement. Michael was so handsome that at every age marker he'd hit—twenty-five, thirty, forty—women eyed him and thought: *that man can't possibly get any sexier.* But he could and did, and now, as he approached fifty, Michael looked better than ever. He was a fine wine, a black Sean Connery.

"An old man, huh? Watch out, David, you'll be forty before you know it." Michael got on the freeway and headed toward downtown Austin. "Then you'll finally be a grown man, qualified to hang out with other grown men, like me," he quipped.

David rubbed one hand across his clean-shaven head. *So far, so good*, he thought. He'd wondered whether he and Michael would be able to pick up their natural banter. So much had changed in both their lives since they last spent time together.

As though he read David's mind, Michael said, "Seriously, it's good to see you, David. I appreciate your coming over to help me. Now that New Word is the biggest black church in the state, I thought you might not be able to spare the time."

"This is a big decision you're about to make and I'm humbled that you asked for my input. I don't care how big my church gets—you ever need my help, you've got it." David removed his sunglasses. "And by the way, New Word is the biggest black church in the Southwest, not just Texas."

They both laughed. Michael turned up the music and they rode in companionable silence until David broached the subject of the big change in Michael's life.

"So, I'm finally going to get to meet Raven," David said.

"You've met her once before, remember?"

David remembered. Back when Michael and Raven's affair was the worst-kept secret in Texas, David had crossed paths with the couple in Houston's airport. It had been an awkward meeting. David had been embarrassed for Michael and moved on as quickly as he could, but not so quickly that he didn't get a good look at Raven. She had worn jeans, stiletto boots, and a form-fitting sleeveless sweater. She might have been fully clothed, but Raven's hips and her butt, hugged by skintight denim, got David's attention the way a bare-breasted woman swinging on a pole entranced other men. From their short encounter he knew one thing: Raven's aura—the way she looked, talked, and moved—was enough to make any man leave his wife's bed for hers, for a little while at least. She was tall and chocolaty with full lips and a stunning figure. David knew so many fine women—black churches were overrun with them—that he wasn't easily impressed. But when he'd met Raven, David understood why Michael was so hot for her. What he couldn't comprehend was why Michael left his wife to marry Raven.

"Look, I know you don't approve," Michael began haltingly, but David cut him off.

"It's not my place to pass judgment on how you live your life. True enough, I wish you had given your marriage to Grace a second chance, but it was none of my business." David could see the state capitol in the distance. "This is the prettiest city in the state," he commented.

"I thought that's what you holy men did," Michael said half-jokingly, "sit around and tell other people when they've crossed the line."

David shook his head. "Nah, we're on the outside looking in. I never forget that. Besides, if I wanted to place blame for what happened between you and Grace, I could start with myself."

Michael looked surprised. "What do you mean?"

David exhaled. "You know how we used to do when you were with Grace. Go out for a drink every now and then, do a little harmless flirting." He looked at the University of Texas tower as they passed it. "At least I thought it was harmless at the time.

"You know my feelings about sin, Michael. It's what all of us, as imperfect beings, do. Hell, if fornication were an unforgivable sin, I'd be on a fast track to hell. All we can do is try every day to be a little better than we were the day before, and try not to hurt others." David looked straight ahead, but in his mind's eye he saw Michael's ex-wife, Grace, crying as she asked him to pray for her family. "Adultery is one of those sins that destroys lives. It can rip a soul as deeply as murder or suicide." David's distress over his possible role in the demise of Michael's first marriage clouded his face. "I had a responsibility to tell you that and I didn't do it. Instead, I ran with you and looked the other way."

"You wouldn't have been saying anything I didn't already know," Michael replied. He paused, then asked, "So you've never done it—never committed adultery?"

"No, and I never will," David replied. He sounded self-righteous to his own ears, so he quipped, "There are enough single women out there to help me avoid the temptation."

"Whatever I did, it was my choice, not yours," Michael said. "We shared a few laughs with women, but that's all. When I cheated, I always flew solo." He glanced at David as he exited the freeway. "And for the record, it would have taken God himself to stop me from getting to Raven."

The men were silent as they separately recollected their history. Back in the day Michael and David had been yin and yang, two sides of the same lucky coin. David was as black as they come—about a quarter past midnight. He wore a neat goatee and clothed his muscular body in clingy sweaters and expensive suits.

Michael was David's exact opposite—the slim, light-skinned pretty boy. Despite having done his share of carousing, Michael had the twinkling eyes of a choirboy. Michael's eyes, along with his white-bright smile, made women say yes to him when their minds were set to tell him no. While Michael conquered women with his innocent eyes, David's weapon of choice was his voice, which was wickedly deep and smooth. Women who ran into them were snared, if not by Michael's compelling wholesomeness, then by David's urbane thug appeal.

"We wasn't nothing nice," Michael finally said.

"Amen to that."

As two doormen approached Michael's car, David looked up at the ornate stone building.

"Impressive, isn't it?" Michael commented. "This used to be a bank building, the finest one in Austin. Raven and I live in a four-thousand-square-foot condo on the top floor. It cost me an arm and a leg, but my baby said she's always wanted to live like a city woman."

"Since when did you become such a big spender?" David asked, humor alive in his eyes. "You used to watch a dollar like it was going to get up and run if you took your eyes off it."

Michael pushed the elevator button. "Grace was pretty basic, but Raven's got classic taste. Classic equals expensive, so she keeps me in a perpetual state of sticker shock." He smiled at David. "But I've got the money, and making Raven happy is definitely worth the price. When you get to know her, you'll see," Michael said as he put his key into the door.

The men found Raven shuttling between the kitchen and the dining room, placing china on the table.

"Smells good in here," David said as he took off his jacket and looked around at the ultramodern, expensive furnishings. "Where are Chris and Evan? Are they having dinner with us?" Christopher and Evan were Michael's sons from his marriage to Grace.

"No. Chris has his own place and Evan's spending the night with him. As for the smell, my woman knows her way around a kitchen," Michael said proudly. "We could hit every top restaurant in this city and I guarantee we wouldn't get a better meal. Not even close."

David looked toward the dining room, saw that Raven wasn't within earshot and joked, "I don't know, if she can't outcook Grace, you may need to rethink this trophy wife thing."

"What are you guys laughing about?" Raven asked as she walked into the room to greet David. He expected a social hug, maybe even a handshake from Raven, since they really didn't know each other, but she extended her arms to him and pulled him close the way one would an old friend.

"David's questioning your cooking skills, and I don't blame

him. Look at you! You don't look like you've been anywhere near pots and pans."

Raven wore a navy pantsuit with a low-cut jacket and a sheer baby-blue camisole beneath. Her hair hung straight down her back and her only makeup was mascara and lipstick.

"Well, I have been in the kitchen, and David, you're just about to find out how good I can be."

"Oh, yeah, what should I expect?"

Raven could cook just about anything, and tonight she'd decided to go Creole. "Chicken and sausage gumbo, shrimp étoufée, and fried catfish." Raven stood in front of David with her arms crossed and a fake smile on her face. She had the idea that he was testing her, measuring her against Grace to make sure she was good enough for Michael.

David ate himself silly. He'd already polished off a slice of sweet potato pie and was considering sampling the bread pudding with bourbon sauce when Raven suggested they move to the great room. "I'll be there in a second," she said.

When Raven joined the men, she was carrying a tray with coffee, and one heaping serving of bread pudding. As she leaned forward to pour David's coffee and place the dessert in front of him, Raven said, "I could tell you wanted to try this. Go ahead, no harm in indulging yourself once in a while." She smiled at David and tossed her long hair out of her face. Since she was thirteen, the hair toss had been Raven's main man-manipulation tool, and it hadn't failed her yet. Her dark-brown hair was shiny and straight with subtle henna streaks. When Raven used her French-tipped nails to throw her hair back, it really was a thing to see. David couldn't help but stare, and Michael, who watched his wife so much he sometimes felt like a stalker, noticed.

Raven poured coffee for Michael and herself. She got a snifter of cognac for each of them, and then sat down next to Michael. *She's practically in his lap*, David thought.

"So tell me what you think, David. Can you imagine me,

skinny little Mike Joseph from the south side of Dallas, in the governor's mansion?" Michael asked.

"I thought your talk about running for governor was a trick to lure me here for dinner," David said lightly. Years of listening to people's problems had turned him into an irrepressible jokester. "I didn't think you were for real."

"I don't know why you're surprised. You and I have talked about me doing something like this before. I like the Senate but I'm ready to try something different."

David ate a spoonful of bread pudding and washed it down with a sip of cognac. "This is sublime," he said to Raven. David's voice was so warm and rich that Raven imagined hot chocolate.

"I'm thinking about running for state treasurer first," Michael continued, "to build some statewide name recognition for my—"

"And I told him to think bigger," Raven interjected. "Michael should run for governor, and he doesn't need to wade through all that other crap before he does it."

"There is such a thing as working your way to the top," David tactfully said.

Raven, her elbows on her knees, clasped her hands and leaned forward. "That's just what Michael and I are about to do. I mean no offense, but being governor of Texas isn't the top, it's just a stepping-stone to better things for us. As for working our way there, President Bush didn't do that, so why should we?"

"That's where we are," Michael said, summing things up. "I'm inclined to take time to raise my name recognition in the state by running for another office, but Raven sees that as a waste of time. What do you think?"

David looked thoughtful for a moment, and then said, "That you'll make a great governor, and you're ready right now." He spread his legs and held his drink with both hands. "Problem is, the state might not be ready for you. Political insiders from

Austin to Washington DC know and respect you, but the average Joe in Brownsville or Amarillo hasn't ever heard of Michael Joseph."

Before he could continue, Raven dismissed David's opinion with a wave of her hand. "My husband has more than fifteen years in the Senate, and during that time he's made a name for himself. He's ready."

"Raven, I already know how you feel. We need to hear David out." Michael nodded for David to continue.

"But I'm not finished," Raven said, and kept right on.

When she paused, David said, "I'm not questioning Michael's credentials, but I'm not the only one who gets to vote." David had been looking at Raven, and now he turned to Michael. "What's your gut telling you?"

"I'm still up in the air."

"Let's just suppose that Michael runs for governor," Raven forged ahead. "What's the first thing he would need to do?"

David pushed his empty snifter away from him and leaned back in his seat. "Sort through dirty laundry."

"I don't have too much—"

"Honey, we've got to face reality," Raven said before Michael could finish his thought. "For one thing, you've got a bitter ex-wife. That could pose a problem, right, David?"

"Women voters are usually more interested in the new wife than the old one," David said.

"I know what you mean," Raven said. She took Michael's hand as she spoke. The simple gesture conveyed so much intimacy that David felt like a voyeur. "Based on what they have heard about how we got together, people might hold the divorce against Michael, but once they find out how good I am for him, they'll change their minds." Raven shook her head regretfully. "I wouldn't say this in front of just anybody, but Grace was nothing but a drag on Michael's career. He's got what it takes to go to the top, and now that we're a team, there's nothing Michael can't do. You'd have no way of knowing it, David, but I'm a hell of a helpmate."

"That she is, has been since the day we met," Michael said. "While my baby was still in law school, she helped me write brilliant speeches and make sharp strategic decisions, all while maintaining the top spot in her class."

"You two are a picture-perfect couple," David admitted. He was absolutely right; Michael and Raven were a striking pair. His light skin was smooth with just enough lines in the right places to give him a distinguished, affluent air. Michael's curly salt-and-pepper hair hadn't thinned a bit, and his body (which had shamed him to no end when he was a teenager) was lightly muscled and wiry.

Raven was an exotic dream come true. All that brown skin! She was in her mid-thirties but had the dewy complexion and clear eyes of a woman ten years younger. Raven was as tall as Michael, and her body was flawless. She had toned, curvaceous legs, a completely flat stomach, tiny waist, and an ass that beckoned men to follow her like she was the Pied Piper. She had generous breasts and the sexiest arms David had ever seen.

David also realized the couple's appeal was more than physical. "You convey a oneness," he said. "It's hard to describe, but I feel it and so will the voters. If the public gets to see you just the way you are now, over and over again, they'll forget Michael was ever married to anyone else."

"So much for dirty laundry," Raven said.

"Well, yeah, for marital dirty laundry, but there are other kinds. Got anything else, Michael? Unpaid taxes, shady financial deals, vices like gambling?" David asked.

"I'm clean," Michael replied.

"Raven, what about you? Is there anything from your past that can hurt Michael?" David eyed her quizzically. He vaguely recalled hearing something negative about her, but so much gossip was thrown David's way, he found it best to forget most of it as soon as he heard it.

"Nope, nothing I can think of," Raven said brightly.

Michael hesitated, then said, "Raven, are you sure? What about—"

"Honey, I said there's nothing." She patted his knee, then stood and began clearing things away. "I think we've covered enough for tonight."

When she left the room, David said, "That's quite a woman you've got."

"I told you."

"Despite what I said in the car, I fought with myself all the way here to keep an open mind." He openly appraised Michael. "But you look happy, man, the happiest I've ever seen you, outside of the birth of your children. Now that I've met Raven I can see why."

"What do you see?" Michael asked. No one whose opinion he valued had congratulated Michael on his union with Raven or had anything good to say about her. He was hungry for validation, for someone he respected to assure him he wasn't an utter fool for tossing Grace aside and marrying Raven.

"Lots of things," David said. "She's beautiful, keenly intelligent, direct, and confident." He loved intelligent women, and he liked them direct, as long as direct meant honest. David grinned at Michael. "And when you add her sexy charm? To me, that's a very cool combination."

"Reverend Capps, you're not allowed to call another man's wife sexy," Michael said, but he had a wide smile on his face.

"Just calling it like I see it. When God called me to the ministry He took away some of my vices, but He left my hormones intact," David quipped. He wanted Michael to feel good about his marriage—might as well since it was a done deal—so he didn't mention that Raven's comment about Grace showed she had a bitchy side as well. He added another compliment. "The thing about Raven that's going to help you right off the bat is that she knows a lot about politics. That's impressive considering this is her first go-round."

"I appreciate the good word, David. I wish other people would give her a chance the way you have," Michael said. "And you know what? The more you get to know her, the more you're going to like her." He stood. "Going back and forth over whether I should run for governor was a good way to flesh out the issues, but it's what you said just now about Raven that's been the most help. I'll be right back," he said and headed toward the kitchen.

Raven was busy rinsing the dishes. Michael walked up behind her and put his arms around her. He kissed Raven's cheek. "I wanted you to be the first to know, I've decided to run for governor. With you by my side, there's nothing I can't accomplish."

She turned to face him. "There's nothing *we* can't accomplish, Michael. We're going to the governor's mansion, and from there straight to the top." Raven burrowed into Michael and kissed him full on the lips.

After Michael returned to the great room to discuss his decision with David, Raven forgot about the dishes and sat down at the kitchen table. She thought about what David had asked her. *Is there anything from your past that can hurt Michael?* Images from Raven's life before she married Michael—her kissing a woman who wore a lab coat, a man doubled up in pain on her apartment floor—flitted through her mind. The memory of the man, whose normally alive, gold-flecked eyes, stared unseeingly at her during his ordeal, caused a tiny knot to take hold in Raven's stomach. She sighed and said softly to herself, "I guess it all depends on whether anyone finds out about Omar Faxton."

# 2

Christopher Joseph beat a rat-a-tat-tat on his steering wheel, grooving to a mixed neo-soul CD. He was stuck in traffic just outside Austin, moving about a mile every five minutes, but he wasn't blaring his horn like the drivers around him. He knew the ride from Austin to Dallas like the back of his hand— just two more miles and the bottleneck would open up; he'd be at the front of the pack in no time. Life was good for Michael and Grace's oldest son. He'd recently graduated from the University of Texas in Austin where he earned dual degrees in history and economics while working as a special assistant to his father. He had a nice apartment, loyal friends, and an extraordinarily promising future.

When Christopher's cell phone rang, he turned down the music and pressed his speaker button.

"Genie, what's up?" Regina 'Genie' Dupree was Raven's appointment secretary. One look at her and Christopher had broken his rule about not dating his colleagues. "You're rockin' an East Coast attitude, West Coast looks, and a Southern heart. I can't resist that," he'd kidded her the first time he asked her out. Genie was almost two years older than Christopher, so she brushed him off in the beginning. But she watched him and quickly discovered that his peers, most of whom were over thirty, treated him with respect, not because he was Michael's son, but because he was good at what he did. They'd been an item for six months.

"Hey, baby. I'm just checking to see what time you want me to come over," Genie asked.

"Come over?"

"Don't try to squirm out of it now, Christopher," she teased him. "You promised me a home-cooked meal tonight, so don't act like we agreed to go out to eat."

*Damn.* "I'm on I-35 headed to Dallas. I forgot to call you; I'm sorry babe."

"What's going on? I checked the newswires just before I left the office, and everything was fine. Did something happen?"

"Not that I know of."

"Then why're you going?" Already Christopher could hear the challenge in Genie's voice.

"To see my mother."

"Christopher, you've got to be kidding! This is the first halfway-free weekend we've had in weeks. What am I supposed to do?"

"Genie, you're a grown woman. I'm sure you'll think of something," Christopher snapped. He'd rather be headed across town to Genie's apartment than to Dallas, and it irritated him to think about what he was missing.

"Have a good time with your mama," Genie snapped back. "Like you said, I'm a big girl. Trust me, I'll find something to do." *Click.*

Christopher turned up his music and tried to recapture his flow but couldn't. He shut off the CD and gripped the wheel like he was in driver's ed.

Christopher had lost a few girlfriends while he was in college. The young women he dated were either hard-core cynics or just keeping it real, depending upon your point of view—

they believed any man who claimed to spend so much time with his mother had to be cheating. Parents were to be checked on by telephone once a week (or biweekly, if one could get away with it). Christopher didn't want his relationship with Genie to end up like the rest; he didn't know where they were headed, but he knew he didn't want to cut short the journey.

An hour later Christopher decided to call Genie back. He got her voicemail and left the message. "You know you're my main girl, but Mom's been vulnerable these past few months. She can't turn anywhere without seeing images of Dad and his new wife on TV and in the newspapers. She needs me."

When she lost her spot as "Senator Joseph's wife," Grace Joseph became a forgotten woman. She loved her sons, Christopher and Evan, and even though depression descended on the house when Michael walked out, Grace did the best she could. Christopher was in college by then, and since Michael was also in Austin most of the time, he spent more time with his father than with his mother.

That left Grace and Evan, the younger son, at home, alone. After a couple of months, the cloud that covered Grace started to dissipate, and on occasion, the sun shone through. Then Raven realized Michael would be easier to control with Evan nearby. She paid Grace a visit, and by week's end Evan had moved from the spacious Dallas home into the two-bedroom Austin apartment Michael lived in at the time.

Right after Evan moved out, Christopher would drive from Austin to Dallas every weekend just so Grace wouldn't be alone. Christopher developed a routine—he'd arrive at Grace's condo as late as possible Friday night and work all day Saturday at his father's Dallas office, then hang out with friends that night. Sunday morning he'd take Grace to church and to brunch afterward. He'd be back on the road to Austin by two.

This weekend he had cajoled Grace into going to dinner.

"My birthday is Wednesday, Mom, and I won't be here. You've got to go out with me," he told her.

As Christopher sat across from Grace at a chic Dallas restaurant, he tried to ignore her lifeless eyes and concentrate on the rest of her. Grace had all the features of an attractive woman in her forties. Her smooth copper-colored skin and almond eyes were accentuated by a stylish haircut. Grace had a curvaceous figure, including breasts that men tended to look at a half-beat too long. Her smile, the one she let out when she was really happy, was blindingly beautiful; however, Christopher hadn't seen it in a while. With her inner light dimmed, Grace reminded her son of a once-beautiful woman stricken by a life-draining disease.

Grace examined her son as closely as he examined her. "Sitting across from you is like sitting across from your father twenty years ago. You've got the same curly hair, tan skin, muscular build."

"But I'm taller, like your side of the family. Thank God for that," he quipped, hoping to be rewarded with at least a slight smile. Grace's expression stayed the same.

When the waiter came, Christopher said, "My mother will have the seafood gumbo." He leaned toward Grace, "Mom, you still like gumbo, don't you?" Getting no response, he added, "I hope this is the right place. I remember you always ordering the gumbo."

"Your father routinely ordered it for me, so I ate it," Grace said glumly. "I think one of his girlfriends told him this place had the best gumbo in town." Grace's response was typical—she rarely said anything that didn't invoke the bitter memory of Michael Joseph.

A young couple and two small children were sitting at the table next to them. The children were restless; one was on a mission to touch every item on the table while the other crawled underneath it and refused to budge. The wife tried, but she could not handle more than one child at a time.

"You see why I don't like to take you and the kids any-where? I let you be a stay-at-home mom, and they're still little animals," barked the husband. "Jerry's wife works and does a great job with their kids." He cut his wife a nasty look. "And she still looks like she did when they were dating."

Grace stiffened, and Christopher immediately picked up on the warning signs.

"Mom, he probably doesn't really mean—"

"Sure he does," she said. Her eyes were not dead anymore.

Grace turned, looked directly at the man, and asked, "What if they were gone?"

"Excuse me?"

"Your wife and your babies, what if they got killed in a car wreck?"

"Lady, please—"

"My husband used to be an asshole, just like you, until my son and I almost died." She gestured toward Christopher. "We were in a wreck. A bad one, and I almost died." Grace's voice was soft, yet filled with missionary zeal. "It took almost losing me for my husband to realize that I'm the light of his life. Don't let that happen to you."

"Mom, why do you say things like that, tell people lies about you and Dad?" Christopher whispered to her. "It's embarrass-ing."

"So? What's a little embarrassment compared to saving a family?" She shook her finger at Christopher. "A little lie never hurt anyone. That man needed a wake-up call, Chris, treating the mother of his children like trash. How dare he?" Grace eyed the family over her shoulder. The husband, having fin-ished his meal while his wife wrestled with the children, held the smallest child in his lap and talked the other one through getting peas from her plate, onto her spoon, and into her mouth. The wife was able to eat her meal in peace.

Grace said, "What did I tell you? A little lie never hurt anyone."

Before Christopher could reply, a tall, hearty-looking man in his sixties came over to their table. He said, "Little Chris, I've heard you sneak in and out of town without calling on your old uncle, but I never believed it!"

Christopher stood and embraced the man. "Uncle John, it's good seeing you."

"You too, son." The man turned to Grace. "My Grace," he said. Grace stood and her eyes welled with tears.

John Reese and Grace held each other for a long moment. Her whole body relaxed, but not for long. "I'm glad we ran into each other. Be sure to tell Maggie I said hello," Grace said as she took her seat. She cast her eyes downward, focusing on her gumbo.

"She'd like it better coming from you," John said. "Mind if I sit?"

Grace looked up at him and quickly asked, "Weren't you on your way out?"

"Yes, but when I saw you, I told the guys to go on without me." John said as he pulled out a chair.

John Reese wasn't Christopher's uncle; he and his wife, Maggie, were his godparents. Although there was no blood between them, the Reeses and Josephs were family in the truest sense of the word. When Michael and Grace were married, they'd gone over to the Reeses at least once a month for Sunday dinner. Every other year they took a family vacation together.

John was like an older brother to Michael, not just any older brother, but the type who raised their younger siblings because the parents ran off or died. John had been his touchstone, his advisor and protector. They stood by each other, come what may, and told one another the truth, even when it hurt.

Since the divorce, John seldom saw Christopher. Now they caught up on everything—John asked Christopher about work and about Evan, but he was careful not to mention Michael.

"Grace, what about you, keeping yourself busy?" John asked.

"Sure," she answered, her eyes still downcast.

"Doing what?"

"Oh, you know, different things," she said in a small voice.

John gave Christopher a look that asked, "Is she any better?" Christopher shook his head. As far as he knew, Grace spent most of her time watching TV.

"I've got a lot going on, myself," John said. "Too much, in fact." He caught Grace's eye and said, "I feel like I'm drowning."

She didn't say anything, so Christopher chimed in. "If anybody can juggle ten things at once, it's you. What's got you so busy?"

John leaned back and sighed. He rubbed a hand across his close-cropped gray hair. "I'm trying to set up a literacy program at the junior high school around the corner from the bookstore."

"For who, adults in the neighborhood?" Christopher asked.

"Nah, for the kids at the school. You'd be surprised at how many twelve-year-olds read like they're in the second grade."

Grace looked up from her gumbo. Christopher, who watched his mother intently whenever they were together, saw interest flicker across her face.

"The kids are eager to get started," John said. "So is the principal of the school, but finding volunteers . . ." John threw his hands up. "It's impossible."

"I guess everybody's at work during the day," Christopher commented.

"Lack of time isn't the problem, it's lack of interest. My retired friends would rather spend their time in the casinos. And college kids aren't like they were back in your day, Grace," John said. "These youngsters would rather zone out on videos than spend a few hours helping a child." He nodded toward Christopher. "Present company excepted."

John stroked his mustache, and stared toward the ceiling. "I need somebody who connects well with children, someone patient and loving."

Grace was listening so intently that it startled her when John said, "What about you, Grace? I realize you're probably quite busy, but if there's any way you can find a little time to help me I'd be grateful."

"I couldn't," Grace said.

"Mom, you'd be great. Evan and I both love to read, and it's all because of you," Christopher said.

John placed his hand over Grace's and said, "These children need somebody, Grace. Can you imagine what it must be like, being locked in your own narrow world, needing help but not having anybody to reach out to? After a while a person starts to feel hopeless, resigned to being left behind. That's how it's going to go for these boys if they don't learn how to read."

Grace looked squarely at John. Her expression was serious, but Christopher could see a glimmer of the beauty she usually hid. "Yes John, I can imagine it," Grace said. "I'll do what I can."

# 3

Christopher wandered around the war room of his father's campaign office while he waited for Michael to complete a phone call. Michael's main campaign headquarters was on the eleventh floor of the nicest office building in Austin. The room was a high-energy mess. Phone bank volunteers plugged one ear with a finger while they called voters; others stuffed mailers. Christopher's practiced eye assured him that beneath the hectic surface, things were being accomplished like clockwork. He stopped in front of a new poster, which read, "Committed To Lead" beneath a photo of Michael.

"He looks like a winner, like a man who knows what he wants and will not be denied," Christopher said to the campaign staffer who was preparing to ship the posters around the state. "I like it."

"It's a good thing you do. You're looking at yourself in another twenty years, you know." She winked at Christopher, picked up a stack of posters, and walked away.

Christopher scanned the room, taking in banners, yard signs, and bumper stickers written in Spanish and Vietnamese. A huge corkboard was filled with "the dailies," which were the day's newspaper clippings from papers all over the nation. The *New*

*York Times* ran an in-depth profile of Michael titled: TEXAS POISED FOR FIRST BLACK GOVERNOR.

The *Wall Street Journal* included an op-ed opinion with the caption: TEXAS PERILOUSLY CLOSE TO FALLING INTO INEXPERIENCED HANDS.

"Chris." Michael stuck his head in the door. "Come on in, son."

Michael's private portion of the headquarters was orderly and tastefully decorated with beautiful African artifacts. The space bespoke power, just like his home and Senate offices did. The only things on display besides art were pictures of Michael at different stages of his career. There was one of him with both Bush presidents at a formal dinner, one with Bill Clinton, and another of him being presented with a humanitarian award by Nelson Mandela. His bookshelves were dotted with plaques and pictures from past campaign victories. The best snapshots from Michael's past Senate races weren't on display because Grace was in them. They'd been replaced by an eight by ten of Michael and Raven, both beaming as Michael gave his victory speech after the Democratic primary.

"How was Dallas? The office running okay?" Michael asked, eager to begin his one-on-one time with his eldest son. He reveled in the young man's every word and movement and still saw Christopher as the miracle that he'd been when Michael first held him over twenty years earlier.

"Yep, the office is fine. We picked up five new volunteers, all about my age," Christopher said as he took a seat before his father's huge mahogany desk. He gave Michael a detailed account of the Dallas headquarters' progress during the prior week. Michael asked about some specific tasks and was pleased, but not surprised, to find out that Christopher had gone over and above what he had been asked to do.

"Everything else going well?" Michael asked, averting his eyes.

"Sure," Christopher lied. Michael's question was a veiled reference to Grace. He asked the same thing every time Christopher returned to Austin, and each time Christopher told him the same lie because he figured it was what his father wanted to hear. Michael knew it wasn't the truth, but he accepted it.

Michael set the stack of papers that were at the center of his desk to one side. "So what's got you so fired up you couldn't wait until later to tell me?" he asked his son.

"I just heard that you've decided to have Dudley Capps as your chief of staff."

"You heard right. I talked to Dudley about it this morning and he's up for the challenge."

"But Dad, why'd you make a decision without at least giving me a shot? I want to be your chief of staff."

Michael was caught off guard. "Christopher, the thought never crossed my mind! You're developing excellent skills, but you're still too young and inexperienced. If we win this election, I'll need someone the legislators respect."

"Since when don't I get respect? I've worked for you since I was sixteen; there's not a senator or state rep I haven't dealt with. When's the last time Dudley stepped foot in Senator Greene's office or had lunch with any lawmaker who's been around for less than three years?"

"What about nepotism?" Michael countered. He stared at Christopher from behind his desk, where he sat with his fingers tented, looking every bit the teacher waiting on a reply from a student who had no answer.

"What about your wife?" Christopher shot back.

Christopher never referred to Raven by name, if he could help it. She was always "the senator's wife" or "my father's wife." If the election went Michael's way, Christopher would have to upgrade Raven to "the governor's wife."

Eyes down, Michael fingered the stack of papers on the edge of his desk. "That's different."

Christopher studied his father and considered his options. Looking at Michael, Christopher felt familiar, mild disgust. He loved and admired everything about his father except for Michael's slavish devotion to Raven.

"Dad, she's your wife. I know you've got to consider her opinion, keep her happy. But she's new at this and doesn't know what type of personality it takes to handle these sharks. Dudley's an introvert; he's fine with the technical stuff, but he's clueless when it comes to getting to know people." Christopher paused, then added, "I could see if Dudley were more like Uncle David."

"Just because Dudley and David are brothers doesn't mean they have to be alike. Just look at you and Evan. And Raven says we need Dudley at the helm because of the technical skill that you don't seem to think much of."

Christopher could have argued the point—he was dead on when it came to reading people and situations. Michael had been a politician all Christopher's life and having shared his father with others for as long as he could remember, Christopher wasn't covetous. Something about Dudley being close to his father, however, disturbed Christopher and always had. No matter how Christopher felt, his father's first two words, "Raven says," ended the matter.

Michael mistook his son's silence for tentative agreement. Another justification popped into his head and Michael started to explain, but Christopher waved him off.

"Dad, it's okay, forget I brought it up. The main thing is that we stick together and kick Jeff Sweeney's ass." Sweeney was Michael's Republican opponent for governor.

Michael laughed and said without thinking, "Your mother wouldn't like to hear you talk like that."

The air between father and son was instantly thick with words they'd never spoken. Michael broke the spell by reaching for his desk calendar. "You're right," he said in a business tone, "It's already mid-April, so for the next seven months we've got to focus on beating Sweeney."

Late that night Michael and Dudley Capps shared a nightcap to celebrate Michael's decision to make Dudley his chief of staff.

"Who was on your short list for the job?" Dudley asked.

"Nobody, really. I wanted you from the start; so did Raven." Michael snapped his fingers. "There was one person. Believe it or not, Chris thought he was up for the job," he said with a small laugh. "According to Chris, you, my friend, are 'clueless' when it comes to getting to know people."

"What?" Dudley said.

"Oh, don't get angry, and for God's sake, don't let him know I told you," Michael said. "He's just a kid, Dudley, but I give him credit, he's an ambitious one."

"I guess so," Dudley said, but he didn't sound reassured.

"Chris is just like me. Remember what a go-getter I was at his age?"

"Sure do. Every student in our law school class knew that Michael Joseph was going places," he chuckled, "at least according to Michael Joseph."

"I wrote you off as a loner," Michael said. "I, on the other hand, was all over the place, president of just about every organization," he reminisced.

"You or Arnold Baker."

"Arnold and I *were* Monroe."

Dudley nodded, his fleshy chin completely hiding his stumpy neck. He wore a budget-priced brown suit, which his nondescript brown face and pudgy body blended right into.

"And there you were, a guy nobody noticed. The first time you spoke to me, I didn't even realize you were my classmate."

"Strange how that changed."

"Not really, Dudley. You were always my boy, listened to me, helped me think things through." Michael set aside his drink, closed his notebook, and loosened his tie. "You and Arnold never got on like that, did you?"

"No." Taking his cue from Michael, Dudley moved around the room, closing blinds and turning off lights.

"Poor guy," Dudley commented.

Arnold Baker was in federal prison serving a four-year sentence for fraud. He was just the type of ignorant fellow Dudley despised. Back in law school, Dudley had never said so much as hello to Arnold.

"Remember when Adel Lenton dumped me? If it weren't for you and John Reese, I'da lost my mind."

Dudley lifted one hand in an "it was nothing" gesture. "We were friends, you'd have done the same for me."

"You and Reese never hit it off either; that always puzzled me. You're a steady guy and so is he."

As they walked through the building's deserted lobby Michael commented, "You lucked out, Dudley. The few friends that you made in law school have done well. Adolpho Rodriguez is a key advisor to the president and Hank Shore is the richest black man in Texas. I know you never thought much of women as friends, but the one you did get close to"—Michael wagged his finger at Dudley—"damned if Veronica Preston isn't one of the best CEOs in the country."

"And here you are, about to be elected governor."

"If—no, *when*—I win, I know it's going to be due in large part to you, Dudley. You've managed how many of my campaigns, five?"

The exact number was six, which Dudley knew very well. "I've lost count," he replied.

"Every campaign you've been involved with, I've won. The tougher the fight the better you get." Michael stopped walking. "Remember when I ran against Ben Jones?"

"Can't forget it. There you were, looking sixteen instead of twenty-six, taking on a black incumbent who'd been in office nearly ten years."

"He sicced his dogs on me, man. Tried every dirty trick in the book and thought up a few new ones." The memory invigorated Michael, and he spoke at the top of his voice, his words bouncing off the vast lobby walls. "But you killed him, Dudley, knocked him so far out of the ring that he left politics for good."

Michael put his hand on Dudley's shoulder. "I need that kind of fire if I'm going to take this thing and you're the best guy to give it to me." Michael sprinkled a little of his charm on Dudley. "Even your brother says so."

"Really? David said that?"

Michael nodded. "I'm scheduled to meet with the editorial board of the *Austin American-Statesman*. They've endorsed me for all my Senate races, so it's a no-brainer that they'll support me. Once they put my name out there, every other paper in the state will follow suit." Michael paused, and suddenly he looked weary. "Things are going fine, and it's still early in the game, but I'm a little worried about the latest poll. Sisters aren't supporting me the way they ought to. And Jeff Sweeney's commercials are starting to hurt me. I knew when we got down to it that the big boys would contribute more to Jeff Sweeney's campaign than to mine, but I didn't know how much more."

Dudley gave an understanding nod. "Let's talk about it tomorrow. We'll figure something out."

As they went their separate ways, it was all Dudley could do not to skip across the parking lot. Having Michael depend on him was so uplifting! And Michael was right about one thing: Dudley was very lucky, and he wasn't going to allow his luck to run out now.

"You're right about losing black women," Dudley told Michael the next night. "They're your core support, but you couldn't tell it by looking at these numbers." Michael,

Christopher, and Dudley sat in the great room of Michael's condo. It was going on midnight, but Michael wasn't thinking about sleep. He couldn't rest until he understood what was going wrong with his campaign. Dudley had spent the day poring over opinion polls, now stacked haphazardly on the coffee table. Black women had always been Michael's top supporters but when it came to elevating him to governor, they weren't standing up and being counted.

"What's their problem?" Michael asked.

Michael and Christopher looked at Dudley and waited for his assessment. Christopher was bone tired and ready to call it a day. That morning he had told Genie they'd go to The Oasis, have a few beers, and watch the sun set; his list of broken promises was growing.

Dudley fumbled through the papers in his folder. "It's hard to say, Michael. The people I talked to in the field couldn't pinpoint the problem. South Oak Cliff women sat out the primary, and"—Dudley licked his index finger and flipped through more papers until he found the one he wanted—"I hadn't noticed before, but you have half the number of female volunteers you had back—"

"C'mon, Dad, you know what the problem is. You left your wife and your family for another woman," Christopher interrupted. "Black women are punishing you for that." When they talked business, Christopher and Michael talked straight to each other. There was no indication that they were father and son. So Christopher conveyed this information to his father without rancor and Michael accepted it that way.

"So? My new woman's a sister too, what's the big deal? It's not like Raven's white."

"Raven's so foreign to the typical South Oak Cliff woman, she may as well be," Dudley offered, and Christopher smiled at the dig.

Michael shook his head. "I've represented Dallas for more

than fifteen years, and every term, I'm reelected by almost ninety-eight percent. It's got to be something else."

"Things are different this time, Dad. People are talking . . . wondering if you're the same guy."

"Why? Because I did what I needed to do to be happy? Raven and I are together and that's that—it's time for sisters to move on, get a life instead of judging mine."

Christopher wasn't letting his father off that easy. "A woman gets hurt, she's going to heal at her own pace. Some women feel like every time they turn around, a brother is putting them down in favor of someone else." Christopher wanted to stay on a professional level, not get personal, but he couldn't get over how nonchalant his father was about having abandoned his mother. "When they see a high-profile black man leaving a black woman, their own hurt surfaces again."

"But Raven is—"

"I know, Dad, she's a black woman, but I agree with Dudley." With effort, Christopher lowered his voice and took the acid edge off his tone. "She's not the type other black women can relate to."

He wanted to tell Michael the truth, as told to him by a white woman who was one of Michael's campaign coordinators: "Most of the women who can bring out the vote for your father have met Raven, and they don't like her. I'm talking about black and white women alike, including me." But Christopher didn't say anything about it. Better to let his father believe that black women didn't like Raven because they felt *less* than her—Michael could live with that explanation. He might not be as comfortable with the idea that his wife was off-putting to women of all stripes.

"Raven is who she is, but I see your point," Michael said and took a deep breath. "What can I do?"

"Don't worry about it," Raven said as she walked into the room. "You're right, baby, I am who I am, and no matter what anybody thinks, I'm taking you straight to the top." She wore a short transparent robe, no makeup, and no slippers. Startled, Michael looked at Dudley, then Christopher, who were both looking at Raven. Christopher picked up a magazine, but Dudley continued to stare. Michael was alarmed to have another man see his woman practically naked. But the look on Dudley's face wasn't lust, it was more like annoyance. Although she had encouraged Michael to offer him the chief of staff position, Dudley didn't trust Raven's political instincts. He had already warned Michael not to let her play too big a role in the campaign.

Michael turned to Raven. "Honey, I thought you were asleep."

"I was, then I got a taste for some ice cream. Want some?"

The men didn't, so Raven fixed herself a heaping bowl of pralines and cream, and joined them. She listened to the trio toss out strategies for jumpstarting Michael's campaign. When she finished eating, Raven said, "I told you when I walked in here, don't worry about it. A black woman will follow a man straight to hell and take the fire meant for him as long as he asks her the right way."

She tossed her hair, smiled at Michael, and said, "We're loyal that way."

"What do you suggest?" Michael asked. He no longer felt tired, but he was ready for bed.

"Get Grace to endorse you."

"You must be out of your mind." Christopher set aside his magazine and stared straight at Raven. He didn't see a beautiful, barely clad woman. All he saw was a threat.

Michael said to Raven, "Baby, I know you want to help, but—"

Dudley held up his hand. "Wait a minute, Michael. I know it sounds crazy, but let's think this through."

"Think all you want, but I'm telling you now, it's not happening. Who the hell do you think could convince her to do something so stupid?" Christopher stood and walked over to where Raven sat on the ottoman in front of Michael's chair. "I'm not surprised that you'd try to use my mother," he snapped, and then turned to Dudley. "But I can't believe you agree with her."

Christopher gave his father a scathing look, shook his head, and walked out.

When Michael started to stand, Raven clasped his ankle. "Let him go, he'll be fine."

Christopher's outburst didn't faze Dudley, but it did help him plot Michael's next move.

"I know. We'll have David talk to Grace," Dudley said.

"Can you believe he told Michael that? 'Dudley's clueless when it comes to getting to know people,'" Dudley Capps said, mocking Christopher. "He's the one who's clueless. Little bastard. No matter what that kid thinks, I know all I need to know about people—they make messes and lack the will to clean up after themselves, I can tell you that," Dudley said as he paced Dr. Laverne's office. He needed a drink and a cigarette.

Dudley plopped down on the sofa and swung his meaty arms along the back of it. "People stick their transgressions in closets and corners and pray that no one will look. But you know what? I *specialize* in hidden corners and locked closets, so I don't give a rat's ass about knowing the name of a legislator's wife or his pet project. When it comes to specifics, only the dirt matters. And I know how to dig it up. That I know. I specialize. Damn right."

"But like his father told you, Christopher's no threat to you. He's just—"

"And you know what else? Know why I don't get to know people? Because I *prefer* not to. I don't like them." Dudley used his fingers to tick off a list. "Not my wife, not those two blood-sucking vampires I call daughters, and certainly not

Michael. I'm the one with the brains, but what do I get to do? Prop up his comatose ass at press conferences, let him be the clever dummy that sits on my knee, does all the talking, and takes credit for my ideas."

Dudley visited Dr. Laverne once a month at which time he'd rant for an hour, take his prescription, and leave. If Dr. Laverne hadn't been afraid of getting in trouble with the medical board, he'd have written Dudley five-year prescriptions for a half-dozen different drugs, shoved him out the door, and dead-bolted it.

Dr. Laverne knew that Dudley didn't need drugs to control his emotions and actions; most of the time Dudley held absolute authority over both. It was just that every once in a while something set Dudley off. And when something set Dudley off, he fantasized about being the central character in a spectacle akin to Columbine or Oklahoma City.

Christopher's comment about Dudley being clueless had set Dudley off. He was in the middle of a pretty decent-sized temper tantrum, so Dr. Laverne stopped trying to ask questions and simply listened. After going nonstop for forty-five minutes, Dudley wiped the sweat from his face with both hands and said, "Whew! That felt good."

"Did you get it all out?"

"Think so. I know I say a lot of crazy stuff when I get wound up, but when it gets down to it, I probably wouldn't kill anybody. Hell, I've never even shot a squirrel. Could you see me in prison with a bunch of ignorant niggers turned jailhouse faggots?" On Dudley's list of things and people he hated, faggots were at the top with ignorant niggers running a close second. "I'd kill myself."

"Remember, Dudley, therapy is the place for honesty."

"What's that supposed to mean?" Dudley said. It sounded like he was ready to go off again.

"Uh, nothing." Dr. Laverne cleared his throat. "Since you're certain you're not going to hurt anyone, have you done what we talked about last time?"

"Gotten rid of my sawed-off? No, it's in my campaign office and when Michael gets elected, it's going to the governor's office with me. There're lots of crazies out there and half of them have a beef with the government. If anything ever goes down, I'm going out like a man, like a hunting man, sporting a sawed-off shotgun."

"The Capitol has top-notch security, Dudley. If anything happens there, the guards are better equipped to handle it than you are. You're making excuses." Dr. Laverne had a lot of patients who were violent, but it was Dudley, who'd never received so much as a speeding ticket, that Dr. Laverne was scared to cross.

"Maybe I am making excuses," Dudley said as he stood and put on his jacket. "But there's something about having one close by. Hell, just the name, *sawed-off shotgun*, is undeniably big dicked." Dudley snatched his prescription from Dr. Laverne's desk and winked at him. "And so am I. All the women say so."


"Will you say something from your pulpit and get the other top preachers to do the same?" Michael asked David. They were in David's sprawling suburban Dallas home, both nursing a glass of Glenlivet 1959 Limited Release.

"Anything for you, Michael, but I'd like to hold a press conference first," David replied.

"Sure you would," Michael said and smiled over the top of his uplifted glass at David. "I was thinking the same thing. How about tomorrow morning?"

They sipped in silence until David asked, "There's something else, isn't there?"

Michael hesitated. He felt slightly embarrassed, but the question had to be asked. "What about Grace? How're you going to explain our divorce to your own congregation? She's been with New Word since the day you married us."

"It wouldn't be a problem if you had kept showing up at Sunday service every now and then. Folks would have gotten over the split by now. Van Thomas over at Second Bethel changes wives every three years." David snapped his fingers and laughed. "Think the women over there care? They'd stroke out if Van talked about leaving the pulpit. If you had only come back, passed out some hugs, kissed a few babies, they would have forgiven you too."

"I hear you, Doc. My heart's still with New Word, but showing up there with Raven? First off, I've only been to church with her once, years back, and I love my baby, but she has no church etiquette whatsoever. And I don't want her bumping into Grace. Raven's high strung, easily upset."

David shrugged. "Don't worry about what other people think about your divorce from Grace. There's some stuff in First Corinthians that I can use, make it sound like it was Grace's decision to get a divorce and that it's biblically acceptable. Make her look good."

"I need you to do more than just make her look good. I need you to get Grace to come out for me."

David sat back and rubbed his chin. David had told Michael that he didn't judge him for divorcing Grace, but privately he thought Michael's decision was selfish and unnecessary. Also, David liked Grace, he couldn't ask for a better church member. But no matter how much Grace supported David and the church, as between her and Michael, David's allegiance was with Michael.

"I might be able to convince her to support you, Michael, but I don't recommend it. Grace is still a wreck. She acts strange, says strange things sometimes. Your best bet is that she goes nowhere near the press."

"She says strange things?" Michael felt a stab in his chest.

"Uh huh. To couples, young ones mainly, if she thinks they're in trouble. Tells them little lies about . . . cherishing each other, I guess you could say. A couple of parishioners have come to me, asked me to get her to stop. No big deal really."

"I didn't know." Michael blushed. "Should I do something, call her maybe?"

"You? Do something for Grace?" David didn't bother to conceal his disbelief. "Don't get all concerned now—you weren't when you left her." Seeing the stricken look on Michael's face, David added, "Don't pay me any mind, I've been in a bad mood all day. Like I told you before, what happened between you and Grace is none of my business." He continued to soothe Michael's feelings. "Grace's situation isn't a big deal. All women go a little bit nuts when they get divorced. Grace'll be all right, but for now she's of no use," David remarked as he freshened their drinks.

"Yeah. Grace probably won't even vote for me herself. But I do need the vote of every other black woman in this state. They're gems, every one of them." He eyed David. "I don't know why you can't find a sister to settle down with. You're good at chasing them, or more precisely, letting them chase you, but sometimes you act like you don't need sisters." Michael sighed. "You just haven't met the right woman. You need someone strong, a woman like Raven." He sipped his drink, and between it and having shifted the talk from his personal life to David's, Michael felt quite comfortable.

"I need black women," David said defensively. A thought came to him, about the kind of mate he craved, but it made him very uncomfortable and he quickly dismissed it from his mind. Trying to smile at Michael, David continued, "It's a good thing for your campaign that I'm not ready to commit to just one woman because that means they're *all* free to love me." David shot his friend a confident look. "Whatever you need from the women in this state—votes, money—I'll get."

# 4

While David Capps worked on rebuilding Michael's reputation with black women, Raven and Dudley tackled the money problem. The campaign had raised a few million, but not enough to counter Sweeney's media blitz.

"We've been to the same wells too many times," Dudley advised Michael. "They're coming up dry."

"*Dry*, my ass. All we're getting is the little bit that spills out of Sweeney's buckets," Raven said as she flipped through television channels. It was commercial break time, and on station after station she encountered Jeff Sweeney—exchanging back slaps with longshoremen, hugging wrinkled little ladies, shaking hands with businesswomen; and of course there was the obligatory shot of Sweeney, surrounded by a miniature rainbow of humanity, jogging to nowhere.

"By my count, for every commercial we run, Sweeney airs six. That money came from somewhere," Raven said.

"Looks like we've hit every interest group," Michael said. "Business owners; Latino leaders; everyone's locked down."

"What about the gun advocates?" Dudley asked.

"What about them?" Michael's voice was tight and the pleasant expression he always wore was nowhere in sight.

"Texans have to have their guns, and they don't mind shelling out money to hold on to the privilege," Dudley said, ignoring Michael's testiness.

"Since when does anyone need a semiautomatic weapon?" Michael abruptly rose from his seat to refresh his drink.

"Only since Congress passed the Second Amendment." Dudley jumped up from his seat and grabbed Michael's glass. "Relax, I'll get your drink," he said obligingly.

"Gun control is the only thing standing between us and the money we need to take the lead in the race," Raven said. She was tired of going over the same ground with Michael. Though he was malleable in their personal lives, Raven had found out at the start of the gubernatorial campaign that her husband stood his ground when it came to his platform. Raven agreed with Michael: handguns and semiautomatic weapons served no purpose outside of law enforcement. Guns were crude, and there were so many more efficient, hard-to-detect weapons to choose from. Still, she wasn't one to begrudge anyone his or her tool of choice. She'd support private citizens' ownership of ballistic weapons if it would get her into the governor's mansion.

"I could place a call to STRAPPED," Dudley said. "They've got so much money—"

Michael's look stopped Dudley in midsentence. "I don't care if STRAPPED is handing out cash on street corners. Do you have *any idea* how many black people were killed by handguns last year?" Michael slammed his drink onto the table and left the room.

"Why can't he get it through his head that those STRAPPED crackers vote?" Dudley complained. "And when they do decide to kill a nigger they don't shoot him, they drag him behind a Ram dualie or give him a lethal injection," Dudley complained.

"Crackers, niggers. You're so articulate," Raven said dryly.

Dudley giggled.

"When we started this race," she said to Dudley without

looking at him, "I promised myself that I would let Michael take the lead." She turned the diamond bracelet on her wrist round and round as she spoke.

"*Let* him take the lead in his own race. How big of you," Dudley replied.

"Not on everything, but issues involving ethics, definitely," Raven said, ignoring Dudley's sarcasm. She stopped playing with her bracelet and looked him in the eye. "When I want something, Dudley, I want it. Period. At times I'm not all that"—Raven paused, searching for the right word—"*particular* about how I get my way. What do you think about that?"

"I think that in politics people who are too particular, who don't realize that this is a business in which the ends often justify the means—those folks get left behind." He got up to refresh his drink again, and with his back to Raven, added, "I don't want Michael to be one of those folks."

"If Michael keeps on making irrational decisions based on emotion we're going to be," Raven said worriedly. She ran both hands through her luxurious mane, sighed, and then said, "Tell me about STRAPPED."

He nodded, glad that in Raven's internal tug-of-war, her practical side won over her follow-the-rules side. "I thought you'd never ask. STRAPPED is a huge organization, but one person controls it. Erika Whittier. It's time the two of you met."

Erika Chaseworth Whittier was a fourth-generation west Texan, progeny of the Chaseworth-Stilton family. Unlike many rich Texans, Erika's family money didn't come from the oil industry; it came from banking and assorted black-market enterprises that served oilmen. Erika was free, white, over twenty-one, *and* rich—in other words, accustomed to having her way.

Erika had seen Raven on television and once or twice from a distance, so she knew that Raven was a good-looking woman. As Erika watched Raven make her way toward her table, she saw that in person Raven was more than just attractive—she moved like a dancer and looked like a model, only healthier.

Erika herself was a very good-looking woman. She was a brunette who'd never given in to the hype that to be beautiful, one had to be blond. She was on the good side of 40, yet her hair had lost none of its thickness and luster. In high school Erika's had been voted "prettiest smile." Her father blamed it on the fact that every other girl in the class wore braces. But when braces came off the others, Erika still had the best teeth and lips in three counties. She'd been a cheerleader back when it was okay for cheerleaders to look athletic, and she maintained her body as easily as she maintained her love of west Texas, by hiking, river rafting, and biking.

Although she was a Texas gal who could bring down a six-point buck with a clean shot, Erika hung with the jet set when she felt like it. She was a patron of the arts, owned a villa in the south of France, and was on a first-name basis with Donatella and Oprah. On the professional front, Erika headed the Austin office of a New York-based investment-banking firm.

"It's good to meet you," Erika said as they shook hands. "I thought maybe I'd been stood up."

Raven never apologized to anyone but she made an exception in Erika's case. "Oh, no. Thank you for agreeing to meet me. I'm so sorry that I'm a little late. Something came up that I needed to take care of. Our staff usually stays on top of things, but . . ." Raven gave a bemused smile. "Some days . . . whew!"

"I'm sure it's a good staff."

"I'd like to think so; I handpicked every member," Raven said.

"Well then, I guess we know who's running things," Erika said jovially.

"I do what I can to help, but it's my husband's show," Raven said, deciding there was no time like the present to start selling Erika on Michael's qualities. "The senator's a visionary, always looking at the big picture." She shrugged, reached for her water glass, "I manage the details."

As they looked at their menus, Raven said, "I've never been here, but I sure like this menu." She read a few entrées aloud. "Pan-seared sirloin, braised pork chops, crab cakes with butter infused chipotle sauce. Sounds delicious."

"Sure does, for later. For lunch, I prefer lighter dishes, don't you?" Erika asked.

Raven put on a fake smile and nodded. When the waiter came they both ordered salads. Raven detested salad.

As was her habit with every woman she came into contact with, Raven sized Erika up. *She's decent looking*, Raven decided, *especially for her age. Probably has had some work done*. She studied Erika's clothing and her jewelry and grudgingly admitted to herself that the woman had style. Erika had on simple, expensive diamond studs and a platinum and diamond ring, which she wore on her right hand. *She shouldn't wear such flashy jewelry; it shows a lack of class*, Raven thought. Raven looked at Erika's earrings only once, and wished that she'd worn her own diamond studs, which she judged to be slightly larger than Erika's. Raven had to make herself stop sneaking glances at Erika's ring. She noticed a Greek-lettered pinkie ring on Erika's left hand.

"Sorority girl?" Raven asked.

"Yes, I was," Erika looked down at her ring. "I know it's silly to still wear this, but no matter how hectic things get, I can look at this ring and instantly feel calm. I still talk to two of my sorority sisters at least once a week, and no matter what's going on we all get together twice a year." She looked up at Raven and inquired, "You must be a sorority girl too. It usually takes one to recognize one."

"I am," Raven said. She looked into the distance and hoped her eyes appeared to be alight with memories. "Thrown in with women you've never met, and you become friends for life. Incredible," Raven said even though she hadn't had a thing to do with her own line sisters since the day they went over.

"Did you go to school here in Texas?" Raven asked.

"No, I went to Wellesley, then to Wharton."

Raven shook her head. "It shows," she said in a low conspiratorial tone. "I've only been in Texas a few years, and I love it here, but the culture is a little insular, don't you think? It's people like you, who've experienced how things are done in other parts of the country, who can help Texas reach its full potential."

"How so?" Erika asked. The slight smile on Erika's lips made Raven think that maybe she was being laughed at, but she pressed on.

Raven set her fork down. "By helping to open the eyes of all Texans so they can see beyond my husband's color. I'm talking about whites, Latinos, and blacks. They've all got to come together, realize that the senator's the best man for the job."

"And you think I can help with that?"

"Erika, I know you can," Raven said, her voice taking on the fervor of an evangelist. "You head the one organization that touches every demographic group in this state. The people here, whether they're rich or poor, black or white, educated or not, are fiercely independent. They don't like being told what to do, and they especially dislike being told they can't own guns. If STRAPPED gets behind Michael, he's sure to win."

Erika said, "The Committee to Save Texans' Rifles And Pistols wants to support Michael, but he's making it difficult. By the way, we don't like that name. STRAPPED? It sounds too Wild West-ish, and it doesn't fit our updated image."

Raven gritted her teeth. "I'm sorry," she said. "The good thing is you and I are on the same page: you want to support the senator, and I want you to do it. All we've got to do is figure out a way to make that happen."

Erika smirked. "I don't see how I can help Michael's platform. He hasn't made a big deal of it so far, but I know he's for gun control."

"I know it seems that way, Erika, but face it; in this election STRAP—your organization—is looking at the lesser of two evils. Can you imagine what will happen to gun rights if Jeff Sweeney is elected?"

Erika knew what Raven meant. Michael's opponent, Jeff Sweeney, had a defect that no gun-toting man or woman could ignore. He hadn't touched a gun since, at age sixteen, he'd seen his father's face blown off by an errant shot from a deer rifle. Sweeney believed in gun control, and couldn't be persuaded to change his mind or mute his voice. Erika had already tried.

Erika didn't want Sweeney in office and having Michael as governor would be almost as bad, if it weren't for Ted Ballentine. Ballentine won the Democratic primary race for lieutenant governor and now he and Michael, like it or not, were ticket mates. Michael didn't like it. Having Ted Ballentine elected lieutenant governor mattered a great deal to Erika and her friends. Ballentine was ambivalent about guns, but he loved gun-lobby money. Once elected, Ballentine would do whatever he could to keep that money flowing into his bank account. Michael's winning was a guaranteed means to that end.

But all Erika told Raven was, "I'm not sure Sweeney would be as bad for us as some people think. But for the sake of argument, let's just suppose that my organization decides to throw its support behind Michael. I think he'd throw it right back at us."

"Oh, Erika, I don't know. He could always be noncommittal."

"You mean Michael says nothing, one way or the other, about gun control?"

"Right."

"You'll never get him to do that."

Raven had kept herself in check during the entire lunch, but Erika telling her what she could and could not do, well, it was just too damn much. "You have no idea what I'm able to do," Raven said. When she'd decided to marry Michael, Raven underestimated the degree of self-control required of a politician's wife. Self-control had never been her strong suit.

She motioned for the waiter. "Key lime pie, please." Forget all this meatless, no sugar shit. Raven shifted the conversation away from the governor's race to other races going on around the state. After the waiter set the generous wedge of pie topped with whipped cream in front of her and she'd had a chance to let its smooth sweetness tame her tongue, Raven took up the subject of Michael again.

"Erika, I know we're just getting to know each other, but I can already tell that we're the same type of woman. Strong, driven. What I said before about what I'm able to do—I'm sure you understand what I meant." She put a hand to her chest, to emphasize her sincerity, but quickly lowered it when she thought about the size of her ring compared to Erika's. "I'm not only Michael's wife, I'm his confidante and his sounding board. He values my opinion, so if I advise him that it's in his best interest to stay away from the gun control issue, he will."

"If Michael backed away from the issue, that would be all that we need. If you can get him to do that, I'll get him the votes."

"We'll need more than votes."

"You want my organization to publicly support Michael?"

Raven sighed regretfully and said, "I wish it were possible but an endorsement from STRA—from your organization might kill our campaign. If you're serious about helping Michael, I think the only way to do it is by making a contribution."

Erika was taken aback. Up to this point she'd been impressed by Raven's savvy courting of her because she hadn't promised anything that—theoretically, at least—she couldn't deliver. But if money changed hands Erika would expect firm results. "Raven, I may not know exactly what you can or can't do, but I do know that Michael won't accept a contribution he can't explain."

*Here the bitch goes again*, Raven thought but she didn't become flustered. "Don't worry, Erika, I told you from the beginning: I'm running things. My husband doesn't need to know everything, he just needs to win." Raven took a note from her purse and gave it to Erika. "Here are the details."

Erika studied the note and said, "Five hundred thousand. I'm impressed. You certainly don't underestimate Michael's worth."

"And you shouldn't underestimate mine," Raven said. She had a big smile on her face and her tone was friendly, but Raven's eyes were dead serious. "You come through for my husband, and I'll come through for you. I promise."

"For Michael, anything," Erika said magnanimously.

"One last thing," Raven said. Now that she and Erika had reached an agreement she felt comfortable setting aside her good political wife act and being herself. "Why do you keep calling my husband by his first name? You don't call Jeff Sweeney by his first name."

"I know your husband a lot better than I know Sweeney," Erika said. In fact, Erika used to know every inch of Michael's body, and although it had been ten years or so since the last time she'd seen him naked, from outward appearances not much had changed. She signed for the check and then stood, not waiting to see whether Raven was ready to leave. "I'll be in touch," she said, and walked away.

# 5

As soon as she got the STRAPPED money, delivered in cash by Erika herself, Raven organized a series of small, lavish "platform meetings" held with black sorority chapters throughout the state. Michael and David, the dangerous duo, swooped through Texas with such speed that at times it was hard for them to remember where they were.

As they watched a beautiful young woman address a standing-room-only crowd of sorority women—Deltas, AKAs, and Zetas sat side by side—David yawned and asked Michael. "Where are we? Longview?"

"Longview's tomorrow. We're in Lufkin," Michael said. The men were just to the left of the stage, and couldn't be seen by the audience.

"Better get it right, man. She's really building you up," Michael said of the woman on stage, who was making a long-winded flowery speech in praise of David, who would then introduce Michael. "Go out there and call this town by the wrong name, you'll probably be booed off stage."

David let out an easy laugh, and smoothed his goatee. "Sisters boo me? Not likely."

David was right. Everywhere the two men went David was received with open arms. Michael wasn't surprised by how warmly women, from eighteen to eighty, embraced David, but he was shocked by their lukewarm response to himself. Before he married Raven, Michael had been as popular with black women as David. He'd had it like Denzel—some women liked his family image, and supported him for it, while other women couldn't care less if his wife and kids dropped dead; he was their fantasy man, their personal lover who could do no wrong. Michael had played both advantages, giving chaste kisses to single women who admired him as a husband and father, and dropping a little something extra on the ones who wanted more.

In his run for governor, Michael no longer had his double edge with women—he still had a wife, albeit a new one, but sisters saw her as a man-stealing, classless tramp. And because Raven satisfied him the way no other woman could, Michael didn't sleep around. He lost out on both counts.

Michael surveyed the crowd. The women who were all immaculately dressed sported campaign hats and waved little flags bearing Michael's picture. Although he couldn't see it from backstage, Michael knew that a huge banner reading, "Joseph for Governor" hung across the stage.

He noticed something amiss. "Most of them aren't wearing campaign buttons."

David nodded absently. "Pin-on buttons and silk don't mix. The crowd loves you, but not enough to ruin a new suit."

A relieved Michael peeked out again and commented, "I never knew there were so many good-looking women in small towns. I'da run for governor a long time ago, if I had known it would've brought me face to face with so many fine women."

"Whatever you *were* missing, you still are, Michael, going straight to your room every night. You ought to get out more, see the sights." David thought about getting out and about in Lufkin himself. He'd seen a nice little waitress in their hotel lobby when they checked in the night before. He hoped she was on duty tonight.

Michael turned his attention from the crowd and looked at David. "If I haven't said so before, I really appreciate what you're doing for me. Taking time away from New Word and your personal life to bring out the vote for me. I won't forget it."

David said, "It's not me, Michael. It's God. He's just using me to help you fulfill your mission in this state." David grabbed Michael's hand. "As a matter of fact, let's pray. We should've been doing this all along." He uttered a short prayer.

Finally, with the dramatic flair unique to black sorority women, the young beauty announced, "Sisters of the Greater Panhellenic Council of Eastern Texas! REVEREND! DAAVID!! CAAAPPS!!!"

David bounded onto the stage amid wild applause and spoke for a mere ten minutes, but for every second of that time, he worked his Capps magic. He prowled the stage. He hollered. He spoke so softly that women stepped on one another's heels as they leaned forward to hear him. He didn't say a word about himself—his sleek, pantherlike control of the entire room spoke for him quite well. David's message was all about his best friend, Senator Michael Joseph. About Michael's past service to the state. About how, if given the chance, Michael would be the greatest governor Texas had ever seen.

When he whispered, David whispered to the women about themselves. About how they had the power, *only* they had the power to put Michael in office. He spoke a little louder when he told them what Michael would give in return for their support. Michael would create jobs. Michael would preserve minority set-asides, see that blacks got their fair share of government contracts. Michael would stop the Texas judicial system from devouring their sons whole, while giving white boys a pat on the butt for the same offense.

Shouting again, David reminded the women that it was about time. About time for a black man to run the state! About time for black women to *flex*, hallelujah, thank you, Jesus!

David put on the same show in every city and small town he
and Michael visited, and he was on like Hollywood every single time. Michael never tired of watching his friend. The Capps
magic mesmerized even him.

By the time David introduced Michael, the women were so
fired up all Michael had to do was wave and smile. Many times
that was all he did, then he and David would work the crowd,
woman by woman, gathering campaign workers, garnering promises of votes and cash.

"The tide has officially turned," Michael said. He raised his
glass and clinked it against David's. The men were drinking
red wine, neither man's favorite, but it was the only thing David
felt comfortable drinking in public. They were in the lobby of
their hotel rehashing the day's events.

Their waitress came over and asked, "You fellas need anything else?" She was a perky blue-eyed little something, with
blond hair swept back into a ponytail.

"I still want to know what you're doing serving drinks?"
David asked. He'd been teasing her all evening. "Looks like
we ought to be carding you."

"Honey, I'm full grown," she said, all Southern sass.

"I can see that." David, having finished his second glass of
wine, roamed her body with his eyes.

Michael looked from David to the waitress and back again.
He clamped his hand onto David's arm. "Ready to call it a
night? We've got another big day tomorrow."

"Not yet," David said, never taking his eyes off the waitress
as she walked away.

"David," Michael spoke slowly and forced David to look at
him. "Are you sure?"

David waved him off. "I'm fine, Michael. I'm right behind
you. Just want to sit here a minute, think through a couple
of church matters I'll need to handle by phone tomorrow
morning."

"Okay, but watch yourself. What might fly in Houston or Austin could cause you to end up with a rope around your neck in this part of the state," Michael said half-jokingly before he left for his room.

As soon as Michael walked off the waitress came back and, to David's pleasant surprise, she sat down. "Where's your friend?"

"Turned in for the night."

"In that case, this is for you. My treat." She slid a drink, which David had assumed was for another customer, across the table to him. "I can tell what a man likes, and you're definitely a single-malt-scotch type." She leaned back, reached into her cleavage and pulled out one cigarette. "No pockets," she explained to David, who watched her every move.

"Are you off for the night?" David asked as he took a sip of the drink. It was his first taste of hard liquor in two weeks, and my, it was good.

The waitress exhaled, sending a cloud of smoke toward the ceiling. "Ten-minute break." She looked at David and smiled. He noticed her dimples. "I get off in an hour."

David leaned forward. "How old are you anyway?"

"Twenty-six. And when I said I'm full grown, I meant it." She took another drag on the cigarette, let it out. "You're one hell of a good-looking man. Anybody ever tell you that?"

"All the time," a feminine voice answered before David could respond.

Startled, David looked up to see Raven standing just behind his chair. "Raven," he sputtered. "What are you doing here?"

"Just thought I'd check up on you boys." She pulled up a chair and sat down. "My meeting for this afternoon got cancelled, and I don't have anything on my agenda for tomorrow." She directed all her attention to David as though the waitress didn't exist. "So I decided to join you, see what life's like on the road."

The waitress didn't move. She eyed Raven and kept on smoking.

"Sweetie, do you work here?" Raven finally asked.

"Yes, I do."

"Great, I'll have a rum and soda, please." Raven leaned back and crossed her legs. She had on a knee-length skirt and she didn't seem to care that it was riding up pretty high.

"I'm on a break."

Raven gave her a wicked smile. "Well, I'm not. I want my drink now." Raven stared at the waitress until the woman stood, put out her cigarette, and stomped off.

"Oh, and sweetie? Make that a double," Raven yelled after her.

David took a sip of his drink. "Nice."

"What?" Raven shot her thumb toward the bar. "Her? Don't worry, I'll give her a good tip." Raven grinned wryly. "And from the looks of things when I walked in, Reverend Capps, you were about to give her even more than that."

"I don't know what you're talking about," David replied.

Raven shook her finger. "Uh-uh. If there's one thing I know, it's men. The look you were giving her"—she nodded her head toward the waitress, who was headed back their way with Raven's drink—"means one thing. You're on panty patrol."

"Panty patrol? That's a quaint way to put it, coming from a woman who supposedly knows men," David said, feeling the alcohol.

"White pussy patrol. Is that plain enough for you?" Raven asked just as the waitress sloshed the drink down in front of her.

"Would you like anything else, sir?" she asked David without so much as looking at Raven.

Raven took in David's eyes and half-empty shot glass. "He'll have a bottled water," she said. The waitress didn't move, so

Raven, her hands clutching the sides of her chair, turned toward the waitress. "Bambi, Tinker Bell, whatever the hell your name is, you can bring us the water or not. Just get away from this table." She looked at David, but spoke to the waitress. "I'm here now, so you might as well move on."

When the waitress left, David burst out laughing. "Raven! I'll never be able to show my face in this place again. She's just a girl. Why'd you go off on her like that?"

Raven laughed too. "She pissed me off, that's why."

"How?"

"Trying to push up on you. Then when I show up, she acts likes she's still the hottest thing in the room?" Raven pursed her lips and tossed her hair. "She must be out of her mind."

"You sound jealous," David said, a slight smile on his face. "Why would that be?"

She shrugged. "What can I say? I like being the center of attention." Raven leaned across the table, suddenly serious. "I think you've had a little too much of this," she said as she pushed his drink away from him. "I didn't want the waitress to take advantage. It wouldn't be good for you, or for Michael."

David looked shamefaced, so Raven started flirting again, to ease the tension. "And like she said, you're a fine-looking man. I'd hate to see you waste yourself on the likes of her. Even for one night."

"Oh, yeah? Why is that?"

"Because." Raven tipped her glass up, partly obscuring her face.

David waited. He felt flushed and didn't know whether it was because of what he'd had to drink or the conversation.

"Because," she repeated when she put her glass down. "You . . . are . . . one . . . *fine* black man. Trust me, I'm an expert."

David cleared his throat. He felt hot all right, and it wasn't because of the alcohol. "Michael went up about ten minutes ago," he said. "You might want to join him."

Raven kept her eyes on David, willing him to squirm but he stared back at her as boldly as she stared at him. Finally she said, "Want to or not, I think I'd *better* go up."

As she passed David, Raven bent and kissed him on the cheek, close to his mouth. "Good night."

# 6

"Christopher, you may as well get it over with. Call her." Genie held Christopher's cell phone out to him. "Maybe she'll have time to make other plans."

"Other plans? She's got no one to make other plans with. My mother stays shut up in her condo. The only time she gets out, other than when I'm in town, is when she goes to church."

It was Friday afternoon and Christopher and Genie were on their way to Houston to attend a baby shower. Genie, who had helped the expectant parents coordinate a full schedule of events for their out-of-town guests, had been looking forward to the weekend for months. When they got to Houston they'd have dinner at the young couple's new home. The shower on Saturday was going to be at the husband's parents' country club. Christopher barely knew the couple, but he insisted on attending the coed shower with Genie.

Genie reminded him of it. "If you didn't want your mother to spend this weekend alone, you should've made plans with her, not me."

"Nah, girl, this is your weekend. And don't act like you've got an attitude. You know you want me with you." He playfully pinched her arm. "Besides, if you think I'm letting you go solo around all those single Houston men, you're crazy."

Genie slapped his hand away, "Single men aren't interested in going to showers!"

"Wrong. Wherever there are single women, if men can get into the mix, they're there." Christopher grinned and said, "Shows how much you know about men."

Christopher's real reason for going to Houston with Genie was that he didn't want to be with Grace. His mother lived for his visits; she reminded Christopher of a sad, old dog waiting for its owner to come home. He'd seen her two weekends in a row and her bleakness nearly suffocated him.

"Make the call," Genie said.

"All right."

Genie dialed the number and put the earpiece to Christopher's ear.

"Hey, Mom. What are you doing?"

Grace sighed. "Nothing. Sounds like you're on the road already. What time are you getting here?"

"That's why I'm calling, Mom. I don't think I'm going to be able to make it this weekend."

"But you promised." Grace's voice hovered between disappointment and resignation. She was aware that being with her was something short of a good time.

"I know, Mom, and I'm really, really sorry." Christopher darted his eyes at Genie, then said, "Genie's hosting a baby shower for some friends and I promised to help her out. I got the dates mixed up and now I'm stuck. I'm sorry." Christopher dodged Genie's punches as he laid out his lie. "We're on our way to Houston and probably won't leave there until Saturday afternoon."

"Well." Grace sighed again. "I'd hoped you'd come for the whole weekend, but if you can't get here until Saturday afternoon, that'll be okay."

"But Dad's sponsoring a town hall meeting Saturday night. Remember, I told you about it? He's going to need my help."

"Right." Grace spoke so softly that Christopher had to strain to hear her. Guilt beat at his temples, but he held firm. He'd told a partial truth about getting his dates confused—if he had things to do all over again, Christopher wouldn't have spent two consecutive weekends with Grace. Now she wanted three weekends in a row? He couldn't take it. He wouldn't do it.

Grace forced herself to sound cheerful. "I understand, Chris. You and Genie have a good time in Houston. I'll see you next weekend."

*Next weekend? Shit.* "Okay, Mom. Next weekend."

"Here," Genie said as she handed Christopher a small plate of pasta and chicken. "I noticed you didn't eat much at dinner. Thought you'd like this." She took a seat beside him on the backyard deck of their friends' home.

"Thanks," he said. Christopher took the plate but didn't touch the food.

"I looked around for you inside." She gave a little laugh. "People are all over the place, even in Kent and Jaime's bedroom. I thought maybe you were taking a tour."

"Nah," Christopher looked up toward the second-story window. He could see the other guests milling around in the game room. "I'm sure it's a nice place but, nah."

Genie picked up his fork and speared a piece of chicken. "They're getting ready to play charades," Genie said between bites. "I don't think the men are too into it, though. Charlie and Mitch already sneaked into the other room and turned on ESPN."

"Oh, yeah," Christopher commented in a distant voice.

Genie slapped a mosquito that landed on her thigh. A minute later she used Christopher's napkin to wipe the perspiration from her neck.

"It's hot out here, Genie. You should go back inside."

"I'm okay." Genie said. She hesitated, then asked, "Thinking about your mother?"

Genie had never seen Christopher look so sad. "I'm supposed to be able to have my own life, Genie. I'm not her husband, I'm not responsible for making her happy all the time."

"I hear you."

"My fucking dumb-ass dad. How could he just leave her like that? To treat a woman who's been nothing but good to you the way my dad treated my mom, I'll never understand it." He motioned toward his chest with both hands. "Then when I get ready to have some fun, I can't even enjoy myself for feeling guilty. It's not fair!"

"I know," Genie said. "And I know that despite their shortcomings, you love both your parents with all your heart."

Christopher nodded and wiped his eyes with the back of his hand.

"Chris?"

"Huh?" He didn't look at her.

"If we leave here right after breakfast tomorrow, we can get to Dallas in time to take your mom to lunch and we'll still make it back to Austin in time for the rally."

"Really?" Sometimes Christopher couldn't believe his luck, landing a girl as good as Genie. "But what about the shower tomorrow? Jamie's going to be hurt if we leave."

"Jamie's my girl. She'll understand." Genie reached out her hand to Chris. "Come on, let's go inside."

# 7

When Michael walked into the room, Raven could tell from the look on his face that the meeting with the *Austin American-Stateman*'s editorial board hadn't gone as planned. Acceptance rejuvenated Michael. He was at his best, attractive in every way, when he won a key endorsement, or when he pressed his way through a crowd that loved him. But rejection beat Michael up three times as much as acceptance restored him. His meeting with the editorial board must have been brutal, because Michael's normally youthful face looked haggard. Raven knew politics aged a man, would turn his hair white at warp speed, but she thought that happened after the man got into office. If Michael kept having bad days, Raven would have to start calling him "grandpa" behind closed doors, instead of "naughty boy."

She asked anyway. "How was it?"

Michael stopped in the middle of the room. He threw his keys on the coffee table—not a good idea, considering that it was glass—and said, "It was all right."

"Really?" Raven said. "Why don't I fix you a drink while you tell me about it."

Raven poured them each a glass of scotch, straight up, and

squeezed onto the love seat with Michael. She rubbed the back of his neck as he talked.

"It started out fine. I know all of them; hell, I can't count the number of times I've met with the members of that board, as a group, or individually, for lunch or what not. So I felt pretty comfortable, know what I mean?" Michael swirled the scotch around in his glass.

"I put on my show, ran through my routine, and the response was good. It was good." He pounded the air with his fist. "I got tough questions, but they were fair ones, and I didn't have a problem with any of them." Michael stopped, drank a little. "Then, bam! Out of the blue . . ." He abruptly slammed his glass onto the coffee table.

"Baby, I know you're upset, but if you shatter my table, things will only get worse," Raven said crossly. "Finish telling me what happened."

Michael looked to the ceiling and let out a labored breath. "Jerry Minshew is what happened. Guy ought to be working for one of those sleazy tabloids instead of a major daily. He's not interested in real news, all he wants to do is sling mud."

"Hmm. That's usually left up to the candidates."

"I know." Michael's expression said *See what I'm saying?* He shook his head, mentally chastising Jerry Minshew. "Sweeney and I made a deal at the beginning of the race that we'd fight fair. I'm out to whip Sweeney, but I'll be the first to tell anybody he's a decent man. Even if I did find out something dirty about him, I wouldn't use it unless it had something to do with his ability to govern. If Sweeney's not trying to throw dirt on me, then Jerry Minshew has no business doing it either."

Fighting fair was something Raven and Michael had gone round and round about. She and Dudley wanted to get into the gutter if that's what it took to win the race. But Michael had other ideas. He and Sweeney had a private meeting, just the two of them, and they emerged with a pact to wage a hard-fighting, clean campaign that focused on the issues.

"I don't know what I resent worse," Michael continued, "the fact that Minshew goes around acting like he's Mr. Black America and then stabs me in the back, or the way he chose to attack me."

*Sometimes it's so easy for Michael to get sidetracked,* Raven thought irritably, and didn't bother to hide her impatience. "I don't even have to know what happened, but I can tell you, the fact that he's the only black man on the board, and that he's the one to come out against you? That's the worst. Publicly he's given blacks the impression that he supports you, but behind closed doors, he does this? The fact that he attacked you at all is unforgivable. How he went about it is beside the point," she said dismissively.

Michael gripped his glass in anger. "You think that because you didn't hear what Minshew said."

Seeing his agitation, Raven softened her voice. "Okay. Tell me."

Michael picked up his glass and drained it. He didn't say anything.

"Michael?" Raven changed positions—she folded her legs beneath her on the love seat and turned her body so that she faced her husband. "It was me, wasn't it? Minshew asked questions about me."

Michael nodded. "Every other word out of his mouth had to do with you. With your past."

"What sorts of things did he ask?"

"There was the usual, you know—what you had to do with my divorce from Grace. And then he brought up some shit about your work for the Department of Defense when you lived in Washington DC. Something about a Dr. Vakar. I didn't know what the hell he was talking about."

*Dr. Vakar! How the heck did Minshew find out about that? What lies did he hear about me?* Raven's thoughts were all jumbled and her insides were tied in knots.

"Then he asked about Omar Faxton," Michael added.

"What did you say?" she asked, hoping that her voice sounded matter of fact.

Michael looked embarrassed. "I was caught off guard, didn't know what to say. I threw out some lines about focusing on the issues. I sounded like a fool to my own ears." He leaned back and closed his eyes.

"Things went downhill from there," Michael said. "I expected to get the paper's endorsement—I had it in the palm of my hand until Minshew started talking nonsense. The editorial board's got this custom: when they're going to endorse you, they all stand and shake your hand before you leave the room. The head of the board escorts you out. Hell, the head of the board didn't even stand up. I had to walk over to him, shake his hand. Then I saw myself out."

Michael looked at Raven, worry etched in every line of his face. "Honey?" Pause. "Should I be concerned? Not about the board's endorsement—I'll figure something out—but about you?" He continued in a hesitant voice, "We've never talked about what happened to Omar. What took place between you and him? Did he really come to see you the night he disappeared?"

Raven leaned over and kissed him. "No, Michael. The rumors about Omar and me were nothing but lies. I've got no skeletons. Everything there is to know about me, you already know."

Even though Michael had told Raven that he'd blown the chance to get the paper's endorsement, he was still disappointed when he opened the *Austin American-Statesman* the next morning and failed to find, in bold print across the top of the editorial page: JOSEPH FOR GOVERNOR.

"At least they didn't endorse Sweeney," Raven said as she threw the newspaper to the floor. She and Michael were having breakfast. Raven's plate was piled high—three pancakes, bacon, sausage, and two eggs over easy. She slathered butter onto her pancakes and drowned them in syrup. Raven took a bite and closed her eyes. Heaven.

"You don't know what you're missing," she said to Michael, who hadn't touched his food. "I fixed your favorite breakfast because I knew you'd need cheering up, and you're ignoring it."

He sat motionless, giving no sign he had heard what she said.

"Don't trip, Michael. Can't you see what the newspaper's doing? They met with Sweeney the day before they met with you, right? And they still haven't issued an endorsement. They're playing coy, waiting for something to happen to tip the scales, let them know which way to go."

Michael sighed at her optimism. "The majority of the board knows which way to go, it's just that Minshew's so influential and he's determined that I'm not going to get their support. I don't think the paper's ever issued an endorsement that he didn't agree with."

With one finger Raven absently twisted the ends of her hair. She squinted, her eyes turning into catlike slits. "Okay, we know Minshew is the problem. We've just got to figure out how to get him on our side. Figure out what he wants and give it to him."

Raven had attended the same events as Jerry Minshew had, but they'd never been introduced. When Raven entered a room, it was natural for men to let their eyes linger on her. Eventually they would turn back to their own wives or pick up their conversations where they'd left off. But there were a few, like Minshew, who never managed to pull themselves away. They ogled her breasts and legs, and couldn't stop, even when Raven looked them in the eye, or Michael tried to stare them down. Their hunger for her was so raw it was ugly. Raven had an idea or two on how to get Minshew to change his mind. She just needed to hear Michael confirm her thoughts.

Michael was still trying to puzzle out the problem. "Minshew and I move in the same circles, we share the same politics; at least I thought we did. Judging how he treated me in the meeting, maybe I'm wrong. For all I know he's one of those neoconservative black houseboys."

"I don't buy that, Michael. This sounds personal, not political."

He looked sharply at Raven. "You're right. Even if Minshew disagrees with me on a few things he knows I'd make a better governor than Sweeney. He didn't kill me on the issues. All Minshew was interested in was finding out more about you. I swear the man's obsessed."

She nodded to herself. Just as she thought. A plan started to unfold in her mind. If Minshew wanted to know what Raven Holloway Joseph was all about, then she was ready to give him the uncut version.

That night when Raven made her ritual refrigerator raid, she found Dudley and Michael in the same seats they'd been in for the past three nights.

"Another sleepless night, huh? Dudley, you should go home to your wife, and Michael, you need to come to bed with yours." She winked at Dudley and looked directly at him as she said to her husband, "It's been—what?—three days? I'm missing you."

"Honey, I'm sorry, it's just that I'm in serious trouble here. David's helping to get votes from black women, but without the newspaper's endorsement I could still lose." Michael looked so miserable that Dudley thought he might actually cry. Dudley wished for a tear, just one, but Michael braced himself and the moment passed.

Raven returned from the kitchen with a slice of apple pie. She stooped and rubbed Michael's shoulder. "I keep telling you, don't worry about it. Things are going to turn your way. You've got my word."

Raven and Dudley exchanged a look that Michael didn't notice, and then she headed back to bed.

"Raven's trying to help, but she doesn't understand," Michael said when he was sure Raven was out of earshot.

"I don't know, Michael, your wife's something else. If she says you'll get a break, I don't doubt it."

"I'm surprised you value her opinion. What's that you used to say in law school, brains and breasts don't mix? Tell you the truth, I'm shocked that you two get along at all."

"We do okay."

"Too short. Not short enough. Way too much—might kill him." Raven was in her walk-in closet, going through her man-hunting clothes. She slid outfit after outfit along the rack, looking for the perfect bait. She had ensembles suitable for catching men of all persuasions, and she was experienced enough to know that a girl couldn't put on just any sexy little thing, it had to be the *right* sexy little thing. Some men didn't even want a sexily attired woman—they wanted a women dressed like their mother, or like a man.

She thought about Jerry Minshew. A loser like him would definitely want sexy; he'd probably never dated anyone who wasn't as funny-looking as he was. And Minshew was plenty funny in the looks department. He was one of those men who wore his blackness on his sleeve because at first glance he was often mistaken for white. Minshew was very fair-skinned and had gray eyes. The look worked well for some black men, but he wasn't one of them. He'd been partially bald for years, with a horseshoe shaped gap in the middle of his oddly shaped head. One day he up and decided to get hair plugs. Minshew's swollen scalp hadn't completely healed from getting the plugs put in before he started getting the luxurious locks taken out. Journalists are cruel people, and even within that group the folks at the *Austin American-Statesman* were a mean-spirited breed all their own. They made fun of Minshew to his face, behind his back and, although they didn't know it, in Minshew's dreams. Ms. Piggy with a pen, they called him. His scalp wasn't bare anymore, but now it was covered with scars rather than hair. It looked like a dog's chew toy.

Minshew's body was harder to look at than his angry red scalp. He carried about eighty extra pounds on his ordinary frame, and he wore the weight more like a woman than a man. Fat ass. Pregnant, low-slung gut. Enormous saddlebags and spare tires all around. Minshew was a major ugh, a uck, a make-a-woman-throw-up type guy.

"The things we do for love," Raven muttered under her breath as she rejected another ensemble in her closet. Michael needed the paper's endorsement, and if she had to turn Minshew out to get Michael the nod, well, that's just the way it was. That's why her outfit was so important. "If I choose just the right getup," she continued talking to herself, "maybe all I'll have to do is let him look at me." But Raven was a soldier with a strong stomach, and if Minshew needed more than a look and a quick feel, she fully intended to rub her beautiful, bare body against his unfortunate one.

Raven changed course and decided to select her shoes first. Shoes talk to men, scream at them or whisper to them, telling them all sorts of things about women that may or may not be true. She chose a pair of lavender snakeskin Jimmy Choo's with five-inch heels and ankle straps. Once she picked her shoes, the rest was easy. When Raven walked out of the house she had on a sheer black La Perla bustier and matching thong, fishnets, and a little white linen jacket that barely covered her ass.

Jerry Minshew was about to get punked, Raven style.

"Mrs. Joseph, what are you doing here?" The people who rang Jerry Minshew's doorbell were usually selling cookies or salvation. So he was understandably frazzled to find Raven on his doorstep.

"I came to talk about my husband. May I come in?" As Raven talked she made her way into Minshew's apartment. It was spacious and had a great layout, but Minshew didn't know what to do with it, any more than he knew what to do with his own body. He had a pleather sofa; an ancient, wooden, floor-model television; and dingy walls. Raven glanced toward the kitchen, which was just as outdated. The only thing she liked about the place was the bookshelf against one wall. Not that the shelf looked good, but it gave the room a little personality.

Raven walked over and read the titles. *At least he's got good taste in books*, she thought. The idea put her at ease, humanized Minshew enough to help her do what she had to do.

"I understand you've got reservations about endorsing my husband for governor." Raven stood with her jacket closed and her hands in her pockets. Her voice was throaty. "And I hear that those reservations have to do with me."

"Mrs. Joseph," Minshew began in an officious voice, "this is quite inappropriate. I'll have to ask you to—"

"To what?" Raven challenged. By now she'd unbuttoned her jacket and let it fall open, just a bit. Just enough to let Minshew get a peek. "Whatever you ask me to do, Jerry, that's what I'll do."

Minshew, bless his heart, was speechless.

Raven stayed where she was and kept talking. As she talked, she let her jacket open more, more, more. With every inch of her body that she revealed, Raven hoped that Minshew would lose it, that he'd turn and run to the bathroom, sparing her from having to go further. But it wasn't working out that way.

"Michael said that you seem interested in my past. Is that true?"

Minshew found a tiny piece of his voice. "Well, I . . . I think it's newsworthy, that's all."

"Jerry, I don't mind letting you know me better, but I don't want my information going public. I'd like for whatever I tell you, or show you, to be our secret. Can we do that?" Raven spoke as though she were talking to a child. "Why don't you sit down?"

Minshew just stood there, mouth agape.

"Go on, sit." Raven motioned toward the sofa. Minshew sat and Raven walked up behind him.

She slowly rubbed his bald, disfigured head. "From what

Michael told me, you've discovered that I'm a naughty girl, who's done some naughty things. I can't lie, Jerry, I *am* a naughty girl. The worst. But I'm also good, and very smart. You know what I mean?"

When Minshew didn't reply, Raven patted his head and said, "I know. Kind of hard to talk right now, huh? That's understandable. But we've got to figure out a way to communicate, Jerry. Because before I let you know what I'm all about, we've got to reach an agreement about the paper's endorsement. Now I'm going to ask you a series of questions, and if you agree with me, just nod yes, okay? If you disagree, shake your head no. Let's begin.

"Do you think Michael is more qualified than Sweeney to be governor?" Raven fondled Minshew's ear as she spoke.

He shook, No.

"Wrong answer," Raven said. She squeezed Minshew's earlobe.

"Ouch! That hurts!" he said, pulling away and grabbing his ear.

"I can't help it if you gave the wrong answer, Jerry." Minshew had halfway turned around to look up at Raven, but she took both hands and turned his head face forward. Raven would do what she had to do, but she didn't have to look at the pig while she did it.

"I didn't mean to hurt you." Raven again massaged Minshew's earlobe. "Let's try again, and this time be honest. Do you think Michael's more qualified than Sweeney to be governor?"

"Yes."

Raven rolled her eyes, leaned down, and gently sucked Minshew's earlobe.

"Good." She massaged Minshew's temple and whispered in his ear. "Question number two. And this is a very important question, Jerry, so pay attention. Is there any chance, any at all, that I can do something to help you convince your colleagues at the paper to endorse Michael?"

"Yes." Now that he'd been shocked into speaking by having his ear pinched, Minshew barely waited for Raven to finish her sentence before he answered. He'd thought about saying no, to see what Raven would do. When she squeezed his earlobe it hurt, but not in a bad way; the way she punished him for saying no was almost as good as the way she rewarded him for agreeing with her. But he was in a hurry to get to the ultimate question and the ultimate reward, so he didn't have time to say no.

Raven used one hand to unfasten her bustier. She leaned her cool bare breasts against the back of Minshew's head. *Surely this ought to do it*, she thought. Although he groaned and sank into the pleather sofa like a wounded animal, Minshew held on.

"What do you want me to do?" Raven asked.

"Anything. Just, please hurry!"

"Well then, I'll skip the details of my past life and give you the big picture. Show you what I'm about. If you're happy—well, happy isn't the right word; *satisfied*, I should say—if I satisfy you, Michael gets the endorsement and my past is forgotten. Agreed?"

Minshew squeezed his already-closed eyes even tighter and murmured, "Agreed."

She licked Minshew's bald spot, and suddenly he was thankful for supersensitive nerves that his botched hair implant experiment left behind. Jacket and bustier now discarded, Raven and her badassed Jimmy Choo's walked around the sofa and faced Minshew. "Tell me how you like it, Jerry."

Two hours later, after he'd closed the door behind Raven, Minshew managed to take two shaky steps toward his sofa before he fainted from exhaustion.

Raven pranced into the master bedroom bearing breakfast and the *Austin American-Statesman*.

"Where'd you get that so early—why'd you get it so early?" Michael asked as he yawned.

"Special delivery," she replied and dropped the paper into his lap. "Look at this." JOSEPH BEST CHOICE FOR GOVERNOR

"Unbelievable," Michael said as he read the banner across the front page of the paper. He relaxed as his body released tension he wasn't aware he carried. "For this to happen, Minshew had to change his mind about me. Wonder what made him do that?"

"I had a talk with him," Raven said as she took a bite of French toast. "He's a weird guy, but quite reasonable, once you get to know him."

Michael looked surprised. "You?"

Raven licked syrup from her lips. "Don't look at me like that. You know damn well that I want to be the governor's wife. You didn't seriously think I was going to let a loser like Jerry Minshew stand in my way."

"Aren't you worried that, well, maybe this could turn on us?"

"How, Michael?" Raven thumped the newspaper. "Look at this, they've already committed, and besides, it's true; you are the best choice for governor." Michael watched his wife lick her fingers as she spoke. There was a carafe filled with warm syrup on her breakfast tray. They kept a chef's torch in their nightstand.

She asked him, "Are you having some sort of black man's inferiority complex? Feeling like you're getting something you don't deserve, not qualified for?"

"Of course not!"

"Well then, accept this victory and move on to the next one."

Michael leaned forward and kissed Raven. "You're right. I deserve to be the big man in the governor's office, but in this room I'm nothing but a servant to my queen. My wicked queen. Feel like showing me how undeserving I am?"

Raven smiled at Michael. Sometimes they were so compatible. "I'll make a deal with you," she said sweetly. "Let me have your French toast and when I finish, I'll treat you like the worthless scum you are."

# 8

"Son, come on in." Michael took off his reading glasses and stood. He'd felt someone watching him and looked up to find an infrequent visitor—Evan.

Evan took a step into the room, then just stood there. Michael's internal alarm bells went off. Evan must have gotten himself into a scrap he couldn't get out of on his own. Even if Evan was about to give him bad news, Michael was happy for the rare visit.

"Something going on I need to know about?"

"Naw. Just wondering about the Juneteenth party."

"You mean the fund-raising gala? Oh, that's tomorrow night." Michael relaxed and sat down again. "It's going to be—what's that you young people say—off the chain?"

"Yeah. I heard." Evan scratched his head and studied the floor. "I was thinking, you know, a Juneteenth party. That's tight." He looked at his father and asked, "What ya'll wearing?"

"I'm wearing a tuxedo."

"Chris too?"

"I'm sure he is. Did you ask him?"

"Naw. Him and Genie, they went to Vegas for the weekend. They ain't coming back till tomorrow afternoon."

Evan's grammar was killing Michael, but this was the longest conversation they'd had in weeks, and Michael wasn't going to disrupt it by harping on Evan's slang. When he was a toddler, Evan had the vocabulary and reading skills of a seven-year-old. Evan's eagerness to learn was so remarkable that Grace and Michael had started to worry that Christopher was a little slow until the pediatrician told them, "Chris is exceptionally bright for a child his age, but don't compare him to his little brother. Evan's the smartest little boy I've seen in the last ten years."

"I was thinking about going, but I ain't got no tux. My old one's too small."

Michael looked at the clock. It was ten o'clock on a Friday night. "I'll have Lawrence meet us out front."

Minutes later Michael, Evan, and Michael's driver, Lawrence, were tooling down Tenth Street toward a downtown men's store. The owner, Rudolpho "Rudy" Dominica, was a tailor for Austin's powerful men and a longtime supporter of Michael. When he first moved to Austin thirty years before, Rudy had jumped when his clients called, but these days he didn't get out of his bed for just anybody.

"Rudy, my friend, thank you for helping me," Michael said as he embraced the tailor. "My son needs a tuxedo for tomorrow night."

"Have you been to Italy, son?" Rudy asked Evan as he measured him.

"No, sir," Evan replied. "We went to Europe when I was a boy, but we only visited the UK, France, and Germany. I wished we'd have gotten as far south as Italy, but we didn't."

*I knew it; perfect English and accurate geography when the time is right*, Michael thought.

"The most beautiful people, the best-dressed people in the world, are in Italy!" Rudy exclaimed.

"No? Why are you laughing? It's no lie!" Rudy said to

Michael and Lawrence. They were laughing because they'd heard Rudy's spiel before and knew what was coming next.

Rudy hung his tape measure around his neck, so that he could use both hands to gesture as he talked. "The black man, he has style, yes! Much style! But it comes from Italy. Black men have Italian blood in them, I'm sure of it!"

Michael egged Rudy on because he always did, and also because he wanted to stretch the moment out for as long as he could. Michael took advantage of the time to study his son and saw that although Evan had inherited his own lean body, the rest of him was Grace made over. He had Grace's quiet, fluid way of moving, but masculine athleticism replaced feminine charm. He'd gotten his height and coloring from Grace's side of the family. Grace was barely five three, but her father had been a tall man, and so was Evan. He had Grace's father's deep-brown hue, which set him apart from Grace, Michael, and Christopher, who were all fair skinned.

Evan was shy, too, like his mother, and it took him a while before he'd look the tailor in the eye as Rudy asked whether the jacket was comfortable along the shoulders and whether the trousers pinched his crotch when he sat down.

"You're Italian here too, son, you need plenty of room," Rudy teased as he measured Evan's inseam.

By the time he'd finished being measured, Evan was as loose as the other men. He dropped his mask of surly nonchalance and softly sang along with the Joe Williams CD while Rudy made the alterations.

Rudy looked up from his work and said, "Michael, your son sings like an angel."

Evan looked alarmed. "Naw, I ain't—"

Rudy stopped him. "Your voice is a gift from God, do not be ashamed." He nodded knowingly. "With a voice like that you will go to Italy one day. Sing at La Scala, maybe." Rudy gave Michael a look that said, Wouldn't that be something? He turned back to Evan and told him, "And when you do, think of old Rudy, eh?"

On their way out of the shop, Michael said, "I'm still wide awake. What about you guys?"

They all nodded, then Lawrence said, "A Burns's link sandwich would be pretty good right about now."

"Or an order of ribs," Michael said.

"With potato salad, beans, and a strawberry soda on the side," Evan added.

As they rolled toward Burns's, Evan leaned forward and asked Lawrence, "Is that Parliament I hear?"

"What you know about P-Funk, youngster? Yeah, that's Parliament."

"George Clinton? Man, I haven't heard Parliament in years. Turn it up!" Michael ordered. Pretty soon all three men were making their funk the P-funk, getting all funked up.

"Dad! I didn't know you could get down like that," Evan said. He flashed a smile so brilliant that it stopped Michael mid-bop and wiped the smile right off his face.

"What? What'd I do?" Evan asked.

"Nothing . . . It's just—your smile—it's just like your mother's. It's beautiful."

Christopher banged on Evan's door. "It's me, Ev! Let me in!" He could hardly hear his own voice above the bass line blasting from Evan's room. Christopher opened the door and found Evan lying on the floor with his eyes closed and his beautiful voice shouting to the beat, something about mutherfuckers, gats, and hos.

Christopher slowly turned down the volume.

"The fuck you want, Chris? Cain't a nigga knock?"

Christopher playfully kicked his brother. Evan was the biggest thug wannabe in the world. He talked hard, but Christopher had caught the soft surprise on Evan's face before he slipped on his gangsta mask. Christopher rarely visited his father's home except for business. When he and Evan spent time together they went somewhere or hung out at Christopher's apartment.

"I did knock, but you got it thumpin' up in here." Christopher bobbed his head for a beat or two before turning the sound even lower.

"'Sup? Dad send you in here 'bout that thing I got into at school?"

"What thing?" Christopher asked, then waved both hands, palms open. "On second thought, I don't even want to know."

Christopher sat on Evan's bed. "Dad didn't send me." He paused, then said, "I talked to Mom this morning. She asked about you. Mom misses you, Evan. She'd love it if you rode down with me to spend the weekend with her. At least do it every once in a while."

"It's boring at her house."

"I know she's not as much fun to be around as she used to be, but she's our mother."

"Does she still cry every day?" Evan asked.

Christopher blinked and they both looked away at the same time. The brothers didn't say anything for a while. The air was thick with shared and individual memories and hurt—there was no room for words.

"You said she asked about me." Evan's voice came out high-pitched and cracked.

"I told her you're trying out for the city choir."

"Is she going to come to my audition?" Evan still sounded funny, but there was something else in his voice, too. Hope for Grace.

"I wouldn't count on it, Ev. Mom's still not . . . she's not right. Besides, I'll go with—"

Evan cut Christopher off by lying back on the floor with a thud. He reached behind him and turned up his music. Christopher stayed just long enough to watch his little brother mumble hateful lyrics—something about "bitches ain't shit."

\* \* \*

Grace sat in the center of the small reading circle. She was surrounded by boys at their terrible best. At twelve and thirteen years old they were victims of the havoc wreaked by surging testosterone. Squeaky voices, hair in strange places. Caught between wanting to hit a girl or kiss her. The boys' mix of emotional impulsiveness and burgeoning intellectual maturity made for an energetic, hard-to-control group.

"Boys! Boys! Please calm down!" If there was such a thing as a timid shout, Grace used it. The students ignored her. They threw balled up wads of paper at each other and refused to stay in their seats. They raised hell.

John Reese, drawn by all the commotion, walked in and asked, "What's going on in here?" He didn't shout, and his voice wasn't particularly deep, but it was authoritative.

"Nothing, Mr. Reese," James said as he and the rest of the boys scurried to their seats.

John looked around the room, giving each of the six boys an evil eye meant especially for him. "I don't want to have to come in here again."

He looked at Grace. *Everything okay?* his eyes asked.

"We're fine, John. Thanks."

"Now boys, where were we?" Grace opened her third-grade reader. "Oh, yes. Open your books to page sixteen, please." Grace didn't look at the youngsters as she spoke.

Grace cleared her throat. "Wallace, will you please read for us?" She never looked up from her book.

Silence.

"Wallace?" Grace looked in the direction of the boy she'd asked to read. She fixed her eyes on his ear.

The boy stared back at her, his face blank. A few of the others snickered.

"Ain't nobody up in here named Wallace," James said. James was thirteen and the boy Grace asked to read was his younger brother. "His name is Waleed."

"I'm sorry," Grace said. "Waleed, please read the first two paragraphs."

The young man stumbled through the first paragraph. Grace helped him out with one or two words, but mainly she left poor Waleed on his own. Grace's mind was far away, brooding over an article she'd seen in the morning paper: JOSEPH AND WIFE TO BE HONORED AT JUNETEENTH FETE

*I used to be the "and wife,"* Grace thought miserably.

Waleed was about to begin the second paragraph, but James broke in. "Can I read the rest of it?" he asked.

Waleed looked at James, clearly relieved, but Grace didn't catch it.

"You'll get your turn in a minute, son," Grace said absently. "Waleed?"

Waleed slammed his book shut. "Read if you want to, James. She ain't gon' be able to tell the difference no way."

"No shit," said Trey, just loud enough for Grace to hear.

Grace finally took a good look at the students sitting around her. Every boy had a surly expression on his face.

"But you're here to improve your reading," said Grace, a puzzled expression on her face. "The only way you're going to learn is to try."

"That's why we here. What you here for? You did some kinda crime, got some kinda community service you gotta do?" Trey said, a smirk on his face.

Emboldened, another student cracked on Grace. "She probably got a child abuse case. We ought to call 911 on her right now!"

Everybody laughed except for James. One boy started rapping—something about calling 911—and two others stood and stalked about the room, waving their arms and reciting the lyrics like they were on stage at a hip-hop concert.

"Boys, please sit down! Eric, why would you say something like that?" She fought to be heard.

"'Cause his name ain't Eric, that's why. It's Aaron," James said. Everybody turned to look at him. James hadn't said anything since he asked to read for his brother. James waved a hand toward the window. "Everybody else out enjoying summer vacation. But we here. Ain't nobody made us come. We came because we want to—" James's voice got a little shaky and his eyes glistened—"to do better. But you act like we ain't nothing. You don't even try to remember our names."

"Yeah, and you don't care if we get embarrassed. When Waleed messed up you barely tried to help him out," Trey added.

"Probably think I'm too dumb to help," Waleed mumbled under his breath.

Grace's top lip trembled. "I'm sorry. What can I do to make the class better?"

"Get us a tutor who likes kids," Trey said. That set the boys off on another laughing jag, but Grace knew it was no joke. She picked up her book and walked out.

"Hey, hey, where are you rushing off to?" John Reese asked as he trotted to catch up with Grace in the parking lot. He got to her just as she opened her car door.

He grabbed the door handle. "Don't leave, Grace. Don't run. Talk to me."

She turned to face him, tears streaming down her face, "I'm sorry, John, but I can't do this." She slammed her fist on the top of the car. "I should've known better! Look at me! What do I have to offer to anybody? Not a damn thing." Grace motioned toward the school. "Even those kids can see that." She covered her face with both hands.

John put his arm around her. "There's nothing wrong with you that can't be fixed," he said. "Come on. Let's go back inside."

John set a cup of coffee in front of Grace. They were in the little room the school set aside for the literacy program.

"It hurt me so bad, me and Maggie both, when you and

Michael broke up. I can't even imagine how much it hurt you."

Grace let out a low moan. She hadn't talked to anyone about her divorce.

"You've been in the valley, all by yourself, and that's to be expected. You lost something important and you needed to grieve that loss." John grabbed Grace's hand and forced her to look at him. "But Grace," he said in an urgent voice, "you've been wandering in the valley for too long. If you don't come out now, you might just stay lost there forever."

"And what would be so bad about that, John? Michael was my life." She shook her head as she remembered the last year of her marriage. "I tried. You don't know how much I tried. I prayed. I fought. I tried to cook better meals, to have better sex. But nothing I did was good enough to make him want me."

"Michael wasn't your life, and you were wrong to ever put him on a pedestal like that. God gave life to you directly, Grace, not through Michael. You can't spit in God's eye by letting your spirit die just because Michael walked out."

Grace stood and walked over to the window. Her class, the boys who wanted "to do better" were outside playing basketball. "I feel so empty," Grace said as she watched them. "Those boys thought I didn't care about them, and you know what? They were right. But it's not just them. Since Michael and I broke up, I can honestly say that I haven't cared much about anything, except trying to figure out where I went wrong." She turned and faced John. "I'm not even as interested in my own sons as I should be, especially Evan." Grace picked up her handbag. "Find another tutor for the boys, John. I won't be back."

The Juneteenth gala, held on the nineteenth of June, turned out to be Michael's coming out party, the preinaugural ball, as black radio stations called it the next day. The guest list was a

Who's Who of black America—actors rubbed shoulders with scholars, ministers danced with hip-hop queens, and politicians wheedled money out of millionaires. Everyone else in Texas who mattered was there as well, and in a reversal of roles, it was the whites who had to fit in. Most of them handled it— what was the Cha Cha Slide, after all, but the Cotton-Eyed Joe minus the flair?—but a few fled the scene in confusion.

When Michael and Raven entered the hotel lobby and Raven loosened her wrap and let it fall into the bend of her elbows, Michael was mildly shocked and thoroughly turned on. As usual, his wife walked the thin line between sexily tasteful and slightly slutty. Raven checked her lipstick, turned to her husband, and smiled. "This is my moment, Michael."

"It's for all of us, honey," Michael said. He half turned, looking for Christopher and Evan. "Here they are," Michael said as he watched the limousine carrying Christopher, Genie, and Evan, along with Dudley, his wife, and two other staffers, drive up. Raven hadn't wanted anyone to ride with her and Michael, even though they'd been in the super stretch. Dudley's wife started standing before she'd completely emerged from the limousine and got stuck in the doorway.

"It'll take that fat cow five minutes to get out," Raven said as she watched Dudley's wife struggle to free herself. "Let's go."

"Not yet. I want my sons with us."

Just then Raven caught a glimpse of Evan, who had gotten out of the limousine from the other side. She saw him all the time, but dressed up it struck her. *He looks just like Grace. If he and Christopher walk in with us, it'll remind everybody of her. I'll be an outsider.*

Raven motioned for the attendants to throw open the ornate double doors, and stepped forward, pulling Michael with her.

"Wait on them? For what? When I'm with you, you don't

need anyone else," she said. By now the doors were wide open and the guests were on their feet, loud and bodacious, clamoring for Michael.

"Are you going to stand here like an idiot or are we going in?" Raven whispered.

Michael, who could smile and cut like a knife at the same time, commenced doing both. He got his feet moving and said, "I don't have a choice, do I? After we do the happy couple routine, you need to stay the hell out of my way. I let you get away with murder with me all the time, but you're going to learn, Raven, not to mess with my sons."

Michael looked back one last time, directly into Evan's eyes. His son's broad smile faded when he realized that his father was going ahead without him.

Michael and Raven knew how to work a room, and even their detractors had to admit that the senator and his wife were a charismatic team. Raven charmed every man whose equipment still worked, and women who'd expected the worst whispered to each other, "She's not so bad."

Raven and Erika Whittier were within arm's distance a few times—while Erika talked to the head of Hub Oil, Raven was just behind her greeting a congressman from Tyler. During dinner, Raven stopped at Erika's table, but turned away after she greeted Tina Boss, who was seated next to Erika. Tina was the young wife of one of Erika's best friends. He was out of the country, but he had called Erika that morning to ask her to keep an eye on Tina.

Tina turned to Erika and said, "I wanted you to meet Senator Joseph's wife. She's, like, the most fabulous woman ever!"

"There'll be time," Erika said. She looked toward the podium. "Isn't that the minister David Capps?"

"Absolutely. Don't tell me you've never met him?"

"Never, but I've heard plenty about him."

"I guess he's going to introduce the senator." Tina leaned

toward Erika's ear and continued, "He wouldn't have been my choice. When a black preacher opens his mouth he's going to, like, whine first and beg second."

"Shhh! You're going to get us thrown out!" Erika said as she lightly tapped Tina's knee. As she listened to David speak, Erika realized that he was not a preacher by default; David was a natural leader: compelling, intelligent, and decisive.

"No whining yet," she whispered to Tina.

"Who'd notice if he did? The guy's a hottie, don't you think?"

Erika's table was just to the left of the stage, so from her vantage point she was able to inspect David from the top of his clean-shaven head to the toes of his Cole Haan shoes. Her eyes traced the length of his body. He wore a tailored tuxedo that perfectly draped his well-built frame. Always one for the athletes, she judged him to be a sprinter or a basketball player when he was in college. Given his height, she settled on basketball. Erika imagined long, spindly legs, which didn't do much for her, but the high, tight butt of a baller had always been one of her favorite parts of a man's anatomy.

"A hottie? I don't know, Tina. If you like his type, then I guess so," Erika whispered back.

"Of course he's not *my* type, but, you know, he's got the look of those black guys in the videos. Kind of like, you know, like a caged animal that'll rip you to shreds if you let it out." Tina shook her head, certain she was right. "Yeah, that's how he looks. Dangerous and sexy." She giggled, cupped her hand to her mouth, and whispered, even lower, "He looks like a pimp, like a dangerous pimp looking for some hos."

Erika looked at young Tina's super-sized breast implants and thought: *And you look like a ho looking for a brain.*

When David finished the introduction and Michael rose to speak, Erika examined him too, but not as closely. Although he was much shorter than David, and on the slim side, Michael Joseph held his own when it came to good-looking men. Yet his sexiness didn't impress Erika. She hadn't been attracted to him in years.

After Raven and Michael made their rounds, he ditched her and kept Christopher and Evan at his side. Raven was getting so much attention from their guests that she didn't mind being on her own; she didn't have to share compliments with Michael or patiently wait while someone showered him with praise. This is my night, she constantly reminded herself, and yes, she was on. Still, although she was glad Michael had left her alone, he had to pay for choosing his sons over her. Raven prowled the room looking for something to get into, something juicy.

She spotted David Capps and thought about the flirting they'd done in the bar in Lufkin. The next day David had avoided being alone with her, but she'd caught him staring at her a few times. She looked over at Michael, who was across the room with one arm slung around each of his sons' necks. What better payback to him than to light a fire in the middle of the room with his friend as kindling?

"Reverend, you sure are wearing that tuxedo." Raven took David's hand in both of hers.

Raven watched his eyes. At his height, all David had to do was look down, and he'd be instantly lost in two mounds of buttery bliss.

"Thank you." His voice was warm, but his eyes didn't really focus on Raven or her breasts, which were practically screaming for attention.

Raven looked down at herself, and thought, *Yep, still there and still awesome. Is he blind?* She forged ahead. "Everything's been so hectic, we haven't had a chance to talk, just the two of us, since that night in the hotel lobby. We should get together over lunch."

"I'd love to," he said with as much enthusiasm as a man scheduling a root canal. Raven didn't know it but David had scoped out her breasts and every other inch of her as soon as she and Michael walked into the ballroom. She looked so stunning that David didn't dare let himself be drawn into a conversation with her. Not here, anyway. He wasn't sure of what he might say.

He scanned the room, desperately searching for Michael. He needed a powerful antidote to fight his attraction to Raven. A glimpse of her husband just might do it.

David's eyes fell on the ultimate cure. His eyes lit up.

"Spotted someone important?" she asked.

Before he could reply Raven heard a familiar voice.

"Mrs. Joseph, I've been trying to get to you all night. My, that's a beautiful dress. So daring."

David yanked his hand from Raven's grasp. "Reverend David Capps," he said, extending his hand. "I don't believe we've met."

"Erika Whittier, Reverend Capps. I've heard a lot about you."

"Then you should've heard that my friends call me David." He didn't eye Erika in a disrespectful way, but he did notice everything about her, and he couldn't hide the fact that he appreciated what he saw.

Raven flung her hair and posted herself closer to David. "Erika, great to see you." She threaded her arm through David's. "We're just finishing a little business, if you don't mind."

"Business comes first, that's my motto. Call me," she said to Raven and walked away.

"Now, about lunch," Raven said, but David barely heard her. He was too busy watching Erika's teardrop of a derriere saunter away.

# 9

"Just look at the crime rate in black communities. They ought to be the first in line to bear arms," Erika said.

"So they can do what? Shoot Lil' Man and Pookie from the next block over?" David asked. He smiled when he said it, which added to Erika's confusion.

David sat back with his arms folded. He'd been that way for much of the hour that he and Erika had been together. They were in David's office at New Word. After the Juneteenth gala, she'd approached him and offered to fly to Dallas to meet with him on an issue that she said was "important to the African American community."

David sat on the sofa and Erika sat in the chair to his left. The coffee table was strewn with documents—think-tank reports, poll results, and statistics. Erika went through each one in detail, but David didn't pay much attention. Before Erika arrived, David had wanted to have a drink to calm his nerves but he talked himself out of it. His resolve weakened when she walked in wearing a white pantsuit with an embroidered pattern that ran down the front of her outfit, from the shoulders of her jacket to the slight flair at the bottom of her pants. When Erika sat down David got a good look at her strappy white sandals, perfect feet, and little gold ankle bracelet. He broke down and headed straight for his private stash. Now they both nursed bourbon and Cokes and Erika matched him, sip for sip.

"Questions?" she said after explaining the final report.

"No."

"Judging from your body language we're not going to agree."

David shook his head. *No.*

Erika frowned. "In my world you're reputed to be flexible. I was told it was worth a try."

David wasn't sure what Erika meant, but he felt a little offended. He leaned forward, elbows on thighs, and slowly turned his glass round and round with his fingertips. "I'm flexible under the right circumstances, but there's no way I'm coming out in support of citizens being able to pack any type of gun anywhere, anytime. That goes against everything I believe in."

Erika looked disappointed. "So . . . I guess we have nothing more to talk about. There's nothing I can do? Come back with a better proposal, maybe?"

David gave her the smile that he used on church sisters when delivering bad news that he wanted them to accept with a good attitude. "Any proposal involving guns you can keep, but that doesn't mean we have nothing to talk about. We're both interested in the welfare of our state. I'm always looking to make friends in influential places, and I'm sure you are too. We should stay in touch."

Erika, thinking she was getting the brush-off said, "Sure thing, Reverend Capps. We'll have to get together sometime."

David kept twirling his glass. He cleared his throat. "I was thinking of something more definite. Like dinner."

Erika stopped gathering her things. She thought, *What's going on here?* One look at David told the whole story. The all-powerful David Capps was gone, replaced by a self-conscious man with the hots. "Tonight?" Erika asked.

"No, no," David said quickly. He shifted in his seat. "Let's do it in Austin. I'll give you a call."

On her flight home to Austin, Erika thought about the way David kept staring at her throughout their meeting. Many Southern white women felt uneasy under a black man's gaze, but not Erika. Although she was a lot of things, Erika wasn't a racist despite having been bred in a culture of casual racism. She didn't pretend to be colorblind, but since she was a child, Erika had seen people as individuals, neither bridled nor crowned with racial stereotypes. Erika knew she'd been a showstopper in her day, but she also knew that beauty and sexual attraction spanned the rainbow. She'd had plenty of non-white lovers—her Blackberry was a mini United Nations log.

Years back, Erika had had a three-month fling with Michael Joseph because he captured her with his wit and with what she admired most in men—power. David was even sexier than Michael and wielded considerable influence across the state. What bothered Erika about David wasn't that he was black; it was the hungry way he looked at her. She'd seen that look too many times and it meant only one thing: her primary draw for David was her white skin.

She imagined what her girlfriends would say if they had been able to observe her and David together. Among Erika's friends, the word was that single black men of David's age and stature all wanted a white woman. When Erika and her friends got to drinking and talking about men, the talk would some-times (but not nearly as often as one might think) turn to what they called their "blacklist." They'd snicker as they ran through the list of black men, from entertainers to coworkers, to guys who sold newspapers on street corners, who lusted after white women. Their list didn't include black men who dated whom-ever they liked irrespective of race. It was limited to guys who had a *thing*, an addiction, a real problem, when it came to white women. The women's blacklist had many categories and they moved the men back and forth from group to group: too scared to chase, actively chasing, about to get in trouble for chasing, and about to go to jail for chasing. Erika played the game because she thought men who made the list deserved to be mocked.

When she had been seeing Michael, Erika didn't tell her friends because although they talked about black men dating white women, they never admitted to having crossed the color line themselves. It was always someone else, a friend of a friend. Also, back then, the good senator had been looking to take down any woman he could. She could be red, white, and blue all over, for all he cared, as long as she was sexy, willing, and discreet.

As she pulled into her garage, Erika's thoughts again turned to David. *I could be wrong about him,* she reminded herself. Erika had her doubts about David, but she couldn't get the image of his supple fingers twirling the glass round and round out of her mind.

One of the things that Raven didn't like about being a candidate's wife was that she had to pretend to like everybody, including citizens who were stuck in the old South. Civil War Southerners, Raven called them, folks who would prefer to see her in the kitchen of the governor's mansion rather than the sitting room. So when Raven received an invitation to a high tea and fashion show hosted by the Texas Daughters of the Succession Society, she didn't want to go to the affair, which was and forever would be all white.

"What will I be?" she asked Michael when he told her about the event. "The honorary negress? What if they decide they need to make a human sacrifice?"

Michael chuckled at her appraisal of the invitation. "I wish I didn't have to ask you to do this, but it's a big deal. Historically the wives of the candidates not only attend, they're asked to play an active role. At least I was able to get you out of being on the program."

"Bet that wasn't too hard to finagle. Sweeney's wife refuses to speak at any public events, so there's no way they were going to let a black woman take charge of the microphone by herself. Who knows what I might say?"

Raven was right. The society extended the invitation to Raven as grudgingly as she accepted it—neither side wanted to start a controversy. The members of the society didn't have anything against Raven personally, or black people in general. In fact, Raven ran into most of the women on a regular basis. She'd even been an invited guest at many of their homes. Exclusivity, as the members preferred to call their segregation policy, wasn't meant to discriminate against anyone. It was merely a tradition that had to be maintained.

"C'mon, honey. Go for me," Michael pleaded.

Raven was still skeptical until Michael came up with an idea. "You're making history, baby, being an integrationist. Why don't we use this as an opportunity to add a serious splash of color to the society's white cream?"

And so, there Raven found herself, the black host of the only multicultural table in a sea of fifty or so tables filled with designer-clad women. Instead of having Raven sit on the dais, as the candidates' wives usually did, Michael bought Raven the best table on the floor, front and center.

When Raven and her guests walked in, one young member whispered to her mother, "Mom, can you believe this? Here comes the rainbow coalition."

The mother arched one eyebrow and said to her daughter, "It's long overdue, don't you think?"

Raven's table represented just about every minority that had a substantial presence in Texas—and Michael didn't have to look beyond his own staff to fill the seats. Genie Dupree sat next to Raven. They filled out the table with Chin Le Quan,

Dr. Melissa Alvarez, Laurie Fritzman, Maya Abouda, and other top-level women.

As they ate their salads, Genie said to Raven, "This is a good thing you're doing, Mrs. Joseph." She looked around the room. "I see so many people I know." She craned her neck for a better view. "There's Jessica Amarault! She lived next door to me in the dorms."

"Why don't you go over and say hello? We need to make contact with as many people as we can while we're here," Raven suggested. "Who knows, maybe your friend will nominate you for membership."

"Doubt it," Genie said as she stood to join the rest of the people who were milling around, exchanging air kisses and hugs. "Somehow I don't think I fit their member profile."

Raven thought about taking her own advice, getting up and working the room, but decided against it. *I'm going to be governor's wife. Let them come to me,* she thought. She pushed her chair a little away from the table and angled it to get a better view of the room.

"Hey, you," someone said and tapped Raven on her shoulder. Erika Whittier scooted into Genie's seat. "You're a hard woman to catch up with."

*Damn.*

"Hello, Erika. You're a member of this group, I suppose."

Erika gave a little shrug, as if to say "Wouldn't you know it?" but her eyes were alight with pride. "Inducted into their hall of fame two years ago."

"I'm not surprised."

Erika wore a green Tahari suit, set off by a pair of the finest sling-backs that Raven had wanted to buy but didn't because she couldn't find them in her size. When Erika crossed her legs, Raven thought, *I hope she doesn't think her legs look better than mine.*

"How're things going?" Erika asked.

"Rolling along pretty well."

"Rolling along! I'm sure your days are more hectic than that. You're so busy these days you don't even have time to return phone calls, at least not mine." Someone called Erika's name and when she turned to say hello, her beautiful hair swung from side to side, like she was starring in a slow-motion shampoo commercial.

*Why is she shaking her big bobble head like that? My hair is every bit as silky as hers.* When Erika turned back around, Raven tossed her own mane for good measure. Raven *owned* the hair toss.

While Erika made small talk, Raven dissected her. Her criticisms of Erika came in rapid succession. *How old is she? Way older than me, that's for damn sure. Look at the way her top lip wrinkles when she talks. Hasn't she heard of Botox? I look better than her and I'm smarter than her, too. Rich bitch.*

"I've been keeping up with the campaign, and I have to say, I'm a little concerned. Michael hasn't been as noncommittal on gun control as I hoped he'd be," Erika said.

Raven forced herself to keep smiling. So far her subtle attempts to steer Michael away from gun control had fallen flat. She promised herself to get Michael in line within the week. "Erika, it might be hard to tell from the outside looking in, but I've got it covered." Raven waved the subject away, "Don't worry about it."

Erika looked doubtful. "When can we get together?" She leaned toward Raven and whispered, "For half a million dollars, I'm afraid I need to hear something more definite than, 'I've got it covered.'"

"Umm, I don't know when, but you're right, let's talk soon." Raven waved at the state comptroller, a stylish woman in her mid-sixties, and motioned for the woman to come over to the table. "Erika, I'm so sorry, but I've been trying to catch up with Carol for a month." Erika gave Raven an understanding look and turned her back.

Erika's smile never faltered, but her eyes glinted fire. *For her own sake, Raven damn sure better be a woman of her word,* she thought.

David exited the elevator on the eighth floor and strolled toward the door at the end of the hallway. His casual air covered the fact that he perfectly timed his stride so that by the time he got to the door, which read, "Dr. Cheryl Flanoy, Obstetrics and Gynecology," the hallway would be empty.

David glanced behind him to make sure he was alone, then ducked into the stairway next to the doctor's office. He bounded up two flights of stairs, looked at his watch, and at exactly 12:35:10 stepped quietly out of the stairwell and across the hall into Dr. Laverne's office. The doctor's reception area was empty; the receptionist, whom David had never met (and never would, if he kept to his schedule), had just left for lunch. She'd be back at her desk at exactly 1:30 just as David, having taken the stairs to the third floor, and ridden the elevator down the rest of the way, emerged onto the street.

David entered Dr. Laverne's office without knocking. The doctor sat behind his desk, waiting for David.

"I keep telling you, David, no one places a stigma on your being here except for you. There's no need to go to the trouble you do, taking an early morning flight here, sneaking in and out of my office so you won't be seen. I know several Dallas therapists I can recommend. Excellent doctors." The doctor twirled a pen as he spoke. "Including a couple of black men. You might find it—"

"C'mon, Laverne, you're wasting my time." David had taken a hard-backed chair from a corner and placed it in front of Dr. Laverne's desk. David refused to sit on the sofa or in a comfortable chair, the way Dr. Laverne's other patients did. He preferred to sit across the desk from the doctor, man to man, rather than doctor to patient. If David could have his way 100 percent, Dr. Laverne wouldn't be sitting behind his desk; the two of them would be seated at a conference table, acting as though they were hammering out a deal. David had instructed Dr. Laverne not to take any notes during their meetings; he didn't want any evidence, not a file or so much as a shred of paper to link him to Dr. Laverne. The only way David could stay in therapy was to pretend he wasn't in therapy.

"I don't know why we have to go through this every couple of months. Every black therapist in Dallas is a member of my congregation. Every white one knows who I am. I'm too high profile to let it get out that I see a psych—that you and I have these meetings. If you can deal with Dudley's . . . issues, then you can deal with mine."

"I know you're well known, David. It's just that you might find it easier to open up if you didn't stress yourself out by running a marathon to get here. I'm trying to look out for your best interests."

David's stubborn expression never changed, so Dr. Laverne moved right on. "What's on your mind?"

"Being a minister is hard," David said. He rarely got straight to the point. David talked as though he were talking to himself. "You've got to be a negotiator, a financier, a marketing whiz." He gestured toward Dr. Laverne. "A counselor."

"And there's the spiritual realm," the doctor said.

"Of course." David popped his knuckles as he spoke. "Juggling those jobs is difficult, but it's nothing compared to trying to maintain your privacy. Most people don't know that, but it's true.

"I'm single, and I'm human, you know? I need a woman to spend time with. The way I see it, what a woman and I do together is between her, God, and me. Nobody's got the right to judge me, or be in my business," David said. He scratched his temple. "When you're part of the black church scene, it's almost impossible to have a personal life. And if you're as well known as I am—forget it."

"I take it you've met someone," Dr. Laverne said. By now

he knew how to decode David's ramblings. They'd been over variations of David's "poor me, I'm a big fish in a clear pond" shtick many times and it always boiled down to the same thing. "And I assume she's a woman who's not within the black church social circle."

David, who wasn't slumping to begin with, sat up taller. "Erika Chaseworth Whittier," he said. Dr. Laverne heard pride in David's voice. "Certainly you heard the name," David continued. "I'm just getting to know her, but from what I've seen, she's incredible. Smart, beautiful, wealthy. She's the kind of woman I could get into."

"Then why don't you? David, this is the twenty-first century, people don't care about interracial dating the way they used to," the doctor said emphatically.

David wondered, not for the first time, why he bothered seeing Dr. Laverne. The simplest truths seemed to escape the man. "When you use a benign term like, 'interracial dating,' people don't care, but call it what it is—'a black man chasing after a white woman'—and it's another story," David explained.

"Then why put it that way? You're the one who makes it sound ugly, like something you should be ashamed of."

"I wasn't ashamed in the beginning," David mused. "I started dating white women because I was fed up with the hassles I ran into when I dated black women. A white woman will let me hit it once or twice and think nothing of it. But a sister? After two dates, she figures we're engaged, just because I'm a minister."

Dr. Laverne tried to reason with David. "Then dating white women is a practical solution to a real problem. Nothing more, nothing less."

"It *was* a solution." David frowned, self-loathing clouding his handsome face. "Now it's become an obsession."

"Every man has a type of woman he prefers. Some men go for tall women, others for petite ones, or redheads only. You're lucky enough to have discovered a woman with the look you like, not to mention all her other qualities, yet you label it an obsession. Are you sure you aren't being too hard on yourself?" Dr. Laverne asked.

*There he goes again*, David thought. *I really do wish I could find a black doctor.*

"Let me explain something, Dr. Laverne. Within the black race, I can find any kind of woman I want. *Any kind.* I can get a woman who looks like Serena Williams or one like that sister on CNN everybody thinks is white. So my preference isn't about a look. It goes deeper than that. Obviously I'm attracted to the blood running through a woman's veins." David, who had leaned forward while he spoke, slumped back into his seat.

"I'm a so-called icon of black empowerment and all I want to do is find a white woman and put her on a pedestal like I'm some field slave."

"So you're no longer attracted to black women at all?" the doctor asked.

Images of Raven, in the hotel bar that night and at the gala flitted through David's mind. "That's what I was afraid of, but no. A black woman can still get a rise out of me." He exhaled and felt that his vision of Raven somehow redeemed him. "So I guess there's hope after all," he said.

Their time was up, so Dr. Laverne ended their session the way he always did. "What is your Christian nature telling you?" he asked David.

"To be honest, the only voice I hear is one that tells me how tired I am of always being on guard with women. How lonely I am and how much I want to be with somebody who sees me as just plain David." He rubbed his goatee. "I don't know if God is a part of that conversation."

David handed an envelope containing two hundred dollars to Dr. Laverne and walked out.

Dr. Laverne reached in his side drawer and pulled out a file with David's name on it. He didn't care what he'd promised David, Dr. Laverne had no intention of getting hit with a malpractice suit for not keeping accurate medical records. He made a few notes to David's file and put it away.

"You're staring."

"I'm sorry, I didn't mean to," David said. Then he added, "But what man wouldn't? You're beautiful."

Erika and David were on the balcony of The Alamo Restaurant, which despite its warrior name was the most elegant eatery in Austin. They had a sunset view of Lake Travis, nestled in the Texas hill country. David had to sneak away to be with Erika because every time he came to Austin members of the New Word finance committee accompanied him. The committee included women, and as much as he wanted to see Erika, David wasn't ready to kiss his career good-bye by being spotted with her.

The committee spent its time with a lobbyist who would make the pitch for New Word to get a part of the faith-based initiative money. The faith-based initiative was a program operated by the state that encouraged religious organizations to run social programs that, of late, had been run by the government. The organizations would receive grants to do everything from offering prenatal and literacy programs to feeding the homeless. Religious outfits throughout the states were gearing up to plead for a chunk of the money. The newly elected governor, be it Joseph or Sweeney, would have his plate full dealing with the competing churches' proposals.

"I've found that men who're surrounded by beautiful women all the time don't normally stare. They get accustomed to the view," Erika said.

"I'm surrounded by women, yes . . . but days can pass, weeks sometimes, between the times I get to share an evening with a woman as stunning as you." David's voice sounded alien to his ears and his throat felt thick, the way it did whenever he lied and felt bad about it. But David was being honest and it burned his conscience more than lying ever did.

Erika knew she was good-looking but being over forty, she'd reluctantly gotten used to having men look at her appreciatively, though briefly, before their eyes settled on a woman twenty years younger. She remembered what it was like to have a man focus on her like she was the only woman on earth, but that hadn't happened in over five years. Despite being flattered, she began to feel self-conscious beneath David's intense gaze.

"What a line," Erika said, laughing uncomfortably. "Every Sunday you get to see hundreds—excuse me—thousands of women, and I'm sure there's a bit of eye candy in the bunch. Doesn't that news anchor, Kema Mitchell, attend your church? Kema's incredibly beautiful, don't you think? She looks like an African princess."

"She does," David agreed. "Kema and I are close friends." David sipped his wine and tried to keep his voice neutral. He and Kema had dated for a while, and at the outset he'd been optimistic that it might work. But when his gaze wandered off once too often, always to follow a white woman's movements, Kema fired David. But as he told Erika, Kema was a gem, and they had managed to build a friendship out of their broken romance.

Erika asked David about another gorgeous woman. "What about Michael Joseph's wife? At the gala, she ushered you away from me like you were her private property."

"Raven? You think she's interested in me?" David asked in what he hoped was a "surely you're kidding" tone.

Erika delicately wiped her mouth with her napkin. "Oh, for sure. She's got a huge crush on you."

*Yes!* David thought, but all he said was, "I didn't notice, and for the record I think you're wrong. Raven strikes me as exciting, which I like, but I'd never get involved with a married woman."

"Reverend Capps, men do a lot of big talk about what they'd never do. But I'm sure you know that." Erika was enjoying

David's company, and she figured based on what he'd said about Kema and Raven, that she had him pegged wrong. He wasn't attracted only to white women, which meant he didn't have to go on her blacklist. David Capps was fair game.

"There's one thing about you that doesn't fit." Erika looked perplexed and fascinated. "You're one of the most dynamic people I've ever met when you're in a crowd or talking business, but here," Erika motioned toward David then toward herself, "one on one? You seem almost—oh, I don't know—almost shy."

"You call it being shy, I call it being reserved and discreet," David said. He'd had enough wine to put him at ease and make him accept the fact that he'd asked Erika out for a reason and it wasn't to become her best pal.

"I guess it's time for me to be direct. I find you incredibly sexy and I want to get to know you better."

"Why me?"

*Isn't it obvious?* David thought. "Why not you?"

Erika cocked her head to one side and thought about it a minute. "You're right. Why not me."

David finished his wine in one gulp. "Ready to go?"

As David walked Erika to her car they made small talk about politics.

"I'm surprised you're going to vote for Michael," David said. "Guns are not high on his agenda."

"Agendas change," Erika said cryptically.

Erika's car was at the far end of the parking lot. As they approached it, Erika kept talking but David fell silent. His eyes roamed the parking lot and although he appeared casual, he made absolutely sure that there were no other blacks milling about and no white person he knew. As far as people he didn't know recognizing him—a man had to take risks sometimes and in David's slightly drunken opinion this risk was worth it.

As she pressed the button to unlock her car, Erika said, "And

if I can just get the African American community to understand—"

David took Erika's hand, slowly raised it to his mouth and
kissed her palm. He closed his eyes and when he opened them
again, Erika found herself drowning in a pool of irresistible
eroticism.

"I've wanted to do that all night. I know your lips taste even
better," David murmured. He pushed Erika against her car,
gently palmed her face with his huge hands and kissed her.
He bent his knees so that he could press himself to her.

David leaned his face against Erika's and whispered, "My
life is already complicated and I'm not interested in bringing
any drama into it, but I have to have you." He buried his face
in her hair and inhaled its fragrance. "My God, you're so perfect!"

Erika ran her hands down David's broad back and ended at
his rock-hard butt, which she held on to for dear life. As turned
on as she was Erika still felt a twinge of disappointment. Although David's hands roamed her body, deftly gliding between her legs and caressing her breasts, he obviously enjoyed
stroking her silky hair more than anything else.

# 10

The next morning David woke up with a pounding in his temples, which wasn't due to his overindulgence in wine. He lay in bed and chided himself for losing control. Fooling around with Erika in the parking lot had been a mistake. During dinner his eyes had constantly roved the restaurant for familiar faces, and seeing none, he'd been lulled into a false sense of security. David was usually more careful and didn't take women like Erika to public places, at least not when he was in Texas. Yet, she was one of the most elegant women he'd ever dated. *I had to show her off*, he thought, and immediately felt ashamed.

David rummaged through his overnight bag in search of Tylenol. He tossed back three, returned to bed, and pulled the covers over his head. As he waited for his headache to go away, David replayed the feel of his body against Erika's and ping-ponged between worry and lust.

When David finally opened his hotel room door, the *Austin American-Stateman*'s front page restarted the jackhammer in his head, and made him completely forget about Erika. THIRTY-TWO DIE IN DEADLIEST WEEKEND EVER

In a perverted confluence of events, thirty-two Texans had been violently killed in a twenty-four-hour period, and there wasn't a mass murder in the bunch. Of the gory total, two of the victims were stabbed and one was bludgeoned. The other twenty-nine were shot to death.

Dudley rapped twice on the door, stuck his head in, and said, "We're ready, Michael."

"Two minutes, I'll be down." Michael and Raven were alone in the minister's study on the second floor of a weathered east-Austin church. On hearing about the bloodbath that had taken place over the weekend, Michael had called an emergency press conference. He chose the church, Saint Mary's, because only hours before, a homeless man on a bicycle had been shot down as he peddled past. Michael cracked the blinds to take a look at the crowd assembled below. Raven came to his side and placed her hand in his.

The media pool covered the church's narrow sidewalk and spilled onto its manicured lawn. The reporters and cameramen who usually smoked, chatted, and looked bored while they waited for a press conference to begin were eerily quiet.

The media pool was ringed by an even larger group of people from the neighborhood. They too stood silent and motionless as though they were waiting for someone to wake them from a forty-eight-hour nightmare.

"Look at them," Michael said quietly. "I've been through enough post-disaster press conferences to know the drill. Something different is going on out there. There's a sense of shared sorrow in the air." He asked Raven, "Can't you see it in their faces? Everybody's emotions are on edge, even the reporters'."

Michael sighed and said, "I fucking hate guns."

"I know." Raven's voice was low. "Like you said, we're all emotional right now, even you. But you've got to rise above emotion and take a stand that's best for the long run. You know that, right?"

Michael turned from the window to Raven, his face questioning. He let go of her hand. "What do you mean, 'the long run'?"

Raven ran her hands down the front of her husband's lapels. "No matter how much you hate guns, there are a lot of voters who don't feel the same way." She paused. "Don't alienate them, Michael." Raven pinched her index finger and thumb so close they almost touched. "We're this close to being in the governor's mansion, but if you go out there and preach gun control, you're going to lose a lot of people. Don't do that to yourself. Once you get elected, you can say whatever you want about guns. But not now."

Michael stepped away from Raven and began buttoning his jacket. His air was dismissive and so were his words. "I know you mean well, but I didn't get this far by lying to the public about my stand on issues. I'm going out there and saying what I know is right," he said, ending the conversation.

But Raven couldn't let it go. *If he goes out there and screws up, Erika's going to be all over my ass*, Raven thought. She blocked her husband's path.

"Well, at least tell me exactly what you're going to say."

Raven was right about one thing: Michael's emotions were running high and he'd had about as much of her meddling as he could stand.

"Move," he said in a voice so unlike his own that Raven practically hopped out of the way. As he closed the door behind him, Michael thought, *Right about now, I sure do miss Grace.*

When Michael exited the doors of St. Mary's, the Democratic nominee for lieutenant governor, Ted Ballentine, was at his side. Usually the candidate for lieutenant governor stayed in the background, and Michael wanted to do things the way they'd always been done, but the party leaders insisted on putting Ballentine out front with Michael.

"We've got to make folks comfortable, Mike," the head of the Texas Democratic Party had told Michael over the phone that morning. "Especially at a time like this."

"The people got me past the primaries," Michael had replied.

"They're comfortable. It's you boys who can't seem to get over it. All Ballentine gets to do is stand there. I'll do the talking."

As he walked to the microphone, Michael was almost blinded by the camera flashes. He didn't need a scripted speech. On this one he could speak from the heart. "Over the past two days, this state experienced unprecedented acts of senseless violence. No area of the state, no social or economic group, was spared. Thirty-two of our citizens are dead. *Thirty-two.*" He paused, letting the number sink in.

"We don't know what caused the carnage; it was senseless and random." Michael paused again and gripped the podium. Christopher, who, with Raven, had come to stand behind him, bowed his head. "Nineteen-year-old Rico Houseman, a student at North Texas State University, shot as he walked from a frat house to his dorm. Ms. Pasha Pardesi, forty-six, was robbed and shot while leaving a baseball game in Houston. Three-year-old . . ." Michael's voice faltered. "Three-year-old Keeley Schuster of Brenham, also shot. The list goes on.

"Thirty-two dead and twenty-nine of them were killed by guns. When I first joined the Senate, I tried, and failed, to pass gun control legislation." Michael put his hand to his heart. "My failure, *our* failure, as a state to do the right thing, cost these people their lives. A bloodbath like this has no place in a civilized society, a society that values education and economic opportunity for all. If you elect me governor, things are going to change in Texas. I pledge to you, as governor of this state, that this will not happen on my watch."

When Michael signaled that he was ready to take questions, a reporter known for stirring things up asked, "Mr. Ballentine, if elected as lieutenant governor, you'll be the one who's responsible for pushing Senator Joseph's agenda on the floor of the legislature. Where will you begin?"

"I'm glad you asked," Ballentine said. He stepped closer to

Michael, edging his way toward the center of the podium. He placed one hand on Michael's shoulder.

"Senator Joseph is a good man and, um, that was heartfelt, heartfelt." Ballentine slapped Michael's shoulder again, buying time until he could think of what to say next. "I agree that things need to change, but the question is, what things? We all know that guns don't kill people, people do. A good economy, education, all that's fine, but first people have got to feel safe in their own homes and in their communities. We need to lock up the thugs who did this and throw away the key, or better yet give them the same death penalty that they gave to their victims." Having found his stride, Ballentine leaned closer to the microphone and said, "If poor Ms. Pardesi had had a way to protect herself, she'd probably be alive today! But in this state it's illegal to protect yourself in a sports arena. That needs to change!"

The press pool went after Ballentine's buzz words—death penalty, protect yourself—like sharks to blood. Cameras flashed and reporters vied for the lieutenant governor's attention. "It sounds like you're advocating more access to guns, not less. Doesn't that put you at odds with Senator Joseph?" the same reporter asked Ballentine.

Christopher knew, without being able to see his father's face, that although Michael's expression never faltered, his eyes had gone neutral. There was no way Michael was going to open tomorrow's newspaper and find Ballentine's agenda and picture on the front page. *Handle your business*, Dad, Christopher thought.

Michael gave Ballentine a bear hug, and at the same time (although he was smaller than Ballentine) managed to reposition himself in front of the microphone with Ballentine at his side. Michael motioned for the press to calm down.

"A civilized society, by definition, puts a premium on the safety and protection of its citizens. A civilized society is also one of enlightenment. Under my leadership, Texas will be safe. Our safety is going to call for a mixture of old-fashioned law enforcement and a new way of looking at things. Under my leadership we will have both. God bless this state!"

As the photographers began taking pictures, Michael let go of Ballentine and motioned for Raven to join him. He reached for her hand, but Raven slipped her arm around Michael's waist and kissed him on the lips. The kiss was the perfect gesture to express security and support, two things that the public desperately needed to believe in at the moment. Christopher, observing his father and stepmother, had to admit that Raven's move was smooth. Senator and Mrs. Joseph's kiss of comfort would be the next day's front-page photo in every newspaper in the state.

Grace sat on the sofa, her Bible on the table in front of her, and watched Michael's press conference. She'd spent the half hour before praying for the victims' families. Her prayer shifted and she'd found herself praying for Michael, too, for his success. Although she'd always stayed in the background when she was Michael's wife, Grace knew politics as well as any highly paid campaign advisor. She knew Michael's position on gun control went against the deeply rooted convictions of many Texans, and she also knew that during his press conference he wouldn't back down on what he believed. So, Grace prayed for her ex.

As Grace watched Michael deftly handle the questions put to him and vanquish Ballentine, she smiled and nodded. He was going to make an excellent governor. She could see Christopher, standing with Raven, in the background. Grace felt lonely, outside the loop of the life that had once been hers, but she didn't give in to it. *You helped make Michael what he is, be proud,* she told herself. She kept self-pity at bay until the kiss. When Raven stepped forward and embraced Michael, Grace's heart fell to her feet. Even to her eyes, Michael and Raven looked liked the perfect couple.

Grace shut off the television and picked up her Bible. She read a few passages and then got on her knees. This time she prayed for herself.

Although his press conference was well received, Michael's camp knew that the real test was the upcoming debate. It was one thing to utter feel-good sentiments right after a tragedy, and a completely different thing to persuade Texans to lay down their weapons.

Dudley was beside himself with worry, "Why'd those idiots have to go on a shooting spree right in the middle of the election season? Why not wait a few months? After this, how's Michael supposed to look into TV cameras and tell people that he's against gun ownership? It's political suicide."

Dudley was talking to Dr. Laverne. He wouldn't have said these things to the election team—Michael wouldn't allow it. Although Michael shared his doubts with whomever he felt like, he couldn't abide a panicky staff.

"I'm surprised at you, Dudley. I expected you to be filled with cheer today. I was really moved by Senator Joseph's speech. And the kiss with his wife was perfect."

Dudley ran his palm across his sweaty face. "The fact that the kiss came off well was just a fluke. When she pranced up to Michael, I halfway thought he'd turn his back on her. They'd been at each other's throats right before that."

"So they're not the happy couple they make themselves out to be?" Dr. Laverne asked.

"Hell no. Raven's a barracuda. She's everything bad that a woman can be: bossy, nosy, and irrational. And she nags Michael to no end."

"Sounds like you feel sorry for him."

Dudley snorted and gave what passed for a smile. The folds of his neck wrinkled. "Nah, Michael's getting what he deserves. I feel sorry for *me*. Raven started out all right—I'd put a bug in her ear and she'd take my advice, no questions asked.

Now she thinks she's so hot that she doesn't need my counsel. The worst thing I could ever have done was set her up with Erika Whittier."

"Oh?" Dr. Laverne, resigned to having to listen to Dudley whine, suddenly perked up. From what David told him, Erika was a fascinating woman and Raven had a mystic air about her that was captivating. The two of them together would be an interesting mix. "What's their connection, are they friends?" the doctor asked.

Dudley's little eyes bulged, which according to Dr. Laverne's notes was a sure sign of nervousness. "Forget about it," Dudley said quickly. "My point is that Raven's in my way. She's trying to get Michael to rely on her rather than on me."

"Maybe you should talk to her. She might not know that she's invading your territory."

"She knows, all right. Besides, Raven's not the type of person who responds to talk. I've got some ideas in mind on how to put her back in her place." Dudley picked up the candy dish on Dr. Laverne's desk. He dug through the M&M's, touching every piece of candy in the process as he scooped out the yellow ones.

"What sort of plans?"

"What do I specialize in, Doc?"

"Dirt," Dr. Laverne said. "Poking around in closets and airing dirty laundry."

Dudley grunted and went back to digging through the M & M's. "Damn right. And it looks like Raven stirred up a bit of dirt when she was in law school. I've got a buddy who works there and according to him, a guy that Raven was doing got mixed up in a scandal with her, then went missing." As an aside Dudley added, "At the same time she was doing Michael, balling his brains out to make him leave his wife. She'll make some First Lady."

"What happened to the guy who went missing?" Dr. Laverne asked. He vowed to throw out his M&M's, candy dish and all.

"Nobody knows, but I intend to find out."

# 11

"This state stands for equal opportunity for all citizens. How can you say to a young boy or girl who studies hard, 'I'm giving your college spot to a student who doesn't work as hard as you, just because of the color of the other student's skin.' It's just not fair." Jeff Sweeney finished on a high note and received a robust round of applause.

"Senator Joseph, two minutes for a rebuttal," the debate moderator said.

"I agree with my opponent. I wouldn't want to tell that to a child because I'd be lying. The young person Jeff Sweeney is talking about is going to get an opportunity for a college education just like she got an opportunity to attend a very good public school or better yet, a private school. The truth is we owe an explanation to the child attending a dilapidated public school with outdated computers and no lab equipment who doesn't get a shot at a college education because he happens to be born poor and black or Latino." Michael looked from his podium to the one where Jeff Sweeney stood. "I understand that child because once upon a time that child was me."

The audience was silent, hanging onto Michael's every word.

"Obviously, when I was in school we didn't have computers. I'm from back in the day when we used carbon paper."

Scattered laughter. "But when I tell you that my school was so poor we had hand-me-down books from the white school across town, believe it." Michael looked directly into the camera as he tried to reach the trucker in Fulshear, the soccer mom in Plano, and the hair stylist in Fifth Ward. "Under the plan advocated by my opponent, I wouldn't have had a chance to become the man I am today."

Michael began his crescendo, his voice ranging with sincerity. "I hope you don't think I'm being arrogant when I say, *I deserved* the chance to become the man I am—an honest, taxpaying, productive member of society!" His voice rose with emotion. "And *every* Texas child, irrespective of who they are, what they look like, what their parents do for a living, *deserves* that same opportunity!"

The audience forgot about the rules established at the beginning of the debate. David Capps was one of the first persons to stand on his feet. He clapped so hard his palms turned red. Erika Whittier was seated two rows behind David and she stood also, with a plastic grin spread across her face. She was furious over Michael's comments about gun control. Erika decided it wouldn't do to show her anger now. She'd deal with Raven later.

Raven, who had been seated in the first row, bounded onto the stage and gave her man a hug and a kiss. She was pleased with the audience's response, but when she'd scanned the auditorium just before the lights were turned down, her eyes had met Erika's. It had not been a heartwarming experience.

"This was it, baby," Michael whispered in Raven's ear as they embraced. "This put me solidly on top."

Raven leased the lobby of the Dallas Anatole Hotel, and threw a debate after-party for Michael. She went all out, spent STRAPPED money like it was free water. Caviar and smoked salmon for the upscalers, barbequed ribs and potato salad for the people keeping it real. Michael gave an emotional speech, then worked the room, accepting congratulatory hugs and kisses.

Later Michael and his inner circle; Raven, Christopher, and Dudley, retreated to the presidential suite, where they enjoyed a champagne toast.

Christopher took off his tie and laid it on the coffee table. "Dad, are you ready for feedback on your performance?"

Raven was standing at the bar next to Dudley. She nodded her head slightly so that only Dudley could see and thumbed toward the door.

Dudley took her cue and said, "It's late, Chris. We can put it off until tomorrow."

"But by then we may have forgotten some of our immediate impressions," Christopher said.

"I'd kind of like to hear what you have to say tonight," Michael said. He hated being criticized and normally fought to delay his performance reviews for as long as possible. But Michael was riding the wave; he felt confident that the group was about to tell him lots of good things about himself. "You're the one who always insists on doing it right away," Michael added to Dudley.

Raven yawned. "I'm so drained I can't think straight. Let's wait."

Christopher grabbed his jacket off the back of his chair. If Raven said wait, that was the end of it. "Breakfast, then? Eight o'clock?"

"Sure, son," Michael said as he walked Christopher to the door. He embraced Christopher and the young man was surprised to find that his father, though shorter and lighter than him, was strong enough to rock him back and forth. "I appreciate everything you've done for me. I love you."

"Love you too, Dad."

Christopher got onto the elevator and looked at his reflection in its mirrored walls. He quickly sliced the air between the closing doors and headed back to the presidential suite.

Evidently Michael hadn't completely closed the door when he let Christopher out, so the young man simply walked in.

"You were pretty good with dividing your attention between the studio audience and the people watching TV, but for the next debate I think you—" Dudley was saying as Christopher walked into the room.

Michael, Raven, and Dudley were huddled in the suite's living room critiquing Michael's performance.

"Forgot my tie," Christopher said curtly as he stepped around Dudley's chair to get it.

"Christopher, this isn't the formal debriefing," Michael tried to explain. "Raven just mentioned—"

"A formal debriefing?" Christopher slung his tie around his neck. "There's no such thing. There's just us, getting together as a *team*, Dad."

"Well, you're here now, pull up a chair," Michael said in a pleading voice.

Christopher looked at Dudley and Raven, neither of whom had said a word since he walked in. Raven wore a slight smirk.

"No, thanks. You started without me, finish that way," he said and stormed out of the room.

Raven picked up their conversation as though they hadn't been interrupted. "Although Sweeney hates guns as much as you do, probably more, considering what happened to his father, he's not able to tap into public emotion the way you do," she said. "The woman sitting next to me crossed her arms when you first started talking about guns, but halfway through I could tell from the look on her face that she agreed with every word you said."

Michael sat back with a satisfied grin on his face. He was the happiest he'd been in a long time, so he quickly forgot about Christopher's hurt feelings. Getting the best of Sweeney had been so easy. Of all the questions the panel had asked Michael, only one caught him off guard.

"How do you think I handled the question on the faith-based initiative? They came out of left field on that one. Did I do okay?"

Raven sat on the corner of Michael's chair and rubbed his back. "Sure, honey. What else can you do but divvy up the money between the major religions and denominations? If you give one group more than the other, you'll be accused of favoritism. You handled it flawlessly." She leaned over and gave him a kiss that most women served up only in private.

Michael took the kiss as his cue. "Time for the next governor of Texas to turn in. He walked over to Dudley, who had moved to his usual spot—the bar—to do his usual thing—nurse a drink.

"Can't thank you enough, man." Michael grabbed his chief of staff's hand and pumped it up and down. "We're on our way, Dudley, straight to the top."

Michael turned to Raven, "Honey, you ready?" He looked at his wife and thought: *I hit the jackpot! After tonight, I'm destined to be governor of Texas. I'm married to a woman who's been through a hell of a day and still looks like she just stepped off the pages of Essence.*

"Not yet, Michael, I'm still amped. I'm going to sit here and talk to Dudley for a little longer. We won't be too long."

After Michael left, Raven walked over to the bar and told Dudley, "Fix me whatever you're drinking."

Dudley handed her the drink and then toasted her. "Congratulations. Michael's showing tonight coupled with those commercials and David's swing through the state put us over the top. All paid for by STRAPPED. Getting their money was smart. Very smart."

Raven took a sip. She could see her reflection in the full-length window next to the bar and had roughly the same thought her husband did. *Twenty hours nonstop and look at me, I look perfect. I am perfect.*

Raven tore herself from staring at her own image and focused on Dudley. "Let's set the record straight—if I hadn't gotten Jerry Minshew on our side, we could've run a million dollars' worth of commercials and still been the underdog. After the *Austin American-Statesman* gave Michael its endorsement, newspapers from all over the state tripped over themselves to support him. That's what pushed us out front: the newspaper coverage, not the TV ads. STRAPPED's money was nice to have, but in the end, it wasn't much of a factor."

"Erika won't see it that way. She'll expect Michael to pay the piper, one way or another. I wouldn't disappoint her if I were you."

Raven felt a knot in the pit of her stomach. All the attention she received at the party and the self-congratulatory atmosphere inside the suite had helped her to forget about Erika. She'd have to figure out a way to deal with Erika, but she wasn't about to let Dudley see her worry.

"Dudley, Dudley, Dudley." Raven put down her glass and turned to her reflection in the window. She rubbed her hands across her cheeks, enjoying the feel and look of her own smooth skin. "Sometimes I think you know me so well, and then you say something stupid. Who gives a shit what Erika expects? Don't you realize she's no match for me?" She gave Dudley an indulgent smile. "Can you think of anyone who is?"

After Christopher got his tie, he headed not to his own room, but to Genie's.

"Hey, hey, hey, slow down," Genie mumbled to Christopher as he barreled past her after she'd stumbled to the door in response to his loud banging. She sleepwalked, her arms groping for him. Genie put her arms around Christopher and laid her head on his chest. "I fell asleep waiting for you." She squinted at the clock, then burrowed closer to him. "Still, it's not that late. The feedback session didn't take as long as I thought it would."

Christopher disentangled himself from Genie, "The session's still going on, but I wasn't invited." He walked over to the bed and fell back.

Genie crawled onto the bed beside him. She stroked his head and asked, "Why not? Your dad values your input."

Christopher flopped over onto his stomach, and as he did so, moved away from Genie's caress.

"It wasn't him who excluded me. It was her," he said. "You know he goes along with whatever she says."

Genie straddled Christopher's back and began massaging his shoulders. "Why would Raven do that?"

"Who knows why the bitch does half the stuff she does? Probably because she hates the idea of anyone being close to my father except for her."

Genie was quiet for a minute, then she asked, "How did it happen? Did Raven come straight out and tell you that she didn't want you doing the debriefing?"

"No, she and Dudley acted like they were too tired to talk to Dad while I was with them, but that was a lie. As soon as I left they started the meeting. I found out when I went back to get my tie."

"Dudley was there? Well heck, Chris, Raven wasn't trying to keep the senator to herself. If she were, Dudley would have had to leave too." Genie laid flat on top of Christopher. She was tired of talking about the campaign. "Sounds to me like you're being paranoid," she said as she reached underneath Christopher to untuck his shirt.

Christopher, who had relaxed to give Genie better access to his shirt and zipper, stiffened and grabbed both her hands. "I'm not paranoid, Genie. You think you know my dad's wife, but you don't. She'll push other people aside in a heartbeat to get what she wants. You should have seen the way she walked all over my mom to get to my dad."

Genie wrenched out of Christopher's grasp. "You can't put all the blame on Raven. If your parents' relationship had been strong, no woman would have been able to come between them."

Christopher bolted up, causing Genie to move before she got thrown off. "Genie Dupree, the know-it-all. You got some nerve trying to speak on my parents' marriage," Christopher said as he grabbed his jacket and tie. He looked Genie up and down. Her robe had fallen open and she didn't have on anything beneath it. Christopher reached over and yanked the lapels of Genie's robe together and pulled the belt tight. "Since you know so much, figure out how you're going to get what you want from me tonight once I walk out that door." He opened the door and turned to her. "Oh, I forgot. You're a superwoman, just like Raven. I'm sure you can get the job done without my help."

# 12

For their fourth "meeting," Erika and David had dinner in the lobby of Erika's hotel. She was in Dallas for a conference, and although David promised himself from the start that he'd never be seen alone with her in his own backyard, he couldn't resist Erika's offer to share a meal.

"It'll have to be late," she told him when she called. "I won't get out of my last meeting until nine, so we're talking tenish."

David made it a habit never to eat after eight. He moved his food around on his plate without actually eating anything, a habit he'd picked up from his very first white girlfriend, and listened to Erika drone on about state politics.

Erika abruptly put down her fork and asked, "Why are we going through this?"

"What do you mean?" David asked. On the outside he was smooth, but he felt his heart pick up its pace.

"This charade." Erika sat back and motioned to the table. "This is just a front for what's really going on between us.

"We've got our routine down. After dinner, I'll find an excuse to walk to your car with you. I'm sure you parked in a corner away from the other cars, the way I do when you're in Austin." Erika studied David. He sat there trying to look cool and professional, but steam may as well have been blowing out of his ears.

"We're going to grind like a couple of teenagers while you whisper some bullshit lines about how much you want me," Erika added.

David dropped his head.

"Then you'll drive off and I'll go upstairs. We'll lie in separate beds and get ourselves off while we think about each other."

The truth was too much for David. He had intended to limit himself to two drinks, but what the hell. He grabbed Erika's glass and took a swig.

"Look," he said to Erika in a voice so low that she had to strain to hear him. "You have to understand my situation. I—" David stopped. Erika had taken off her shoe and placed her foot in his crotch.

Erika said, "Come to my room."

Between what Erika was doing with her foot and the inscrutable look on her face, David was about to pop. He slouched in his seat and opened his legs. David was about to give it up, throw his head back and enjoy, when he spotted a familiar face. The head of the hotel's banquet facilities passed by their table and gave David a slight nod.

David straightened up and knocked Erika's toes off his private parts in the process. "I want to, Erika. But I can't. Not tonight."

Erika picked up her fork and stabbed at her food.

David motioned for the waiter. "Another Glenlivet, straight up, please."

Erika didn't have anything else to say and David couldn't think of what to say. He sat there and tried to figure out how he could sneak in and out of Erika's room without being seen.

After he paid the check, David went to stand, and teetered.

"What's wrong?" Erika asked as she jumped to her feet to catch David's arm.

David gingerly sat back down. "I feel a little dizzy. I must be coming down with the summer flu. I'll be okay in a minute."

Erika scoffed. "The flu? Come on, David, you've had too much to drink. You don't have to drive tonight. Stay with me."

"Erika, I can't, especially not now. I'm going to have hell to pay tomorrow if anybody notices that I'm drunk." He hit the table with his fist. "And if I'm seen going to your room?" David shook his head. He looked as sorry as he sounded.

Erika knew that David was right. Besides, she didn't want to have sex with him if he wasn't in peak condition. "I've got a rental car, want me to drive you home?"

"Me? Being driven to my home in the wee hours by a white woman? No thanks." David tried to stand again, but his head started spinning. "All right," he agreed. "Let's sit here for a few minutes, until I can get my legs to cooperate. Then I'll meet you in the parking garage."

Erika had rented an Escalade. When she reached the vehicle, David was already there, standing on the passenger side. "Come here," he said, his arms stretched toward her.

"Uh-uh," Erica said, and went straight to the driver's side.

As they headed to David's house, he reached over and stroked her thigh. They reversed the roles they played in the restaurant and now it was Erika who opened her legs wider as David's hand went higher. Even though he was drunk, David might have driven as well as Erika, who had trouble staying in her lane.

*This is as far as I'm going,* David said to himself as he used his free hand to direct Erika into his subdivision.

David wasn't the only one having second thoughts about what would happen when they got to his house. Erika was insulted because David seemed to want her to beg him for sex. She'd become more selective about who she let sample her goodies and she was beginning to wonder whether David, with his hard-to-get attitude and his drinking, was worth it.

*What number will he be? Sixty-two? Sixty-six? Damn.* From the time she was fifteen until she turned forty, Erika had dated like a man, like Samantha Jones on *Sex and the City*. If she ran across a man she liked, Erika bedded him, and she never confused good sex with love. When she turned forty, Erika realized that she had racked up some serious numbers. She vowed to have only "meaningful" trysts from then on. Trouble was, Erika's libido wasn't on board with her new, restrained lifestyle. David's nimble fingers, working overtime, didn't help.

*I don't know what number he'd be, but I know it's too close to seventy,* Erika thought as she killed the engine. In one smooth move she climbed across the console and straddled David. She slid her hands beneath his ass and kissed him hard.

"We can't do this here," David mumbled as he reached to pull Erika's skirt up to her waist. "What about my neighbors?"

"The neighbors. Right. I guess we'd better make it look like you're alone," Erika replied. Before David knew what was happening, Erika had hit the floorboard and deftly unzipped his pants. David groaned and lay his head back. He'd had at least three drinks at dinner, but David's body responded to Erika like he was a teetotaling Olympic athlete. A neighbor could have come up and rapped on his window and he wouldn't have cared. He grabbed a handful of Erika's hair, but quickly let it go because just the feel of all that downy softness brought him to the brink of exploding.

Only when he felt Erika dig her fingernails into him did David dare touch her hair again. He let out a primal scream that made Erika think—with the small part of her brain that wasn't occupied with getting hers—that a neighbor just might hear the commotion and decide to call 911.

Erika got off her knees and gave David another deep kiss.

"Come inside, please," he begged.

"Uh-uh. You might end up being number seventy, but it won't happen tonight."

"Huh?"

Erika climbed back into the driver's seat and waited for

David to get out. "Like you said, what would the neighbors think?"

After he showered, David's normal practice was to towel off in front of his full-length mirror. But after his tryst with Erika he couldn't bear to look at himself. As he dried off in the dark, he asked himself over and over again, *How could I risk everything just to be with her?* After David tore himself down, he latched onto one redeeming thought.

*At least it wasn't real sex.*

Michael's strong show of leadership during the post-massacre press conference and the debate gave him a huge boost over Jeff Sweeney, just as he'd predicted. He won the allegiance of thousands of Texans simply by being the eye of calm in the storm. Endorsements and money poured in. Legislation that Michael favored sailed through the House and the Senate. Even Richard Torres, Michael's opponent in the primaries, got on board. He sent Michael a note a week after the debate. "When you get ready to meet with the Latino leaders, I'll pave the way. Call me."

So, by mid-July, Michael was practically unbeatable.

"I needed this. Seems I spend all my time in a suit, even in what's supposed to be a casual atmosphere. I'm never relaxed," Michael said. He and David were aboard David's sixty-foot sailboat in the Gulf of Mexico, just off the shore of Padre Island. "Feels like I've had my guard up constantly, for—hell—forever. This is the first time in months I've not been hounded by a reporter with a camera, ready to record every move I make."

David took a swig of his beer and laughed. "You and me, looking to avoid a photo op. Who'd believe it?"

Michael laughed too. It felt good to be on open water with just the two-man crew and his friend.

They watched the water in silence for a few minutes, then

David said, "This isn't the break you think, Michael. I still want to talk business."

"It's so good just to be out here, I can talk about anything and still feel like I'm on vacation," Michael said, his eyes on the horizon. "What's on your mind?"

"I've done what you asked—sisters all over the state are organized and energized, working on bringing out the vote for you. When we started, you told me you wouldn't forget about me, and I know that's the truth. It's time for us to discuss some things."

"You're thinking about the faith-based initiative, right?"

"It's not a lot of money, Michael. Forty million spread too thinly would be a waste." David's voice took on the authoritative tone he used when in the pulpit imparting wisdom. "You already know what white churches will use the money for. To build more 'religious' schools," he said as he made quotation marks with his hands. "They've single-handedly kept segregation alive since the sixties. Why should they get government funds to perpetuate a system that's illegal?

"And you know I believe God calls all types to preach, because it takes all kinds to reach the masses, but half the uneducated hustlers out there calling themselves preachers will take the money, go buy a Cadillac, a week's worth of shiny suits, and tacky jewelry."

Michael, who was quite good at lecturing, himself, was tired of being on the receiving end from David. "Not every man can drive a two-seater Lexus and wear Armani."

David conceded the point. "I admit I live well, but you know that I always put the people's welfare first. And I've got a vision, Michael. All I need is money and I guarantee you, I'll transform all of south Dallas."

Michael finally stopped watching the water and turned to David. "I believe you, because I've got a vision too. Your vision is spiritual and mine is secular, and they're pretty much the same. You know I'll be fair to New Word. You and your congregation have been good to me."

David had preached fairness all his life, but under the circumstances he wasn't sure that mere fairness would get the job done. "I need you to be more than fair, Michael. I need you to show some faith in me, go a little farther with me than you would with anybody else. You know I won't let you down."

"To implement your ideas, how much are we talking?"

"Can't put an exact price on it," David replied. "I'm just asking you to give me a chance to transform this state, just like I provided the chance to you."

David added, "But, if I could put a price on it, that chance is worth at least fifteen million."

"That almost forty percent of the money!" Michael turned back to the water and realized that he'd been wrong. The calm waters of the Gulf didn't immunize him against stress. He shook his head. "I wish I could, but you know that if I win this election, folks are going to be looking for any excuse to call me crooked. I'm going to get enough flack for putting Raven in charge of my faith-based platform."

"She's running things?" David was surprised.

"Yeah, believe it or not, Dudley suggested that I put her to work on the issue full time. I think he's trying to get her out of his hair, but I thought about it and it's not a bad idea. Raven's smart"—Michael's smile became broader the more he talked about his wife—"but you already know that. And she's still an outsider for the most part, so she'll be immune to pressure tactics from the different churches." He held up his palms to David and said, "No offense."

"None taken. I'd be the last one to want to bring even a whiff of impropriety into your administration. Are there any restrictions on how much Raven can award to one church?" David asked.

"No, she's free to use her own judgment. But honestly,

David, different communities have different needs, so I expect her to choose a cross section of people to figure out how to address those needs," Michael said.

David tossed back the last of his beer and threw the bottle into a nearby trash can. "If I need to enter the fray with the rest of the churches and convince Raven that my plan is the best one, then I will." He winked at his friend and risked a joke. "You know how persuasive women find me."

"I do," Michael said and laughed heartily. "But my Raven isn't just any woman. You're going to have to come correct to get a dime of that money." Michael looked at his watch. "David, I appreciate you bringing me out here for a little down time, but I've got a million things to do. Mind if we head back now?"

"No, man, whatever you want," David said, but he was disappointed. Now that he knew the rules of the faith-based initiative game, David was starting to relax, himself. While David went to talk to the boat's captain, Michael fixed his eyes on the horizon. He may as well have been a blind man because the singular thought turning round in his head blocked his vision. *Did I see a glint in David's eyes when I mentioned Raven?* He felt the boat change course and head back to shore. Michael checked his watch again. What was supposed to be a day of relaxation had lasted all of three hours.

"Michael's taking a hands-off approach with the faith-based money," David told Dudley during one of their late-night phone calls.

Dudley's relationship with his younger brother existed after dark. Talking after midnight was a habit they had developed during childhood and one that Dudley fully incorporated into his life. He stayed on the phone all night long, or if he wasn't on the phone, he'd sneak out of the house. Early in his marriage, Dudley gave his wife the two children they both wanted—she wanted to make a real family, and he wanted her focused on someone other than him. After doing his duty, Dudley felt no obligation, and certainly no desire, to sleep with his wife, and so his nights belonged to him.

The men's habit of talking after dark stemmed from being raised by their mother, Sue Capps, who went by the name Baby Sue, and their grandmother, also named Sue Capps, known as Big Sue. Big Sue was an elephant of a woman. By the time she was forty-five she was so huge she could barely get out of bed. Baby Sue, who was as scrawny and dried up as Big Sue was ample, had a habit of dragging home stray men.

When the welfare check came on the first of the month, Baby Sue bought steak for her boyfriend and Spam for her sons. Whatever her current lover put on her—a black eye, a slap across the mouth—she took out on Dudley and David. Despite the way their mother mistreated them, their main reason for hating Baby Sue didn't have anything to do with a man. They despised their mother because she stank, smelled like the funky side of rich fertilizer. The neighborhood children called her Stinky Baby Sue.

"How could he?" Dudley would whisper to David whenever a man entered their mother's bedroom.

Dudley and David dealt with Big Sue and Baby Sue by staying out of their way. They didn't play or talk until Big Sue's snoring competed with the grunts and yelps coming from Baby Sue's room, usually after midnight.

Following their childhood pattern, the brothers commiserated about Michael after dark.

"How long have I been telling you that Michael's only out for himself?" Dudley said. "Now that you've solved his problem with women, he's riding high and acting like he made it this far on his own. As long as he's on top, Michael's not interested in anybody else's agenda."

"Be realistic, Dudley. It's not like Michael can simply cut me a check. The public might not look too kindly on my church

ending up with the bulk of the money if he's personally involved in the process. I don't want him to get jumped for passing out favors to his friends."

Dudley snorted. "Bullshit. This state was built on cronyism
and a governor is expected to throw a little business his friends'
way. Michael's just one of those Negroes who locks the door
behind him once he's gotten in."

"Dudley, you really need to stop hating on Michael." David
never understood why Dudley criticized Michael so harshly.
"He always looks out for you and I know he values your advice. When did you become so bitter?"

"I'm the same man I've always been, but Michael has
changed. Since the debate, he's been walking around like he's
the Second Coming," Dudley said. "And maybe he used to take
my advice, but to tell you the truth, I don't have Michael's ear
anymore."

"That not true," David said. He was eager to convince his
brother of Michael's loyalty. "In fact, because he liked your
idea about putting Raven over his faith-based initiative platform, I still have a shot at getting a good chunk of the funds."

"Oh, yeah? He told you he's giving the job to Raven?"
Dudley was pleased. He couldn't care less about the politics
of throwing crumbs to Holy Rollers. But the media was fixated
on the initiative and Raven was eager to be involved in any
project that would keep her name on the front page, so to
Dudley it seemed the perfect fit. And it would keep Raven
out of his way.

"Yep."

"Then talk to her. I know she likes you. Better yet, hit her
with the Capps' magic wand and the money's yours." Dudley
guffawed. "You know how we do it."

David was taken aback. "How could you even suggest that?
You know I'd never fool around with Michael's wife. We're
more than political colleagues, we're friends!"

"So I keep hearing," Dudley said, his voice dry. "But if my

idea is so far-fetched, why are you getting so agitated?" Dudley cradled the phone between his shoulder and head while he freshened his drink. "Besides, I haven't seen you out and about with any eligible women lately, which means that you're probably doing something that can get you in a lot more trouble than flirting with Raven." Dudley laughed to soften his words, but if he could have seen David's eyes, he would've known that they hit the mark.

David wiped his brow and thought about Erika. Since their driveway escapade he'd driven to Austin three times in two weeks. They ordered in and spent all their time in Erika's bed. David felt like a field hand more than ever, but he was hooked.

"As a matter of fact, Dudley," he began, "there is something you should know about, just in case I ever need a quick alibi."

As they sat across from each other, Raven and David were pictures of perfection. David's royal blue sweater enhanced the blackness of his smooth skin and his goatee brought attention to his lips, which were thin by Raven's standards, but sexy nonetheless. He looked hot, but Raven was hotter. She hadn't forgotten the way David looked at her at the Juneteenth fund-raiser when Erika walked up. In the hotel lobby in Lufkin, she'd gotten under his skin and she knew it. Since then David had been polite but distant, and Raven wasn't used to men holding her at arm's length. David needed to be initiated into the Raven Holloway Joseph Fan Club. He'd flubbed his prior invitations, but no man could permanently resist Raven's offer to worship her. She wasn't having it.

As soon as David called to ask her to lunch, Raven had buzzed Genie. "Call the salon, tell them I'm coming and I want everything: hair, nails, makeup. Then call Cheryl at Saks and tell her to pick out something ultrasexy for me. Have her bring it to the salon." She started to hang up, but then added, "I doubt that anyone needs reminding, but just in case, tell them I'm not one to be kept waiting."

Raven and Michael made a striking couple, but Raven and David looked like a world-famous photographer had paired them for the ultimate photo shoot. David could feel the buzz they generated. When he'd been close to her on other occasions David had deliberately avoided really looking at Raven. But sitting directly across from her now, he couldn't tear himself away from her catlike, deep-set eyes, her full lips, and her flawless skin. *As dark chocolate goes, Raven's on the ultrasweet side*, he thought.

"You look . . ." David's words hung between them because her beauty struck him speechless. "That's a nice dress," he finally said.

Raven didn't say anything. She knew how to make a man squirm.

David started over. "It's good to see you. How's Michael?" He retreated to non-flirtatious ground and stayed there. When the waiter brought their meals, Raven looked at hers and said, "Excuse me, I ordered the mandarin chicken."

"No, no," the waiter told her in rushed, broken English. "You order black bean chicken."

Before Raven could reply, David said to the waiter, "She's right, she ordered the mandarin chicken."

"No. Black bean," the waiter insisted.

"You know what—" Raven began, only to be interrupted by David again.

"He doesn't mean any harm, Raven. It's the language barrier—"

"I realize that," she said, speaking over him in the same light tone she'd been using all along. She looked at the waiter and said, "Black bean chicken is fine. Thank you."

"That was good of you," David said once the waiter walked away. "Thanks for not making a scene."

"What makes you think I'd do that?" Raven asked. She

made scenes all the time and enjoyed herself immensely when she did. Raven was the queen of scenes.

"Because I've seen you in action! Remember how you treated that little waitress in Lufkin?" he said. "And black women are scene-makers by definition. You love going off on people who're providing a service. Waiters, flight attendants, store clerks, but especially waiters."

When Raven didn't respond, he said, "I'm just kidding! You know how much I like to joke around."

"If you think you can pigeonhole me or any black woman into some definition you've made up, then you're very naive. And you need new jokes." Raven took a bite of her chicken and then she said, "I ran off that waitress to save you from yourself, David. Something was about to happen that you, as a minister and a key part of my husband's campaign, should have no part of."

David refused to concede that he might not have been in control of the situation with the waitress in Lufkin. "I still say you misread what was going on, but I know you were trying to help me."

"Then would you mind treating me with a little respect?"

David blinked. "Not at all," he said. For a man who ran his mouth all the time, David found himself at a loss for words. Finally, he said, "I'm sorry. I didn't mean to be rude."

"You were, but, no problem," Raven said. She smiled at him and to David, her lips looked like ripe fruit, ready to be nibbled.

"I assume you asked me to lunch to talk about the faith-based initiative?" Raven asked.

He began by telling Raven about New Word. David started out slowly, because he was still taken aback by the way she'd called him out. But once he started talking about the things he wanted to do with the money, David quickly warmed to the topic.

"I want to start a program that pairs retired businesspeople with young entrepreneurs. And I want to bring in retired teachers to help students study for the SAT. My goal is to get Ivy League scholarships for at least five south Dallas kids every year. And every child with natural intelligence and a drive to succeed who comes through the New Word program is going to get into somebody's college. "

Raven was impressed. "I've met with about five ministers so far, and they've got some good ideas, but they're all the same. Nobody's come up with ideas as far reaching as yours." Raven leaned forward with her elbows on the table and her hands clasped together. "You've got a passion for these things, I can tell. You get this look in your eyes just like Michael does."

"Michael and I aren't the only ones," David replied. Raven was displaying more than a little passion herself. David's energy was contagious, and as she listened to him, Raven forgot about how nice her hair looked and how her new dress showed off her cleavage. She didn't make any moves calculated to be sexy the way she usually did; she just acted naturally. Which, of course, made her even more alluring.

David stopped talking and listened to Raven expound on his dream. She posed questions on everything from when David thought he could get his program up and running to how he'd convince an A-list, black filmmaker to do a documentary on New Word. Then she helped David figure out the answers.

In January, when he and Raven had debated whether Michael should run for governor, David had realized that Raven was smart, but he hadn't appreciated how her intellect changed her. Raven's eyes alight with a fresh idea were infinitely more alluring than her usual sexy gaze. When she unself-consciously brushed her hair from her face, as opposed to performing her studied hair toss, David felt the urge to reach across the table and caress her cheek.

When their desserts came, Raven sat back in her seat. She

enjoyed a spoonful of her ice cream. "Ahh," she sighed. "Wouldn't it be nice if you could really do all those things?"

"I can," David said with quiet confidence. "And if I didn't believe it before, I do now. You've convinced me."

"David, your church's share of the money probably won't fully fund one of your programs, let alone everything we've talked about."

David threw up his hands in exasperation. "But what about what you just said? Every idea I pitched, you loved. And any holes in my plans, you filled in. How could you be so into my program and not get behind it?"

"Helping you talk through the kinks wasn't personal, it was an academic exercise for me," Raven said blithely. "Just because I enjoy figuring things out doesn't mean I'd be willing to award your church more money than it deserves." She licked her spoon and gave David a mischievous smile. "At least not without a whole lot more information."

David, who had ordered a slice of pie for dessert, took his spoon, reached over, and dug into Raven's ice cream. "I should be annoyed with you," he said. "I have a feeling that would get me nowhere fast. If it's more information you need, then I'm going to do my personal best to give it to you."

Minshew knew that this time, Raven wouldn't hang up on him. He could feel it—today would be his lucky day. Just in case his luck didn't hold, Minshew had a backup plan. He had a crib sheet with key lines to his speech written on it to prevent him from fumbling around for the right words the way he had during his prior calls to her. He might be able to write a newspaper column in under two hours, but it took Minshew two days to perfect his conversational tidbits for his call to Raven. He went over it again (really, six more times) before he dialed the number.

"Hello?"

"Hi, this is Jerry Mi—"
*Click.*

"I didn't realize we had an appointment," Raven said. She was sitting in her office at Michael's campaign headquarters. She made a mental note to give Genie a stern dressing down as soon as her unexpected guest left.

"We don't," Erika said. "Just happened to be in the neighborhood, as they say." She put her handbag on Raven's end table and looked around the office. "No art on the walls. No figurines. I've never seen an office quite so bare," she said, and finally sat down. "Reflects your personality, I guess."

"I like it spare. Too much fluff only serves to hide things." Raven crossed her arms, uncrossed them, and placed her hands, her fingers intertwined, in her lap. Erika was a socialite, to be sure, but not the easily ruffled type Raven usually encountered. Raven wanted to project the same level of coolness.

"In that case we don't have to go through the whole 'so nice to see you' routine, do we?"

Raven looked surprised. "Erika, it *is* nice to see you. I'm glad you decided to drop by. I've got a meeting in an hour, but I'd love to treat you to a quick lunch."

"If your time is that tight, I don't want to waste any of it on lunch," Erika said. Raven had been smiling but she stopped. She hoped her face didn't show how much she wanted to rip Erika's head right off.

"I know you've been busy," Erika went on, "but that's no excuse for ignoring my calls. And because it'll get us nowhere, I'm not even going to address how you snubbed me at that tea the other week. After what happened at Michael's debate, I decided it's time to talk, whether you want to or not."

"I have been busy, Erika, and at the tea we talked." Raven dug her fingers into her palm. "I apologize if you felt snubbed, but I had at least a dozen women I needed to have face time with during the tea."

"Okay, then. Forget about the tea and explain what went wrong during the debate. Were my eyes playing tricks on me, or did Michael practically come out and say that if he's elected, he's going to see to it that our current gun laws are repealed? My organization wants *more* freedom to own weapons, not less."

"That's not exactly what he said."

"Damnit, Raven—"

Raven held up one hand. "I know. Michael got excited and went a little farther than he should have. I talked to him about it afterward, and he realized his mistake. Don't worry, you won't be hearing him say anything like that again." As Raven spun her tale, her mind raced as she calculated the number of remaining debates and public appearances Michael had before the election. She thought, *How the hell am I going to get him to shut up about gun control?*

"But I do worry, because you keep telling me you've got the situation under control, yet every time I turn on the TV there Michael is, flapping his gums about gun control."

"You can't very well expect Michael to side with STRAPPED after twenty-nine people are gunned down." Out of habit, she added, "That's just plain stupid."

Erika hadn't been called stupid to her face in a long time. Raven was toying with her, making Erika itch, making her want to let off a round, just one. But Erika decided instead to wrap her anger in a Southern smile.

"What's stupid, Raven, is that you're pretending you don't remember our agreement," Erika said in a sugar-coated voice. "I never asked for Michael to endorse my organization's agenda. He was to sit by and say nothing, but now he's actively fighting against us! People are scared, Raven. They want to arm themselves without restrictions on where they can carry their guns, or what kind of guns they can own. The legislature's ready to give in. Michael's the one making problems, when all he needed to do was get out of the way." Erika said all this in a quiet voice.

Raven tried to look earnest. "I've tried everything I can, Erika, and I'll keep trying. I'm not sure what more you expect me to do."

"Well then, let me make it plain. I *expect* you to get Michael to shut the hell up and stop making speeches about how evil handguns are. I *expect* my organization to get its money's worth." Erika, whose posture was elite private school proper, sat up even straighter in her chair as she issued orders to Raven. Erika tapped Raven's desk with her index finger to get her point across. "I *expect* to get what I paid for, and I damn well better get it soon."

Raven had been as nice as she could for as long as she could. "I get your point, Erika." Raven looked at her watch. "It's about time for my meeting, but I promise you one thing." She looked Erika in the eye with what she knew was an unreadable stare. "I'm going to make good on what I owe you."

# 13

Christopher decided that if he couldn't be his father's chief of staff, he'd be in charge of something else. That something was his father's Dallas office, which, once he had announced his bid for governor, Michael renamed the Neighborhood Assistance Center. Instead of going to Michael's Dallas office every Saturday, the way he used to, Christopher now went during the week and stayed for at least two days. Once a month he went down on the weekend so that he could go to first Sunday communion with Grace. The rest of his weekends were for Genie.

Christopher walked into the Dallas office and found someone new sitting at the receptionist's desk.

"Hello, I'm Christopher Joseph." He put out his hand, but she didn't take it.

"Oh, hey. What's up?" The young woman dragged her words along like they weighed a ton. "Let me get a look at you." She stood and walked around the desk.

Christopher checked her out. Killer body; sweet, heart-shaped face; and a weave that was a little over the top for his taste, but not bad. Tattoo of a rose on her left breast.

She looked him up and down. "They told me to be on the lookout for you, but hell, Chris, you went and got fine on a sister." Her words kept dragging along, but now that he had a full view of her, Chris thought of a slow, warm trail of molasses rather than a heavy load.

Christopher smiled. He loved around-the-way girls. So fresh and so fine. From the way she talked, and carried herself, Chris guessed the young woman must be a high-school student.

"Why are you here this early? Shouldn't you be in school?" he asked her.

"Nah, I took this semester off. So I'm just chilling, checking out this situation. We're moving to new office space pretty soon, right? I was hired to help with the move."

"Since when do you get to take a semester off in high school?"

"High school?" She waved one hand at him. "You're tripping, Chris. I'm a college junior." When he still looked confused, the young woman said, "Chris, you don't remember me? I'm Monica!" She raised her arms and did a fashion turn. "Monica Fowler, Buddy Fowler's granddaughter."

"Monica! I'm so sorry. You're not that much younger than me." Christopher whistled. "Girl, you've grown up."

"So have you," she said as she sauntered back to her chair, letting her booty do the rest of the talking.

If it had been anyone but John Reese, Grace wouldn't have opened her front door.

"What are you doing here?" she asked.

"It's good to see you, too," John said as he bent to kiss Grace. "I brought lunch." He waved the brown bag beneath Grace's nose. "Since when can you resist a Dewberry's cheeseburger?"

"Come on in." Grace uncrossed her arms and pulled her bathrobe tight.

Although it was his first time at her place, John moved around Grace's kitchen as though it were his own. "Are you sick?" he asked as he poured them each a soda.

"No. Why do you ask?"

"It's the middle of the day and you're still in your pjs," he said kindly as he sat down across from her. "You look like you just got out of bed."

"I did, but that doesn't mean I'm sick."

John nibbled a Creole fry. "Beautiful Saturday like this, the Grace I know would be out doing something. Remember how you and Maggie used to drag Chris and Evan to the mall with you every Saturday?" John chuckled. "I put a stop to that the day little Chris told me that my shoes were the wrong shade of brown for the pants I had on."

"I remember," Grace said. "After that you'd take the boys to the bookstore with you, or Michael would take them to his office." The memory seemed to deflate Grace even further. "Why are you here?" she asked.

John stretched his legs out to the side of the table, his ankles crossed. "Because I need you back. I looked for another volunteer to tutor the boys in reading, just like you asked. But I haven't been able to find anybody. I've been teaching the class myself, but with my other duties I'm in over my head."

Grace forced down a bite of her burger. It was as flavorful as cardboard to her, but she hadn't eaten anything since lunchtime the day before. "I told you I wasn't coming back, John. Keep looking, something will turn up."

"Maybe," he replied, "but in the meantime those young men are suffering."

A guilty look crossed Grace's face. She thought about the students every day and kicked herself for making them feel insignificant. She knew all about feeling worthless, and it wasn't an emotion she'd wish on her worst enemy.

"You say you've been teaching the class," she said as she swirled a fry in ketchup. "How's Waleed, is his reading any better?"

"He's still trying hard. When he gets overwhelmed, I let his brother James help him out. That seems to work for him."

"Oh. I'm sure it does." Grace blushed as she remembered

how she'd refused to allow James to read for Waleed. "And what about Trey, is he still the class clown?"

"They told me you didn't know their names," John said with mild surprise. "You care about these children, I can tell. Why won't you come back?"

Grace shook her head. She didn't have an answer. "To tell you the truth, John, I find it hard enough to go through the motions of living. I think about the boys all the time, but I can't help them. I don't have the energy to help myself."

John was alarmed. "But you know you've got to keep on living, keep putting one foot in front of the other."

Grace sniffed. "I do. You don't have to worry about me hurting myself, John. Every day of the rest of my life might be a living hell, but I'll not cut one day short by my own hand."

"I had to ask," he said. "There's no need for you to resign yourself to a life of misery, Grace. Your family and friends love you. You're healthy, beautiful, and blessed with many gifts, including the gift of working with children." He chucked her under the chin, and said with a twinkle in his eyes, "And you used to be fun to be around."

"I know." Grace said. She sighed and smiled a little. "I just can't seem to move the knowledge of the things I've got going for me from my brain to my heart." She sat there in her bathrobe with her head tilted to the side and had no inkling that her inner light, though dimmed by sorrow, still flickered.

John cleared the table, then went over to Grace's chair and hugged her. "You need more of these," he said.

Grace saw John to the door. As he turned to walk away Grace called out, "John?"

He turned back to her.

She hesitantly reached her arms out to him. "May I have another hug?"

"Dad, I just heard. How'd we end up losing the Rice Association endorsement?" Christopher asked. He'd knocked and walked into his father's office without waiting for a reply. Dudley and Raven were already there, and they looked as shocked as Christopher felt.

Michael shook his head. "We can't figure it out, Chris." He looked at Dudley. "Their support was locked down, right?"

"Tight as a drum."

"Damn." Christopher stood there, hands on his waist. "What are we going to do?"

Michael surprised Christopher by laughing. "You sound like you just got in this game, man. Win some, lose some. We don't have to do anything. Those guys sell *rice*. Nobody listens to them anyway." He waved his hand like a king granting a special privilege to peasants. "They prefer to endorse Sweeney, let 'em have it."

Raven frowned. "I don't know about that, Michael. I think we need to knock some heads. I mean, look at who screwed us on this one." She counted the legislators' names out. "Addison, Riley, that dust for brains Watkins. Their counties are the ones with the rice fields; as much as you've done for them, there's no way the association's endorsement should've been withdrawn. We need to call those three on the carpet now, pull them back in line." Raven crossed her arms. "Just say the word, Michael, and I'm on it."

Dudley waved his arms signaling time out. "And I'm sure you'd be quite effective," he said sarcastically, "but now's not the time. Michael's right—this is a penny-ante loss, doesn't mean much in the scheme of things." Dudley had been quiet until now. He hated to lose as much as Raven did, and he loathed being double crossed. Addison and the rest would get theirs, he'd make sure of it, but right now Michael was on a roll. This wasn't the time to start a civil war.

Michael leaned back in his chair, his arms behind him, interlaced fingers cradling his head. "Yep. How many endorsements have I lost until now?"

"None," Christopher said.

Michael, one hand cupped to his ear, leaned forward. "Huh? I can't hear you."

Christopher smiled at his father. "None, as in, *not one*," he said loudly. He loved his father so much.

"Correct. This is just a blip on the radar screen. By next week we won't even remember it." Michael stood, walked over and kissed Raven. "Enough of this. I'm starving. How about Italian?"

By the time his driver, Lawrence, dropped them at Antonio's for dinner—less than twenty minutes later—the lost endorsement was already forgotten.

You'd have thought Raven was the candidate for governor from the way she conducted Michael's staff meeting. The group was in Michael's conference room, drinking coffee, eating Krispy Kremes, and going over the day's agenda. Michael began the meeting the way he usually did, by commending his staff for their hard work and encouraging them to work even harder. "I know that you did everything you could to keep the Rice Association from pulling its endorsement. I appreciate the effort."

"I don't see how you can say that, Michael," Raven interrupted. "If they'd worked hard, you wouldn't have gotten a call last night telling you the association's endorsing Sweeney."

The few eyes that weren't already on her turned Raven's way. Early on, the staff had taken to watching Raven, because that's what Michael did, especially when he was speaking. The men enjoyed looking at Raven because she was one of the finest women they'd ever seen. The women studied Raven's manner—decisive, fierce, condescending with staff and smooth with contributors—and to varying degrees, they modeled themselves after her. After all, they weren't in politics for the bumper stickers and funny hats.

"Elsa, Pete, and Juanita, it was your job to hold onto that endorsement. You were stunningly ineffective," Raven said. "Maybe it's time you faced the fact that major league politics aren't for you. Time to go back to the minors."

The three staffers were dumbstruck. Pete was the first to break the trance. "Senator, what's going on?" Pete blurted. "I've been with you for six years."

"And based on your performance, we're going to stay "*senator*," Raven said sharply. "My husband and I want to be *the governor*, Pete. *The fucking governor*. And you're unable to keep up. The three of you screwed up for the first time in El Paso, during the primary, remember that? Your performance has been downhill since then." Raven coolly paced the room, holding her coffee mug with both hands.

"I may have made a . . . a miscalculation with the Rice Association, Mrs. Joseph. I apologize," Pete said.

Raven banged her mug down on the conference table with so much force that coffee sloshed over the rim. Raven used her hands, spread wide and tented on either side of her mug, to lean forward across the table.

"A miscalculation?" Raven screamed. "You think I've got time for your fucking miscalculations? Or that I want your sorry-ass apology?"

That shut Pete up. For once, everyone was looking at Michael instead of at his wife. Michael's professional loyalty was one of his best assets. His staffers and supporters would do anything for him, because he wasn't one to abandon a friend or colleague when things got tough.

Michael was seething. How dare Raven undercut his authority with his staff? The thing that irritated him the most was that Raven was right—the three hadn't earned their keep for months. He, Raven, and Dudley had discussed firing the trio but he'd turned around and thought of an excuse to give them one last chance.

"Elsa, Juanita, Pete," Michael looked each in the eye as he spoke their names. "Over the years you've been good to me, and for that I'm grateful. This should've been handled differently, but what's done is done. Think about whether you'd rather stay here in Austin or go back to Dallas. Once you decide, let me know and I'll make some calls. You'll each be situated somewhere else by the end of the week, I promise."

"You're fired. Please leave now," Raven said.

Michael grabbed Raven by the arm. "Come here, let me show you something."

She tried to jerk away. "Michael, stop it! You're hurting me!" They were in Michael's office, just the two of them, after the staff meeting.

"Hurt you? In my wildest dreams," he said as he marched Raven over to a wall mirror. He pointed at their reflections with one hand and squeezed her arm with the other. "You know what I see? Huh? I see Senator Michael Joseph and his wife! I don't see Senator *Raven* Joseph and spouse, and I damn sure don't see two candidates for governor!"

When Michael spun Raven around to face him, he was so incensed that his lips trembled and his words came out shaky. "I might love you, and you might be the commander in our bedroom, but not here. You understand? Not here!"

"The only reason I fired them was because you weren't man enough to do it!"

Michael's eyes flashed, and he abruptly let go of Raven's arm, put both hands in his pockets and took several steps backward. "I suggest," he said evenly, "that you stay the hell out of my sight for the rest of the day."

Raven wasn't ready to leave—she thought of half a dozen insults, any one of which would have taken their argument to a new low, but the brutality in Michael's eyes unnerved her. "Fine with me. I've got too much to do today to be bothered with you anyway."

"I could've been like you," Michael mused.

"What do you mean?"

Michael rubbed his eyes with his fists. "Happily married. How long have you and Mary been together?"

"Thirty years, just about," Dudley said vaguely. As soon as he had finished high school, Dudley rushed out and married the only girl who would have him.

"Come next month, Grace and I would've celebrated twenty-three years together."

"You fell in love with someone else. It happens."

Michael stood near the window that provided his favorite view of Austin. His kingdom. "But the price," he said as he looked into the distance, seeing nothing. "I heard from David that Grace hasn't been the same since the divorce. When we split, I didn't give much thought to how it would affect her. I was, you know, trying to get to Raven. She was the only person on my mind."

He turned to Dudley. "And my new wife. Half the time I can't think straight, always worried about what Raven—aah." Michael stopped himself, because he'd learned that complaining about Raven was a waste of time.

"Evan's got problems, did you know that?" Michael asked. "He has Grace's sensitive temperament."

Dudley didn't reply.

"When he was younger, I was busy with other things. Now this race sucks up all my time. I missed Evan's city-choir audition and Grace didn't show up, either. Christopher was the only one there. A big brother, taking the parents' place. It's not right."

"You would've been there if you could've," Dudley said. He'd said the same thing to Michael hundreds of times: "You would have (Dudley would fill in the blank with whatever the situation called for) if you could have."

"Look at your life," Michael continued. "Still married to your high-school sweetheart. One daughter at Yale, another married with a baby on the way."

Dudley's daughter was at Harvard, not Yale, and his youngest grandson was a month old. He'd told Michael about his birth, but Dudley himself couldn't care less about the little bastard, so what did it matter?

"At least Chris is doing fine," Dudley said.

"Fifty-percent success rate, is that acceptable for a father? But you're right, Chris is a good kid. A better man than I was at his age." Michael looked uplifted. "He'll make a name for himself and someday he's going to be a good husband and father. He's going to outshine me, and for that I'm thankful."

While Michael boo hooed on Dudley's shoulder, Raven was in her own office, opening her mail. She was so angry that her hands shook. Michael hadn't ever hit a woman, and although she knew he'd never hit her, no matter how far she went, his roughness rattled her. It made her feel like he was the one in control.

The first thing she opened was a card from her mother, Jacqueline. She'd seen a picture of Raven and Michael in the *San Diego Union-Tribune*. Had Raven put on weight, her mother wanted to know. Why was she standing so awkwardly, and what was wrong with her hair? Raven ripped up the note and put it in the trash can. She closed her eyes and felt the familiar hunger, the emptiness that had gnawed at her insides since she was a girl. Her impulse was to eat to the point of nausea, purge, and hurt someone, in that order. Never one to deny herself whatever her body craved, she took a bag of Dove bars from the back of her bottom drawer (where she tried to hide it from herself) and began the process.

As she ate the chocolate, Raven went through the rest of her mail. This time she started with the invitations. As she read invitation after invitation, Raven regained her composure. All these people—the Texarkana Chamber of Commerce, the Wichita Falls Philanthropic Society, 100 Black Women of Houston—wanted her. By the time Raven got to the tenth envelope, she was no longer gripping the letter opener like it was a weapon. She shoved the bag of Dove bars back into its hiding place, leaned back, crossed her legs, and assured herself that she wasn't fat or awkward as Jacqueline's note implied. How could she be? She was the future governor's wife.

\* \* \*

*David is a tough nut to crack*, Raven thought as she enjoyed yet another lunch with him. He managed to have lunch with her once a week, and from the start, Raven enjoyed their conversations. One minute she flirted with him and the next they commiserated like old friends. They talked about everything from world events and economics to movies and hip-hop culture.

As they finished their meal, Raven boldly went out on a limb. "I probably shouldn't say this, but we ignite a spark when we're together. Remember the first time we had lunch? And that night in the Lufkin hotel lobby? Whew. Have you noticed?" she asked. Raven was surprised to find that she felt shy. "What do you think it means and what should we do about it?"

"It means we click," David replied. "We shouldn't read more into it than that."

"I'm not reading anything into it, David, and you know it." Raven challenged him. "Are you denying that you're attracted to me?"

"No," David quietly said. "I can't deny that you're incredibly intriguing to me."

Raven threw up her hands in exasperation. "Okay, then what's the problem? I'm not saying we need to do anything drastic, but if you're feeling me, David, you could at least show it."

David grabbed her hand across the table. He was completely confident and at ease because he was doing what he did best, providing moral guidance to a confused soul. "Ever heard of one thing leading to another? If we were to start acting like more than just friends, the next thing you know we might decide to act on our feelings. I don't want that to happen and neither do you. It would be wrong, Raven."

She sighed. "So, just friends?"

"The best," David said.

"Let me get this one," he said when the check came.

"Oh, no, you got the last one," Raven said. She quickly added, "But if you insist, go right ahead."

It was their private joke. Raven let David know early on that she didn't believe a woman should ever pay for anything. "The pleasure of our company ought to be enough," she had said. David told her that her attitude was old-fashioned, but he liked it a lot.

As they left the restaurant, David's hand brushed against Raven's bare skin. The electricity between them had been hot enough to burn down a brick house.

"Come here," she said and pulled David into the empty coatroom.

Raven kissed him, and he kissed her back, briefly, passionately. She felt him rise, but when Raven reached for David's crotch, he pulled away, leaving her standing there with her eyes closed and arms groping for him, like a blind woman.

"David, I don't get you. Why won't you just go with the feeling? Is it because of Michael?"

"In part, but mainly because it would be wrong." David didn't feel as sure of himself as he had moments before. As much to reassure himself as to get Raven in check, he said, "We're both adults. We can be friends without letting our hormones take over."

"That's not what your kiss just said." Raven moved toward David again. He grabbed her hand, but then disappointed her by leading her out of the coatroom.

"Let me walk you to your car."

As David closed her car door, Raven looked up and said to him, "You say one thing, David, but the fire in your eyes tells another story."

"Maybe so," David admitted. He was still so rock hard that it hurt. "But this is one story that won't end the way you want it to."

# 14

Grace, concentrating on picking bruise-free tomatoes from the grocery bin, didn't notice the woman standing near the onions. The woman waited until Grace turned so that she could get a better view of her face, then she rushed forward.

"Grace? Grace, girl! I thought that was you!" Before Grace could react, the woman reached out and hugged her.

"Hi, Carolyn. You're looking great." Grace was right. Carolyn, almost six feet tall, was one solid sister. Carolyn had been thick and curvy when they were in college, and now she was even thicker. She was still curvy too, and showing it. Carolyn had on tight black pants that gripped her huge behind and a low-cut bright orange blouse that her double-D-cup breasts all but popped out of. She had on diva lashes and wore her natural hair twisted. Carolyn's look matched her personality, outsized in every way. Neither Carolyn's disposition nor her fashion sense were for everybody to emulate or to like, but they worked for her.

"Thanks, hun. I'm feeling good, too," Carolyn said.

Grace looked down at her own baggy sweats and sneakers. No wonder Carolyn didn't return the compliment.

"How's Jimmy?" Grace asked.

Carolyn waved one jeweled hand dramatically. "Girl, that

fool is fine, last I heard from him. You know he quit me for a woman who works at the car wash around the corner from our house." Carolyn's big grin never wavered. "*My* house, I should say."

Grace put her hand on Carolyn's arm. "I'm sorry, I hadn't heard. I know how hard it is."

"It was in the beginning. I kept trying to figure out what I did wrong. I look good, I've got a good job, and like Betty Wright said, I was a mother to the children and you-know-what in the sheets." Carolyn had started out serious, but by the time she finished her sentence, she was smiling again. "What could a man want with a bone like that car wash girl when he had a juicy, thick T-bone steak like me at home?"

Grace tsk-tsked, and started to say something, but Carolyn kept on talking.

"And you know what I said to myself? Who gives a damn! I mean, really, Jimmy's stupid as hell anyway, so he went and did some more stupid shit—so what!"

Other shoppers were starting to look at them and Grace was getting a little self-conscious, but she wanted to hear more. In the back of her mind she'd always believed that Michael left her because she was boring, couldn't hold a candle to Raven when it came to excitement. But here was Carolyn, sexy, vibrant, and larger than life, saying that Jimmy dumped her. Men didn't leave women like Carolyn, they only left women like Grace, or so Grace had thought.

"I'm not handling my divorce so well, Carolyn," Grace blurted out.

Carolyn cocked her head to one side and looked at Grace. "I can see that." Suddenly she interlocked her arm with Grace's and said, "Come on, girl, I'm taking you to lunch."

"But what about our groceries?"

"This store will be here when we get back," she said as she and Grace walked out of the store. "Besides, grocery stores don't sell the kind of nourishment you need."

Grace and Carolyn went to a Thai restaurant across the street from the store. Carolyn promptly ordered for both of them: white wine, spring rolls, and hot fish.

"How did you do it?" Grace asked as she looked out the window.

"Do what?"

"Become happy again, find your joy."

"You're talking about two different things, Grace. When Jimmy walked out, it made me unhappy. I was so hurt—I can't put into words how hurt I was. But my joy? He never touched that." Carolyn patted her chest. "Joy is mine, and Jimmy—nobody, for that matter—can take it from me."

Grace felt a tear slip down her face. "Michael took my happiness and my joy. He walked off with my children, with my whole life."

"Michael doesn't have anything that belongs to you, Grace. Everything that's yours, you've still got. Your joy and happiness are buried, and you're refusing to dig them up."

"So it's my fault, is that what you're saying?" Grace angrily asked. "That's not true. I'm not going to sit here and listen to you blame me. I put my soul into saving my marriage."

Grace moved to stand, but Carolyn grabbed her hand. "Sit down, Grace. You're mad and that's a good thing. But it's time to move beyond the anger and the hurt and do something."

Grace wilted and said miserably, "I don't know what to do. I'm not like you, Carolyn. I don't bounce back as easily. I still feel beaten down by what I've been through."

"Just because you feel beaten down doesn't mean you have to look it," Carolyn said. "When you were going through tough times, battling to hold on to Michael, you looked liked a star."

Grace looked surprised. "You knew?"

"Of course, sweetie, we all did. But you didn't want to talk about it, so we didn't say anything." Carolyn ordered them both another glass of wine. She added more Thai pepper to her dish, and enjoyed a few bites before she went on. "I remember running into you once, right when things were really bad with you and Michael. You had on a royal blue St. John suit and a pair of two-toned patent shoes. I still remember those shoes." Carolyn shook her head as she recalled the moment. "You were fabulous."

Grace didn't remember the suit Carolyn was talking about but she was sure it was in her closet, way in the back. Most things about that time in her life were a blur, but she vaguely recalled that she had looked outstanding.

"Even if you don't feel good, you've got to look good." The wine had gotten to Carolyn, and it took her back to her roots. "We're South Oak Cliff girls who moved to ritzy North Dallas. But no matter where we live, *this*"—she made an up and down motion toward Grace's sweat suit ensemble—"is *not* how we roll."

Carolyn dug a fifty out of her handbag and put it on the table. "Come on. We're going shopping, and I don't mean for groceries."

"Genie, will you grab me a beer?"

"Already got that covered," she said as she walked into the room with two cold beers and paper plates.

Christopher opened the pizza box that sat on the coffee table in front of them. He fixed Genie's plate, then his, while she flipped through TV channels.

"The preseason game between the Patriots and the Eagles should be on," Christopher said as he took a swig of beer.

"Here it is," Genie said. She laid the remote on her TV tray and bit into a slice of pizza. "Hey," she said to Chris. "Slow down, you're halfway through your second slice already! We should've ordered two."

He ended up eating twice the number of slices Genie ate. As Christopher went into Genie's kitchen to get two more beers, he said over his shoulder, "Your boss has been in rare form lately, hasn't she?"

"For sure. That staff meeting was pretty intense."

Chris sat down next to Genie. "Whenever I think she's hit her limit, that she can't possibly do anything more outrageous than some of the things she's already done, she surprises me."

Genie placed one leg on the sofa, knee bent, and turned so that she faced Christopher. "Shouldn't have been a big surprise. Those guys had been screwing up for months, especially Pete. I couldn't believe he had the nerve to question Raven's decision."

"Well, honey, it wasn't her decision to make and Pete knew it. Key staffers shouldn't be fired without my father's say-so, and it was obvious that Raven hadn't consulted him beforehand."

"Thank goodness for that," Genie said dryly.

Chris stared at Genie. "What's that supposed to mean?"

Genie put her hand on Christopher's arm. "Chris, I don't mean any harm, you know that. But your father was . . . hesitant . . . to tackle the problem, even though he'd been told umpteen times that it needed to be done. Heck, he's said it himself. It's a good thing Raven took charge, that's all I'm saying. There's no telling how many more endorsements we would've lost if she hadn't stepped in and let them go."

"Whatever. Let's see what else is on TV," Christopher said, and reached across Genie to get the remote.

Christopher lay back and Genie reclined in his arms. They watched a silly sitcom, and Christopher found his good mood restored.

"This is cool, just the two of us spending private time together. Guess we better enjoy it while it lasts," Christopher said.

"You planning on going somewhere?"

"No. I'm talking about this phase of our relationship, when we don't have anything else to worry about. It's great. How long are we going to be able to sit in front of the TV and eat off paper plates?"

Genie shrugged. It wasn't a big deal to her. "For as long as we want to, I suppose."

Christopher hesitated, then plunged in. "Well, I don't want my kids sitting on the floor with their paper plates on the coffee table, yelling, 'Hey, Mom, bring me some more juice.'"

Genie had been looking at TV and half-listening to Christopher but now she gave him all her attention. "Kids?"

"Don't get it twisted, Miss Dupree, I'm just talking. No way am I ready for diaper detail." Christopher cautiously felt his way forward. "But we've got something special, Genie, I recognize that. Things are going good, we've got Dad on track, for the most part." Christopher went for the gold. "I think we ought to start thinking about the future. At least about getting engaged."

Genie abruptly sat up. "I'm in no hurry, Chris. Getting engaged, marriage, children—maybe all that will come in time. I love you, but I love me, too, and I love my life right now, just the way it is. A demanding career, my own space—those are the things I've dreamed about since the day I graduated from high school."

*She sounds like I'm talking about putting her in prison*, he thought. "You're older than me, Genie, I just assumed you'd be on the fast track when it comes to planning for the future." Although Christopher had been nervous about bringing up marriage, this wasn't the reaction he expected. Wasn't a woman supposed to be happy—overjoyed—when a man made up his mind to take their relationship seriously?

"I don't want to rush through my life." She lay against him again and added, "And you shouldn't want to rush through yours, either. You're way too young to be thinking about starting a family."

One of the reasons Christopher loved Genie was because she knew her own mind and wasn't afraid to speak it. But those same traits annoyed him, too, when Genie turned dismissive. "I don't know about all that," Christopher replied in a cautious tone. He wasn't in the mood for a debate. "My parents married when they were young."

"We see what a huge success that was," Genie quipped.

This time Christopher was the one to sit up, all but shoving Genie off him.

She put her hand over her mouth and said, "I'm sorry, Chris, that didn't come out the right way."

"No problem," Christopher said. He burrowed into the sofa and finished his beer. Genie tried to strike up a new conversation but Christopher wouldn't bite. Finally he put his hands on his knees and pushed himself up. "I think I'll tackle that environmental commission report tonight."

"Is it in your car?" The authority in her voice was gone, replaced by worry.

"No. At my apartment."

"But I thought you were spending the night."

As Christopher put on his jacket, he gave Genie a look she didn't like, a look she'd seen his father toss at Raven, and said, "I wouldn't want to encroach on your space. Maybe some other time."

Dudley had hoped that putting Raven in charge of the faith-based initiative would keep her out of his way, but he was wrong. She ran the staff meetings and placed calls to key legislators and lobbyists without consulting him first. He kicked his plan to get the goods on Raven into high gear. He started by visiting an acquaintance at Monroe School of Law.

The man who was director of admissions was not happy to have Dudley drop by his office. "I can't give you information from student files. That's a crime!"

"Calm down, Crawford, I don't want anything out of the files, at least not yet," Dudley assured the man. Crawford was a married man on the down low. Dudley had so much dirt on Crawford that the poor man would have given Dudley the key to the student files if Dudley had asked.

Dudley tried to get his squat body comfortable in the cheap chair in Crawford's office. "I want to find out what you know about Raven, Senator Joseph's wife."

Crawford lit up. The scandal that Raven left in her wake hadn't been forgotten. "That Raven was something else," he said as he closed his office door. "She had her little clique: Callie Stephens, a guy name Keith something, and Omar Faxton," Crawford explained. "When you saw Raven, you saw Callie, but Raven was the queen bee. Top of her class, beautiful, and screwing a powerful man."

Rather than sit behind his desk Crawford took the seat next to Dudley. "Everyone got along fine as long as Raven was the lead pony, but when Callie pulled out front by proving herself an awesome litigator, Raven decided to get rid of her." Crawford spread his hands in the air as he painted an imaginary picture. "Now get this. Omar and Callie had a thing: she called it love but Omar didn't love anybody but himself." Crawford paused and arched his brows at Dudley. "You should have seen him. Fine as shit. What I wouldn't have done—"

"Crawford! You know I can't stand that faggot talk!" Dudley barked. "Get back to the story!"

"Anyway, Callie was a real nice young lady, real nice." Crawford shook his head as he remembered Callie Stephens. "Raven somehow convinced Omar to help her get Callie kicked out of school. They say she was slipping Omar a little bit through the back door."

Dudley wondered whether Michael knew that Raven was sleeping with one of her classmates at the same time she was sleeping with him. *He probably did, the punk*, Dudley concluded. "Keep going," he said to Crawford.

"Raven and Omar set up Callie in a cheating scandal. There was a big hearing. You should have seen it, child," Crawford said as he slapped Dudley on his wrist. "In the end Callie got off and Omar went missing."

Dudley was disappointed. He'd heard rumors that Raven was a true bad actor, but this crap didn't even qualify for honorable mention.

"Thanks, Crawford. See you around," Dudley said as he started to squeeze himself out of his seat.

"Don't leave! You haven't heard the best part," Crawford said. "Six months passed and no Omar. Although Raven denied it, the police and Omar's acquaintances believed that the last time anyone saw him, he'd been on his way to meet Raven."

A slight smile crossed Dudley's lips. As best he could, he got settled into his seat. "Really?" Dudley drawled. "Tell me more."

"From what I heard, Omar's fiancées suspected foul play, but they mainly relied on their intuition."

"Fiancées? He had more than one?"

"I'm telling you, Dudley, Omar was a straight-up dick slinger." Crawford sighed. "Too straight, unfortunately." He put himself back on track before Dudley could snap at him again. "But to answer your question, he had three women. Callie Stephens—I'm not sure whether they were ever engaged. But he was engaged to two other women at the same time, a married white girl—her husband owns that big computer company, what's the name?—Huffmeyer? Yeah, Huffmeyer. And he had another one, a little Louisiana girl. What was her name?" Crawford snapped his fingers as he tried to remember. "Boudreaux? Micheaux? Hold on a minute," he told Dudley as he went and sat behind his desk. After a few strokes on his computer, Crawford said, "Tanisha Malveaux. She was nice, too." As though he had personal insight into Omar's preferences, Crawford added, "Omar liked them nice, except for when it came to Raven."

"I can't believe our luck," Michael said to Christopher as Lawrence shuttled them both to the airport. Christopher was headed to Dallas, and Michael, to Washington DC. "I shouldn't call it luck, though; I knew you did a lot of work to get that new office space. Good job," Michael said.

Michael was talking about Christopher's successful bid to have Michael's Dallas office moved into a larger facility. Christopher called on Dallas-area business leaders and convinced them that a larger, better-equipped Neighborhood Assistance Center would benefit their businesses as well as the community. Christopher did everything above board, followed all the campaign finance rules, and was about to oversee the actual move.

"Thanks, Dad. I can't wait to get things off the ground. We've got lots to do, but Monica's a great help. It'll take over a week to get everything set up. Genie's coming up Wednesday or Thursday to take our communications system offline. Then I'll have her come back the week after that to put us back online."

"Good deal; when Genie does something, it's always right. She's about the only person in the world meticulous enough to work for Raven and diplomatic enough to get along with her. Genie's a hell of a young woman."

"She's all right," Christopher said with a marked absence of enthusiasm.

"Just all right?" Michael closed his portfolio and put his electronic organizer in his breast pocket. "I thought I noticed a little strain between the two of you." He rubbed Christopher's shoulder as he prepared to step from the limousine. "I know you don't think much of my choices when it comes to love, but your old man's still good for some decent advice. Let's talk about it when we both get back to town, okay?"

"Sure, Dad. Have a safe one."

Christopher spent the day working side by side with Monica Fowler. She might be all hip-hop on the outside, but inside, Monica was pure brains. She oversaw the packing of the boxes, supervised the movers, and, rather than waiting for Genie to come to town, personally took the communication systems offline. All in one day.

That night Christopher took Monica to dinner. They planned their setup strategy for the next day, and when Christopher mentioned that he'd be there about nine, Monica drawled, "The building opens at seven. What's up with wasting two hours?"

"You're a workaholic, Miss Monica. Why aren't you finishing your degree instead of working as a receptionist?"

Monica put her elbows on the table and formed a tent with her fingers. "Got into a little trouble." She momentarily seemed lost in her own thoughts, so Christopher kept quiet and watched the tattoo on Monica's breast rise and fall. He kept watching it.

"To tell the truth, I'm not sitting out this semester of my own free will. I'll be enrolled next semester, though. In the meantime, my grandfather called your dad and hooked me up. Grampa Buddy's always trying to tame me." Monica used her straw to dig at the ice in her glass as she spoke.

She gave Christopher a wicked grin. "I'm trouble, true enough, but I'm the best kind of trouble, Chris, because I'm smart. And I'm as good on the inside as I look on the outside." She noticed him watching her tattoo, and glanced down at it herself, to let him know she caught him staring and didn't care. "I've got more, but I don't show them to just anybody."

*Genie wouldn't get a tattoo, not even a hidden one, if her life depended on it*, Christopher thought. He'd once joked with her about getting a tattoo in a private spot, but she said she would feel unprofessional, even if other people couldn't see it. "Yeah. Whatcha got?" he asked.

Monica rolled her eyes up toward the ceiling as she thought. "Well, I've got an hourglass in the small of my back."

"What does it mean?"

"Private joke. Drunken mistake." Monica grinned. "And I've got a butterfly that's off the chain. It's filled in."

"What color?" Christopher asked.

"Dark brown, the same color as this," Monica flipped one hand through her hair. "Outlined in deep red. Can you imagine how good that looks against my skin?"

Monica was a golden girl—her skin looked like honey. And yes, Christopher could imagine it.

"And I'm about keeping it real, so other than the ink outline, my butterfly is all natural, the same dark brown as the hair on my head," she giggled. "Except it's not permed," Monica said.

It took Christopher a minute to catch on, and when he did, he blushed. "Oh."

"You're so cute. It's been a long time since I hung out with a brother like you. It's nice," Monica said. "Now, let's finish talking about tomorrow."

By the time Genie flew in Thursday, there wasn't much for her to do. She breezed in wearing a Prada ensemble and Gucci shoes. Monica's gear was expensive too, all Sean John. Monica showed Genie around and told her that she'd already taken the computer system offline. All Genie would have to do was connect the system to Michael's network once the move was complete.

"Monica, this is good. You're really a bright young lady." Monica was sitting at her desk, and as Genie walked by, she patted Monica's shoulder. "Good job!" she said in a cheery corporate voice.

"Gee, thanks," Monica said.

As Christopher drove Genie back to the airport, Genie asked him, "When are you going to have a talk with Monica?"

"About what?"

"Her attire, for one thing. Now that the center's high profile a lot more people will be going through there, businesspeople who'll expect to be greeted professionally. Monica seems like a smart girl, so maybe she'll be good at accepting constructive criticism. Unless she does though, you should think about getting someone new to be the first face people see when they walk into the center, put Monica in the back."

Christopher came to Monica's defense. "Genie, Monica's not a girl, she's a woman. She's a college student who's taking a break, and what you saw today? She's twice as smart as that. Monica's the main reason that the move to the new space is going without a wrinkle." Christopher laid out his case as a lawyer would, but he was a little miffed that Genie felt like he needed her advice. *If it weren't for Monica, you'd still be down on your hands and knees, unplugging wires*, he thought. Christopher kept going. "Monica is Buddy Fowler's granddaughter, and after all Buddy's done for my dad, I wouldn't disrespect him or Monica by putting her 'in the back' as you say."

Genie took the point. "I'm sorry, Chris, you're right. I fly in here for half a day and start making judgments and recommendations. This office is your thing, and you're working it. If Monica's all you say she is, you'd be a fool to move her." She leaned over and kissed the side of his mouth. "I'm probably just being a hater. Did you check out Monica's pants? I couldn't fit into those if I tried."

"She doesn't dress like that every day," he said, still feeling defensive. "Those were her moving clothes."

"Pretty skintight for moving but she got the job done. Heck. I wish I could dress like that *any* day." Before she got out of the car, Genie pulled Christopher to her and gave him a real kiss. "See you Sunday evening?"

"Yeah, babe. I can't wait." On his way back to the center, Christopher thought about his father's offer to have a talk about Genie. No need for that. Genie's kiss, and the way she backed off about Monica, proved it. Their relationship was heading back on track.

# 15

"Mrs. Joseph, to what do I owe the pleasure?" State Representative Charlie Smotes said as he ushered Raven into his office using the cigar he held as a pointer.

"Pleasure's all mine," Raven said in a honeyed voice. She'd been in Texas long enough to mimic a Southern drawl when she needed to. She made sure she passed close enough for Smotes to smell her perfume.

Raven had on pants, so sitting back and crossing her legs wouldn't do. She knew every fashion rule including the one that dictated that when the bottom was covered the top had to be exposed. Raven leaned forward as she spoke.

"I'm here on pension protection, Charlie."

"You are?" He feigned surprise and ogled her breasts at the same time. "Why?"

"Because I hear you still haven't made up your mind how you're going to vote."

Smotes stood and poured himself a drink to go with his cigar. Raven's breasts were okay but they were too brown for his taste. He'd rather have a drink. "Michael's got you out rounding up votes? I thought that was Dudley's job."

Raven got up and walked over to Smotes. "It is." She took

the drink from him, had a sip, and handed the glass back. "But you're a special case, so I decided to come myself."

Smotes nodded and sat the glass down. A six-piece glassware set, ruined, he thought. "A special case, huh. Michael said that?"

Michael had said nothing of the sort and Dudley hadn't either. Raven hadn't talked to either of them about her plan to visit Smotes. She knew that next to gun control, pension protection was the project closest to her husband's heart. They'd lost so many endorsements and votes lately, she didn't want to take a chance on losing another one.

"We need you on this one, Charlie," Raven said as she mentally sized him up. Although it was early fall, Smotes wore a sky blue seersucker suit. Raven idly wondered where he could have purchased such an atrocity. He waved his cigar like it was a Cohiba, but Raven could tell from the aroma that the cigar was a cheap drugstore brand. *He's for sale*, she thought, *at a bargain basement price.*

Although she had given him back the glass, Raven didn't move out of Smotes's personal space. "You come through for Michael on the pension plan bill and I promise you, he won't forget about you when he becomes governor." She was so close he could feel her breath, which smelled of spearmint.

Smotes took a puff of his cigar and exhaled right into Raven's face. "You mean *if* he becomes governor. And that's a pretty vague promise, don't you think?"

Raven forced herself not to blink. She stared into Smotes's eyes through the smoky haze. "I said *when* he becomes governor, Charlie, and that's what I mean. And as for the promise, it's as good as a slimy slug like you is going to get."

Raven reached into her bag and removed an envelope. "I've heard through the grapevine that you're a poor man. What is it they call you people? Poor white trash or trailer-park trash? I always confuse the two." She shook her lovely hair and laughed in his face. "A poor white politician. You've got to be the dumbest man alive if you can't figure out how to make money in this game."

She waved the envelope in front of Smotes. "Here's a little something to help you make next month's rent on your double-wide. You know what I expect in return."

Raven dropped the envelope on the floor and walked out. She had no way of knowing that Erika had already funneled Smotes more than enough cash to buy himself a little something nice. A car, maybe, or a down payment on a beach house in Galveston. All Smotes had to do was vote against Michael on the pension bill, and keep on voting against him on every piece of legislation that hit the floor.

"He in yet?" Michael demanded of Smotes's secretary.

"Yes sir, he is. But—"

Michael strode to Smotes's door and barged in. "Charlie, what the hell! What happened? I thought we had a deal!"

"Morning, Mike." Charlie Smotes was sitting on his sofa, watching *Good Morning America*. "Just catching up on current events. Join me?" He motioned toward a chair.

Michael stood in front of the TV and held up his fingers like quotation marks. "Senator Joseph's pension board legislation dies on the vine." Michael made a disgusted snort. "Doesn't even make it out of committee. How's that for a current event?"

Smotes turned off the television and walked over to Michael. "Oh, so now I guess it's your turn to bully me. I'm surprised, Michael. You know I don't respond well to being pushed around."

"Pushed around? What are you talking about?"

"I'm talking about your wife." Smotes pulled a cigarette and lighter from his shirt pocket. The cigar between his lips, Smotes cocked his head to the side and lit up. "Sending her over here to strong-arm me. The way she came into my office, talking to me like I'm some damn errand boy—you must've been out of your mind to pull a stunt like that," Smotes said, the cigar bouncing up and down as he spoke. "From now on, when you're lining up votes, count me out."

Smotes went to his door and invited the Democratic candidate for governor of the great state of Texas to get the hell out of his office.

"Raven! What did you do?" Within twenty minutes of leaving Smotes's office, Michael was in his wife's. The brisk walk from Smotes's state capitol office to Michael's campaign headquarters left him red faced. The only time Raven had seen her husband so out of breath and excited was during sex.

"Sit down a minute, Michael. Here." She poured a glass of water and tried to hand it to him, but he wouldn't take it.

"I don't have time to sit down." He looked at his watch. "What in the world possessed you to go talk to Smotes about the pension bill?"

Raven was the picture of innocence. "Honey, I talk to legislators all the time, you know that."

"But I'd already talked to Smotes. You had no business going to him. Do you know how ineffective this makes me look? If I can't push through my agenda as a senator, why the hell should anyone trust me to be governor?"

"If you didn't want my help, you should've told me." By now, Raven was fully on the defensive. "Things have been so raggedy around here, I'd think you'd want all the help you can get."

"I appreciate help, but not the kind of help that makes veteran politicians feel like dirt."

"Michael, you're wrong," she protested. "I don't know what Smotes told you, but I treated him just fine. You know how I can do a man when I want something." She turned her back on Michael, let the innuendo sink in. "If he says anything different, he's a liar."

"You calling somebody else a liar. That's rich." Michael

walked around to where Raven could see him. He'd calmed down, and his voice was matter of fact, but his eyes were as cold as ice. He looked at Raven that way more and more these days.

"I owe you a lot. If it weren't for you, I wouldn't have had the nerve to run for governor in the first place. But sometimes, Raven, you're nothing but an albatross hanging around my neck, messing up everything."

Michael was tired of reminding himself every other day that *he* was the one who'd wanted to get married to Raven, *he* was the one responsible for keeping his marriage to a firecracker on track. He decided to give Raven a quick, hard one below the belt.

"Grace was quiet, not nearly as outgoing as you are. She wasn't one to go out politicking for me, but she'd cut off her arm before she'd do something to hurt my career. The difference between you and Grace is that her main concern would've been me becoming governor." He had his finger in Raven's face by this time. "The main thing, the *only* thing you care about, is being the governor's wife. What I wouldn't give to have a woman like Grace on my side every once in a while."

He broke off and headed toward the door. "I'm in meetings all day. Tonight, too. When you get home, I won't be there. Don't wait up," Michael said and walked out.

"Hey, little lady, what you up to?" David asked as he entered Raven's office. He was in Austin for the day, and as had become his custom, he stopped by to see if Raven was available for lunch. Dinners he reserved for Erika.

"Hey," Raven responded. She was usually a perpetual whirlwind, but for once Raven was sitting at her desk, doing nothing. Except, that is, figuring out how to get back at her husband.

As David took a seat, Raven got up and locked the door. Then she went back and sat down behind her desk. They chatted for a few minutes, but David sensed that Raven was just going through the motions. "How's life treating you today?" he asked her.

"Not too good." Raven didn't say anything else and when David continued to look at her quizzically, she added, "Headache."

"Why didn't you say so?" He got up and went to her. "I've got magic hands. Just tell me where it hurts."

"Here." Raven motioned to her temples. David began rubbing in a circular motion just at the edge of Raven's hairline. She relaxed and closed her eyes. It was so quiet in the room that David could hear her soft breathing.

Raven reached up and guided David's hands into the thick of her hair. As David rubbed his hands through her luxurious mane, his breathing became as audible as hers. Raven leaned forward, flipped her hair up in back, and held it there. "My neck," she said.

*What the hell are you doing!* David's conscience shouted at him, but it was a tiny, faraway shout that was drowned out by all the heavy breathing going on. David bent low and massaged Raven's neck, then her shoulders. She leaned back in her chair then and grabbed David's left hand. She guided his hand inside her shirt.

"No," David managed to say and tried to pull away, but Raven held him firmly.

"Can you feel how fast my heart is beating? Go on, feel it." Raven slowly let go of David's hand and instead of pulling away he squeezed her tighter and groaned deeply. David twirled Raven's chair around, picked her up, sat in it, and placed her in his lap, so that she straddled him. He thrust his hands into her hair again, pulled her to him and kissed her. Raven's lips were as soft as he'd imagined they would be.

David wrapped his arms around Raven. "We can't do this to Michael," he whispered in her ear. His voice was thick with guilt.

"This doesn't have anything to do with Michael. It's between me and you," Raven whispered back. "This has been coming for a long time, David, and we both know it." She backed away from his ear and kissed him again and then looked him in the eye, silently asking him, *Are you down?*

David's expression was a jumbled mixture of sadness and heat. He bowed his head and when he raised it again, Raven was looking at a different man. The brother was up, had been since the moment he opened Raven's door and looked at her, and now he began moving slowly beneath her. Raven thought buck wild was the only way to go and she tried to hurry him along. She tried to unbutton his shirt and take off his belt, but David wouldn't respond. David didn't change the tempo of his own unhurried groove, he just kept kissing her, pulling at her tongue, gently biting her full lips. He kept it up until Raven started moving at his rhythm and started kissing him back.

"Take it slow, pay attention," David whispered to Raven, once he'd subdued her. "You don't want to miss any part of what's about to happen."

David shoved everything off Raven's desk and placed her there. He undid her top and slid her thong to the side. Then he quickly undressed himself. Reverend David Capps, with his thirty-seven-year-old, righteous self, was a specimen. His biceps were pumped, and his upper body was broad and cut. David's stomach wasn't exactly flat, but it was firm. A patch of curly hair dusted his chest, formed a band at his sternum, headed south, and kept going.

He dropped his shorts and there it was.

Raven rose up and held him in her hands as one would a rare jewel. "You should have told me," she said. "I wouldn't have waited so long."

"Is that it, Robert?" Michael asked the representative from the budget office. They were in Michael's Senate office on state capitol grounds.

"Well, actually, there is one more item." He handed Michael a folder.

Michael opened the folder, then snapped it shut. "I need a break." He looked at his watch. It was almost three. "Let's take an hour, hour and a half."

Raven hadn't called or stopped by the way she usually did after one of their arguments. She'd usually come in and fling a bunch of four-letter words, he'd fling around more, and then they'd go to lunch, or slip home for a little midafternoon love. Michael missed that. *Guess I went too far this morning,* he thought.

He decided to walk over to his campaign headquarters and apologize.

"You're a wild one," David said. He and Raven were again seated in her chair, but now they were only half-dressed.

"And I'm bad, too," Raven replied. At least she'd tried to be, but David wasn't having it. He let her smack his butt, but when she dug her fingernails into his shoulder, David grabbed her hand and held it. When she'd reached for his throat with her other hand, he changed positions, pulled her down to the edge of the desk, put her legs over his strong shoulders, and lightly pinned her arms. "Don't get rough with me," he'd growled. "Ain't but one man here."

"I like my women bad," David said, and moved to kiss her again. *Can't get enough of her lips,* he thought.

They were interrupted by a knock on the door.

Raven started to move, but David put his arm around her waist, and motioned, *shhh.* The knocks came again, and then a voice: "Raven, honey, are you in there?"

It was Michael.

Over a late lunch, Christopher told Genie, "She's done it again."

"Who did what?"

"Your boss. She went to State Representative Smotes about the pension bill. Got nasty with him."

Genie put down her fork. She didn't know what went on with Smotes, and she didn't care. Genie was able to work for Raven because she was able to decipher her moods and because she was outstanding at her job. Today Raven was hell on wheels. She'd yelled at Genie twice already, and once even swore for good measure.

Genie couldn't snap back at Raven but she could take her frustration out on Christopher. "Stop being so immature, Chris. Calling Raven "she," "your boss," or "his wife" isn't going to change the fact that Raven has a name. You ought to use it sometimes."

*Immature? She didn't think I was immature last night.* "Okay. How about this: Raven Holloway Joseph, the future governor's wife, went to Representative Smotes and talked to him, or rather, at him, about the pension bill. She—excuse me—Raven Holloway Joseph, the future governor's wife, belittled Representative Smotes and badgered him to the point that he voted against the pension bill. How's that?"

Genie looked skeptical. "Raven wouldn't do that. She wanted the bill to go through as much as your father did."

"Aren't you listening, Genie? I didn't say she intended to make Smotes to vote against us, but her style is so raw, alienating him was the end result. It would be nice if she stayed in her place, stopped messing everything up."

"And what place would that be?" Genie asked sharply.

Christopher was as stressed as Genie. When he had talked to Michael earlier, his father's anxiety had disturbed him.

"I could tell you where Raven's place is, but you're just like her, so it wouldn't do any good," he snapped back.

Christopher didn't often say things that stung Genie, so his words caught her off guard. She felt a twinge in her chest and her lips twisted oddly, but she didn't respond.

"Both of you," Christopher continued, "are so ambitious you can't envision anything about the future except for your own climb to the top."

"Christopher, that's not true!"

"Yes, it is. That's why, no matter what happens, you're always on her side. Why do you always take up for her?"

Genie threw down her napkin and mimicked Christopher in a baby voice. "'Always taking up for her. Always on her side.' You're such a baby, Chris. And you have the audacity to talk about getting married and having kids." Genie stood, took one last sip of her soda and said, "You need to grow up your damn self."

When Michael knocked at her office door, Raven's eyes widened and she tried to move again, but David held her tighter and shook his head back and forth, *No*. He had a little experience with sneaky office sex, and knew the worst thing to do was make a sound. Out of nervousness, Raven felt an irrepressible need to laugh; she couldn't help herself. David put one hand over her mouth, and the look on his face, which had gone from lustful to distressed, made her want to laugh even more. Raven's body shook from the effort of keeping the sound inside; David could feel her stomach muscles contract against his own.

Standing outside the door, Michael took the key to Raven's office from his pocket. He knew she was in there, Dudley had just told him so. Michael slid the key into the lock and gave it a half turn.

Then he thought better of it, tried to figure out how a good husband would handle the situation. *I acted a fool earlier today. If she doesn't want to be bothered with me, that's her right.* Michael put the key away and headed back to his Senate office. *I'll get my secretary to send her roses.*

David counted to twenty, and then took his hand from Raven's mouth. She laughed and he did too, but not for long.

"What's wrong?" Raven asked as she rubbed her hands over his face. "Feeling disloyal to Michael?"

"Yes." *He's not the only one I've betrayed,* David thought. He leaned back in the chair and looked at her. His eyes masked most of what he felt. "You're beautiful, you know that?" David reached out and traced the curve of her beautiful lips with his finger. Remorse and the thrill of almost getting caught got all mixed up together and lit the fire again.

Next door, Dudley walked away from the wall he shared with Raven. He poured himself a drink in the glass he'd been using to try to spy on the couple. They were so loud he didn't need it.

"Are you coming to bed now?" Michael asked sheepishly. It was two in the morning and Raven was sitting at her computer, playing a game.

"Nope," she said without looking up. "I'm working on something important."

"Honey, I said I'm sorry."

Raven kept playing her game. Michael waited for her to say something and when she didn't, he went back to bed. As soon as he left, Raven got up from the computer and got a blanket and pillow from the hall closet. She stripped, got comfortable on the sofa, and drifted off to sleep.

The next thing Raven knew, she had the sensation of being lifted.

"This isn't where you belong," Michael said as he walked toward the bedroom with Raven in his arms.

"I'm sorry about the way I acted today. Honey, please forgive me. Don't deprive yourself of our bed or of all this." Michael took off his boxers.

Raven decided that she and Michael needed to have more fights. He believed in giving his all when it was time to make up.

As she drifted off to sleep, Raven thought, *Seduced by two men in one day. I must be doing something right.*

* * *

A week after they began the move from the old office to the new office, Monica and Christopher prepared to close down for the night. She looked around at the boxes, stacked three levels high, which took up all the space in the main area. The boxes formed a maze around the room. "Okay. We made it into our new office, but we've got our work cut out for us if we want to be open for business Monday morning," she said.

"There must be over a hundred boxes here," said Christopher.

"One hundred six, to be exact." She scooted along one of the narrow aisles created by the rows of boxes and flipped off a light switch at the back of the room.

"Oops!" Monica accidentally bumped one of the boxes and the stack started to tilt.

"I'll get that. You go ahead, hit the lights." Christopher made his way down the aisle and secured the boxes. "I should have asked Genie to fly in and help us. Tomorrow and Saturday are going to be hell."

"We'll be fine without her. She called me with the computer codes, so I'll be able to bring the center online with your dad's network in an hour or two. Prada and unpacking don't mix anyway." Monica turned off the last light and made her way back down the darkened row.

"Where are we going for dinner?" Monica asked.

"Mmm. How about somewhere fun," Christopher said.

Monica was almost next to him now. "Anywhere with you is fun, Chris. Which brings me to a question. Does Genie know how to have a good time?" Monica stood with her thumbs hooked into her pants pockets. "She doesn't look like it, if you ask me." Monica leaned close to Christopher. "She tried to act like she's all that when she was here last week. When we talked on the phone today, she was still on some more.

"Where's she from, Boston, some shitty, stuck-up place like that?" As she talked, Monica began squeezing past Christopher, but the space, filled with boxes on both sides, was too small.

"Let me get out of the way," he said and started to sidestep down the row.

"That's all right, you're good just where you are."

Monica brushed against him and lingered.

Uh-oh.

Monica stayed right in front of him, their bodies barely touching, until she was certain he got the message. "I've been meaning to tell you," she said. "When you come to town, you don't have to stay with your mother. You can come over to my place, check a sister out. Unlike Genie, I'm so much fun I should be illegal."

# 16

Although he was concerned about what Erika might be up to, Dudley hadn't forgotten that with each passing day, Raven became more of an obstacle to his success. It didn't take him long to locate one of Omar's former fiancées, Tanisha Malveaux Sawyer. She had moved back to her hometown of Baton Rouge and was married to the mayor.

"After the drama with Omar, it was hard to go to class every day and endure the whispers and the stares," she told Dudley during a telephone conversation. "I thought about transferring to Southern, here in Baton Rouge, but all my life I'd been the type to run away from hard situations and I didn't want to live that way anymore, so I stuck it out at Monroe."

"Did you ever hear from Omar, or get hang-up calls that could have been him?"

"No. I hoped for a long time that I would but it never happened," Tanisha admitted.

On his end of the line, Dudley smiled, but he made sure that his voice sounded a little sad. "What do you think happened to him?"

She thought for a moment and then said, "Omar left home to meet Raven and no one's seen or heard from him since. I think the situation speaks for itself."

* * *

"I've got no problem whatsoever—let me not exaggerate—I don't have *too* much of a problem when it comes to getting in trouble for the things I do. But to get blamed for something I didn't do, the way Michael blamed me for the Smotes disaster? I can't stand for that, Dudley."

Raven and Dudley were on the telephone. They were obsessed with finding out why Michael's agenda was falling apart. Dudley wasn't trying to get Michael elected for the fun of it and nobody was going to cheat him out of his place of power behind the throne. Raven was just starting to have fun as the future governor's wife, and she wasn't ready for the ride to end any more than Dudley was.

"Who's around us that we can't trust?" Dudley asked.

"Ted Ballentine?" Raven offered.

They sat silently, each thinking the exact same thoughts about Michael's running mate. If Raven and Dudley could be said to revel in the cushy life that would come with a move to the governor's office, Ted Ballentine was drunk with the idea; he'd already become addicted to the advantages that came with being a candidate for the position of second in command. He didn't much care for Texans, but they loved him—at least the ones with money to spend did. Ballentine walked around with a big price tag on his forehead and a "for sale" banner draped across his ass. For anybody who wanted to buy a politician, for any reason, Ted Ballentine was the man to see.

"You really think it's him?" Dudley's tone was doubtful.

"Doesn't make sense, does it? Ballentine's scum, and he's dumb as a drum with a hole in it, but even he's smart enough to know he can't stab Michael in the back until after we win the race. He wants to be in the governor's office as much as we do," Raven said.

"True. It's got to be somebody who can play both ends, who can work their agenda with or without Michael."

"Let's look at the people who've let us down, the endorsements we've lost. The one's we've been able to count on before now." Dudley ticked them off. "Midland Oil, Smotes, the Rice Association, which we can blame on Addison, Riley, and that dust for brains Watkins, as you like to call her.

"Who has the clout to influence them all?" Dudley mused. They said it at the same time. "Erika Whittier."

"Mom, I'm sorry it's so noisy," Christopher said as he looked around Cantina de Carlos. "I didn't know there'd be so many kids here."

"It's Friday night, Chris. Families always take this place over on Fridays. We used to come here all the time when you and Evan were small, always on a Friday. Don't you remember?"

Christopher leaned closer to his mother so he wouldn't have to shout. "A repressed childhood memory, huh? No wonder I like coming here." He leaned to one side to avoid a little girl of three or four, who was running down the aisle, her arms flailing. "If you knew it would be a zoo, why didn't you suggest we go somewhere else?"

"A zoo?" Grace looked around her and smiled. "Maybe to you, but I call it life. I'm glad we came here, Chris. Reminds me of good times."

Her smile shot love through Christopher like a lightning bolt. He felt the urge to get up from his seat and give her a hug, but he settled for saying, "Well, I'm glad you're having a good time." Grace wasn't just having a good time; she'd taken Carolyn's advice and started looking good, too. She had on a tan calfskin jacket—which went quite nicely with her honey-blond streaked hair—jeans and ankle boots.

"That I am. But what about you? You seemed a bit distracted on the drive over. Anything you want to talk about?"

He'd been thinking about Genie. And about Monica's tattoo.

"Nah, I'm straight. Just thinking about the election." Christopher threw out the explanation that he gave Genie whenever he didn't want her to really know what was on his mind. Too late, he realized his mistake. Christopher tried not to mention anything remotely related to his father to his mother.

One corner of Grace's smile dipped, then her eyes widened in surprise. The same little girl who'd run by before, careened directly into Grace.

"Whoa, sweetie. Slow down," Grace said as she pulled the child onto her lap.

"Shinquintana, didn't I tell you to sit your butt down?" The girl's mother said as Grace handed over the child.

Shinquintana broke into loud sobs. The mother jerked the girl by one arm. "Come on here. You so bad!"

Grace reached out and touched the mother's arm. "Oh, I didn't mind her bumping into me. She a precious little thing, just as cute as can be."

"Yeah," the mother's rough exterior gave way under Grace's kind words. "She's been sitting still for hours, getting her hair done. I guess that's why she's got so much energy."

"She looks absolutely beautiful," Grace said.

Christopher looked at Shinquintana. She would have been a cute little girl if her mother had enough sense to leave her alone and let her look like a child. Christopher didn't know much about children, but he did know that one of the prettiest sights on earth was a little black girl, too young to have her hair permed, who still wore thick puffy plaits. Poor Shinquintana was wearing enough weave to give long locks to two grown women. The hair was braided, and it curlicued down her back all the way past her tiny shoulder blades.

Shinquintana's mother picked her up and kissed her. "Come on, boo boo. Let's finish eating."

"Mom!" Christopher whispered after Shinquintana and her mother went back to their table. "Why'd you tell her that hairdo looks good? It's ridiculous!"

"You know what I always say, Chris. A little lie never hurt

anyone." Grace tried to look serious but she couldn't hold it. She burst out laughing and kept it up for so long that her eyes watered and she started coughing.

*Thank God for little Shinquinwhatever,* Christopher thought as he watched Grace.

When Christopher got Grace home, he hugged her the way he'd wanted to all night.

"Mmm," Grace said as she held him tightly, "your Uncle John is right. Hugs have healing power."

Christopher held her at arm's length. "And so do you. That girl and her baby at the restaurant sure felt it. You've got a way with people, Mom, especially young ones." He winked at her as he walked off. "Stop wasting it."

He pointed his car in the direction of Austin, but he really didn't want to make the trip back. Not that he was tired, just the opposite. Christopher was a bundle of energy, and didn't really know what to do with himself. He refused to call Genie—they were okay on the surface, but inside Christopher seethed over the flippant way she had treated him. He couldn't get over the disrespectful things she'd said to him recently, like calling him immature. He didn't feel like driving to Austin and he didn't want to go back to Grace's. Where else could he go?

*"You can come over to my place, check a sister out."*

Just the thought of Monica caused shame to knot Christopher's throat and heat to rise in his groin. He had never come close to cheating on Genie. They promised from the beginning that no matter what, they would always be honest with each other.

Christopher recalled Genie, her voice oozing with superiority, telling him what a boy he was. He made his decision. *A little lie never hurt anyone,* Christopher thought, recalling Grace's favorite phrase. He added his own twist, *especially if the person being lied to never finds out.*

He picked up his cell phone.

"Hey, Monica."

"Hey, Chris." Monica didn't sound surprised that Christopher was calling her on a Friday night.

"Look, uh, I'm still in town, nothing to do."

"So you decided to call me as a last resort?" Monica didn't sound pleased, but as she talked to Christopher she walked to her linen closet and took out a set of fresh sheets.

"No, no, it's not like that. I just thought I could stop by, take you for a drink, maybe."

Monica laid the fresh linen on her bed and walked to her lingerie drawer. "I'm not dressed to go out." She had just gotten home from dinner with her girlfriends when her cell phone rang. She hadn't even taken off her shoes.

"Oh." *Cut it off now, before you get into trouble*, Christopher thought, but he said, "We could just talk or watch TV."

"Let me give you directions," Monica said.

On his way to Monica's place Christopher told himself that they were two adults who were perfectly capable of holding a decent conversation or watching a movie without getting physical. He passed a drugstore, made a U-turn, and bought a packet of condoms.

When Christopher knocked on Monica's apartment door his heart was racing. She answered wearing a transparent black teddy. He could see her butterfly tattoo through the flimsy material.

Christopher took one step inside and the next thing he knew Monica was in his arms, her legs circling his waist. He gave a backward kick to close the door and laid Monica on the sofa. Then he went down for a closer look at her tattoo.

# 17

"Here, try this." Raven reached into one of Michael's bureau drawers and tossed his favorite toy on the bed.

"No, thanks, I'll stick with the hot oil," David said.

They were in Michael and Raven's bed, and David had just finished giving Raven a massage with oil that Michael had bought in Paris. Besides the toy, Raven had tried to get David to use other things of Michael's. His slippers. His robe (it would have been too small, anyway). Even his toenail clippers. It turned her on.

But David refused. "It's bad enough that I let you convince me to come here." Shame crossed his face. Sleeping with Raven was over the line, and doing so in Michael's bed was, for David, a brand-new low. He loathed himself for being there, but he and Raven were in deep. They had quickly become addicted to each other and found a way to be together once or twice every week. David didn't know how he was managing, considering the other things he let slide in order to get to Raven.

"I told you I couldn't leave the house today," Raven said as she massaged David's feet. "I'm expecting a special delivery," she lied. "Besides, this is my home, too. Michael's in DC, and Evan's in Houston with his high-school choir. Who are we hurting?"

"Tell that to the pain in my soul," David mumbled.

"What?"

"Nothing, babe," He smiled down at her. "I'm here, so that's that."

"Is it really true you were a boy preacher?" Raven asked.

"That's right. Preached my first sermon at ten. That's when I realized that I was right."

"About what?"

"Everything."

Raven laughed, but David didn't.

"Few men know right from wrong. Plenty pretend that they do, but half of them are more confused than the people they're trying to lead. I happen to be one of the few, one of the real ones. I was born with the responsibility to do great things," he explained.

Raven motioned at the room. "So this is your idea of doing right?"

David felt the pain in his soul again. "I said that I *know* what's right. My name is David for a reason." He nodded to himself and added, "I could have just as easily been called Jacob, I suppose."

"But your mother chose David."

"My mother? No way—about the only thing she ever did for me was lay with some dude so I could get here. I think one of the hospital nurses named me."

"Sounds like you and your mother don't connect."

"We didn't, not for years. She was a piss-poor excuse for a mother when Dudley and I were kids. She's the reason I don't like—I've never liked being around women who remind me of her. I used to hold a lot of things against my mother, but I gave up my resentment a long time ago. We made our peace before she died."

"Did Dudley and your mother make up, too?"

David shook his head. "No. The ability to forgive is a gift from God. It's His grace, nothing else, that helps you through it. Dudley doesn't believe in God, so, once you get on his bad side there's no making peace with him."

Raven understood Dudley's position. She thought about her own mother and wanted to ask David, *How do you do it? How do you make peace with a woman who's hurt you so much you can't really feel hurt, or any other emotion, anymore?*—but the question got stuck in her throat, so she said something else instead.

"You think your name describes you perfectly, huh?"

"Of course, David was the ideal man to name me after, much better than Jacob, when I think about it. That's what I am: a modern-day David, a man after God's own heart." Comparing himself to David of the Old Testament made David feel better about himself. Sure he was sinning now, but he'd get right later on.

"When it comes to a hot woman, I'm like my namesake." David moved closer to his lover and kissed her on his favorite spot. "It's the goodness and the courage in my heart that matters. What I *do* is beside the point."

After they had sex, David's guilt set in. "You know this can't go on forever," he said to Raven as he dressed. "It's not right."

Then he asked, "Can you slip away to Dallas one day next week?"

That night David tossed and turned. When he finally fell asleep he dreamed of being at the Joseph home with both Michael and Raven. In the dream, the couple went about their evening and barely acknowledged his presence. They treated David like an uninvited guest who had overstayed his welcome.

"Dudley?" Raven opened the door to Dudley's office and looked around for him. Certain that he wasn't inside, Raven quietly closed the door behind her. Although she had a key to his door—she'd stolen it from his secretary's desk—Raven was glad that the door was unlocked. Less to explain. She and

Dudley planned to meet in his office at three, and when she found out he was stuck in a committee meeting at the state capitol that started at two and was bound to run over, Raven decided to show up fifteen minutes early so she could snoop around. Dudley was far too close to Michael for her not to know more about him than she did.

She looked around the office. Where to begin? Raven got the desk drawers out of the way first, then went through Dudley's credenza.

"Dudley, you ass. You really shouldn't keep things like this in your office, even if they're under lock and key," Raven said as she picked up a lock box from Dudley's credenza. She used a paper clip to unlock the box and found copies of medical insurance claim forms. She saw the name Dr. Dennis Laverne on several forms. "I wonder what's wrong with Dudley," she said aloud as she went over the forms, line by line. She found what she was looking for: prescription receipts for Melleril.

Raven leaned back in Dudley's chair. *Well, I'll be damned; Dudley's a certified nut case. He's taking antipsychotic drugs,* she thought. Raven looked at her watch: five minutes until three. She moved to Dudley's floor-to-ceiling closets, and unlocked those. She felt around in the corner, where she couldn't see. Raven, who didn't scare easily, touched something that made her nearly jump out of her skin.

Slowly, she pulled out Dudley's sawed-off shotgun. *Dudley's not only a nut case, he's a nut case with a gun.* Raven realized she was starting to sweat. She put the gun back, locked the closet doors (and triple-checked to make sure she'd locked them), and looked around the office. Everything was back in place, but it was too late for her to sneak out. She might run into Dudley on his way in.

Raven walked behind Dudley's desk, where she stared out the window at the beautiful Austin hills and waited.

\* \* \*

Dudley loosened his tie, closed the door behind him, and leaned against it, his eyes closed.

"Don't tell me we lost another endorsement!"

He blinked several times, clearly surprised to see Raven standing behind his desk. "What are you doing in my office?"

"Relax, I just got here. I'm surprised we didn't run into each other in the hallway. The door was unlocked."

"We lost one, and we're on the brink of losing another," he replied. "The Educators for Change pulled out this morning. They're penny ante, have about ten members, so screw them. I'm more worried about a Latino group out of San Antonio. Their leader's getting nervous; the organization has backed losers in the last two elections and they're not anxious to do it again. I expect to hear from them this afternoon and I doubt it'll be good news."

Raven sat in Dudley's chair. "You're telling me we can't even hold onto a bunch of Mexicans?"

"They're Americans. Mexicans don't get to vote in our elections," Dudley dryly commented.

Raven waved her hand dismissively. "Whatever. Instead of making jokes, you ought to be figuring out how we're going to turn this election around. We're in trouble, and it looks like it's because you can't do your job!"

"You're angry, I'm angry, and we're both crazy. If you want to find out which of us is craziest, scream at me again. And by the way, get out of my chair." Dudley never moved and never raised his voice. Raven thought about the sawed-off and took a seat in an armchair.

"I know why this is happening. Erika's pissed off at me because we took the STRAPPED money but couldn't get Michael to keep quiet on gun control," Raven admitted.

"Can we give her back some of the money?" Dudley asked.

Raven raised both palms. "All gone. I've tried reasoning with her, but she wants what she paid for, and honestly, I can't blame her."

Dudley smirked. "I'm surprised that you're so understanding."

Raven shook her head. "I understand Erika, but that doesn't mean I'm willing to let her push me around." She leaned forward on Dudley's desk, her chin resting on her fist. "You know what? Erika's got too much time on her hands. Instead of us trying to get her off our backs we need to jump on hers."

She slapped both hands on the desk. "That's it! Dudley, when it comes to digging up dirt you claim to be the master. Let's see how good you are. Find something nasty on Erika and figure out a way to use it. We need to be in full swing on this by the end of the week."

Raven was relieved to finally have a game plan. And she was pleased that her meeting had yielded unexpected information. Who would have ever guessed that Dudley Capps owned a shotgun?

"Are you going to finish that?" Raven asked.

"No, help yourself," David replied. He propped himself on one elbow and watched Raven eat the rest of his hot brownie à la mode. They were at David's home, cuddled up on his sofa. "I've seen some women put away the sugar, but you set a new record."

Raven took a bite of the brownie and faked a shiver. "It's because this is better than sex. If I were forced to choose which chocolate treat I like the best, you or this brownie, you'd be in trouble."

"Have you always been hooked on the stuff?"

"Since I was a little girl." Raven set down the empty bowl and burrowed deeper into David's arms. "When I was about ten, my parents and I passed by this bakery and I saw a Boston cream pie. It was the prettiest thing I'd ever seen, so I begged my parents to buy it. Jacqueline said no, I wouldn't like it, but my daddy was so happy to see me happy that he bought it anyway. Jacqueline got so upset that she stopped talking to Daddy. We ended up cutting our day short and going home."

Raven blinked her eyes rapidly and whispered to herself, "I should have known then."

David eyes were closed. He rubbed her stomach and said, "So what happened next?" David was only half listening to Raven, but her voice was like warm honey and he wanted to keep it flowing. If he kept feeling like he was feeling, Raven wasn't going to get to finish her story.

"Daddy cut me a huge slice, probably a quarter of the whole thing. I took one bite and started crying. Jacqueline was right: I hated everything about the dessert: the texture, the taste, everything. Jacqueline wanted to make me eat it anyway, 'She wanted it, let her eat it,' she told my daddy, but he's not like that. He told me I didn't have to eat it if I didn't want to, so I threw the rest of my slice into the trash. Jacqueline didn't say a word, just kept chain-smoking those cigarettes of hers, those damn Virginia Slims, and watching me."

Raven's voice didn't sound so sexy anymore and David, after years of hearing parishioners go on and on about their problems, noticed the change. He kept rubbing Raven, but he started listening, too.

"That night—it must have been after midnight because Daddy never got up—Jacqueline jerked me awake. I started crying, but she put her hand over my mouth and marched me into the kitchen, straight to the trash can."

David kept stroking Raven, but there was nothing erotic in his touch. He looked down at her. Tears were sliding from the corners of Raven's eyes.

"Jacqueline made me dig my slice of cake out of that filthy can. Boston cream pie is really a cake, not a pie, did you know that? I'd eaten the dessert early in the afternoon, so by midnight there were all sorts of things on top of my slice of cake. What I remember most is her ashes. That bitch probably smoked ten extra Virginia Slims that day, just for me. By the time I got the Boston cream pie out, my fingertips were black with ash."

Raven seemed unable to say the actual words, so David said it for her. "Your mother made you eat it."

"Every crumb. And David, it was so big. I'm sure it didn't take me more than a half hour to eat it, but it seemed like it took all night." Raven's eyes, and her voice, were now desert dry. "To make it worse, I had to listen to her fuss at me about how I needed to learn that everything that looks good isn't good for you. Jacqueline compared me to that cake, pretty on the outside . . . you know. She always said things like that. All the time."

David stretched out on the sofa and pulled Raven to him. As they lay face to face, Raven said, "After she made me eat that trash, I threw up for two days. You'd think I'd hate sweets, but," she wiped away a tear, "look at me. Still taking in trash, using my body as a garbage can."

"Oh, baby. Come here," David said as he put his arms around her.

Raven reached for his sex, but he took her hands and put them around his waist. He pulled her to him. "No, just come here."

Raven lay in bed next to Michael and thought about David. She couldn't believe she'd told him the Boston cream pie story. Worse, she'd cried in front of him! Raven didn't even like to cry when she was alone.

David had wanted to talk about Jacqueline but all Raven told him was that Jacqueline was a name-dropping snob and was not welcome in Texas. Jacqueline was beside herself because although she was the mother-in-law of the future governor, she was barred from capitalizing on the connection.

*Something about David . . . I don't know, I'm in a different place when I'm with him, and it's getting that's where I want to be all the time,* Raven thought. The sex was different too. Michael was better at the pure freak action, but when David put his arms around Raven, the feeling that surged through her was soothing beyond anything she'd ever experienced. The closest thing to it was the feeling she'd gotten as a child when her father came home from work and picked her up. Raven stared at her bedroom ceiling and thought, *For the first time in my life, I think I might be in love. What on earth am I going to do?*

"Why would you think I know something about Omar Faxton?" the woman asked.

Dudley licked the cappuccino foam from his top lip. "Well, you were fucking him, weren't you, Mrs. Huffmeyer?"

Shelly looked around the coffee shop to see if anyone had overheard Dudley. The only reason she had agreed to talk to him was because he threatened to call her husband with some old gossip about her and Omar.

Shelly's blue eyes were friendly, in case anyone was watching, as she said, "Mr. Capps, you might have me in a tight spot, but you've got to talk to me better that that. Otherwise I'll walk out of here and deal with whatever comes."

Dudley reeled himself in but he didn't apologize. "Well, let me put it this way: My sources tell me that you and Omar were an item during his first and second years of law school. All I want to find out is what you know about his disappearance."

"Six months after he went missing, Omar's condo was still filled with expensive things, most of which I bought. He liked the high life too much to leave all that behind." She swept her natural blond hair to one shoulder. "And I know for a fact that he was sneaking around with Raven."

She stood. "I hope you find Omar, but I doubt that you will." She dug into her purse. "On the off chance that you do, give him this." She handed Dudley a business card. "My cell number is on the back."

# 18

"My, my. A personal phone call from Mr. Big Shot. I must be coming up in the world."

Michael laughed. "John, you sound like a second-string girlfriend who's not getting enough attention. Don't treat me like that."

"That's what I feel like," John Reese joked back. "You've gone and gotten yourself friends in high places—the President of the United States, and whatnot—how am I supposed to compete?"

"Yeah, right. All I can say is, when I grow up, I want to be just like you." Michael read from the invitation he'd just opened. "Maggie and John Reese request the honor of your presence as they celebrate forty years of marriage." He placed the invitation on the corner of his desk. "Free limousine service for out-of-towners, reception at the Four Seasons Resort. You must be running an illegal business out of the back room at the bookstore."

John Reese laughed so hard, he lost his breath. The sound of Michael's voice, easy and stress free, was like balm on a wound. Once, the two men had talked several times a week. Back then, Michael, Grace, and the boys came over at least once a month for Sunday dinner, and every other year both families took a vacation together. Never mind that there was no blood between them—Michael and John had been family in the truest sense of the word. John was like an older brother to Michael, not just any older brother, but the type who raised his younger siblings because the parents ran off or died. John had been his touchstone, his advisor and protector. They stood by each other, come what may, and told each other the truth, even when it hurt.

The qualities that had held them together for more than twenty years were the same ones that eventually pulled them apart. When Michael found himself falling for Raven, John Reese was the only person he confided in. Michael thought he'd get John's usual speech about not letting his outside affairs cause trouble in his home. John surprised Michael by going much further. John had done some investigating and he knew that Raven was nothing but trouble. When Michael and Raven married, John slipped out of Michael's life. Their weekly talks faded to birthday and holiday calls. Michael used to stop by John Reese's bookstore every time he went to Dallas, but on his last several trips there, he'd made excuses about why he couldn't go.

Although they'd become estranged once Michael left Grace, Michael thought about John almost every day, and Michael crossed John's mind at least as much.

"You know me, Michael, I'd just as soon have flown to Jamaica, had a small ceremony there. This is all Maggie. Forty years ago we got married at the courthouse because we couldn't afford a wedding, not even a small one. I didn't even know she missed being a real bride until we went to a ceremony for old friends in DC."

"Got her to thinking?"

"Yeah. That's all she talked about for weeks, until I finally asked her if she'd like to do the same thing. My Maggie went nuts," John Reese said, laughing at the memory. "I may go broke, but after what she's been to me all these years, how could I say no?"

"I know. I envy you, man. Hope I make it to forty."

An uncomfortable silence followed, during which each man thought about Grace. If Michael had ever had a chance of long-term wedded bliss, he'd already blown it.

"The whole family will be there, John. Wouldn't miss it."

"Speaking of family, two more things before you go. Maggie wants Evan to sing at the ceremony. Would you have him give her a call so she can see if he'll agree to do it?"

"I have no doubt he'll do it," Michael said. "Tell Maggie it's a go. I'll have Evan call her to square away the details. What's the other thing?"

"Just so you know, we're hoping Grace comes."

"She's got an invitation, Chris, Dad told me so. I don't know why I have to call her," Evan reasoned.

He and Christopher had been going back and forth for a week over one question: should Evan call Grace and ask her to come to the wedding? The brothers were cruising the mall, supposedly looking for the perfect present for Uncle John and Aunt Maggie, as they called the Reeses. So far Evan had purchased two pairs of the latest tennis shoes, and Christopher had sexy Victoria's Secret lingerie for Genie and Monica. All they'd done regarding the Reeses so far was talk, but the talk was intense.

"Ev, you know how Mom is. Unless she finds out you're singing, she might stay home. Call her, help me get her out of the house."

They stopped talking for a moment, their attention diverted by a group of well-toned college girls.

"Texas women is throwed, ain't they?" Evan commented as he openly eyed the girls.

"For real." Christopher stared, too. It was the way things went down in the mall.

Then Evan said, "If Mom wants to stay locked up in her apartment, that's her business, man. Dealing with her is a trip.

Seems like every time we talk, it's because you've made me call her. You made me invite her to my city-choir tryout and she didn't show up. I ain't with that."

Christopher slapped Evan on the shoulder. "I know. But right now we're all she's got, and I'm telling you, Ev, she's getting better, crawling out of the hole she's been in. It's because of us. When's the last time you saw her?"

"Couple of months."

"That's too long, Ev." Christopher walked toward a bench. "Tell you what, I'll chill here for a minute while you give her a call." When Evan started to protest, Christopher said the magic words. "Do it for me."

Evan walked a few yards away and flipped his cell phone. "Mom? Hey, how's it going?" His mouth felt like it was filled with cotton.

"Evan! Honey, I'm fine. How are you?"

"I'm cool." Evan was no good at casual conversation with either of his parents, so he got to the point. "I'm s'posed to sing at Uncle John and Aunt Maggie's wedding."

"Baby, that's wonderful! I haven't heard you sing in ages."

"Yeah, well." He thought about his audition. "You ought to come to the wedding, check it out."

"Well, I don't know. I really hadn't—"

"No problem. If you can't make it, you can't make it." *Although we both know you don't have anything else to do*, Evan thought but didn't say.

Grace picked up his vibe, and said, "Evan, I'll be there. I promise."


"I still don't understand why you have to stay, Chris." It was late on a Friday night. Christopher had flown to Dallas Thursday morning, with the promise that he'd be back in Austin with her Friday evening. Now he was telling Genie that he wouldn't be back until Sunday afternoon.

"It can't be helped, Genie, I've got to finish this report. I'm already all set up here, so it'll be easier for me to stay, knock it out, then come home." Christopher wished she'd pitch a fit and demand that he come home right that minute, but Genie was a trusting, independent woman. If he told her he had to stay, she'd take him at his word.

Genie slumped in her chair. "I'll get one of my girlfriends to go to the comedy show with me. I miss you."

"Miss you, too. Have a good time."

Genie took Christopher's advice and had a great time. She and her girlfriend ended up sitting in the front row, which made them prime targets for every comedian who took the stage. The comedians flirted with the women more than they made jokes about them. The one female comedian gave them props for keeping the guys in line.

When Genie got home, she called Christopher on his cell, but didn't get an answer.

"Stop it!" Genie said to herself after she'd called three times. But Genie didn't stop; she took her manhunting to level two. She called Grace.

"Hi, Ms. Joseph," Genie said when Grace answered. "I'm sorry for calling so late, but I've been trying to catch up with Christopher and he's not answering his cell. Is he there?"

"Genie? Hi, baby," Grace sat up and looked at the clock. It was almost one in the morning. *These young girls*, she thought, then remembered that once upon a time, she'd been a pro at tracking down her man. "No, Christopher isn't here. When did he leave Austin to head this way?"

*When did he leave Austin!* Genie repeated in her head. "Thursday morning," she said in a small voice. "He told me he'd be staying with you."

"Oh." Grace didn't know what else to say.

"Thanks, Ms. Joseph. If you hear from him, tell him I called?"

"Sure."

Pause.

"And Genie."

"Ma'am?"

"Don't stay up worrying about Chris. Get a good night's sleep. I'm sure he's fine."

The next morning, not knowing quite how she got there—after all, her mind kept saying no way—Genie found herself on the road to Dallas.

She got to the Neighborhood Assistance Center at ten. Genie looked toward the office that Christopher usually occupied when he was in town. The lights were out. *What about all the nonstop work he's got to do?*

"Hi," she said to the young man at the reception desk. "Is Christopher Joseph here?"

"No. They'll probably be in about twelve, twelve-thirty."

"They?"

"He and Monica."

Genie felt like she was watching herself in a horror movie, making all the wrong moves. She knew that she should wait for Christopher to show up, but instead she whipped out her identification badge. "I need to use your computer for a sec, okay?"

As soon as Genie pulled into the parking lot of the apartment complex, she spotted Christopher's Honda. She looked at the slip of paper in her hand. Monica Fowler, 5412 Finch Way, Apartment 123. This was the address and that was Christopher's car, no doubt about it. No hiding from the truth.

Genie took a compact from her purse and dabbed at her eyes. They weren't red, not yet, but it was clear she'd been crying. She fluffed her hair and got out of the car. As she searched for Monica's apartment, Genie tried to talk herself out of what she was doing. *Hunting down a man; it's degrading. Chris is where he wants to be. I don't want a man who doesn't want me. What if I lose it?* And, most troublesome of all—*What if he puts his arm around Monica and tells me to get the hell out?*

But Genie knew what every woman knows. Unless a man is

cold busted—unless his woman can tell him where he was, who he was with, what he had on, when it happened, and what he said—he'll say, "It wasn't me."

Monica answered the door when Genie knocked. She looked shocked but composed. "Hey, Genie." She wore a red silk robe. Genie had one exactly like it, in blue. Victoria's Secret.

"May I come in?"

Monica tucked her hair behind her ears. "It might be awkward."

"I can handle it if you can."

Monica stepped aside and Genie came in. She didn't sit down.

"Chris," Monica called out and then thought better of it. "No, wait!" Monica hurried toward the bedroom.

Christopher, totally unaware of what was going on, yelled back, "Is breakfast done already? I'm starving."

Then the man Genie knew so well stood in front of her in his bare feet and briefs.

"I was wrong," Genie said, talking to Monica, but looking at Christopher. "I can't handle this."

# 19

The crowd outside New Word was enormous; one would've thought people were flocking to a wedding for a celebrity couple rather than to one for the owner of a small bookstore and his wife. It took four drivers to keep up with the flow of cars waiting to be valet parked. People who decided to self-park had already filled the huge parking lot and were starting to line the curbs of streets near the church. John Reese and his wife weren't New Word members; they belonged to an older, traditional Baptist church. Once the RSVPs had started coming in, however, Maggie Reese realized that New Word was the only black church in Dallas large enough to hold the crowd that would show up to share the day with them.

As Christopher drove toward the church, he kept glancing at Grace. She clutched the handbag on her lap with one hand and the door handle with the other.

"Relax, Mom, you can do this. If you don't let go of that handle, I'm afraid you're going to end up on the highway."

"You're really thinking I'm going to fling this door open on purpose." Grace tried to make a joke of it, but her tight voice revealed how nervous she was. "John and Maggie are good people, the warmest couple I know. Your father and I wouldn't have made it for as long as we did without them. They're not blood, but I knew from the moment Michael introduced me to John and Maggie back when I was pregnant with you that I wanted them to be a big part of my children's lives."

"Pregnant? But Uncle John and Aunt Maggie were at your wedding—I've seen the pictures! Don't tell me you and Dad lied to me and Evan all these years. I thought you got married before you started having babies."

"Before we started having them. Not before we started making them."

"Mom!" Christopher looked so alarmed that Grace had to laugh. It sounded so good to hear his mother laugh, he continued to make a show of being shocked. Christopher knew that his mother was pregnant when she and his father married—he and a group of friends had counted out the months when they were preteens. Seemed to him that back in the day, a hot night was quickly followed by a rushed wedding day. His generation's tradition, in contrast, was to get pregnant, then say goodbye.

"I'm just saying, son, when I met the Reeses, your father and I were dating, and I was already starting to fall for him. I decided then that if Michael and I got together, John and Maggie would definitely be a part of our family."

Grace noticed that Christopher didn't seem to be listening to her. "Chris? Honey, what is it? What's wrong?"

Christopher's head throbbed. The talk about marriage and babies made him think about Genie. Since she had caught him with Monica, Christopher hadn't had any peace. The freeway traffic looked surreal to him, just like everything else, everything he'd touched or seen, every conversation he'd had over the last few days. He was moving in slow motion, looking at the world from the other side of an invisible wall. Christopher wanted to cry, to scream, to hit something, but he couldn't bring himself to act. He felt locked inside himself and was too ashamed to talk to anyone, even Michael, about how he'd gotten busted.

"It's nothing, Mom."

They drove a little farther, then Grace asked, "Ready to tell me yet?" Christopher said no again, but this time his answer came out weak.

Although Grace didn't say anything, Christopher could feel his defenses breaking down. He realized that what he was experiencing on a small scale, Grace lived through every day. If he expected her to stop holding back, he decided, the least he could do was lead by example.

Christopher put on his right-turn signal as they neared their exit. "Mom, I told you my reason for asking you to come to the wedding with me was because you need to get back out into the world." He slowed as he merged into the frontage road traffic. "You do need to get out, face the people you used to know, but that wasn't my main reason. I kind of need to talk to you." He told her what happened between Genie and him.

"I suspected that. Genie called me that Friday night looking for you."

Christopher was taken aback. "Why didn't you say something?"

"Not my business. But I see it's tearing you up, which by the way, is a good thing. Christopher, if you love the girl, you've got to show her. And if you have a problem with her, then you have to work it out. Running to another woman is not the way."

"Why did I do something so stupid?" he asked then answered his own question. "I was pissed at Genie because I'm ready to get married and she's not. What kind of husband will I be if I've already started cheating?" Christopher was completely down on himself. He hit the steering wheel with his palm. "I'm so much like him!"

"Yes, you are your father's son, which means basically you're a good man. But Genie's right, you're pretty young to be talking about marriage. By the way, I ran into Monica the other week. Hadn't seen her since she was about twelve. I can see why you are attracted to her."

Pause.

"Why the rush, Chris? Why do you want to get married so soon?"

"I just . . . I want a family again, Mom."

"You've got a family."

"I mean a real one."

"No, son. You mean a perfect one. Not gonna happen. Not with Genie, or any other woman, for that matter."

"Guess I've still got a lot to learn," Christopher said. He turned onto the boulevard leading to New Word. "This, this . . . *thing* that happened with Genie—what I did to her—it's killing me, Mom."

"I know that, Chris. I'm your mother, I know my sons." She reached over and caressed the back of his neck. "It's going to be okay. I know what happened between you and Genie hurts, but having a broken heart from time to time is a part of life. You need to do the right thing, and she'll take you back or she won't. Either way, you'll get past it."

Christopher wiped his eyes with the back of his hand. "Here," Grace said, and handed him a tissue.

Christopher smiled as he wiped his tears away. "I'm just a big baby, huh? That's what Genie says."

Grace patted Christopher's knee and began humming a tune—not for him, specifically, but absently, the way a mother does when she's packing a lunch, combing hair, or bandaging an elbow. Just to assure him that she was by his side.

As they neared New Word, the traffic slowed, then stopped. "Man. I know Uncle John and Aunt Maggie know a lot of people, but I never expected this." Glancing at his mother he saw that she'd gone rigid. Her stare was fixed straight ahead.

"Take me home."

"Huh?"

"I said get me out of here, Christopher, right now, and I mean it."

Christopher followed Grace's gaze. Up ahead, his father and Raven emerged from a limousine, arm in arm. Raven, with her cool sunglasses and dramatic cloak, looked like something out of *The Matrix*, except that her suit was vivid blue, not black.

"But Mom, what about Evan? You promised him."

"There are so many people, Evan won't know that I'm not here. What he doesn't know won't hurt him. Take me home." She sounded flat, like someone had steamrolled the Southern melody right out of her.

Christopher put the car in park and turned to face his mother. "Just a minute ago you said I'll get past my hurt over Genie. What about you, why can't you at least try? I'm not going to let anybody disrespect you in any way. Mom, please. With me by your side, can't you take this small step?"

"Christopher Aaron Joseph, you turn this car around right now, or I'm calling a cab." She pulled out her cell phone.

Christopher made a U-turn and headed back the way he'd just come. He didn't see Evan, who'd just emerged from the limousine, but Evan saw them.

By the time they got back to the freeway, Christopher, whose temper had flared when Grace made him turn around, felt calmer. He snuck a glance at his watch. If, within the next ten minutes, he could convince Grace to change her mind, they'd still make the ceremony.

"Mom, so many people love you. They miss you, too. Can you imagine how happy Uncle John and Aunt Maggie would be to have you there? Not to mention Evan. You're wrong about him not being able to spot us. What's he going to think when he looks out into the audience and you're not there?" Christopher looked at Grace and realized that she'd tuned him out. The sight of Raven had driven her back to wherever she hid when life overwhelmed her. *What the hell. She's making me miss the wedding, I may as well speak my mind.* Christopher kept talking, trying to convince his mother that she deserved a full life, a life filled with friends and love. This was her time. He didn't stop talking until he dropped Grace at her front door twenty minutes later.

David and Reverend Pope, John Reese's pastor, agreed that David would open the ceremony and that Reverend Pope would lead the couple in reciting their vows. David didn't try to be the center of attention—he knew the Reeses mainly through Michael, and he had enormous respect for them. He made sure the ceremony was all about John and Maggie.

"We'll go through the ceremony as printed in the program."

Everything went as planned—the first soloist caused the audience to break into applause, and the praise dance to a song by Yolanda Adams had women wiping away tears. Raven yawned and rolled her eyes.

When the church lights dimmed, Michael leaned over to Raven and said, "The wedding procession is about to enter. Evan should step to the mike any second."

But Evan didn't. The organist played through the introduction twice, and still no Evan. The wedding guests started to whisper, and David rose halfway out of his chair, about to ask the usher to throw open the double doors, when Evan finally appeared.

"Aunt Maggie asked me to sing whatever I wanted, and to put my own twist on it." He shifted his weight and cleared his throat. "Here goes."

The boy closed his eyes and sang.

*Love.*

*So many people use your name in vain.*

Evan worked "Love," a romantic, spiritual classic by Musiq, and by the time he hit the part about crying from the things love does, about wanting to die from the thought of losing love, every head in the church was nodding, keeping time with the simple melody.

If that wasn't moving enough, halfway through that song he took up another Musiq classic about love lasting a lifetime, through graying hair and thickening waistlines, then he switched back to lyrics from "Love." As he wove a new tapestry from the familiar, beautiful songs, he had everybody thinking about love—new love, lost love, lover-done-me-wrong love. Mostly looking at Maggie and John standing at the altar, the crowd collectively longed for once-in-a-lifetime, until-death-do-us-part love that so few of them would ever experience. Even Raven could feel it.

As he sang his heart out, Evan didn't envision a sweet little honey who wanted to be down with him. He pictured Grace and better days.

When Evan finished, the crowd was too wrung out to move. David stepped to the pulpit microphone and said, "That's my godson." He looked down at Maggie and John Reese, both of whom were wiping away tears.

Time for some laughter. "Sorry, folks," David said to Maggie and John, "but you've been upstaged."

The first thing Raven did when she, Michael, Evan, and Dudley got into their limousine was to slip off her pumps. "That wedding was way too long," she said as she grabbed a glass and rummaged around for a soda. "And I don't know what John's wife was thinking when she bought that dress; it was at least two sizes too tight."

When she finally found a soda, Raven said, "Sprite? I don't want a Sprite, where's the Coke?" She shouted, "Lawrence? Lawrence!"

"Hold on, Raven, let me open the partition so he can hear you," Evan said as he pushed the button to open the panel separating the driver and passenger sections.

"Where's the damn Coke? You know I like Coke in my drink."

Lawrence wasn't in the mood for one of Raven's fits. He might be an assistant to Michael, but he was also an invited guest at the wedding. He and John Reese had struck up a friendship when John loaned him five hundred dollars, behind Michael's back, to pay off a gambling debt. At the time, Lawrence, barely out of high school, was an eighteen-year-old with a wife and twin babies to take care of, and he'd just started working for Michael.

"This isn't just money I'm putting in your hand, son, it's my investment in your future," John had told Lawrence when he handed him the money. "I'm putting my faith in you that you'll get your business straight and start carrying yourself like a responsible family man."

Although the partition between the front and back of the limousine had been closed, Raven talked so loudly that Lawrence heard every word she said about Maggie Reese. *Why doesn't he put her ass in check?* Lawrence thought for what must have been the thousandth time, but as he always did when Raven got on his nerves, Lawrence ignored Raven's attitude. "Look in the cooler in the back, Mrs. Joseph," he said when Evan opened the partition. "I put three Cokes in there this morning, just for you."

Raven filled her tumbler with scotch and added a touch of soda. "And white!" she said, starting in on Maggie Reese again. "Are women who've been giving it up for forty years entitled to wear white? Maybe she shut down on John Reese twenty years ago, earned her way back into a white dress. I know if he were my husband, I'd turn my back on him every night." Raven drank more and complained more. "Then there's the way she pranced down the aisle, waving and blowing kisses, grandstanding like she was walking the red carpet at an awards show."

When no one said anything, Raven said, "I swear, men have

no taste at all. Am I the only one who noticed what a tacky little ceremony that was?"

Therein lay the problem. The wedding wasn't little or tacky. Maggie Reese wore white, and she looked marvelous, like a woman who'd carried around one man's whole, passionate heart for forty years and who'd given hers to him in return.

"Maggie's not tacky, and neither is John," Michael said wearily. "Staying together for forty years, and being in love every step of the way, that's something to celebrate. They could've had jugglers and dancing showgirls precede them down the aisle, for all I care. I'm just happy they're happy."

Michael turned to Evan. "Speaking of which, your song was awesome, son. Spectacular. I'm so proud of you."

Evan, whose face was turned toward the window, merely grunted.

As the limousine made its way toward the reception, Michael thought about John Reese. He liked to joke that he judged his friends by whether he could call them in the middle of the night. Michael had a short list of people who, if it ever came down to it, would get out of their beds at 3:00 AM, no questions asked, if he called and said, "I need you." John was at the top of the list. David was on the list too.

*Why has it taken me so long to reconnect with John? If not for this wedding, who knows when we would've talked?* Michael chided himself.

Raven downed her drink so fast that it didn't take her long to start feeling it. When Michael said he was glad John and Maggie were happy, Raven leaned over to Dudley, who was seated across from her, and slapped his knee. "You hear that, Dudley? Michael thinks a long marriage means a happy marriage." She leaned back and elbowed Michael. "You've got a few things to learn, mister." Raven giggled and poured more scotch into her glass.

"Oh, I know about marriage, Raven. I know how hard it is to find that once-in-a-lifetime love, but let's forget about that for now." Michael gently took Raven's glass and said, "I need you to behave, baby. Okay? We've got a long evening ahead of us and I need you at your best. I want to be able to be proud of you—of us—okay?"

Michael's gentleness embarrassed Raven, made her feel like a scolded child. And like a brat who'd been shamed in front of others, she decided to do just the opposite of what her husband asked.

"Come on, Ev, there wasn't anything I could do about it." Christopher and Evan were standing outside the ballroom. Inside, hundreds of the Reeses' guests ate, mingled, and swapped stories about the couple. Christopher had missed the wedding, but as soon as he walked into the ballroom, Evan grabbed his arm and led him back outside.

"That's bullshit, Chris, and you know it. You could've taken me with you to pick her up. You could've made her get out of the car."

"Ev, I couldn't make her—"

Evan got in Christopher's personal space and looked down on his older brother. "You could!" Evan stood so close that Christopher felt Evan's spit on his cheeks. "You could have—"

"Boy, you better get out of my face," Christopher growled. Evan and Christopher eyeballed each other for a moment, then Evan backed off.

"Look, Evan, I tried to get her to stay, but she wouldn't. It didn't have anything to do with you."

"It should have. She should've stayed because she wanted to hear me sing." Evan's voice cracked. "She promised."

"I hear you," Christopher said. He bent, picked up a pebble, and rolled it around in his fingers as he spoke. "It's taking Mom a long time to get up the courage to face the crowd she used to be part of. I think—no, I *know*—she's a little intimidated by them, concerned about what they think of her, of what they might say to her." Christopher tossed the tiny pebble back and forth. "She felt overwhelmed, Ev, that's all. And the thought of being in the same room with Raven and Dad makes her nervous. Seeing Raven is what made her run off."

Christopher tried to coax a smile from his brother. "Come on, man. If you were Mom, wouldn't Raven scare you? Look at that Twilight Zone, Prince, end-of-the-world shit Raven's wearing today. Walking around looking like she's about to pull out a lion-tamer's whip any minute." Actually, Christopher had to admit he liked Raven's outfit: The woman had style, and she stepped dramatic more often than not, but she never stepped wrong.

"Scare me? Hell, no. At least Raven was there to hear me sing. Mom's being a selfish bitch. She doesn't care about how I feel."

Christopher felt his body involuntarily flex. He dropped the pebble he'd been playing with and crushed it beneath his heel. "That's not true, Ev. Mom shielded you from all the stuff she went through. I'm just finding out about a lot of it myself. Those hard times changed her, but Mom loves us, Ev; she's never stopped."

Christopher found himself again in the position of having to share more of his feelings than he wanted to in order to get someone else to open up, let life in. "When you saw us in the car? I wasn't handling this thing going on between Genie and me very well. Not at all. Mom was her old self. If it hadn't been for her there with me—"

"She was there for *you*, Chris, not for me. What about *me*? Why doesn't Mom give a fuck about *me*?" Evan pointed to himself as he spoke, and his eyes were bright with tears he refused to shed. He sniffed, and because Christopher let him get away with calling Grace a bitch, said, "You know what? Fuck Mom. I don't need her."

In lieu of gifts, the Reeses had asked for flowers. "We really don't want anything but your presence," Maggie Reese told people who inquired about a gift. When their friends wouldn't take no for an answer, Maggie said, "Well, if you must do something, give us flowers."

They received enough flowers to fill a florist shop and had to have the resort employees set up two extra tables for gifts. Michael had left it up to Raven to order the flowers from them. "Get something extravagant," he told her. At the reception, he slipped John Reese tickets for a seven-day package to a Jamaican resort.

John Reese tapped his champagne glass to get everyone's attention. "My beautiful bride and I want to thank all of you for coming out." He paused and kissed Maggie, who stood beside him, her arm encircling his waist. John was extremely happy and more than a little tipsy. He motioned toward the gifts and the flowers. "Look at all this. More flowers than at a pimp's funeral." Maggie playfully swatted him.

"Woman, you'd better save those love taps for later," John said. People laughed and clapped.

"And the gifts." John turned around and stared at the small mountain on the table next to the flowers. "All I can say is, I hope there's some lingerie and Viagra somewhere in there." Having gotten one more good laugh, John prepared to say his final thank-you, but Michael interrupted him.

"Uh-uh, old man. You don't get to have the last word," Michael said as he joined the couple at the microphone. "We're not done yet. You asked for your flowers while you're living. Fair enough. But if you get the flowers, you've gotta have the thorns, too."

Michael raised his champagne glass. "Let the roast begin."

Guest after guest proceeded to the microphone to tell a funny story about either John or Maggie. After the funny stories came the heart-tugging ones in which people thanked John for some kindness he'd shown them over the years. When one lady choked up in the middle of her story, Michael decided it was time to change the pace.

"Come on, John, Maggie." He motioned for them to come back to the mike. "One last thank-you and then we'll let the band get started, show these north Dallas elites how we do it on the south side."

John, sobered by the love his guests showered upon him during their testimonials, made up his mind to say something heartfelt but brief.

What came out of his mouth was, "Grace?"

John handed the microphone to Michael and walked toward the ballroom door. Every eye in the room followed him. Grace Joseph stood alone in the doorway.

"Grace," he said again when he got to her. He gave her a big, warm hug.

"I'm sorry I missed the wedding, John, I—"

He held Grace at arm's length and looked at her. "You're here now, that's the only thing that counts."

"Grace," Maggie Reese said as she came up on Grace's left. "We've missed you, girl," she said as she hugged her friend.

Then another friend said it. *Grace.* And another. *Grace.* In an instant, Grace Joseph was enveloped in love, just as Christopher had predicted she would be.

When Grace walked into the room, Michael was caught off guard by the huge lump that developed in his throat and the way his heart dropped to the floor. Like a man in a trance, he moved closer to Grace, until he stood just outside the circle surrounding her. Michael noticed that Grace had lost a little weight—no more than ten or fifteen pounds, but it was enough to remove the love handles that turn women's waistlines from small curvy things into square blocks. She wore her hair up and rays from the ballroom chandeliers seemed to bounce off her blond highlights. She had on an ecru-colored pantsuit with rhinestone buttons. Although she'd lost the war against Raven for Michael's heart, Grace held onto some of her tools of combat, including her designer clothes.

One of Grace's well-wishers stepped aside, and Michael got a clear view of her face for the first time since the judge granted their divorce. Grace had looked worn then, and she'd cried the whole time. He looked at her now and thought, *Whoever said light-skinned women don't age well should've met Grace.* Her skin was luminous, as were her eyes. When she smiled, which she did more and more with each friendship renewed, Grace looked timelessly beautiful.

Michael didn't mean to stare, but he couldn't help himself. Grace looked up quickly, as though she sensed that she was being watched, and she and Michael locked eyes. He lost himself and continued to stare until Grace, turning away, broke the spell.

Michael completely forgot that when other women were around, Raven watched his every move. And she was watching now.

Raven saw Michael standing there, staring at Grace like a big dummy. *I ought to go over and snatch his ass back into reality,* she thought. But she realized that Michael was as shocked to see Grace as she was. What other reason could he have for giving her a second glance? It wasn't like she looked good— Raven figured that the suit Grace was wearing was at least two seasons old, and her shoes!—hideous.

Raven walked over to Michael, close enough to touch him, and said plainly, "Michael," but he didn't hear her. She decided to deal with the situation a different way. If Michael could gawk at his ex-wife in her face, then she could do far worse in his.

Raven scanned the room for David, who was in a corner talking to Erika. He kept looking around the room like a thief but then he would turn his attention back to Erika, and Raven's gut told her David was enjoying himself way too much. Now she had two men and an ex-wife to put in their places.

\* \* \*

Michael wasn't the only one transfixed by Grace. Evan looked across the room at his mother, and even though he was angry with her, the young man's heart was talking to him, telling him to forget his pride and hurt feelings, to go to her. He'd just convinced his feet to get moving when Raven sidled up to him. "I see your mom decided to show up. Too bad she chose to make a grand entrance here instead of coming to the church to hear you sing. I wouldn't have missed your song for anything."

Evan was doubtful. "You think she skipped the wedding on purpose?"

Raven nodded toward Grace, still accepting hugs from long-lost friends. "Look at her, she hasn't even taken the time to seek you out. Too busy socializing."

Before Evan could make up his mind what to do, Raven pointed across the room to a portrait of John and Maggie, surrounded by flowers. "Isn't that cute," Raven said to Evan in a mocking tone. "Come on," she grabbed his hand, "let's go see."

In another corner of the ballroom, David talked to Erika Whittier. She'd been one of the guests to tell a funny story about John Reese. "For a while there, I thought you were going to bomb," David half-jokingly told her.

"Who couldn't give those two a proper wedding toast? They're such an adorable couple, they make it easy," she said.

"But yours was one of the best—*the* best. I'd heard you were good, but with this crowd." David smiled and shook his head. "I'm proud of you. You were surprisingly effective."

"Was I?" Erika crossed her arms and asked, "What was so surprising about it?"

"Like I said, this crowd," David said, feebly. He wished he'd never brought up the subject.

"All I see is people, David. Look around, what do you see?"

David looked, and what he saw made him uncomfortable. There was Raven, standing before the flower display with Evan. Something seemed wrong but at first David couldn't pinpoint what it was. Then it came to him. Raven wasn't very steady on her feet.

"Excuse me, Erika. I need to speak to Michael's son."

Erika followed his gaze. "Over there with Raven Joseph? He's an awesome talent. Good-looking kid, too."

"Nice running into you," David said. His eyes roamed the room as he looked for New Word members who might be watching him. He extended his hand to Erika.

"This time yesterday you were sucking my toes. Today I had to practically run you down to get you to speak to me, and now you want to give me a handshake?" She turned her nose up at David. "No, thanks." Erika nodded toward Raven and Evan and said, "You'd better hurry before someone notices you talking to a white woman."

Surprise flashed across David's face. He didn't realize that Erika was aware of his discomfort. "You're wrong," he said and then he hurried away.

"Hey Ev, Raven," David said when he walked up.

"What's up, Uncle David?" Evan said, and bobbed his head backward as he spoke.

"What's up? Boy, I know you've got more for me than that," David said as he embraced Evan. At the same time, David managed to position himself between Evan and Raven.

"I'm looking for our floral arrangement. What'd they do with it?" Raven asked.

"What does it look like?" David asked.

"I have no idea, but I'm sure it's probably the biggest one here."

"That one there?" Evan asked.

"That's got to be it. It's not the biggest one, but it's definitely the best," Raven said and walked toward the fullest, most beautiful arrangement, a cornucopia of deep-colored roses. Evan followed close behind.

Raven turned away from the arrangement so quickly that she stumbled, knocking over a smaller plant. When Evan bent to right the plant, he looked at the card. "This one is ours," he said.

Evan grabbed Raven's hand, then her waist as they walked back toward David. Raven really needed Evan's help. Between being drunk and having spun around too fast, she was about to create a spectacle.

"The big one wasn't yours?" David said.

"It's from some woman named Callie," Evan answered.

"That bitch," Raven said loud enough to be heard by others.

David looked around him. A few other people were openly staring at the trio.

"Evan, I see your mother. Why don't you go over and talk to her?"

"Looks like she doesn't need me." The crowd around Grace had thinned, but there were still enough hangers-on to form a small entourage. Evan snorted and said, "I don't wanna talk to her anyway."

David got along well with young people, and part of the reason was he never let them forget who was the adult and who was the child. He gave Evan a cool look and said, "Did I ask what you wanted? Get over there. Now."

Evan looked like he wanted to say something back, but he knew better. He looked toward Grace.

"Evan?" David's voice was gentler. "It's time, man. Past time. It'll be fine, I promise."

Evan started the long walk across the room with his head down. Words from the song he'd just sung came back to him: *Love, there's so many things I've got to tell you, but I'm afraid I don't know how.* He had a million things he wanted to tell his mother, to ask her. *I miss you, Mom. Why'd you leave me, Mom? I love you, Mom.* Evan didn't think he'd have courage to say any of what was in his heart right away, but he agreed with his Uncle David, it was about time he got started.

When Evan walked away, David told Raven, "In a couple of

minutes, I'm going to stroll outside for some air. I expect to see you out there, not on the side of the building where the cars are parked; on the other side, near the golf course."

"What do you think you're doing?"

"I don't know what you're talking about."

Raven and David were outside. They walked slowly, side by side, toward the back of the building.

"You've been drinking?"

"So what, David. You drink more than I do."

David stopped and faced Raven. He rubbed his chin and looked at the sky as he spoke. "I do. And I pray to God, literally pray, for the taste to be taken away. When I drink too much it's because I'm trying to get up the nerve to do something stupid."

Raven sulked.

David asked her, "What's got you so stirred up? Who are you trying to piss off?"

"David, that's silly. I'm not doing anything." Raven started to walk again, but David blocked her path.

"Then why are you making a fool of yourself?"

Raven leaned against the side of the building, her hands behind her so that her suit wouldn't touch the surface. "I'm surprised you noticed, the way you let Erika Whittier climb all over you." Something flashed across David's face that Raven couldn't quite put her finger on.

"I don't know what you're talking about," David said defensively. "Whatever you're upset about doesn't have anything to do with me."

Raven inhaled. "This is a bad day for me, David." By now they'd walked to the back of the building. "Mr. Reese did everything he could to stop Michael from marrying me. I hate him. But Michael loves him, loves what Mr. Reese and his wife have together. Then that damn Grace shows up, walking in like she's Princess Grace instead of some old, dried-up broad nobody wants.

"I can tell—I can feel it—Michael's regretting he ever parted ways with Reese, that old bastard. For all I know, maybe he's even reminiscing about being married to Grace." She looked at David. "That means he's thinking he never should have married me."

Raven sniffled. "Weird, isn't it? Me complaining about my husband to my lover. Telling you things I can't tell anyone else feels natural."

"Because it is natural. We're more than just lovers, Raven." Forgetting where they were, David embraced Raven. "It's okay," he said. "It's okay to have those kinds of thoughts, baby, it is, really. But that doesn't mean you have to act out. You're too beautiful a woman to treat yourself so poorly. When you're feeling bad, when you feel like doing something crazy, talk to me instead. That's what I'm here for. Talk to me, Raven. Promise me you will."

"David, I can't—"

"Yes. *You can*. Promise me."

"Okay."

David kissed Raven on her forehead, and held her to him a moment more.

Grace couldn't sleep, because her brain wouldn't shut down. Nothing unusual there; she was accustomed to lying awake against her will, recounting past hurts, beating herself up for not being stronger. Instead of tossing around trying to make her thoughts go away, Grace lay still and summoned them. She went over the wedding reception again and again, starting from the first moment John Reese stepped forward to welcome her, to the last, when Evan and Christopher walked her to her car. She relived every hug and kind word in between. When she got to the end, the part where her sons bent and kissed her before closing her door, Grace would go back to the beginning.

The only dicey part of the evening had been when she looked across the room and saw Evan, *her* son, standing with Raven. Grace's heart had lurched then, and she'd wanted to either run to Evan and snatch him from Raven, or run straight out the giant ballroom doors. She didn't know which. But then someone called her name, and when she turned around again, Evan had been crossing the room, heading her way.

There had been the other thing, too—the way she'd found Michael staring at her. A million times, Grace had imagined what it would be like the first time she and Michael saw each other. Half the reason Grace became a hermit was because she dreaded the day she'd have to see Michael with Raven on his arm. Seeing them on television and in print was brutal enough. Face to face, Grace imagined, would be more than she could stand, so she prayed that God would spare her that indignity until she was ready.

She'd daydreamed dozens of scenarios, including the one that actually took place—Michael fixated on her from across a crowded room. That it actually happened was too good! Grace was about to replay the look that passed between Michael and her, when the telephone rang.

"It's almost midnight. Who's calling this late?" Grace said aloud. After the divorce, she had picked up the habit of talking to herself.

"Hello."

When no one responded, Grace repeated, "Hello, who is this?"

"Grace, it's me."

Shock hit her first, then panic. Grace sat up and switched on her nightstand lamp.

"Michael! What's wrong? Are the boys okay?"

"Yeah, yeah. Sure, they're fine."

"Then what—"

"I'm sorry. I didn't mean to upset you. I should have known . . . calling this late . . . I didn't mean . . . " Michael stammered through the little speech he'd spent the last two hours going over.

He started over. "I wanted to tell you how good it was to see you today. You look good, Grace. How have you been?"

"How have I—?" Before she realized what she was doing, Grace pressed the END CALL button. She placed the phone on her nightstand and stared at it. Grace willed the phone to ring again, just to be sure she wasn't dreaming or that she hadn't lost her mind. And she willed it to ring again so she could hear Michael say her name. It had been so long.

The phone didn't ring. Grace sighed, and, wide awake now, sank into her pillow. It was going to be a long night.

# 20

"How are things going with your woman?"

David laughed uncomfortably. "My woman. I don't have one to call my own, do I? Are you talking about Raven or Erika?"

"Raven, of course," Dudley replied. He looked understandingly at David. "A woman like Erika wouldn't ever really be yours."

The brothers were seated in Dudley's office late in the afternoon. Even though David regularly had business in Austin and Dudley was often in Dallas, they rarely spent time together. Dudley's fleshy grin and fish eyes reminded David of Big Sue, which, in turn, reminded him of being cold and hungry. Dudley never seemed to want to see him either, so David assumed that he himself reminded Dudley of the past. David feared that if his brother brought Big Sue to mind, then maybe he made Dudley think of Baby Sue. The only memorable thing about her, though, was her overpowering funk. At least once every day, David, in spite of himself, would take a quick whiff under each arm to make sure that he wasn't carrying on Stanky Baby Sue's dubious legacy.

"Raven and I are okay." David didn't want to have this conversation with Dudley and he kicked himself for having confided in him. He'd told Dr. Laverne about his affair but that wasn't the same as telling a real person. If it had been any woman but Raven, David may have even shared his secret with Michael. He needed to let someone know about Raven and about Erika. Dudley was his only choice.

"Okay? What kind of answer is that? I want to know if she's getting you what you want," Dudley said.

"More than what I want, and almost more than I can handle. Raven's probably the smartest woman I've ever met—when I've got a problem she comes up with a good idea. And in the bed, she gives me so much of herself, I can't imagine what's left over for Michael.

"I started out dealing with her on a strictly business basis, trying to get her on my side with the faith-based money, but Dudley, now I'm in deep"—David shifted in his seat—"and I don't want to get out." *Shut up*, he told himself and kept going. "The guilt is killing me. I'm no angel, but I never thought I'd commit adultery and I never intended to take Michael's woman from him. Over the years he's done good by me and I've tried to do likewise."

Dudley leaned over his desk. "Sex? Brains? Guilt? What the hell are you talking about? Let me remind you, brother, that your main goal was to get *the money*. The sex is just gravy. What's Raven going to do for you?"

"We haven't had a chance to iron out the details."

"*Haven't had a chance!* You've spent all this time with the spiteful bitch and *you haven't had a chance* to talk about money?"

David bristled at Dudley's harsh words. "Raven's just high-strung. She's not that bad, once you get to know her."

"*Get to know her!*"

"Damnit, Dudley, will you stop acting like a parrot! Raven's ready to make a decision about how much to award New Word; I just haven't followed up. We'll get our fair share." By now David was as agitated as Dudley because he realized that the faith-based initiative hadn't crossed his mind since the day he first kissed Raven. The knowledge unsettled him because it meant he was losing focus. David's ministry was his life; he couldn't put his desire for Raven ahead of New Word. He made a mental note to mention the initiative to her the next time they talked.

Dudley settled into his first-class seat and thought about his upcoming meeting with Callie Stephens. He had done a little research on her before deciding to fly to Atlanta. He began dropping her name casually during conversations and everyone who knew Callie, including Michael, spoke highly of her. According to him, Callie was warm and generous, an all-around good woman. He implied that Callie's relationship with Raven proved that Raven possessed those same traits.

When Dudley mentioned Callie's name to Raven, she had turned on him and sharply asked, "Why are you bringing her up? She's an ungrateful bitch. End of story."

Finding Callie had been easy. She lived in Atlanta, where she was a district court judge. Dudley's sources told him that Callie had a stellar, though short, career as a litigator before taking the bench. Although she had been easy to locate, Callie had been hell to contact by phone. During their sole conversation, Callie had been cordial until Dudley had said, "I want to know about Raven." Callie, speaking curtly, had told him that she had nothing to say about Raven, and that furthermore, she was needed in court. After that Callie wouldn't take his calls.

Dudley's instincts told him that he was on to something juicy so he boarded a flight to Atlanta. He vowed to camp out on the front row of Callie's courtroom until she talked to him just to get rid of his ugly mug. Dudley hoped that wouldn't take long because the campaign had entered the final stretch and he could spare only one day in Atlanta.

Dudley gave his name to Callie's clerk and was immediately ushered into her chambers. Things happened so quickly that he thought maybe he'd been set up.

Before he could settle into his seat, Callie asked him, "Has Raven done something?" Her pretty face was clouded with worry.

"Maybe," Dudley hedged. "I'm surprised you agreed to see me. To tell you the truth, I expected to be escorted out of the building as soon as I announced myself."

"I figured that for you to fly here something serious must be going on. I couldn't live with myself if I sat by and let Raven hurt someone else."

Callie had always been a quick study of people, and after her fiasco of a friendship with Raven, she was even better. She looked at Dudley's liverish smirk and dead eyes and was immediately wary.

"You said *maybe* Raven's done something." She asked, her voice strictly business. "What is it?"

*What's wrong with her? Why is she cross-examining me? I'm not one of her criminals,* Dudley thought. He knew he came up short in the charm department, but still. If real men like him didn't stand up and do something, stuck-up bitches like Raven and Callie would end up ruling the world.

"We don't know yet. Michael thinks—and this is a very sensitive matter, you understand, not to be repeated—he thinks Raven may have done something illegal during the course of his campaign. If she has, it'll ruin him." Dudley hoped he sounded convincing. "He asked me to come and find out what you think Raven is capable of."

Callie was a striking woman who was as beautiful as Raven, but in a quieter way. She was a shade or two lighter than Raven's dark brown, and not quite as tall. Someone once described them as two unique, stunning garments—one soft and delicate, the other daring and demanding—cut from the same cloth. The major difference between them was that Callie radiated a peace that Raven didn't have. When Dudley asked what Raven was capable of, Callie's serenity cracked and an ugly expression flickered across her face.

"He knows damn well what she's capable of," Callie commented dryly. She leaned back in her chair and unfastened the top three buttons of her judicial robe. "But since you asked, I'll tell you. Raven is shrewd, self-centered, and definitely dangerous."

*Bingo*, Dudley thought. "Strong words coming from a best friend."

"Raven's best friend." Callie laughed bitterly. "Imagine that."

"Trouble is, I can't. You strike me as gracious and self-confident," Dudley said, "whereas Raven is petty and egotistical." Dudley held his hands up like a scale. "Raven, here. Best friend, over here. It doesn't balance. She'd hate a woman like you."

"Which is why we're no longer friends."

"I know about the cheating scandal and that some guy named Omar Faxton helped Raven try to take you down. Beyond that, all I hear is rumors about Omar leaving town. What really happened?" Dudley asked. He already knew a lot but he wanted confirmation from Callie. Based on what everyone had told him, Dudley believed that if anyone knew what really happened to Omar, it was Callie.

"Six months after Omar's disappearance, a detective named Coolidge began tracing his last known activities and found out that he'd probably been with her. The police pinned Raven under a microscope and between that and what she tried to do to me, she became an outcast during our final year."

"Coffee?" Callie asked Dudley. She poured a cup for each of them as she continued her story. "The first two years of law school, Raven had been quite popular. But that third year Raven slid comfortably into the role of pariah, like she enjoyed it." Callie handed Dudley a mug.

"So what do you think happened to Omar?" Dudley asked as he sipped his coffee. Despite his natural aversion to people, especially women, Dudley felt like he could sit all day and talk to Callie. She had an ease about her that even he was drawn to.

Callie looked down into her mug as she spoke. "I loved Omar and I think Raven did something really bad to him because she found out that he loved me, too."

"Bad like what?"

Callie's eyes darted to Dudley and then away from him. "All I know is even though Omar was in a lot of trouble with the law school, he wouldn't have just walked away. He was smart enough to talk his way out of anything, so he would have stayed around, fixed the situation. Somehow Raven made sure that never happened."

When Callie looked at Dudley again, her mouth was set in a grim line. "I promised Raven that if she had done anything to Omar she'd have to deal with me, but I never followed up."

"How could you give up? Didn't you want her to pay for what she did?" Dudley asked.

Callie took a deep breath, and although her eyes were on him, she was looking into the past. "I moved here with Keith and let go of all that. When we were in school, I allowed a different situation that I couldn't do anything about eat away at me. I felt like I was losing my mind. After that I refused"— Callie corrected herself—"I *refuse* to ever let something from the past rule my life. So I put my episode with Raven and Omar behind me. I haven't set foot in Dallas since Keith and I left."

"So Michael was right; he said you'd probably married a guy named Keith," he said.

Callie threw her head back and laughed. "No, I didn't. Keith ran into an old friend soon after we moved here. They're married now."

There was a brief knock on the door and then it opened. "Callie, you've got—oh, sorry, I thought you were alone." A young man stood in the doorway. He looked like Callie, but was clearly too old to be her son. "Judge Stephens, your next case starts in five minutes."

"Thank you, Jason." After Callie rebuttoned her judicial robe she extended her hand to Dudley. "I made a promise, years ago, to do exactly what you're doing now, but I didn't follow through. Good luck." Although Dudley had become drawn to Callie during their short time together, she didn't like him any more than she had when he first entered her chambers. Nonetheless she felt compelled to add, "And for your own sake, be careful."

"What are we doing for your birthday?" Raven asked David that evening.

It was dusk and they were seated in the courtyard of a hotel in San Antonio. The mid-September evening was cool and dry. David was the speaker at a leadership conference for ministers from around the country and he'd invited Raven to drive over. When they first started seeing each other, David and Raven made sure to meet only in very public places like restaurants, or in the private space provided by double-bolted hotel-room doors. But as their relationship progressed, they blinded themselves, and earnestly believed that no one could tell what was going on.

"Most of the ministers who'll be here are white; they won't notice you," David said, as though white ministers were, by definition, blind eunuchs. "If anyone asks, I'll tell them you and I had a meeting that couldn't be postponed." The hotel front-desk manager who rang David's room for Raven did happen to be a little on the dim side, but she still recognized the most photographed woman in the state. She was also a veteran hotel employee and knew that if Raven didn't identify herself, then she didn't want to be recognized.

So Raven and David sat in the courtyard, the air surrounding them heavy with emotional intimacy, and believed that anyone who saw them would think they were conducting business.

"I asked you what we're doing for your birthday, David," Raven said as she slapped his arm. "What are you thinking about?"

He was thinking about his conversation with Dudley regarding the faith-based initiative. David didn't know how he'd let his goal of getting more faith-based money slip away, but he had, and he needed to get back on track. David decided that he would broach the subject, but he didn't know where to begin. Today the conference had adjourned at noon so the attendees could go sightseeing. He and Raven had been together since the conference ended, and David still hadn't said a word about the money. Raven's question about his birthday gave him another opportunity to delay his own mission.

"My birthday's not until October seventh, that's almost a month away. I don't know what we'll do—go to dinner maybe?"

"Of course we'll do that, but I'm talking about doing something special. Let me take you somewhere." Because she wasn't concerned about being recognized, the way she was when she and David were together in Austin, Raven was relaxed, which made her as beautiful as she'd ever been.

"I haven't been to southern California for a while. How about we go there?" Raven suggested.

"A little over three weeks before the election? I can't imagine Michael letting you go anywhere."

"He'll do okay without me for a couple of days," Raven said. After the Smotes incident, Michael had marginalized Raven to the point where she had to snoop around to find out what was going on. "While we're there I can get a few donors to send checks in. Michael will be happy with that."

Raven looked at her watch. "It's later than I thought. I'd better get on the road." She stood.

"Don't be in such a hurry," David said as he got to his feet. "We have to finish talking about my birthday." He looked around the courtyard and up at the hotel windows, then kissed Raven. "Let's go to my room."

Raven was putty in David's hands. "We shouldn't," she said, sounding as though there was nothing she'd like better. "I spent the night with you two nights ago, David. If we keep this up, we're going to get caught."

"I didn't say anything about spending the night," he said as his hands moved down her body and pulled her closer. He was grateful for the darkness.

"I just want to talk," David whispered.

By now, Michael, followed by the New Word gospel choir, could have walked into the courtyard and the couple wouldn't have noticed.

"Okay. But just for a minute," Raven said.

The next morning, David asked, "What did we have to discuss that was so important we had to sleep on it? We'd better think of something good."

Raven stretched but she didn't open her eyes. She lay next to David, with her head just below his chin. "I could tell Michael that we had to decide where we're running off to for your birthday, but he might want to come with us."

David chuckled. "Why not tell Michael the truth, or at least half of it. The other ministers wanted to know what's going on with the faith-based initiative, and you needed to stay over to brief me on it."

Raven opened her eyes and pushed back from David. "What? I thought we were playing a game."

"We are, honey, but hey, as an alibi, it's hard to beat. This afternoon I'm scheduled to speak and I would like to touch on the subject. Why don't you give me a primer on it?"

Raven frowned. "Now?"

"Sure, why not?"

Raven rolled onto her back. "For one thing, you haven't wanted to talk about it in weeks. I assumed that's because you know I'm going to be fair to New Word. You've attended all the faith-based presentations that I've put on for Michael's campaign and at least half the ones done by Sweeney. I should know—we always end up in your hotel room afterward."

Raven was only partly right. David had attended not half, but every one of Sweeney's hearings. She was in the dark about how frequently David was in Austin because if he wasn't going to be with Raven, he didn't let her know he was in town. On the trips Raven didn't know about, David spent the night with Erika.

"There are things I still don't know," he said.

"Such as what?"

"Well, like how effective is this thing really going to be? I understand that the money needs to be spread around, but if it's divided up too much, all the state will have done is create a lot of underfunded programs. It's hard to have an impact when things are done that way."

"If Michael wins this election, the initiative is going to be more successful than you think. Let me tell you why," Raven said. She sat up, and David saw that she was all business, which made her sexy in a completely different, yet equally stimulating way. He listened to Raven explain the way the initiative would work, and although he knew she was responsible for implementing the plan he was nonetheless impressed by Raven's perfect grasp of how religious organizations operated. She instantly answered questions that he'd put to Sweeney's people weeks earlier and for which he was still awaiting a response. David and Raven became so engrossed in their conversation they lost track of time.

"I hear what you're saying—the plan is workable just as it is—but I'm not so sure you're right. Let's finish this conversation the next time we get together," David said as he tucked his sweater into his slacks.

"What's left to say? You didn't come up with a single reason not to distribute the money evenly that I wasn't able to knock down." Raven was still in bed. Her habit was to let David get dressed and leave the room first, and she told him she did it to stay out of his way. Raven's real reason was that kissing David good-bye just as he stepped over the threshold made her feel like she was his wife, sending him off into the world while she stayed behind and kept the home fires burning. It was very un-Raven of her, and she couldn't have cared less.

David strode to the bed and kissed the top of Raven's head. "Don't get up. Drive safely, baby. I'll call you later."

For the rest of the day David mulled over his conversation with Raven. As much as he wanted to get a huge chunk of the faith-based money, he had to admit that she was right: The current plan to divvy up the money was fair. And as she had talked about the program, she'd looked completely guileless, so devoid of the slyness that usually marked every word she said that David felt a little bit ashamed. Although he told her that they would take up the subject later, David decided that he'd never again mention the faith-based money to Raven.

# 21

Christopher took Grace to a movie, then asked where she'd like to go for dinner. She surprised him by offering to cook.

"Mom, this is a new side of you. I didn't know you liked to cook," Christopher said. He sat at the bar and watched his mother dice tomatoes.

Grace's eyes glowed as she recalled good times. "When your father and I first married, I cooked all the time. Dinner was our time together. He'd come in from his job at the district attorney's office, and make a beeline for the kitchen."

"Starved after a long day, huh?"

"Not really. Back then I was the big attraction, and I could be found in the kitchen." Grace smiled at Christopher. *She's beautiful*, he thought. He'd never noticed her as a woman before; she'd always been just Mom. But sitting there, watching Grace prepare a simple, elegant meal, Christopher saw his mother through his father's eyes. Grace was as magnificent to her son as she'd been to his father when Michael was in his early twenties. Grace Joseph was a sweet heartbreaker.

"We planned his entire career, sitting much the same way you and I are sitting here now. Michael would watch me cook and he'd talk—dream, really—and I'd tell him he could do whatever he set his mind to."

"Why'd you stop?" He watched as Grace expertly diced vegetables: onions, celery, bell pepper, and garlic. Now she browned flour as Christopher kept talking. "From the look of things, you know your way around a kitchen."

"After you were born, I didn't have time," Grace said after a while. She looked up again, and this time she wasn't smiling, but she didn't look hurt or slightly unhinged the way she had been. She sighed and said, "Even with you running around the house—Evan too, when he was born—I could prepare a five-course meal in no time. Truth is, once your father got his first elected position, when you were about three, he lost interest in spending that quiet time with me. So I stopped doing it." Grace took fresh shrimp from the refrigerator and added them to a skillet that already contained vegetables and a half-dozen spices.

"I know I shouldn't tell you this, but I started being afraid of losing him back then, when you were a toddler. From my first date with Michael, I was crazy about him, and I thought he was crazy for wanting to be with me."

"Why would you—"

Grace held up her hand. "I know, I know, it sounds stupid. After all, I've got all this." She moved her hands across her body with a flourish, but the gesture seemed insincere. "Or I had it, back then." Grace wiped her hands on a dish towel and said, "I'm sorry, Chris, I shouldn't be saying these things to you."

"Mom, all I know is you need to talk to somebody, get all the crap out of your system and walk away. I'm your son, but I'm also a grown man and your best friend. You can tell me anything."

"What if I told you I got pregnant with Evan on purpose, to save my marriage?"

"You what?" Christopher was so surprised he forgot what he'd just said about no subject being taboo. His personal code said that good women—be they wife, girlfriend, or one-night stand—did not trap a man by getting pregnant.

"I know what you're thinking, Chris. But you'd be surprised how many babies are conceived for their glue power. Sometimes the couple makes the decision together, sometimes it's just the woman, and sometimes, just the man."

Christopher thought about how much he wanted to marry Genie and start a family, how desperate he'd been to get her attention. "Is it a mistake, making a baby like that?" he asked.

"Yes and no. The baby's not a mistake, but using a baby to cement a relationship? Making a decision that affects another person without their permission? Those things are wrong." Grace turned back to her cooking. "In my case, I realized, too late, that I should've talked to Michael. He would've been ecstatic at the thought of another child, I know that now. But the way I went about it made things worse, not better."

She prepared their plates. "Let's eat."

Christopher was accustomed to banquet meals and the unimaginative dishes cooked by the cafeteria in his father's office building. He savored Grace's dish, for the flavor and for the normalcy that preparing it brought out in her.

Christopher ate seconds and thirds. "Mom, would you cook this again the next time I'm in town?"

Grace laughed. "If you want me to. But, Chris, I've got dozens of recipes." She began clearing the table. "Whatever you have a taste for, I'll cook."

Christopher leaned back in his seat and watched his mother as she cleaned the kitchen. He'd offered to do it, but she insisted. As she worked, Grace sang along to the CD that she'd put on during dinner. Evan got his amazing voice from his mother.

When Grace brought in coffee for each of them and sat across from him, Christopher said, "You look happy."

She reached across and covered Christopher's hand with her own. "Getting there. Because of you."

"Mom?"

Grace waited.

"Mom, why did you let us go?"

Grace stirred her coffee, took a sip. She held her mug with both hands, grateful for its weight. She didn't want Christopher to notice that she was trembling. When she trusted her voice to sound normal, Grace said, "There were a lot of reasons why, but it came down to the fact that Raven knew our schedules."

"I don't get it," Christopher said.

"Your father . . . I was accustomed to . . . his ways. I figured it was just the price I paid for being married to a politician." Grace shook her head and peered into her mug as she spoke. "I see young girls doing the same thing today—accepting disrespect just to hold on to their men. Used to be only high-profile men got away with cheating right out in the open. Now even sorry, broke, ugly men have two and three women."

Grace hadn't meant it to come out sounding funny, but it did, so they both laughed.

Grace shifted her gaze to Christopher, "Looking the other way back then was so stupid, and it's damn sure stupid now." She shook her head again, remembering.

Christopher had never seen this side of her personality. She was always so appropriate; he couldn't believe she'd just said *damn*. He liked it.

"I wish Genie were stupid enough to forget about seeing me at Monica's, but . . ." He shrugged. "You were saying."

Grace resumed her story. "I knew there were other women, but there was something different about this one, I could tell from the start," Grace said. "So I went to see her."

"How did that go?" Christopher asked, but he already knew. Even if Grace were twenty times more self-assured than he'd ever realized, she was no match for Raven.

"Not good. That's when I found out she knew our schedules. I didn't mind so much about mine, but for her to know your baseball coach's name and what time I dropped Evan off at choir practice." Grace hesitated, then said, "She knew what

Evan had worn to a birthday party the Saturday before. That shook me," Grace said.

"I can understand that," Christopher said, although he couldn't. So Raven was a stalker, so what? That should have given Grace even more reason to keep her children away from Raven. Christopher knew that he should let it go, but his scars from the divorce demanded answers. If pressing Grace meant taking a chance that she'd dive back into her shell, then so be it.

As though she could read Christopher's mind, Grace said, "I know it sounds like a poor excuse, but my mother's intuition kicked in and told me not to take Raven for granted. When your father said he wanted you boys to live with him, I knew Raven was behind it." As Grace talked, Christopher noticed fear creep into her eyes. "I wasn't sure what she'd do if she didn't get her way."

Grace abruptly stood, took both their mugs, and headed for the kitchen. "So I let you and Evan go rather than see you hurt."

Raven and David sat at the bar of a San Diego nightspot. The music was good—old school, like Johnny Gill and Anita Baker, mixed with neo-soul and the latest hip-hop. They danced until they got thirsty, went to the bar for drinks, and then danced some more.

"How'd you find a place like this in San Diego?" David asked.

"My parents live near here. This is my escape when I visit them."

"Speaking of which—"

"I haven't changed my mind, David. Maybe if my father were home, but he's out of town. I have no desire to see Jacqueline," Raven snapped.

"Okay," David said, realizing that he needed to tread carefully. He and Raven had been in southern California since Thursday night, celebrating David's birthday, and they were in the middle of having the time of their lives. Even on her best behavior, Raven was self-centered and easily upset, but David accepted that about her. *The good with the bad*, he thought whenever she got an attitude. The good times were Raven's brief moments of naked vulnerability. David was convinced that Raven was essentially a decent person and that, since she showed her true, sensitive nature only to him, it was his mission to take that goodness and cultivate it.

Since they'd landed at the San Diego airport, everything had been perfect. David didn't get to see only glimpses of the good Raven; she gave him one hundred percent of the best inside her, without even being aware that she did. They laughed until they cried, made love until they fell away from each other utterly exhausted, and sat quietly together on the beach, listening to the roar of the Pacific, until their souls were united and at peace.

They'd discussed Raven's relationship with her mother many times, and although David wanted her to get past her hurt, he knew better than to push. He swiveled in his seat and looked around the club.

"There was a time you couldn't get me into a place like this."

"Partying and pastoring don't mix, I suppose."

David hoisted his drink, "The drinking, having a good time, I can deal with. It's who's doing the partying that would've bothered me."

Raven surveyed the room. It was filled with the people she felt most comfortable around—they were good-looking, mostly middle class, and mostly black.

"You have a problem with your people?" Raven jokingly asked. She patted her hand against her thigh, keeping time to the music.

David surprised her, and himself, by admitting, "Yeah, I do."

He swiveled back around so that he faced Raven. "I know I give you a hard time about your mother, but actually, I know where you're coming from." David screwed up his face. "I grew up with two loud . . . mean, ignorant women. The way my grandmother looked, and the way my mother carried herself—I couldn't bring friends home. They were a disgrace. Once I got out of that house, I made up my mind not to spend more than five minutes with people like them." He asked the bartender for another drink.

"I thought you forgave your mother?"

"I forgave her, but then I started blaming other women."

David didn't want to keep looking at Raven, but he felt compelled to. "In the back of my mind I began thinking that women who were the total opposite of my grandmother and mother were better."

"White women?" Raven asked softly.

David looked into his glass. "Yeah. When I first started dating them, my excuse was that I needed to date women who couldn't possibly know any of my church members. But I really did it because I wanted to. Because I thought they were somehow better than black women." He started to drain his glass, changed his mind and set it on the bar.

David looked embarrassed. "I can imagine what you must think of me. I hope you're not offended."

"No, I'm not offended. I can hold my own against any woman. As for what I think of you, I figured you had issues with white women when I ran into you with that Lufkin waitress," she said. "My daddy would say it like this: Issues are like ears; everybody's got them. It's nothing to make a big deal about."

"I've never told any of my friends why I'm attracted to white women—who would understand?" David made a sad little smile. "Michael knows. I think that's why he trusts me around you."

David wanted to be in the here and now with Raven, so he

stopped thinking about Michael. "But I can tell you my secret, because you've cured me. Laverne would be impressed."

*Laverne?* The name seemed familiar to Raven. She tried to
figure out where she'd heard the name before, but she couldn't.

"Who's Laverne?"

"Nobody you know," David said.

Raven took David's hand. "I know about being judged and
misunderstood. A lot has been said about me." Raven started
to say more, then thought better of it. "You've heard the rumors, right?"

David had and he'd spent hours trying to reconcile the Raven
people gossiped about with the Raven he knew. He decided
that his Raven was the real one.

"I know you," he told her, "so I know that what they say are
lies."

Raven kept her eyes on the dance floor. "Would it matter if
they weren't?"

While the lovers talked, the DJ slid into slow songs. "Love,"
the song Evan sang at the Reeses' wedding, had just begun.
*Love, there are so many things I've got to tell you, but I'm afraid I
don't know how, 'cause there's a possibility that you'll look at me differently.*

David grabbed Raven and pulled her off her bar stool. "Let's
dance."


"Hey, please don't hang up," Michael said.

Grace wasn't going to hang up. She'd waited for Michael to
call her again. Every time the phone rang, she hoped (and be-
rated herself for hoping) that Michael was on the other end.

Now that he was, Grace didn't know what to say. Neither
did Michael, but after a few uncomfortable seconds, he said,
"I apologize for the way I called the last time. I was out of line."

"That's okay," Grace heard herself say. *That's okay? That's
not what I planned to say.*

"Look, I know you probably hate me, but I'm just . . . seeing you was just so good. I know it may not seem like it, but I've always wanted the best for you. Looks like you're doing well." Michael paused, then softly asked, "Are you?"

"I'm fine."

"Well, good. That's all I wanted to say. I'll let you go."

"Bye."

"Bye," Michael said and hurriedly added, "Grace? I think about you all the time. Good night."

Grace tried to figure out what Michael's calls meant. Did he want them to be friends? If he was so happy with Raven, why was he calling her? Would he call again? All her questions did was lead her to more questions. She ended up with dozens of "whys" and "what ifs" but not with any answers.

# 22

"You want my opinion, he's dead."

"What makes you so sure?" Dudley asked. He was talking to the retired detective who'd investigated Omar's disappearance.

"It was pretty obvious. Raven's place was the last place he was believed to be," the detective said. He spoke in the officious twang used exclusively by Texas law enforcement types.

"And?" Dudley pressed.

"And all the little gals he was tomcatting around with said he wasn't the type to up and disappear."

"What evidence did you get from Raven's home?"

"Whatcha mean?"

Dudley exhaled. He hated dealing with slow people. "From the search of her apartment. What did you find out?"

"Well, er. I don't rightly recall getting a warrant," the detective said. He didn't sound as blustery as before.

"How could you not get a warrant to search her place?" Dudley asked.

"As I recall it was the end of the year, so I ran out of time."

Dudley was incredulous. "How on earth could you run out of time? The guy had only been missing for six months!"

"I retired the end of that year. I had a lot of paperwork to fill out."

Dudley couldn't take any more. He hung up and reached for the notebook he kept on Omar Faxton.

He had checked name and social security number databases using the Internet and there was no record of Omar Faxton. All three of Omar's women said that he had to be dead. And now the detective, sorry though he might be, said he believed the same thing. One way or another, Omar had fallen off the face of the earth. As far as Dudley was concerned, Omar Faxton was dead.

*I'm so good at shoveling dirt I should've been a gravedigger,* he said to himself.

Dudley placed his call at exactly noon. "So, brother, what mischief are you planning to get into while you're here?" Dudley asked. He had taken to checking Raven's schedule behind her back and learned that she had set aside a block of time from one until five during which she was "unavailable." That could mean only one thing: David was in Austin.

"I had a meeting with a minister's coalition," David said, then added a lie. "I started to call you for lunch, but I've been sidetracked."

"By Raven, I presume," Dudley wisecracked.

"No, by business," David replied curtly. The more Dudley dug, the more tight lipped David became. He was actually on his way to meet Raven. She had rented a suite at the Driskill Hotel. Before he could think of how to change the subject, Dudley did it for him.

"By the way, when's the last time you saw Erika?"

"Couple weeks ago, why?"

"Oh, no reason," Dudley said casually. "A friend of mine saw her out last night, said she was with a black guy. I thought maybe it was you."

"Wasn't me. I just got here this morning." David hoped that his voice sounded natural.

"Mmm. I guess she's moved on." Dudley struck a cheery tone. "I've got to run, David. I'll talk to you later."

David slid his phone into the inside pocket of his jacket. Although it was a cool October day, his face felt flushed. *Is she fucking another man? Another* black *man?* David thought. He knew he didn't have a right to question Erika's activities because he'd put her on the back burner since he and Raven had returned from San Diego.

When David walked into the Driskill Hotel his plan had been to go straight to the bank of elevators and make it to the suite as quickly as possible. Instead he stopped in the lobby and pulled out his cell phone.

"Hey. It's me," he whispered. "Are you available for a late-night dinner?"


When the elevator doors opened, Grace stepped to one side to let the UPS man get on.

"Ladies first," he said. When he smiled at Grace, she found that he looked only a year or so older than Christopher.

"No. I'm not the one with the heavy load. Go on," she said as she put her hand on the door to keep it open. As the UPS man rolled his cart onto the elevator, Grace absently noted that he had strong, sturdy legs, a luminous smile like Evan, and broad shoulders like Christopher.

"What floor?" Grace asked as she pressed floor twenty-five for herself.

"Twenty-two."

"Sure is unseasonably warm today. It feels more like June than October," Grace said, making conversation. "Hope you're keeping cool."

"I was, until we got on the elevator."

Grace heard something familiar in the young man's tone,

but it had been so long, she wasn't sure what it was. She turned and looked at him.

She may have forgotten the tone, but Grace remembered the look. He was coming on to her!

"I like your dress, it fits well," he said. "I thought I'd have a chance to cool off on my ride up, but it's hotter in here than it is outside."

He looked her up and down appreciatively.

"Son, I've got children almost as old as you."

"So? You're not my mama."

He smiled that smile that she loved to see on Evan. It struck her for the first time that one day some girl was going to find her baby boy sexy as hell. Of course, Evan got his smile from his mother, but when she looked in the mirror, Grace didn't see a sensual being. She had no idea that the sexy, Evanlike smile the UPS man flashed at her was pretty much the same as the smile she gave back to him.

"Don't let my baby face fool you, I'm twenty-eight." The UPS man leaned against the elevator wall, with one leg bent, and the bottom of his foot on the wall. He balanced his clipboard on his raised thigh and cocked his head to one side. "And I happen to like good-looking grown women."

When he said that, the UPS man reminded Grace less of her son, and more of the young man on the cover of one of Christopher's CDs—what was his name? Tyrese. She had turned the CD facedown the first time she saw it because looking at Tyrese's ripped body made her feel like a child molester. But she never forgot his name.

When the elevator door opened, the UPS man pressed a card into her hand as he backed out. "My cell number is on the back. Call me."

Grace looked him in the eye and said, "Have a good day."

*Oh, my goodness, I just flirted with a kid!* Grace thought, but she couldn't stop smiling. She folded the UPS card in half, intending to tear it up, changed her mind, and slid it into her handbag. Then she exited the elevator at her doctor's office.

At the end of Grace's examination, her doctor said, "You're in great shape, Grace, but your blood pressure's a little elevated. What's the story?"

"Oh, doctor, there's nothing to worry about. I'm sure it's just the heat."

"Why do you have to drive back to Dallas this evening? It's already too late to do anything but get caught in traffic. Look, it's piling up already. You could at least stay the night and leave early Saturday morning."

David joined Raven at the window of the Driskill and embraced her from behind. "That's just the rush hour traffic, baby. It'll ease up soon, so my drive won't be too bad. I have a late-night meeting with a Dallas school board member, otherwise you know I'd stay."

"But I want more," she said and playfully tried to push him back to the bed. "We never do it just once."

"I know." David put his powerful arms around her and stopped her in her tracks. "But you wear a brother out. Another round with you and I might fall asleep on my drive back to Dallas."

"You won't believe what my sources dug up on Erika," Dudley told Raven. When he'd called her, Raven insisted that Dudley meet her in the relaxation room of the Driskill Hotel spa, where she lounged while waiting for her fingernails and toenails to dry. When she'd called from her suite to book her services, the receptionist had asked, "No massage today?" Raven's skin still tingled from David's nimble touch, so she smiled to herself and said, "Not today."

"It'd better be something good, Dudley. Erika's killing us, knocking down every piece of legislation Michael wants pushed through, even small items. I don't understand how she can be so petty," Raven added, talking more to herself than to Dudley. "And I didn't realize she was so powerful."

"Erika's got three things going for her. Number one, she's got deep pockets. Forget about STRAPPED's money, I'm talking her own inheritance, which I'm sure she's using now." Dudley was using his fingers to tick off Erika's advantages. He moved from his pinkie finger to the one next to it. "Politicians—many of them Democrats—who don't mind under-cutting Michael. No matter how much they smile in his face, some of these good old boys still aren't ready for a black governor." Dudley went to his middle finger. "And she's a home girl with a reputation for loyalty. These guys know that if they come through for her now, Erika will help them out later."

Raven listened closely because she found Erika's reach as instructive as it was disturbing. Like a very good chess player up against a grand master, Raven wanted to remember every move Erika made.

When Dudley finished, Raven asked, "And you think you've uncovered something good enough to overcome all that?"

Dudley delivered his news with triumphant flair. "Erika's into black men. How's that for good?"

Raven rolled her eyes. "It's mediocre, that's what it is. We need something that's going to bring her down, Dudley, not just make people talk about her behind her back."

"Raven, how long are you going to have to live in this state before you catch on to the way things work? How many prominent mixed-race couples do you know?"

Raven thought about it. She shrugged, conceding the point. She knew a few black judges with white wives, but the men deliberately kept their spouses in the background as though they were shameful family secrets.

"I've always suspected that Erika liked dark meat, I just had no idea she had such poor judgment."

Raven sat up. "Meaning?"

"Meaning that she's got a thing going with a STRAPPED employee. The young man works for STRAPPED and spends a lot of time with Erika. He's just a kid, only seventeen, eighteen at the most, his folks are dead and Erika's set herself up as a mentor. She's taken to having the young man over every Friday night. From what I hear, he doesn't know enough to keep his mouth shut and Erika is too into the relationship to see that people are starting to talk."

*If Erika's anything like me she couldn't care less about what people are saying,* Raven thought. "If it's common knowledge around the office, why hasn't anyone said anything?"

"You'd be surprised at the things people close their eyes to." Dudley realized he'd gotten carried away, made his story too juicy. *The best lies are simple ones,* he reminded himself. "Only a core group knows, and they're all loyal to Erika. They won't tell."

Raven threw up her hands in frustration. "Then it's not a big deal after all. Jeez, Dudley!"

"It will be if the rank-and-file faithful get wind of it. Guys who are pro-gun are generally anti everything else. Anti-abortion, anti-immigration, and anti-race mixing. STRAPPED has to be the most conservative group in Texas. That's saying a lot."

"So you think I should expose Erika—get her out of the way?"

"Not necessarily. Just like Erika's hurting us, she can help us, given the right motivation. You think Erika opened STRAPPED's purse for you before? Just think how much it'll be worth to her, in money and influence, to keep her secret a secret." As Dudley spoke, he thought, *Raven's losing her edge. Six months ago, she wouldn't have had to ask me what to do.*

Just as Dudley began to think he was wasting his time, Raven rewarded him by saying, "Don't just sit there, Dudley, it's already six o'clock. You've hired an investigator, right? See if he can catch Erika in the act. Getting caught with a black man who's practically a kid probably won't ruin her, but it'll get her off our backs long enough to win the election."

Dudley gave Raven a confident nod, and prayed that he knew his brother as well as he assumed. Right about now David should be going crazy with jealousy that Erika had found another black man to spend time with. He wouldn't leave Austin without reclaiming Erika as his property.

Dudley assured himself that he knew David's weaknesses like the back of his hand. He set aside his doubts and thought about the future. *Once I get rid of Erika, it'll be one down, one to go.*

"Come on," Erika said. She took David's hand, intending to lead him toward her bedroom. When David had called out of the blue, Erika hadn't asked why he'd been scarce because she didn't care. She had no love for him, but it had been a taxing week and he was the best stress alleviator a woman could ask for.

David stayed where he was. "I need to ask you something."

Silence.

"Are you screwing somebody else?"

Erika let go of his hand and crossed her arms. "That wouldn't be your business, seeing as how there's not much going on between us."

David stuck his hands in his pockets. "If you plan on me going in there"—he nodded toward the bedroom—"then it is my business."

While David had been spending time with Raven, Erika had made it up to lover number seventy-two. "David, I'm a grown woman with a healthy libido. There's always somebody."

David's eyes flashed with anger. "Who?"

"That," Erika said, her own anger flaring, "really isn't for you to know." She moved to walk past David, but he grabbed her arm.

"Tell me right now," he said sternly. David was so worried about who else might be doing Erika that he wouldn't be able to enjoy himself until he found out. His mind wouldn't stop replaying the kaleidoscope of images banging around in his head: flashes of another man, with lighter skin and larger where it counted, devouring her.

True, he'd made his confession to Raven in San Diego, faced his emotional baggage. David had named his demon, but that wasn't the same as exorcising it. Because he loved Raven, David had thought he was over Erika, but the notion that she'd replaced him was more than he could stand.

"Reverend Capps, I didn't know jealousy made you lose control. I thought only alcohol did that," Erika snapped as she jerked away from him. "It's nobody you know. He's a colleague of mine, an investment banker from Sweden who's detailed here for a month." She looked at him accusingly. "What did you expect? It's not like you've been knocking down my bedroom door lately."

"He's Swedish?" David stammered. "But I thought—never mind, forget I asked." David blinked and the jealousy in his eyes morphed into confusion. Then his confusion disappeared and David was left with . . . nothing.

"Now that we've resolved that," Erika said as she reached for David. "I know what you need." She began unbuttoning his shirt.

David tried to push her away. "Why don't we sit down. Have a drink, talk for a minute," he said feebly.

"Uh-uh," Erika said as she undid his pants and gently pushed him against the wall. She knew that David got primal satisfaction from having her kneel before him so that he could grasp her hair with both hands, holding her in place while he did his thing. For her it was okay, but she did it mainly because afterward David put all his energy into satisfying her.

David looked through half-opened blinds across Erika's backyard as he tried to figure out what to do. Erika's dim garden lights twinkled romantically. The lights reminded David of a restaurant that he and Raven had gone to in San Diego.

When Erika's knees hit the hardwood, she got a very irritating surprise. "What's wrong?" Erika asked. She looked up at him. "What do you expect me to do with this?"

"I don't—I think this might not be the right time," David said. He wished for a drink.

Erika got to her feet and pressed herself to David. She kissed him, stuck her tongue in his ear and said, "Don't worry. I'll fix it." She went back down and tried to bring David to life.

So when it happened, neither Erika nor David was prepared. David was still limp, and it's a good thing he was, because he yanked Erika's hair so hard that she instinctively clenched her jaw.

"Ouch!" David shoved Erika and crouched down beside her. "Someone's out there!"

"David, that's impossible!" Erika whispered.

"Tell that to whoever's outside with a camera! See, there it goes again."

Erika and David watched the nonstop camera flashes as they crouched behind the sofa. "David, we've got to stop this guy. How am I going to deny it's me in those pictures if he's got a dozen shots of my house?"

David's fantasies about white women didn't include his turning light-skinned enough to play white knight to a damsel in distress—he wished Erika would figure out a way to stop the intruder that didn't include him, but he couldn't say so.

David cursed the dim garden lights. Whoever was outside could probably see inside.

"When I count to three, I want you to create a distraction, scream and throw something. I'll run straight toward the doors. That ought to scare him off," David said.

"One . . . two . . . three!"

Erika screamed and threw a statuette of Sam Houston toward

the French doors that opened onto the patio. David scrambled from behind the sofa, and screaming like a warrior, ran directly toward the patio.

More camera flashes blinded them both, then the photographer ran off. He'd run out of film.

David freaked. "People can't find out I'm fooling around with you! This would ruin—"

Erika stepped in front of David. "You're not fooling anyone, David. Everyone knows you've got a thing for white women, so cut the *me, me, me* bullshit."

Erika was lying, in a way—she'd heard plenty of rumors about David, but nothing about white women.

*People knew?* That bit of information stoked David's panic. Living the fantasy wasn't turning out the way David thought it would. Definitely not.

"I should go," he said. He took a step and came firmly down on a piece of glass from Erika's shattered French doors.

"Ouch!" He hopped from that piece of glass onto another one. "OUCH! Oh my God, I'm cutting my feet to shreds!"

"Then stop moving around, you idiot," Erika said. "Let me clear you a path to the sofa."

As Erika picked shards of glass out of David's feet, they didn't say much, but they shared the same thought. *We're screwed.*

When Dudley printed the photos, he got so excited he could feel blood pounding in his ears. He took two of his wife's blood pressure pills, then called Dr. Laverne.

"I have an emergency, I'll see you in twenty minutes."

"Dudley, it's Saturday, I don't see patients today."

"I'll pay whatever you want. I'm on my way."

A short while later Dr. Laverne flipped through the photos of David and Erika while he and Dudley talked. "I don't understand why you had to do this," Dr. Laverne said.

"Who said anything about having to? I'm pulling everybody's strings because I want to. It's fun." Dudley sat comfortably on Dr. Laverne's sofa as he spoke. Although Dudley had called Dr. Laverne practically beside himself with the need to talk to someone, once Dr. Laverne began looking at the pictures, Dudley stopped being his usual wound-up self. No pacing back and forth. No agitation. No grievances to air. Not today. Dudley was the original cool cucumber. And why shouldn't he be? The world was turning, and finally, Dudley would be the lucky one.

"Maybe your intentions are good, Dudley. You want Michael to win the election, and bringing Ms. Whittier down is the only way to do that. But these photos . . . can't you see how they could destroy your brother?"

Dudley frowned, clearly offended by Dr. Laverne's questions. "I've spent my whole life helping David. That's all I ever did: stand in the background, use my brains to help my little brother succeed. So no, Doc, don't twist what I'm saying. I don't give a shit about what happens to David when these pictures come out."

Dr. Laverne hesitated when he got to a full frontal shot of David. No wonder the man was so fixated on women. That thing had to be fed.

Dr. Laverne removed his glasses and wiped his eyes. "Okay, Dudley. Let's go over it again. Tell me why you find it necessary to destroy your brother."

They talked for another two hours, and at the end of the session, the only thing Dr. Laverne knew for sure was that he had earned every penny, and then some. He made a mental note to raise Dudley's hourly rate.

As Dudley prepared to leave, Dr. Laverne said, "One last question. Did your private investigator happen to follow David when he was with Raven?"

"Why, Doc?" Dudley was preoccupied with putting the photos in their correct order. He didn't bother to look up.

"I was wondering . . . did your investigator . . . do you have any pictures of those two . . . like these?"

That made Dudley look up. He was happy to find out that Dr. Laverne was as messed up as everybody else. Dudley's day couldn't get any better.

"No?" Dr. Laverne said when Dudley continued to stare at him without saying anything. "That's fine, just thought I'd ask."

Since Genie had caught Christopher with Monica, Genie and Christopher had worked together, sometimes side by side, sometimes talking by phone a half dozen times a day, and through it all they acted like complete strangers. Professional, polite strangers, but strangers nonetheless. A person who didn't know their history had only one clue that something was amiss between them: Christopher and Genie never looked each other in the eye.

When Genie ran out of Monica's apartment, Christopher didn't follow her. He didn't call her for three days—couldn't get up the nerve. When he finally called, his apology fell somewhere between contrite and defensive. Genie hung up on him, and from that point they never spoke of it again.

Christopher found himself driving aimlessly one afternoon and the next thing he knew he was at Genie's doorstep. "Thought I'd stop by, see how you've been," Christopher said as soon as Genie undid her deadbolt and let him in.

"You see me every day, Chris. Can't you tell from looking at me? I'm just fine," she replied with no trace of emotion.

Genie did look good. She never missed a beat on the outside. But on the inside she'd changed. It was her first time being hurt by a man, having her trust hurled back in her face. She couldn't help but change after feeling that type of pain.

"Can we talk?" Christopher asked.

"Sure."

Christopher sat, but Genie remained standing, with her arms rigidly at her sides.

"I'm sorry, Genie. I know when I apologized before, I made

it sound like you pushed me to Monica. You didn't; I made the decision to get with her on my own. I'm sorry I cheated on you, and I'm sorry I was such an asshole about it when we talked before."

Genie sat down. "You were an asshole, and I accept your apology, at least on that part. What else?"

"I need you to forgive me because I want you back. I miss everything about you," Christopher gave a half chuckle. "Even the stuff I used to complain about. You're older than me, smarter than me, maybe even more ambitious than me. I couldn't handle it."

"So you ran to a woman who was less than me? Is that what you're saying, that Monica was nothing but a way to get by whenever I bruised your ego?"

"Monica? She's okay . . ." Christopher stammered. "I mean she's all right, she's not . . ."

Christopher looked at Genie. Her eyes said, *Tell me the truth*.

He started over. "Monica's different from you but she's like you, too, in a lot of ways. Smart, strong." He looked into Genie's eyes and watched her wince as he added, "Kind.

"She's not as focused as you are. But no, I can't honestly say that she's less than you." Monica, Christopher found out when Genie left her apartment, was more woman than he'd realized. Just like Genie had never been on the receiving end of heartbreak, Monica had never seen herself as the other woman until she looked into Genie's eyes. Genie's eyes were magic mirrors reflecting Genie's hurt and Monica's role in it.

"I can't be a part of bringing a sister down like that," she'd told Christopher as he gathered his things to leave.

Christopher urgently needed Genie to pay attention to his next words. "Monica's not the one I love, and she never will be. We broke it off the same day you came by her apartment. Monica doesn't even work in the Dallas office any more."

He gestured with both hands. "I love you, Genie, and you're the only woman I want."

"I love you too, Chris, and I forgive you."

Christopher moved toward her, but Genie put her hand up, a stop sign.

"This experience has me thinking about what I want out of life."

"And?" Christopher felt anxiety rise in his chest. *Why'd she have to go and start thinking?*

"I forgive you, but that doesn't mean I want to get back with you. You hurt me, Chris." Her voice cracked. She cleared her throat. "And you're right about me, I'm ambitious. I've got a million dreams, and I'm not ready to settle down with one man." Seeing the look on Christopher's face, it was now Genie's turn to plead for him to understand her. "Chris, I meet men every day—fine men, interesting men. And not once, *not once,* have I so much as given out my cell phone number." She paused, "But I've wanted to."

Christopher looked shocked. How could Genie even think about another man?

"Oh, so now you're ready to get out there, mingle with other men because of the mistake I made?" Christopher was on the defensive again. "Sounds like a recipe for HIV if you ask me."

"Nobody's asking you." Genie felt the urge to spare Christopher's feelings but she fought it. "I'm not saying I want to sleep around, but do other men catch my eye? Yes, the same way Monica caught yours. And this isn't only about me wanting to date other men."

Christopher threw up his hands in exasperation. "What else, then? What else do I need to do?"

"It's not what you need to do, it's what I need to do for myself. I'm going back to school, Chris. Starting on my master's, next semester." Genie looked away from Christopher and said words that hurt them both. "I'm going to move to Washington DC as soon as the election is over. I've been accepted at Georgetown."

When Christopher left Genie's apartment he had his head down and his hands shoved deep into his pockets. He could barely see through the tears that brimmed in his eyes.

Now he knew what men meant when they talked about the one that got away.

After he'd talked to Dr. Laverne, Dudley had a hard time deciding whether to have another bite of his treat immediately or savor it until later in the day. The idea of waiting a few more hours so that he could serve up his news in person appealed to Dudley. That way he'd have the entire morning to imagine what might happen once he set things in motion. Dudley picked up the phone and made a lunch date.

"You won't believe what I have to show you," Dudley said as Raven rushed to his table and stowed her sunglasses in her bag.

"Yeah, what?" She picked up the menu and ran her finger down the selections. "This had better be good. I had to postpone my salon appointment for you."

"Look at you, acting all bored and distracted," Dudley said as he took the envelope from his portfolio. He pushed the envelope across the table to Raven. "Check these out, see if they pique your interest. They were taken last night."

Raven found herself staring at David's penis and the blurred image of a woman. When she finally looked at Dudley, the pain and bewilderment on her face sent a delicious shiver down his spine.

"It's David," she said. "I mean, is it David? Those look like his hands."

"I had a feeling you'd recognize him, and I suspect it isn't because of his hands," Dudley said as he reached across the table and rubbed her hand. "I thought something was going on between the two of you, I could feel it."

"He was the one with Erika?"

Dudley nodded. "Yes, my source had it all wrong." Dudley turned the photo sideways so that he could see it. "But looking at my baby brother, I can see why he'd be mistaken for a young buck."

"You're sure these were taken last night?"

"Positive." Dudley noticed that Raven had stopped at the second picture. "Go on, look at all of them."

Raven flipped through a few more shots, then shoved the stack across the table to Dudley. She motioned for the waiter. "That Death by Chocolate on your dessert menu—please bring one for me, and bring him the crème brûlée," she ordered.

Raven drummed her fingers on the table. "These pictures, if they were to get out, they'd hurt David as much as Erika."

"Maybe, but what choice do we have? If you want Michael to win, David's got to suffer the consequences."

Raven didn't say anything, just sat there shocked. Finally, she looked at Dudley with her stunning, icy eyes and asked, "Do you think he loves her?"

"It wouldn't surprise me. David's been waiting his whole life for a woman like Erika—someone smart, beautiful, and powerful."

*What about me? I'm all those things*, Raven wanted to scream. "There are lots of women around who fit that description. What's so special about Erika?"

"She's white," Dudley said softly. He shook his head as though it pained him to speak of his brother's foible. "David's always had a thing for white women. You want to hear a man go on and on about white women, just buy my brother a six-pack." Dudley laughed and feigned surprise at Raven's surprised look. "What? Don't tell me you didn't know?" Dudley laughed again. "David just plays the sisters. That's how he built New Word."

*He told me I cured him*, Raven remembered. *He lied to me.* By now she had finished her Death by Chocolate and started on

Dudley's crème brûlée. The more she ate, the calmer she became. "So when he spends time with a black woman, say a woman like me, he's looking for something?"

Dudley waved his hand, "Well, yeah, but let's face it, David couldn't take advantage of you if he tried. You guys had some sort of "You wash my back, I'll wash yours" thing going on. Right?"

Raven sat back and folded her arms across her chest. "Let's just say we did. What would be in it for me?"

"If I had to guess?"

She nodded. "If you had to guess."

Dudley was having such a delightful time, he had to remind himself not to overdo it. "I may be closing in on fifty, but nothing's wrong with my eyes or my memory. When Michael snubbed you at the Juneteenth gala this summer, I saw you make a play for David to get back at him. Now you're even more pissed off because Michael hasn't appreciated the way you've tried to help him win the election. What better revenge than to screw one of his closest friends?"

"And David. What would be in it for him?"

"Money. I don't know if you and I ever talked about it, but I'm sure you know David's mission in life is to get the bulk of the faith-based money. Michael told him he'd have to go through you to get funding. That's why he came onto you so strong. I guess my clever brother decided to bang Michael's woman and pick his pocket at the same time."

Raven asked Dudley more questions, but she didn't ask him why he would give up his own brother. Having spent most of her lifetime turning on people, she didn't need a reason why.

Raven threw off so much heat as she paced, her bedroom should've burst into flames. How dare David! She thought about how she turned her back on Michael every night and all the while David was running around with Erika. *They've both lost their minds if they think I'm taking this shit lying down.*

Raven was ready to deal with them both and she wanted to get Erika first, but she couldn't find her. She called Erika's home and cell phones, but all she got was her voice mail. Raven wanted to leave Erika a message—oh, did she!—but catching her off guard would be better.

Raven grabbed her keys and headed to Erika's.

Erika loaded her CD player with Bonnie Raitt and roamed around her house, searching for something to keep her mind off the pictures. Maybe the lighting wasn't right, so they wouldn't come out clearly. Maybe he dropped his camera in a puddle of water when he ran away. Maybe. Maybe. Maybe.

Erika kept wandering. She had lived in her home for ten years and she'd never so much as mopped the kitchen floor. She found where her housekeeper kept the cleaning supplies and cleaned her house from top to bottom. Erika lost herself in discovering her home. Her last job was to sweep up the glass from her broken French doors. As she swept, Erika tried to sing along with Raitt's "I Can't Make You Love Me" but the words making tracks in her head didn't match what came from her mouth. All she could think of was when and where the photos would show up.

When the doorbell rang and Erika answered it, seeing that it was Raven, she put one latex-gloved hand on her hip and asked, "What are you doing here?"

Erika reluctantly stepped aside for Raven, who walked in like she was the homeowner and Erika, the downstairs maid.

"Why haven't you returned my calls?" Raven asked. She threw her handbag on the sofa.

"That's how we do things, isn't it? One of us," Erika pointed at herself, "usually me, makes a call, and the other one, normally you, doesn't return it. We've reversed roles, that's all."

Raven walked over to Erika's shattered French doors. "Looks like you had a break-in. That's too bad."

Erika didn't move from the entrance. She wasn't in the mood to play Raven's game; finding out who took those pictures was far more important. She decided to allow Raven enough time to do some moderately degrading groveling.

"Since you're here, I guess you've changed your mind. It took you long enough." Erika took off her housecleaning gloves and tucked them in the back pocket of her jeans.

"Changed my mind about what?" Raven's intention was to tear Erika limb from limb, and on that point, her mind was made up.

"About making sure my organization gets its money's worth out of Michael. You almost waited too long, but I'll make some calls tomorrow, get his endorsements back on track."

"STRAPPED? Erika, screw STRAPPED. I'm here about you and David."

Erika, who was not shy, felt her neck turn scarlet. "David who?"

"Let me refresh your recollection." Raven grabbed her handbag off the sofa. She whipped out one of the photos, and held it in one hand while she stabbed at it with her index finger. "*This* David. Reverend David Capps. Who do you think you are, sleeping with David?" Raven shouted.

The photographer had captured David in a stance that was particularly flattering. Erika was in the photo too, breasts swinging, stomach bulging, as she reached for the Sam Houston statuette she'd thrown through her French doors. If Erika looked like that in real life, David (or any self-respecting man) would've chased the photographer down and confiscated his camera rather than let anyone know he'd slept with her.

"Why do you care about me and David?" Erika shouted back.

"Because he's mine!" Raven blurted. That shut the both of them up.

Then Erika started to laugh. "Yours. Are you kidding? The man's a whore, or haven't you heard?"

Raven felt anger rise in her throat. She forced herself to calm down. She leaned the photo of David and Erika in front of a framed picture of Erika and a horse. "You can scream, shout, break everything in this house for all I care," Raven said as she straightened the propped-up photo, stepped back, stepped forward, and readjusted it. While Raven displayed the picture of David and Erika to her liking, she talked to Erika in a shaky voice. "But the one thing you cannot do is laugh at me. It makes me angry."

Erika thought about the stories she'd heard about Raven. *Those stories are so bizarre, they can't be true*, she told herself. And if they were, well, Erika wasn't just a STRAPPED member, she was its top-rated female marksman.

Erika backed down, but only so much. "I don't care about David one way or another, but obviously you do, so I'll give you a choice—Michael or David."

"Explain." Raven's voice was steady now. Her glossy stare of moments before was gone.

Erika relaxed. "You think you deserve to have everything you want, but you don't. So here's the deal. I let bygones be bygones as far as the STRAPPED money is concerned, which means I'll stop messing with Michael. In exchange, I keep David, exclusively. Or, I'll give you David, but Michael loses the election."

Raven stared at Erika for a few beats, then said, "Okay, how about this? I keep David, you call your dogs off Michael so that he can win this election, and in return I don't expose the fact that you sleep black," Raven shot back.

Erika called Raven's bluff. "People don't care who I sleep with, but when they find out that you're involved with David, Michael would be lucky to be elected president of a rock-collecting club." The alarm on Raven's face told Erika she'd hit the mark. She continued, "I'll keep David around for as long as I want to, then when I'm done, you can have him."

Erika reminded herself of who she was: Erika Chaseworth Whittier, a woman who cut the nuts off bulls and chopped the heads off snakes. She couldn't let a pest like Raven disrespect her in her own house and get away unhurt. "I've got no problem giving you my leftovers, especially since they suit you so well. When I got tired of Michael, he ran right to you, so I'm sure David will do the same."

Raven wanted to hit Erika. But she'd learned a few things on the campaign trail; things like patience and how to wait for the right time to stick in the dagger.

"Fuck you, Erika, I'll get what I deserve, and so will you." Raven grabbed her handbag and left.

Raven sped through Erika's quiet neighborhood, her entire being concentrated on one thing: hurting Erika. A small child chasing a ball or an old lady crossing the street would've been road kill, because Raven didn't stop for shit, not indecisive squirrels, not stop signs.

Her cell phone rang.

"What!"

"Raven, it's Jerry Minshew. Please don't hang up. Listen, I can't get you off my mind. I have to see you. I'll do anything you want—write another column, give you money—whatever, I don't care." Minshew stopped begging, not because he'd run out of things to say, but because he was shocked that Raven hadn't hung up in his face.

Raven didn't hang up because she needed a target for her rage, and Minshew, with his unlucky self, was it.

"You're the most disgusting man I've ever let touch me, why would I put myself through that again? Why would any woman want you—have you checked a mirror lately?" Another call came in. "Hold on," Raven said.

And the fool did.

Dudley was on the other line. He was having second thoughts

about having shown Raven the pictures so soon. He wanted to plan their strategy for approaching Erika first before Raven did something stupid.

"Hey, sweetie." Dudley tried to sound compassionate.

"I'm on the other line with Jerry Minshew. What's up?"

*Why is she talking to Jerry Minshew?* Dudley thought. "Just wanted to check on you, see how you're doing."

"I'm fine." Raven had reached the freeway and she hit the entrance ramp going eighty. "I just left Erika's house. Can you believe she tried to make a deal with me? She'll *let* Michael win the election if I give up David."

"You did what! Raven, why didn't you wait and let me talk to her? Now all you've done is make Erika angrier!"

Raven talked right over Dudley. "And she implied that she used to be involved with Michael. That's just one more reason for me to smash her into the ground. I don't care if it was before I met Michael. When I finish with her, she'll have to move out of the state of Texas. I told her that I'm going to make sure she gets what she deserves." Raven moved across three lanes without looking into her mirrors. She was going ninety and picking up speed.

"What did she say to that?" Dudley asked. He was upset with Raven but also with himself for rushing to her with the photos. There was nothing he could do now except to gather information and do damage control.

"I've got to give it to the tramp, she's ready for a fight, and so am I. It's been a long time since I've had somebody stand up to me the way she tried to."

Dudley and Raven talked for another couple of minutes, then she clicked back to Minshew.

"Jerry?"

"Yes."

"One more thing. You're a lousy fuck." Raven hung up in his face.

# 23

"Good afternoon. Reverend David Capps' res—"
"Put that son-of-a-bitch on the phone!"
"I beg your—"
"Bitch, don't beg, just put his ass on the phone right now!" Raven screamed at Vera Jean, David's housekeeper. Vera Jean was known to use a few choice cuss words herself, and she definitely took issue with being called a bitch for no reason, but she was getting dressed for Saturday night service and she wasn't about to let Rev's problems steal her joy. She took him the phone.

David was also accustomed to a fair amount of profanity—but not since Stanky Sue had caught him in the garage with the girl next door had he been on the receiving end of such a vile, low-down tongue lashing like the one Raven put on him.

"Tell me another lie, David, and I'll catch a plane to Dallas right now and be there before evening service lets out. I'll show these pictures of you and your white piece of—"

*Pictures!* There went David's hope that it was all a bad dream.

"Okay, okay. Just calm down. It's me, but it's not what you think."

"What! It's not what I think! You must think I'm a fool. See you at church, lover."

"Raven, wait!" But he was talking to the dial tone.

David called for Vera Jean. "I feel sick. Call the church and tell Reverend Greene I won't be back tonight," he told her. It wasn't a lie. David had to drag himself to New Word earlier that day—an irrational conviction told him that everyone he came into contact with had copies of the pictures of him with Erika. Raven's tirade sealed the deal; he wasn't going anywhere near New Word. David would have canceled Saturday night and Sunday services, but that wasn't possible.

He didn't doubt that Raven was on her way to Dallas. She'd flown in once before and taken a taxi directly to the church. That day, they spent many unholy hours in almost every area of the church except for the sanctuary and the chapel. No matter what Raven offered, David had never let her so much as peek into those areas. That was where he drew the line.

*How did Raven got hold of those pictures?* he wondered as he raced to the airport. He'd worry about that later. He didn't consider that Raven might be the one behind his troubles. Although he knew Raven had done some scandalous things in her time, David didn't believe she'd do anything to hurt him. Raven loved him.

As soon as Raven exited the terminal, David came up behind her, grabbed her arm, and squeezed. "You're coming with me."

Raven gave him a cool look. "Or I could scream and cause a scene right here. Get your hand off me."

David didn't let go, but he loosened his grip. "Raven, I'm *asking* you not to ruin my life. Please don't go to my church."

Raven was accustomed to seeing lust or pride in David's eyes, but all she saw was fear and desperation. Her feelings, already all over the place, jangled some more.

"Where's your car?" she asked.

They went to David's home. David locked the door leading from the garage to the kitchen and turned to find Raven's open hand fast approaching his face. He grabbed her wrist.

"I'm not Michael," he said. "Raise your hand to me again, and I'll hurt you."

"You couldn't hurt me if you tried," Raven said, and looking into his eyes she knew she was right.

The couple fought without touching, flinging bitter words at each other. Raven accused David of being a dressed-up field nigger sniffing after massa's woman. He told her he'd rather be with a beautiful, rich, white, *sane* woman than with a married sociopath. Raven broke dishes. David put his fist through a wall.

Then Raven smirked at David and said, "So this is what a false prophet looks like."

David's face crumpled under the weight of Raven's accusation. She gave a voice to David's deepest fear—that he had become a fake, a man who lived by his passions rather than by The Word. How could he lead others to God when he'd lost the way himself? David abruptly turned from Raven, tears stinging his eyes.

Seeing how hurt he was, Raven stopped. "I didn't mean it. None of it." She removed her coat and threw it across a kitchen chair. "David, look at me." She wore a red wool dress that zipped up the front. She took off her dress and stood there in her heels, hose, and bra.

When he turned to face her, Raven said, "I don't understand you, David. How could you want Erika when you've got all this?"

David gently put his hands on either side of Raven's face, bent and kissed her. Within seconds everything they dragged around with them—their problems, their pride, their pretensions—was stripped away. They sank to David's kitchen floor, but for all the lovers knew, they could have been anywhere in the world.

After she caught her breath, Raven repeated, "How could you be with her, David? After what just happened between us?"

They were seated side by side on the floor, their backs resting against the kitchen cabinets. David looked at her and said, "You know how, Raven. I started seeing Erika before you and I got together. She chased me from day one. You and I are alike. If somebody gives us something, we take it. I'll bet you've never given yourself to only one man at a time."

"I do now."

David was surprised. "You do? What about Michael? What about all the freaky stuff you like to make him do?"

"Gave it up for you," she said quietly.

David still couldn't believe all he'd taken away from Michael. "He told me once that I needed to find myself a woman like you. Who would have imagined . . ." His voice trailed off. He brushed his hand over Raven's hair. "And there hasn't been anyone else but me?"

"No." Raven told the truth. Her transaction with Minshew took place before David. Since David, Raven didn't think she could abide the touch of another man.

"Damn." David slung his arm around Raven's shoulder.

"Yeah," she agreed.

"Let's do this," David spun around and with his legs akimbo, faced Raven. He took her hands in his. "I promise you, from this day forward, I will not give myself to anyone but you. Do you promise the same thing?"

"I do."

Michael leaned over and pawed Raven. She slapped his hand away.

"Get off me!" she whispered in her sleep and scooted to the far side of their king-sized bed.

Michael did as he was told. Lately Raven rejected his advances more and more. They hadn't made love in over a month. Michael was on his most servile behavior, but it wasn't enough to get Raven in the mood. When they did make love, she went through the motions, but clearly didn't enjoy herself. Lately she'd given up the pretense of being interested in Michael. Except, that is, when it came to his gubernatorial race.

Michael suspected that the cause of his sexual problems with Raven was their constant bickering over how to stop the flow of blood from his campaign. She wanted to use strong-arm tactics, but after what happened with Smotes, he wouldn't allow her to talk to anyone of importance. Michael knew that Raven wasn't accustomed to being told no, especially not by him. She didn't know when she married him that Michael had a dual nature—bedroom slave, boardroom king.

He looked at her, curled in a fetal position, her hair clasped in a thick, beautiful ponytail, and wished he could change his nature, or hers. But it wasn't happening. Michael was his own master when it came to politics, and even if Raven never let him near her again, he wasn't giving up control of his professional dream. Raven, Michael knew, would never change. No way, no how.

He got out of bed and went down to get the Sunday *Austin American-Statesman*. The news for Michael these days was usually no news, or bad news—in the form of another endorsement lost. Even though he was conditioned to expect the worst, Michael's heart skipped a few beats and his mouth went dry when he read the opinion page. IS IMPOTENT GOVERNOR TEXAS' DESTINY?

"Texas is a great state," the article began. "A strong, virile (if I may use the word) state. Whatever Texas does, she does in a big way. Can we, given our size, our strength, and our dreams, afford to have as governor a man who is professionally impotent?"

The editorial continued, "I speak, regretfully, of Michael Joseph. Although it was only a short time ago that I used this page to endorse him as the best candidate for governor, events that have taken place since then cause me to question my own judgment. Senator Joseph began on a high note, but his campaign of late has been mediocre, his message unfocused, and his ability to hold onto key endorsements, pitiful. Senator Joseph even managed to lose the endorsement of the Rice Association. It's *rice*, for crying out loud!"

The opinion piece went on to recount every lost endorsement and lost vote that plagued Michael's campaign since the day Erika decided that he shouldn't be governor. The article was mean spirited and unbalanced. It was also factually accurate and stunningly effective. The best thing that Jerry Minshew had ever written.

Grace put on her favorite Boney James CD, prepared a bubble bath, lit her candles, and poured herself a glass of wine. She let her robe drop to the floor and stepped into the fragrant, steamy water. She didn't want to think about anything, but Michael was on her mind and she decided to soak, drink her wine, and deal with it.

They'd started out with so much promise, two good people who were deeply in love. Tears slid down Grace's cheeks as she recalled a young Michael, his naked body pressed to hers, whispering in her ear, "I've had sex plenty of times, but this was my first time making love." She could feel his tears on her shoulder. She pictured the fear on his face during her rough labor with Evan, the way he'd wiped her brow and muttered nervous words of encouragement. Grace and Michael had shared so much: vacations alone when they'd left the boys with the Reeses, family reunions, professional successes and setbacks, secret dreams and fears. Michael and Grace Joseph had been true intimate friends.

But over time, their relationship changed. Michael demoted Grace from best friend to live-in acquaintance. From lover to infrequent semen receptacle. From one hundred to zero in what seemed to Grace like the blink of an eye.

Now Michael wanted her to be his friend again. "Good enough to be his friend, but not good enough to be his wife," Grace muttered as she took a sip of wine. She lay there, getting a buzz from the wine, letting the tears and memories flow. *Please, God,* she prayed, *let me cry until I cry Michael out of my system. I know you can heal a broken heart—you said it in your word. Please, Father, let this be my last time crying over that man.*

But crying Michael away wasn't to be. The doorbell interrupted Grace's soul-cleansing ritual. Still wet, she pulled on her robe and hurried to the door.

"Hello, Grace," Michael said when she opened it. "We need to talk."

"Can I get you a drink?" Grace asked Michael.

"Rum and Coke would be good." Michael wandered around the room, looking at Grace's photos. "This place looks great," he said. "You've always had a good eye."

Grace started to make Michael's drink, but thought better of it. "Why don't I make us some coffee?"

Michael wandered over to the breakfast nook and watched Grace start the coffeemaker. "Remember when we used to do this? Sit in the kitchen, stay there until one, two o'clock in the morning, talking about our future. Those were good times."

"Let's sit in the living room," Grace said. Although she'd been revisiting the good old days when Michael arrived, she had no desire to go on a nostalgia trip with him. She placed the coffee on the table between them.

"Why are you here, Michael?"

Michael wiped his hand over his face. *He's aged,* Grace thought. "Don't know," he finally said. "I felt the walls closing in on me earlier this evening, so I jumped in my car with no intention other than to drive around, release some stress. Next thing I know, I'm on the highway, headed to Dallas." He looked at Grace. "To you, I guess."

Michael put down his coffee mug and rubbed his temples. "Jerry Minshew's latest opinion piece drove the last nail into my coffin. Looks like I'm going to lose the election."

"Yes, I read it this morning. I'm sorry, Michael, I know how hard you've worked. Maybe you'll lose this go-round, but you'll get to the governor's office eventually. Remember your first race for public office? Your opponent wiped the floor with you. But you're a fighter—you're going to be governor, if not this time, then the next."

"You always believed in me, and after all we've been through, you still do." Michael met he ex-wife's gaze. "I miss that, Grace."

He stopped for a moment, and then admitted. "My career isn't the only thing falling apart. My marriage isn't what I expected. Raven and I don't really talk anymore and she's stopped—we don't share things like we used to."

*What does he expect me to say to that? I'm sorry?*

"I made a mistake, getting mixed up with Raven." He hung his head. The notion that Raven might be seeing someone else crossed Michael's mind, but he didn't tell Grace. All he said was, "She's nothing like you. Not at all."

Although she tried to fight it off, hope surged through Grace. These days she was praying for God to take Michael out of her heart, but in the beginning she'd prayed for Him to put her in Michael's. Every night for the first year after their divorce, every single night, Grace fell asleep imagining Michael on his knees begging her back. When she'd finally given up hope, it looked like her dream was about to come true.

"What are you saying, Michael?"

He moved from his place in the chair across from Grace onto the sofa, next to her. "In life, things happen that we don't expect. I knew all the fooling around I did during our marriage was wrong, but I didn't expect for it to destroy us."

"I never should have put up with your behavior," Grace said. Except for John Reese and her own sons, Grace hadn't been this close to a man since Michael walked out. Her body knew it was him—the one who could make her feel again. It started calling to him. The long-forgotten sensation of moisture between her legs took Grace by surprise. At first she didn't realize what was going on, then the throbbing began in her groin and spread to her breasts.

Michael saw it in her face. "Grace." He caressed her neck and then slowly slid her robe off one shoulder. When Michael bent and brushed her nipple with his lips, Grace's whole body trembled. She cradled his head to her for a moment, then pulled his face up to hers.

"Why are you doing this?" Tears flowed freely from her clear brown eyes." She shook her head. "Michael, don't do this to me."

"I wouldn't hurt you again for anything in the world, Grace." He undid her robe and cast it aside, leaving her naked. "I've always loved you, and I always will."

Grace's body was flushed from head to toe, anticipating the moment Michael would release her from the loneliness that had plagued her for so long. And then Michael kissed her. Grace kissed him back and it was the best kiss of her life. She prolonged the kiss, drew every ounce of passion from it that she could, then pulled away.

"Stop, Michael. Things are moving too fast!"

"Not for me," he said as he tried to nibble at her breast again. Michael knew her weak spot.

Grace pushed him away again. "Not for me," he repeated as he sat up. Grace was so discombobulated she didn't move to put on her robe. Michael looked at her and thought, *She's beautiful. How did I forget?*

Michael handed Grace her robe. "I'll leave if you want me to, but I need you to think about me, Grace. Think about us." He picked up his jacket and gently kissed Grace on the top of her head. "I'm begging you, Grace, don't let what happened in the past ruin what we could have in the future."

# 24

As Michael walked the half-empty Corpus Christi community hall with Christopher at his side, shaking hands and accepting best wishes, he hoped his smile hid his disappointment. The election was two weeks away and the sparse crowd that showed up to hear him speak brought his hidden fears to the surface. People were not interested in him. If they didn't care enough to come out and meet him in person, they wouldn't take time on a dreary November Tuesday to go to the polls. As he listened to an elderly white man complain about property taxes, Michael thought, *God help me if it rains on election day.*

Raven and Dudley were standing on the sidelines watching Michael work the crowd.

"I know it looks bad, but the election's going to turn around, now that we've got Erika under control," Raven said. Dudley gritted his teeth. Raven looked at his balding, sweaty head and forced herself to say, "Look, Dudley, I'm sorry about not letting you talk to Erika first. The bottom line is, she's got no choice but to back off."

Dudley looked up at her. "And you think that two weeks before the election, simply backing off is going to be enough to make Michael win?" His eyes were filled with disdain. "There are two key votes in the legislature between now and the election. I could have persuaded Erika to make sure Michael's side won those votes. There are a couple of organizations in central Texas that still haven't endorsed Michael or Sweeney. I could have gotten her to make some calls, to get them to endorse Michael."

Raven stood with her arms crossed. "I get your point, but you know I'm not into constructive criticism, Dudley. What's done is done."

"And all you've done is piss Erika off. We'll be lucky if she doesn't come after Michael even harder. When you add our problems with Erika to the Molotov cocktail Minshew threw at Michael in his latest editorial, we're in deep trouble."

They cut off their argument as Michael and Christopher approached. The toll of running a losing campaign showed on both men's faces. Michael stood next to Raven and looked at the crowd filing out of the hall. "I don't understand what happened," he said, sounding genuinely puzzled. "I had such a strong start."

"It's not over yet, Michael. We've got to keep fighting, do something bold," Dudley suggested.

Michael nodded and determination slowly seeped back into his face. "That's what I'm thinking." He and Christopher turned to Dudley, unintentionally putting their backs to Raven.

Raven walked around the group to stand where she could be seen. "Michael, you need to let me handle it. Maybe I can get Minshew to retract the editorial about you."

Dudley, addressing Michael, said, "That's an awful idea. Remember what happened when she interfered with Smotes. Besides, we can let the Minshew issue die because you're already carrying Austin."

"True," Christopher interjected. He was grateful to Dudley for reminding Michael that Raven was more destructive than helpful. "We need something to attract people in the Panhandle states."

"And to make sure the faithful show up on election day," Dudley said.

"Don't just blow me off! I still think Minshew—" Raven began.

Michael held up his hand, "Honey, we've got this covered." He gave his full attention to Dudley and Christopher. "Dudley, do we still have time to set up something in Wichita Falls?"

"Sure do," Dudley said. "I'll make the call right now." He pulled out his cell phone and stepped away from the group.

"Christopher, you know my Dallas constituency better than anybody. I need you on a plane now, and I need you to get people on the phones and in the streets, making sure that everybody goes to the polls on election day. You hear me? *Everybody.*"

Michael was catching fire and it was contagious. Christopher said, "I hear you, Dad. We've got to make sure the seniors get out—I'm talking high-school seniors and senior citizens. I'm going to start with those groups and work my way to every other one. Then I'll fly to Houston, do the same thing there." As an afterthought he added, "Do you want me to get Genie to go to east Texas?"

Michael gripped Christopher's shoulder. "No, son. She's got enough things to wrap up before she leaves." Michael's eyes conveyed the message, *Sorry about you and Genie.*

Christopher shrugged. The two men walked away with their heads together as they continued making plans.

As they wandered off, Dudley came back over to Raven.

"Dudley, I don't appreciate being exed out! Getting Minshew to run a retraction is a great idea. You and Christopher are just pissed that I'm the one who thought of it." She moved to step around Dudley. "I'm calling Minshew right now."

Dudley blocked her path. "You're doing no such thing! Come over here!" Dudley ordered as he stepped out of earshot of the few people left in the hall.

Dudley breathed heavily and his entire face was bathed in sweat. "I'm tired of you screwing things up. That's all you've done from the beginning! I've got a feeling that you're the cause of Minshew writing the opinion piece attacking Michael." Dudley screwed his face up like a scary clown. "We had this election won from the start until you decided to take Erika's money and get her on our asses. Then you started running around with David, being seen all over the state. Do you know what could have happened if that got out?"

Raven couldn't believe her ears. *No, this midget's not going off on me,* she thought. "You're the one who suggested that I talk to Erika. And as for David and me, that doesn't concern you," she said coldly.

"Yeah, I did introduce you to Erika, but I didn't tell you to make promises to her you couldn't keep." Dudley turned in an angry little circle and ended with his finger in Raven's face. "I certainly didn't tell you to get into a catfight with her over David."

Raven grabbed Dudley's finger and bent it down. "Don't do that," she said. "It disturbs me."

Dudley's finger popped back up. It shook because he was so angry. "Listen to me, from now on you're going to do what I say when I say. I know about Omar Faxton, Raven. I know what you did to him."

Raven felt the blood drain from her face. Her insides became a heated mass of knots.

"I tracked down Callie Stephens and a few other people. They told me everything."

Raven tossed her hair and began popping her knuckles one by one. "I don't know what you're talking about," she said defiantly.

"Like hell you don't," Dudley said loudly. He looked around, then repeated in a furious whisper, *"Like hell you don't!* You killed Omar so he wouldn't tell about your scheme to destroy Callie. And I've got the proof!"

Dudley slowed down and tried to calm himself. He wanted to make sure that his message to Raven was crystal clear. He smoothed the front of his sweater as he spoke. "I don't know how you got away with it, but you did, so good for you. Your secrets are safe with me as long as you do what I say."

Dudley pulled himself up to his full five feet two. He'd never felt more manly. "For the rest of the campaign, I want you on the sidelines, playing the part of the sexy supportive wife. No more stupid suggestions and no more conversations with anyone about anything. You'd better not so much as say hello to the mailman." He enunciated slowly. "When—*if,* thanks to you—Michael wins, you're going to play the dutiful, empty-headed governor's wife. And," he said, delivering the coup de grâce, "you're going to break it off with David."

Raven bit her lip. She stood over Dudley, so close to him that he could smell her minty breath. "If you take back everything you said, right now, I won't hold it against you," she said.

Dudley felt himself start to sweat again. *She can't punk me,* he told himself over and over again as he made himself stare Raven down.

"Fine," Raven finally said. She smiled at Dudley in a way he hadn't seen before. "Just remember, I gave you a chance." She turned and walked away.

If Raven had been certain that her body wouldn't stage an all-out revolt, she'd have driven to the nearest Marble Slab Creamery and eaten until the store ran out of ice cream. She settled for going to a movie. Raven wanted to sit in the darkened theater, with the Dolby Surround Sound threatening to take away thirty percent of her hearing. Maybe then she could think. She tried to concentrate on her problems, but couldn't. Something else tickled at her brain, distracting her. When she got a feeling like that, Raven knew that whatever it was would eventually come to her.

Her life wasn't going as planned. Michael's campaign was

disintegrating. Erika was ready for war over the money and over David. And now Dudley had found out about Omar.

Raven stared at the theater marquee, trying to decide which movie would have the loudest soundtrack. Screeching car tires, bombs going off, screams, and gunfire would help Raven think, go deep inside herself. She had to go deep in order to figure out how to annihilate Dudley.

"One, please." Raven was about to place her change in her wallet when, like solving a simple riddle, her mind put things together.

*Dr. Laverne.*

Raven remembered from snooping around in Dudley's office that his psycho drugs were prescribed by a Dr. Laverne. If anyone in the world knew how to disable Dudley it would be his psychiatrist.

When Raven called Dr. Laverne on his private line and made her appointment, he immediately said yes. He'd always wondered if a laser peel would make him look younger and he decided now would be the time to experiment. As a result, Dr. Laverne's thin face looked like he'd been pummeled with small rocks. He called one of his patients, a makeup artist, and had him make the best of a bad situation.

Raven arrived dressed down, at least by her standards. She had flat-ironed her hair so that it was long and bone straight. She put on a burgundy Dolce & Gabbana pique skirt suit and Michael Kors ankle-wrap pumps. This was to be a professional meeting.

"Mrs. Joseph, so good to finally meet you." Dr. Laverne walked up on Raven so closely and quickly, he almost stepped on her toes. He hit her full in the face with a blast of Listerine, and it wasn't the cool mint flavor. "Please, let's sit." He ushered her toward the sofa.

Raven laid her handbag on the table, and studied her surroundings. She took in Dr. Laverne's made-up face, new suit, and fresh, boy-band haircut, and had the thought: *All spiffed up, but his teeth look like buttered popcorn.* Maybe this meeting wasn't to be professional after all. Raven crossed her legs, and let her skirt ride up. High.

"Doctor, I really appreciate your agreeing to see me on such short notice."

"Anytime. My door's always open for you."

"But you hardly know me," she said, sounding completely naive.

"Ah, but that's not quite true," Dr. Laverne said. "I hear about you all the time." He rushed to add, "Our conversation is confidential, you understand. So when I said that I hear about you, that's, uh, I'm ethically bound to keep that a secret."

"Sure, your secrets are safe with me," Raven said. She giggled and smiled. "Who talks about me?"

"The Capps brothers, David and Dudley."

*David!* Raven was taken aback. Then she remembered that when they were in San Diego, David mentioned Dr. Laverne's name.

"What do they say?"

"Well . . . lots of things. David for example, couldn't imagine his life without you. He thinks you're terrific and Dudley does too. They both admire the heck out of you, think you're the nicest person. Why, just the other day—"

"Doctor? Excuse me." Raven raised one finger like a student. "I don't have a lot of time, so why don't we cut to the chase. What you're saying is a bunch of bullshit. I'm sure David and Dudley have said lots about me, but neither of them called me nice. Nobody calls me nice. I'm a lot of things, but nice isn't one of them."

The doctor looked shocked. "Okay."

"Good. So here's the deal. I'm sure David has good things to say about me, but not Dudley. He's out to destroy me and I'm here to find out how I can get to him first."

"Well, I can't—"

"Doctor, I'm not kidding. I really don't have time for this crap." She sighed. *Damn.* Raven loved David, she really, truly did. And the doctor had all but told her that David loved her, too. She believed David when he promised to stop seeing Erika. She meant it when she promised him in return never, ever to have sex with another man, not even Michael. But hey, when dealing with a man like Dr. Laverne, a girl's got to bring some to get some.

"Dr. Laverne, do you want to have sex with me?"

"Mrs. Joseph." He said her name quietly. Dr. Laverne couldn't think straight. His mind was racing through all the freaky stories Dudley had told him about Raven. David didn't give him the details of his intimate encounters with Raven, but to make a white-woman-loving man like him fall in love? Well, Raven had to be something else.

"I know my name, Doctor. That's not what I asked you. Do you want to have sex? Yes or no will do."

Dr. Laverne didn't need to be asked again. "Yes."

"And afterward you'll let me have a copy of Dudley's file."

"Yes." Dr. Laverne nearly choked on his answer.

Raven swung her legs onto the sofa that Dudley loved so much. "Okay, come on."

Dr. Laverne kept his word. He sat quietly while Raven flipped through Dudley's file, speaking only when spoken to.

"So, good old Dudley is gay," she said. "And he hates himself for it."

Dr. Laverne spoke in what he hoped was a scholarly tone. "We'd have to create a new word to describe how much Dudley detests himself for being gay. First off, he won't admit that he is. All his life Dudley has wanted to be thought of as a powerful man. It's what he lives for. But not only is he gay, he enjoys being the passive partner. What he craves sexually is at odds with his idea of what makes a real man. He despises himself for who he is and lives in constant fear that he'll be exposed."

"A depraved brownie queen, huh," Raven said as she continued to flip through his file. "If I were a gay man, I sure wouldn't want to have anything to do with his big wide ass."

"Evidently he's good at all submissive roles," Dr. Laverne added helpfully. "His street name is Bugle Boy. He hates the name. He'd die if he knew I told you."

Raven gave the doctor a charming smile. She shook her head and frowned as she read page after page about how much Dudley resented her. "Slimy slug," she said when she got to the end of the file. Raven looked at Dr. Laverne. "I underestimated him."

"And based on what he told me about you, I'm surprised that you did." Dr. Laverne averted his eyes after he said this.

Raven smiled at the doctor's shyness. After what they'd just done, why be shy? She sort of liked him, wouldn't mind stopping by from time to time, just to talk.

"How did what you were told about me compare to the real thing?" Raven asked the question just to make conversation. She walked to the doctor's copier, fully expecting him to entertain her by singing her praises while she copied Dudley's file.

"It was okay."

Raven spun around. "What did you say?"

"I said it was okay. Good—I should have used the word, good. It was good." Dr. Laverne looked a little frightened. "Really."

"Don't get all bent out of shape," Raven said as she walked toward him. "I just want to know what was lacking."

Dr. Laverne had never felt so naked. He stuttered and stammered so much that Raven lost interest in him and started back toward the copier. The doctor finally spit it out.

"Dudley tells me you can really hurt a man, when you put your mind to it."

"It's true, I can. But Doctor, I'm in love with David; I can't go around having sex with other men just for the fun of it.

Especially not that kind of sex. There has to be something in it for me, and you've already given me all I need." She resumed her copying.

"I've got things you need, and you don't even know it," he said.

"How's that?" Still bored with him. Still copying

"Jeff Sweeney's my patient too. Talk about a man with problems."

"Well, then," Raven dropped her papers and strode over to Dr. Laverne. She grabbed a handful of his perfectly coifed hair, and put her knee in his groin. "In that case, let's get this party started."

# 25

"Well, well, you're the last person I expected to see at my doorstep," Jerry Minshew said. "Since when does a lousy fuck rate a home visit?"

"Just let me in," Raven said.

"Why should I?"

"Because I'm about to make you a very happy man."

Minshew tried to look cool, but his neck turned red. "It's a little late for that, isn't it? I've been asking you to make me happy for weeks. If you'd returned my calls, maybe I wouldn't have had to take back the paper's endorsement. Maybe you and your husband wouldn't be about to get trampled a few days from now."

Minshew had intended to end his speech by closing the door in Raven's face. But he didn't; he just stood there like a horny idiot.

"Think about it, Jerry. If it were too late for you to help me, I wouldn't be here, would I?" Raven gave him a winning smile and stepped very close to him. "And you know if I say I can make you happy, then I can. Let me in."

Raven sat on the pleather sofa and Minshew sat next to her, so close that his sweaty blubber pressed into her side. After their "romantic interlude," as Minshew called it in the messages he left on Raven's cell phone, she'd tried hard to forget about his pale, jiggly stomach, but it was the sort of grotesque sight (not to mention feel) that stays with a person. Twenty-four hours earlier, she would have cringed at the thought of being this close to Minshew. But after her encounter with Dr. Laverne, Raven wouldn't ever again call any man nasty. Dr. Laverne set a new low.

Raven turned and looked Minshew in the eyes. "What do you want more than anything?"

Now Minshew's whole face was flushed. "You mean what kind of . . . uh . . . I don't know." Gone was the eloquent newspaper editor, replaced by a stammering boy. "Whatever you want." He scooted over, away from Raven.

"I'm talking no limits, Jerry."

Minshew's face went from red to white. "No limits?" He was struck dumb by the very idea.

*Let me quit before he dies of anticipation,* Raven thought. She took the envelope from her handbag.

"How about a Pulitzer?"

Grace combed her hair just so, and then studied her reflection. She fluffed her hair so that a few strands hung seductively over her left eyebrow, changed her mind and pushed the strands behind her ear. "Ugh!" she said in frustration. She picked up her comb and started over again.

"Stop it," she said aloud and tossed the comb aside. She leaned close to the mirror to make sure her makeup was perfect. "You look fine."

Michael was on his way over. She hadn't seen him since he almost seduced her on her living-room sofa. Michael had begged to come back, but Grace put him off, so he began seducing her in a different way. He remembered everything about her, like which florist she preferred and the type of jewelry she liked. Michael played those memories for all they were worth by showering Grace with flowers and gifts.

Michael also called Grace every day. His conversation was always the same. "Believe me, Grace, I'm serious about us being together. Believe me."

At first Grace didn't want to believe, because the idea of her and Michael getting back together was, by definition, *un*believable. She knew that God answered prayers, but once she emerged from her shell, Grace had stopped praying for Michael to come back. She was scared to death that now that she'd finally gotten herself together, Michael was going to come into her life like a twister, tearing up her insides and leaving as quickly as he came.

But Michael Joseph was one persistent ex-husband. He chipped away at Grace's doubts about his sincerity. And although it had taken him years to truly break Grace's heart, he put it back together and took up room inside it in an amazingly short time.

"There's still a lot to talk about," Grace assured herself as she looked around the room to make sure everything was perfect. Grace was a wine drinker, but she had stocked her bar with Michael's favorite scotch and cognac. She'd carefully selected the music for her CD—The Whispers, Luther, Phyllis Hyman—it was the music they made their babies to.

*How will the boys take the news?* Grace wondered as she checked on her leg of lamb. Michael loved leg of lamb. "We'll have to talk about how to tell the boys," Grace said aloud as she lit the candles on the dining room table. She felt butterflies as she looked around the room one last time. No matter what Grace said, the ambience in her condo did not lend itself to conversation.

When the doorbell rang, Grace took a moment to look at herself one last time. Her Tahari pantsuit perfectly complemented her figure. *You're beautiful.* She was finally able to acknowledge what John Reese and Christopher had been telling her all along. *You're beautiful, inside and out.*

\* \* \*

"This is the best date I've ever had," Michael said as he sipped cognac after dinner.

"I know," Grace admitted. She had never enjoyed Michael's company more, not even when they were on their honeymoon. Since the moment he arrived, Michael had been thoughtful, witty, and unabashedly romantic.

They were in Grace's living room, seated across from each other. Michael put down his glass and went over and sat next to Grace. He kissed and caressed Grace until telltale blushing rose in her face.

Michael took her hand. He glanced toward the back of the condo, where Grace's bedroom was, then back at her. "Are you ready?" he asked.

"I am." Grace kissed Michael on the side of his mouth. "But I have some things on my mind, Michael."

He sat back, still holding her hand. "Okay, shoot."

"Well, for one thing, it's going to come as quite a shock to the public that we're back together. How are you planning to handle that?"

A strange looked passed across Michael's face. "The public?" He chose his words carefully. "I don't think we need to let the public know anything right away, Grace. This is between us."

Grace thought for a moment, and then asked. "What about our friends?"

"Honey, they're part of the public. If we let them know, our relationship will be common knowledge in no time."

"Okay then, what about Chris and Evan?"

Michael let go of Grace's hand. "Grace, don't you think you're moving a little too fast?"

Grace felt a heavy thump in her chest. "What do you mean?"

Michael looked cornered. "It's like you just said, Grace, the public wouldn't understand if we got back together right away. Even though you'd have to be patient—"

"Be patient? Michael, I've been patient for years. Through

your marriage to Raven and through all your other affairs before her. What else is there to wait on?"

"I've got to figure out what's going on in my marriage, for one thing."

Grace was struck speechless.

Then Michael had the nerve to say, "We're talking about my marriage, Grace. Raven and I haven't even talked about our problems. I owe it to her to have a conversation before I up and leave."

Grace knew her mouth was hanging open, but she couldn't help herself. She was furious. "I agree, Michael, if a husband's going to walk out on his wife, he ought to at least talk to her first. Maybe they can work it out. I only wish you'd cherished your marriage to me half as much as you cherish your marriage to Raven."

Michael had never seen Grace so angry and he wasn't sure how to react. "I did, honey, I cherished what we had, but I was also a fool, messing around with all those women. I didn't expect to fall in love."

*No. He. Didn't.* She edged further away from him and said, "Excuse me?"

"I didn't expect to fall in love with Raven, but I did." When he saw the outraged look on Grace's face Michael added, "But believe me, Grace, everything I've been telling you is true. I never stopped loving you. I always loved you, and I still do."

"You've got some fucking nerve," was all Grace could say.

"Honey, don't say that," he said in a quiet voice. "Believe me, if I could turn back time, I would. But you know how crazy Raven is—if I tried to leave her right now . . . but eventually I'll be able to . . . uh . . . figure something out."

"So basically, you're offering me the position of babies' mama, ex-wife, tramp on the side to the almost governor. How's this for an answer!" Mild-mannered Grace reached over and slapped the hell out of Michael.

He grabbed his scarlet cheek with one hand and reached

out to her with the other. "Grace, no! You make it sound so ugly."

"Only because it is." She caught a glimpse of herself in the mirror on the wall. Something about her was different. Grace's face was flushed with desire and anger, but the mirror reflected something else, an inner quality—a strength beaming off her like sunlight.

Grace took a good, long look at Michael. "Michael, I'll always love you, and not just because you're the father of my sons." Michael looked hopeful but not confident. He could see that he was talking to a new Grace, and it would be her, not him, who set the rules.

"I've forgiven you, and myself, for the things that went wrong in our marriage. We're intertwined for life. But I refuse to be your back-door lover. And after the way you've played with my feelings, I don't want to be your friend. When you need a shoulder to cry on, mine is not available. Understand?" She got up and walked out of the room.

Michael sat by himself, for how long he didn't know. He was losing the race, maybe his wife, and he had stupidly alienated the one woman who'd always been on his side.

He rose from the sofa and went into the kitchen, where Grace sat. "I'm sorry, Grace. It was foolish and selfish of me to expect more from you, when I never gave you what you deserved in the first place. I disrespected you, and I apologize for that." Michael kneeled before Grace, and she thought about how many times she'd prayed for that moment. He took her hands in his own. "I know we'll see each other, because of the children. But aside from that, may I call you once in a blue moon, just to see how you're doing?"

"I don't know. You'll just have to wait and see."

Grace let Michael out. She took the baby-making music out of the CD player and put on Angie Stone. She moved the lighted candles from the living room to the bathroom and prepared herself a hot bath.

Grace thought she would cry, but she didn't. "I'm free," she said aloud. She blew at the bubbles beneath her chin and laid her head back. "I'm free."

"Why don't you try the next paragraph, son," John Reese suggested.

The boy read slowly but clearly. He stumbled a bit, but since the summer his confidence and his ability to read had improved dramatically.

"Excellent, Waleed," a woman's voice said.

The boys and John Reese looked up and found Grace standing at the door.

"John," Grace nodded to him in greeting, then she went around the room, calling names—Waleed, Trey, James, Aaron—and dispensing hugs.

"I missed you guys. I apologize for not being more concerned about you the first time around, but I'd like another chance."

"I don't know," Trey said. "We need more than a simple apology."

"Yeah, yeah," the other boys chimed in, and John did, too.

Grace held up her hands to stop the commotion. "How about I start tomorrow and bring brownies as a peace offering?"

Mr. Reese stood and extended his hand toward his seat. "You don't have to wait, Grace, you can start right now."

"Can't," she said as she walked toward the door. "I've got to catch a flight to Austin. Evan's singing with the all-city choir tonight. I promised him I'd be front and center." She threw the boys a megawatt smile and said, "Nuts in the brownies, right? I'll see you tomorrow."

# 26

"Dudley, it can't be done!"
Dudley leaned back in his chair and twirled a cigar between his fat fingers. "Oh, you'll do it, Miles," Dudley said to the mayor of Laredo, "or my next call will be to the IRS. You really don't want them to know that you've cheated on your taxes for the last five years, do you?"

"That's a lie! How dare you—"

"How much are we talking, Miles? At least thirty thousand a year under the table from farmers who'd rather grow marijuana than corn?"

Miles got quiet then. Dudley laid down the rules. "I want every taco bender with a pulse at the polls voting for Michael, you hear me? I don't care how you do it, but Michael damn well better carry Laredo, or I'm coming after your ass."

"Fine, Dudley, you'll get your votes, but you'd better pray Michael wins," Miles said, his voice filled with venom. "I heard you've been out burning bridges, but this is ridiculous."

"Burning bridges is fine as long as you're already on the other side," Dudley retorted. "Crooked politicians like you are the ones who carried me across," Dudley said and hung up the phone.

He went down his list. Ten calls already made and a dozen

more to go. Dudley was finally using all the dirt he knew on Texas' movers and shakers. Gambling debts. Kept Korean girlfriends. Illegal kickbacks. He knew about them all, and used them to get Michael elected.

He was about to make another call when someone said, "Hey, Dudley. What's cracking?"

Dudley glanced up to find Raven standing in his doorway with her hands on her hips. He was surprised that she'd show up at his office after he told her off in Corpus Christi, but what the hell, if Raven wanted to fight some more, he was ready. *She thinks she's so smart, but I'm beating her at her own game.*

"I decided to take things into my own hands," Dudley said. "So I've been working the phone, using every piece of trash I've gathered over the years to force influential people to get out the vote for Michael." He waved his cigar. "I'm having a pre-election celebratory smoke. Care to join me?"

"Sure." Raven took the cigar he offered and sat in a leather guest chair. "In another couple of days, I'll be the wife of the governor-elect for the state of Texas. That's worth celebrating."

Dudley poured a drink for both of them before he said anything else. Raven waited. She could wait. These past months on the campaign trail had taught her a lot, including how to be patient. Sometimes waiting was better than bum rushing. This was one of those times.

Dudley handed Raven her drink. "You are one smug bitch, you know that? I can't stand a bitch anyway," he said bitterly, "but a smug one really gets on my nerves." He took a draw on his cigar. "If Michael gets elected, it'll be because of me, not you."

"Oh, I don't know," Raven said, smooth as silk. "I've got a hunch that the election is as good as over already."

Dudley was too caught up in his power trip to wonder what Raven meant. He sat on the arm of her chair and brushed his hand over her hair. "You're smart, but not smart enough to

really help Michael. You're too emotional, too shortsighted."
Dudley sighed. "The way you tried to mess over Erika when
all you had to do was make Michael keep his mouth shut."
Dudley gave a sad shake of his head. "Come to think of it, you
screwed up everything you touched."

"Take your hand off my head before something bad happens." Raven looked directly into Dudley's eyes and added,
"Bugle Boy."

Dudley's heart skipped a beat. He not only moved his hand,
he scurried from Raven's chair and took a seat behind his
desk.

"I should've guessed," Raven said. "You hate gays and you've
never tried to come on to me." She raised her hands like a ma-
gician's assistant. "What else could you be but a bottom boy
who can't stand to look at himself in the mirror."

Dudley poured himself another drink while Raven talked.
His hands shook so badly that he spilled as much whiskey as
he got into his glass. Raven's glass was empty also, but he didn't
offer her a refill. Something about her, the way she looked him
straight in the eye nonstop, her eyes empty of emotion, made
Dudley not want to get close to her again.

"Don't tell," he said. It came out a half command, half plea.
Raven toyed with him. "Why shouldn't I?"

"Because it's not true," he said in a firmer voice. "I'm a married man with daughters. A real man. I don't troll the streets at
night looking for young boys to dominate me."

Raven didn't comment so Dudley rushed to make his second point. "And you need me to win the election." He pushed
the list on his desk forward so Raven could pick it up. "Look
at these names. District attorneys, community leaders, corporate CEOs. I'm the only one who can turn these folks."

Raven made no move to pick up the list. Dudley tried to
keep his cool but his inability to read Raven made it hard.
"Like it or not, maybe you and I have to be partners," he said
in a conciliatory tone. "You keep quiet about the lies you've

heard about me and I'll forget what I found out about you and Omar Faxton."

It took every ounce of Dudley's courage to meet Raven's steely eyes, and say what he said next, but Dudley realized that if he showed a moment's weakness, Raven would eat him alive. "Don't be a stupid bitch, Raven. Take my offer."

Raven stood, one beautiful leg extended through the high slit of her long black skirt. "You've made a lot of mistakes with me, Dudley. But calling me a bitch—I think you've said it about three times now—that's the worst. I don't like being called bitch—makes me feel like one of those poor girls in the rap videos. So, no, we can't make a deal."

She leaned across Dudley's desk until she was nose to nose with him. "I know your kind. If you'd found out anything about Omar you would have used it against me a long time ago. When I tell Michael you tried to blackmail me with rumors about Omar, he's going to cut you off. Once Michael's done with you, you've got nowhere to go because you've made too many enemies.

"I've already hired an investigator to flash your picture around gay bars on Sixth Street, see what kind of stories the boys down there have to tell about you. After that, what'll you have left to live for, Dudley? Nothing."

Dudley couldn't contain his panic any longer. "I've put my career on the line for Michael! A life in politics is the only life I know, Raven. You can't destroy that by spreading rumors about me!"

Raven laughed. "Tell that to Miles in Laredo." As she walked out, Raven said, "Before this election is over one of us is going to be made a bitch, and I promise you, it won't be me."

Dudley leaned back and closed his eyes. *Think!* he ordered himself, but he couldn't because his head was pounding. Dudley began massaging his temples and just as the tension started to ease, his telephone rang. "Not now," he complained aloud, but the 773 area code on his caller ID grabbed his attention.

He pressed his speakerphone button. "Capps here," Dudley said as he continued massaging his head.

"Mr. Capps," a woman's voice said, "Mr. Thompson on the line for you, please hold."

The next voice Dudley heard was so sexy it made Dudley's skin crawl. "Mr. Capps, this is Omar Thompson. I heard you've been looking for me."

"Omar Thompson?" Dudley stammered.

Omar said, "Faxton, to you. My mother's last name was Thompson. When I left Dallas I took her name."

Dudley grabbed the receiver. "But why?" Dudley cried. He sounded offended. "Why would you do that? How are people supposed to find you if you change your name?"

"I'm back in Chicago, my hometown," Omar explained. "It's a long story that doesn't have anything to do with me, but Faxton isn't a very popular name around here and I needed a fresh start anyway. So I changed it and cut all ties to the old me."

"But I couldn't find you! I was positive you were dead!" Dudley's heart was racing. He wished for one of his wife's blood-pressure pills.

"It's hard to find a man who doesn't want to be found. As for me being dead, why would you think something like that?" Omar asked.

"Once you disappeared all trails led back to Raven Holloway Joseph. She was the last person to see you alive and she's crazy as hell. And it's not just me, everyone thinks you're dead, even Callie. She told me that you're not the type of man to simply walk away."

Sitting in his law office overlooking Chicago's Magnificent Mile, Omar hung his head. He had wanted to try to find Callie to let her know he was okay but he couldn't stomach hearing about how happy she and Keith were together.

"Now that we've established that I'm alive," Omar said, in a voice that masked his emotions. "Tell me why you've been trying to find me."

Dudley sat back in his chair. *Too bad he isn't dead but maybe the situation is salvageable,* he thought. "I was looking for you because of Raven. Maybe she didn't kill you, but I know she did something bad to you. I don't care what you say, I know she did!"

Omar loosened the collar on his shirt. He felt claustrophobic at the mention of Raven's name.

Dudley kept talking. "She deserves to be punished for what she did to you, if not by the law, then by you. I can help you get back at her."

Omar forced himself to laugh again. "Mr. Capps, you don't know me, but I'm a pretty tough guy—born and raised in Cabrini-Green. I can take care of myself. It would take a lot more that a hottie like Raven to hurt me. I've got no beef with the woman."

"But there's got to be more to the story—"

"No. I'm sorry, Mr. Capps, but I can't help you."

Dudley sat there, numb, with the telephone receiver still in his hand.

His one shot to destroy Raven missed the mark. His political career was dead. Those things he could deal with, but knowing that his secret, which no one, not even his brother or his wife knew about, was about to come out was more than Dudley could bear. He thought about what Raven asked him. *What do you have left to live for?*

Dudley rocked and cried as he summoned the nerve to do what had to be done.

# 27

Michael pulled the heavy stage curtain back slightly so he could get a look at the audience. He was in Dallas, in Monroe University's auditorium. This was it, the final debate on the final Friday before the election, and Michael was going to lose.

Michael was a master debater, and given a fair playing field, Sweeney wouldn't have had a prayer. Michael thought back to how he'd dominated Sweeney during their first debate. But the field wasn't level. Jerry Minshew was one of the panelists, and after his last opinion piece, Michael knew to expect the worst. Michael still hadn't figured out why Minshew endorsed him one moment and turned on him the next and at this point he didn't care. His brain was a ball of confusion. Things with Raven had been so awful lately that he knew she had to be having an affair. *How could she?*—but what kind of question was that? Raven was what she was.

Michael just wanted to get the debate over with. A slow death wasn't his style. "But I'm going out strong," he said to himself. He was in agony, thinking about how he'd put his heart and soul into the campaign and into his marriage, but when pushed to the wall, Michael set aside his pain and focused on the task before him.

"I'm a fighter." Michael repeated Grace's words, pumping himself up like a boxer about to enter the ring. He didn't have any choice but to talk to himself, because no one was by his side. Dudley had agreed to meet him at the auditorium at four, but it was almost six, and Dudley hadn't arrived. And where the heck was Raven? She'd been in a good mood that morning, which surprised Michael, because Raven was not a gracious loser. He figured she must be in denial regarding the fact that he was about to get slaughtered. Or maybe it was some other man who had her in such a good mood.

At least Michael knew where Christopher and Evan were and what they were doing. They'd arrive in time for the debate, but for now, Senator Michael Joseph was alone.

He flipped through his index cards to have something to do with his hands. Michael didn't need the cards; he knew his position on the issues cold. He knew every statistic, every rule, and every issue, hot button and mundane. As he read the cards, a calm descended on him. He'd been that way, feeling calmer and calmer, since he visited Grace. The second time he ran for office, Grace convinced him that one reason he lost the first time was because he couldn't break away from his notes. She convinced him that he was good enough to master the details, with or without cards. No one else believed he could do it; he didn't believe it himself, but Grace did. She'd been his foundation. No matter how much Raven did for him once she entered his life, Grace was the grand architect, the one who imagined what he could become when he couldn't see it himself. Regret washed over Michael, as he remembered how much he had taken Grace—his wife, lover, and confidant—for granted.

As though he'd conjured her, Grace walked into the auditorium, flanked by Christopher and Evan. The room took on a low buzz as the word traveled from one member of the audience to the next: "Senator Joseph's ex-wife is here." Grace had decided to publicly close the breach between her and

Michael. She finally understood her value—as an individual, a mother, and, in this case, a public opinion shaper. Hundreds of women still held a grudge against Michael on Grace's behalf. She knew that by showing her face at the debate, she would free those women to let go of their own personal hurts. She might even help Michael pick up a few votes. Grace had a whole heap of blessings bestowed upon her; she didn't mind letting a little of her grace rub off on Michael.

Christopher saw his father standing behind the curtain, staring out at them. Michael gave a little wave, and when Grace moved to wave back, Christopher looked shocked. "Mom, I can't believe you insisted on coming. And now you're waving at him?"

"It's okay, son. We've worked it out," Grace said. She made sure that at least one newscamera recorded her wave and easy smile.

The moderator opened the debate. "Good evening, and welcome to the final debate between the candidates for governor. I'll introduce them in a moment, but first, let me introduce our panelists."

He extended his hand to the three panel members one by one. "Lucille VanHoffer is president of the state chapter of the League of Women Voters." Ms. VanHoffer stood and made a half bow as the crowd gave perfunctory applause. "Jerry Minshew, editorial board member, the *Austin American-Statesman*; and C.T. White, editor of blackscribe.com."

Behind the curtain, Jeff Sweeney walked up next to Michael. "This is it," he said. "Make or break time."

"Guess so. Good luck, Jeff," Michael said, extending his hand. In order to return Michael's handshake, Sweeney had to brush aside his handler, who was trying her best to make the perpetually rumpled man look good for the cameras.

Michael smiled as he watched the woman dart around Sweeney, because nothing she did would do any good.

Sweeney's shirt was sure to come untucked inside of five minutes. But tonight it didn't matter; Sweeney was already the winner. Michael did wonder, though, where the heck was Dudley? Not that Michael needed any last-minute primping or prepping, but Dudley lived for moments like these. Where could he be that was more important?

"Reverend Capps, so good to see you. Is this seat taken?" Erika said. The debate moderator was about to call the candidates to the stage, so Erika didn't have time for polite chatting. Once she sat down, Erika whispered, "Why haven't you returned my calls?"

"I needed some time to myself, but that's no excuse for being rude. I should have called," David said evenly. "I'm sorry."

Erika had a biting retort on the tip of her tongue but David's quiet manner threw her off. "Why didn't you tell me about Raven?"

David didn't bother to do his usual glancing around to see who was watching him. He turned a little in his seat so that Erika could see his face and said, "I've been keeping a lot of secrets, Erika. My relationship with Raven was one more. Raven told me that she confronted you about it." David felt an urge to drop his head but he didn't. "I'm sorry you had to find out the way you did. I didn't mean to hurt you."

"I'm not hurt," Erika said even as she felt hot tears well in her eyes. She was grateful that the lights had already been dimmed. She realized that, when she wasn't paying attention, David had stolen her heart.

"I'm not hurt," she repeated, "at least not yet. But someone is going to end up hurt, right?" She stared straight ahead into the darkness and said, "Tell me it's not going to be me."

"I'm sorry, Erika, but I've got to follow my heart and it's not leading me to you."

\* \* \*

Michael was holding his own, and surprisingly, so was Sweeney. The first question had been on education, and Michael was required to respond first. He gave a confident, easy-to-understand explanation of why he was against school vouchers, but Sweeney came back with a commonsense argument in support of vouchers that, even to Michael's ears, sounded well thought out and reasonable.

Next, Minshew asked a question about the death penalty. Sweeney was a Republican, but God bless him, he was not in favor of the death penalty. He got to talk first, and because he said the same thing that Michael would later say, Michael's response sounded like he was seconding a motion made by Sweeney.

As the debate went on, Michael began feeling hopeful. He turned every question asked of him into an opportunity to explain away the endorsements and votes that he'd lost over the past months. So far Minshew had asked him three questions, and although they were tough, they were fair. *If I step up my game, and knock Sweeney off his, I will win this debate. And if I win this debate, I will win the election,* Michael told himself. He made a show of discarding his index cards, and began answering the questions so expertly and passionately that if people hadn't known better they would have sworn that he wrote the questions himself.

Raven slipped into a seat just as Michael hit his stride. She wore a bright red St. John pantsuit, the better for the cameras to spot her. From where she sat, Raven could see David and Erika. She stared at David until he turned and looked at her. David's face was unreadable. Raven couldn't tell whether he was alarmed or amused by being caught sitting next to Erika. It didn't matter. Raven puckered her lips in a silent kiss, then turned her attention to the debate.

Minshew asked Michael a question about welfare, which Michael answered with ease. When Minshew turned to Sweeney everyone expected him to invite Sweeney to make a rebuttal, but instead he asked, "Mr. Sweeney, are you familiar with the name Richard Altoona?"

*Richard Altoona? Who the hell is Richard Altoona?!* Michael's mind raced through the list of state and local government leaders. *Who the hell is Richard Altoona?* Michael could feel his pulse racing. He forced himself to calm down and go through his mental roster once more. He went through every Texas town from Abbott to Zephyr but there was no Richard Altoona anywhere.

Sweeney turned pale. Michael felt another surge of hope. Maybe Sweeney didn't know who Richard Altoona was, either.

But then Sweeney squeaked, "Sir, why do you ask?"

"I ask because, as a member of this panel, I have a right to. Is the name Richard Altoona known to you?" Minshew sounded more like a prosecutor than a newspaper editor. But then again, he was a journalist, a part of the only profession whose members were bigger jerks than lawyers.

Sweeney looked at the moderator, who nodded for Sweeney to answer the question. Sweeney's plastered-down cowlick popped up. A sheen of sweat covered his top lip.

"I knew him, yes."

Minshew took off his glasses with a flourish. He felt like Walter Cronkite announcing President Kennedy's murder. "So you say you knew him, which leads one to believe, does it not, that Mr. Altoona is dead."

"I don't see what Richard Altoona has to do with anything," Sweeney said, in such a defensive tone that he managed to make it sound like Minshew's question had everything to do with everything.

The moderator, who said, "Mr. Sweeney, your time is up," saved Sweeney. "Senator Joseph, your rebuttal, please."

Michael looked at Sweeney and saw trouble in his eyes. The politician in him wanted to exploit whatever was going on, to say he couldn't make an adequate rebuttal because Sweeney hadn't answered the questions. Michael looked into the audience, at Grace. He couldn't do anything for her now except set a good example for their sons.

"I don't know who Richard Altoona is," Michael said.

David turned to Erika. "You know everybody who's anybody," he whispered. "Do you know this Altoona guy?"

"Shit! How did Minshew dig that up?" That was all Erika said, and all the answer David needed.

It was C.T. White's turn to ask a question. He'd planned to throw Michael a hardball question on reparations, but he changed his mind. "Mr. Sweeney, how do you know Richard Altoona?"

"He was my wife's, uh, friend. She knew him from college." Sweeney looked a mess. He looked at his wife, who sat on the front row. Her tiny rounded shoulders slumped.

Lucille VanHoffer ceded her questioning time to Minshew.

"Mr. Sweeney, isn't it true Richard Altoona was a physician who used to supply Mrs. Sweeney with OxyContin?" Minshew asked accusingly.

Sweeney visibly cringed. "Leave my wife out of this!"

"Two years ago Richard Altoona was found dead. His nostrils were clogged with congealed blood and cocaine, were they not? And his, uh, private parts were bound by rubber bands. Isn't that true?" Minshew was so excited, he shot the questions at Sweeney without giving him a chance to answer. But Sweeney tried his best; he kept shouting, "Leave my wife alone!" but he couldn't drown out Minshew.

Minshew dealt the final blow. "Wasn't Mrs. Sweeney questioned about Richard Altoona's death?"

"Those records are supposed to be sealed," Sweeney said quietly and walked off the stage.

Throughout, Michael bowed his head rather than witness the public disembowelment of a man he respected.

\* \* \*

As soon as the lights went up, David turned in the opposite direction from Erika and made his way down the aisle.

"David!" When Erika called his name, there was no command in her voice, but there was a pleading urgency. When he turned, she didn't say anything, but her eyes asked the question: *Is this it? Are we done?*

He smiled at her kindly, turned around and kept walking, making his way toward Raven.

Michael stood with Christopher and Evan, accepting the congratulations of well-wishers. It wasn't the way he wanted to become governor of Texas, but hey, that's politics for you. Michael expected Raven to be at his side, but when he looked around the auditorium, he saw her turning her face up to accept a congratulatory kiss from David. Raven turned and waved but she didn't seem in a hurry to join him.

Michael asked Christopher, "Where's your mother?"

"There she is." Christopher pointed to where Grace stood talking to one of the professors from Monroe's business college. "She and Professor Dupas are going to dinner, then he's dropping her at home."

"Looks like your friend's finally leaving," Raven said as she watched Erika walk out. "Oh, she looks sad." Raven gave Erika a wave and a *so sorry* look.

"Now's not the time or the place," David said, "but I've been doing some soul searching. We need to talk."

"Sure thing, but my time is going to be tight over the next few weeks." Raven smiled radiantly. "Can you believe it? I'm going to be the governor's wife! This is just the beginning for Michael and me. I tell you, David, this has to be the happiest day of my life," she said, accustomed to being able to tell him anything. Raven was oblivious to the pain in David's eyes.

"I love you, Raven," he said.

"Yeah, I love you, too," she said absently, her eyes roving

the room. She pinched David's butt and left his side to be with her husband.

"Come back here!" Michael said early the next morning as Raven got out of bed. She playfully slapped his hands away. "Please, no more. After last night it's a miracle I have the strength to move."

Michael lay back on his pillow and cradled his head in intertwined hands. "It was like when we were first married, or when we were dating." He looked at her with awe. "I've never seen you so . . ."

"Reckless?" Raven pulled on sweats and put her hair up in a ponytail. "I know, Mr. Governor-elect. And you loved every minute of it."

"That I did," Michael said as he recalled how Raven had climbed all over him as soon as they got into their limousine after the debate. She sexed him during the entire ride from Dallas to Austin. That Raven was something else.

"You really think Sweeney is finished?" he asked.

"Of course. You won the debate anyway, but Sweeney's meltdown ended the governor's race." She put on a baseball cap and pulled her ponytail through the back. "I'm headed to Starbucks, back in a minute."

Raven lingered in Starbucks, drinking coffee with a dozen newspapers by her side. The headlines were all the same: JOSEPH WILL BE TEXAS' GOVERNOR! SWEENEY WITHDRAWS AMID SCANDAL.

Raven flipped through the paper until she found another, smaller headline: MAN FOUND DEAD. POLICE SUSPECT SUICIDE.

The latter article said, "Last night patrons of a Sixth Street bar called the police when a man walked in with a sawed-off shotgun. The man reportedly announced, 'This is my last bugle blow,' put the gun in his mouth, and fired. Police are withholding the man's identity pending notification of next of kin."

*David's going to take this pretty hard,* Raven thought as she sipped her latte and read the article again. *He's going to need me.* She thought about it some more and decided that David didn't really need her. It wasn't like she could *do* anything. *Michael's going to be upset too, maybe even more than David. Now that he's practically the governor I really must put him first.*

Raven picked up the *Los Angeles Times,* which featured her and Michael on the front page. She sighed and said aloud, "Life is good."

"Is it, now?" a man replied.

Raven's blood froze in her veins. She turned and found herself staring into the gold-flecked eyes of Omar Faxton.

"You look surprised," he said. "You had to know I'd turn up sooner or later." He sat down across from her.

"But I thought—" Raven blurted and abruptly stopped.

Omar shook his head. "I've got more lives than a cat. You of all people should understand that." He thumped Raven's newspaper. "Congratulations. Word to the wise—enjoy it while it lasts."

"What do you want?" Raven asked, trying to sound tough.

Omar's smooth voice stayed even, but his eyes turned cruel. "I thought about letting bygones be bygones, but I couldn't do it. I changed my last name, but I guess I'm still the same old Omar, and you know how I roll."

He leaned toward Raven, and when she flinched, he grabbed her ponytail to hold her close. Omar's lips brushed against her ear. "I'm back, and I'm not going anywhere until we're even," he whispered. "I hope for your sake you're prepared."

Omar stood and threw Raven the smile that used to drive all the women nuts back when they were law students.

"See you around," he said, and walked away.

# BAD GIRLS FINISH FIRST

## Shelia Dansby Harvey

The following questions are intended to enhance
your group's discussion of
BAD GIRLS FINISH FIRST
by Shelia Dansby Harvey.

We hope they will help enrich your own
reading experience as well as generate lively and
thought-provoking conversations about the book.

# DISCUSSION QUESTIONS

1. Does Raven enjoy sex?

2. Michael said that by leaving Grace for Raven, he did what he needed to do to be happy. Was Michael's decision the right one?

3. If Raven had left Michael for David, would that have destroyed David's ministry? What about if David had openly dated Erika?

4. Considering that Michael was Grace's husband before he married Raven, would it have been wrong for Grace to sleep with Michael?

5. Even though she had been traumatized by her divorce, could Grace have been a better mother? How so?

6. Why didn't anyone realize that Dudley was dangerous?

7. Does Raven have any traits you admire?

8. What disturbed you most about David? What did you like most about him?

9. Should Grace have confronted Raven about destroying Grace and Michael's marriage? What would Grace have gained or lost from a confrontation?

10. If happiness were her goal, should Raven have stayed with Michael or chosen David?

11. Was Raven an asset or a liability to Michael's career?

12. Should Genie have given Chris a second chance?

13. Did you expect Omar to show up sooner than he did? What did you expect him to do?

14. Raven said, "A black woman will follow a man straight to hell and take the fire meant for him as long as he asks her the right way." Is that true? Is it right?